Massacre at
Brewer Lane

Howard Harrison

This book is a work of fiction. No part of the contents
of the story line relate to any real historical event,
or person or persons living or dead.

ISBN: 978-0-9870962-0-3

ABOUT THE AUTHOR

Howard Harrison was born on the outskirts of London, and now, as a widower, lives on the mid north coast NSW Australia. He has lived in many parts of the world, gaining experience in various occupations including successful self-employed businessman, soldier, public speaker, entertainer, senior executive and small business educator. Howard has  worked with many governments at all levels and enjoys a healthy cynicism of the bureaucratic and political systems which is often reflected through the main character of his Detective Chief Inspector Harrigan series.

Dedicated to my darling wife Beverley
and
Granddaughter Libby
Together again in God's hands

Chapter One

The magenta hue of the subdued red lighting outside The Sister's Basement nightclub in London's Brewer Lane, more than served its purpose of increasing the intensity of the two already menacing muscle-bound security guards-cum-doormen. Acutely oblivious of their compliance with the dictates of the stereotypical, each proudly wore their profession's unofficial uniform. Black T- shirt several sizes too small to emphasise their bulging muscles, the word Security emblazoned in bold white letters on the back, and a swagger of self-importance that even existed when standing motionless. And of course, the obligatory shaved head.

Brewer Lane was a quiet street, but not because it was a respectable family neighbourhood, quite the opposite. Brewer Lane was, as they say in the media, 'an area known to police'. Only those with a reason to be there, went there, and with the exception of garbage collectors, street sweepers, service vehicles, black cab taxi drivers, residents, and the occasional geographically challenged tourist, no law-abiding citizen ever had, "a reason to be there". But at ten forty-five on the evening of Tuesday, the first of May, nineteen ninety, the quietness of the street was destined to be shattered and the hidden secrets of London's underworld exposed for all to see.

Sounds of endless streams of diesel powered vehicles filled the area as their drivers fought for supremacy in the pandemonium that is Piccadilly Circus. The security guards sheltered from the drizzling rain in the doorway discussing the recently released Steven Seagal debut movie, *Above the Law*. So engrossed were they in the heroic and often brutal deeds of Nico, the fictitious hardball detective in the Chicago police department's vice squad, they failed to notice the long black vehicle approaching them until it was too late.

The heavy vehicle slammed carelessly into the curb and three hooded men, each carrying a Beretta M12 automatic weapon, jumped from the car. Realising the sudden danger, the two doormen, intent on getting inside the club and locking the security doors, turned towards the front entrance. Sadly, the basic human instinct of self- preservation, the narrowness of the front entrance way and their broad, muscle filled backs, made them easy targets. It took just three seconds for the sudden hail of 9mm bullets to rip into their flesh and send the two bloodied, lifeless bodies crashing to the ground. After dragging the bodies away from the front doorway and leaving their victims staring through sightless eyes into the drizzling rain, the two gunmen replaced the magazines in their Berettas and hurried into the darkened, smoke filled nightclub. The third gunman stood watch, his weapon glinting eagerly in anticipation of the elimination of any innocent passer-by unfortunate enough to be witness to the mayhem.

Up until this point it had been just another night at the Sister's. The sounds of Poison's *"Nothin' But A Good Time"* being crucified by a band looking and sounding a little like the bastard child of KISS and Culture Club, cut through the smoke-filled black light atmosphere. Tortured notes bounced off black walls and crashed carelessly through the ultraviolet light. A light punctuated only by the colourful glow of a variety of those drinks, makeups, materials and drugs, susceptible to the UV rays.

With the exception of the brightly lit stage area, the shadowy blackness made it almost impossible to realistically identify anyone or anything, and nobody even attempted to converse with their friends or partners. But the gunmen needed little light, they knew exactly where they were heading. Without even raising one eyebrow of suspicion in the crowded room, they moved quickly in silhouette between the tables and towards an alcove in the left side wall. When they reached their target, there were no words spoken; no shouts; no threats. They simply raised their Beretta's and under the cover of the band's decibel hell jabbing every eardrum with hot pointed needles, squeezed their triggers. It took the rapid fire weapons just under five seconds to empty their forty round magazines into the couple in their mid-twenties sitting to the left side of the table, the two men of similar age seated directly opposite the shooters, and a younger scantily clad girl sitting between the two men. A third girl, sitting on the end to the right, had fallen outwards in what appeared to be a dead faint, and dropped to the floor just nanoseconds before five 9mm bullets tore into the backrest where she'd been sitting. The gunmen replaced their empty magazines and nine seconds after they'd entered the club, retraced their steps towards the Brewer Lane entrance.

It was almost a minute later the third girl, miraculously saved from the bloody massacre of her colleagues, began rising slowly from the blackness beneath the table. A bolt of fear shot through her as she felt a hand grab her shoulder and drag her to her feet. "Let's go. You're coming with us."

Recognising the familiar voice, she screamed, desperately seeking help from patrons in the crowded room. But no one paid any attention to her screaming, people screaming in The Sister's Basement wasn't all that uncommon; and of course, it could easily have been coming from the band.

***

"Ali's restaurant please driver," Detective Chief Inspector Bill Harrigan, currently on unpaid leave from the London metropolitan police, and acting head of the United Nations International Investigation Agency said to the cabbie. "Not the one in Beckingham, the one in Abby Towers, off Millbank Road near Albert Tower Gardens."

To call Ali's a restaurant was grossly understating the true nature of the place. It was, as Ali had originally envisaged, more of an elite club of unsurpassed luxury and privacy with only known customers and their approved guests being admitted. To be eligible to be considered for the status of being known, a person must firstly be introduced and recommended by another known customer at some previous dinner or attendance. With the exception of a very select few, reservations were always required, even for known customers. Harrigan was one such exception. Bill Harrigan was Ali's number one known customer. In the normal course of events, the likes of Bill Harrigan would never see the inside of such a place, unless on police business of course, and even then it would be doubtful. But there are occasions when fate brings the most unlikely people together, and Harrigan saving Ali from being beaten to death by a gang of hooligans on the streets of London many years previous, was one such occasion.

When he'd arrived at Sarah's apartment two evenings ago, it had been his intention to leave his vehicle in her underground parking area, and for them to then spend a quiet, and hopefully, romantic dinner at Ali's. It was now Tuesday evening, almost forty eight hours later, and details of the events that caused the cancellation of the Sunday booking are a little too personal to pursue, suffice to say that although the subject hadn't actually been broached, there was now no doubt in either of their minds, of the depth of their feelings for each other.

"My dearest friend, William," Ali greeted as they arrived. "I have missed you."

"And I you, Ali," Harrigan replied, a warmth in his voice Sarah had never previously witnessed.

"And Inspector Throgmorton, it is a privilege to welcome you once again." Sarah had only been to Ali's once before; the day of Margaret's funeral.

"And it is indeed a pleasure to return," she replied. "But must we be so formal? Please, call me Sarah."

"Oh dear, oh dear, oh dear, such informality would be contrary to the reputation of Ali's," he replied, but then continued with a smile. "But maybe this time we can come to a compromise, or as you would say in the local vernacular, let's do a deal." He gave a slight but genuine laugh. "I'll forgo Inspector and replace it with Miss?"

"It's a deal," Sarah replied with a smile on her lips and a sparkle in her eyes.

Ali led Sarah and Harrigan through the most lavish of restaurants the overall size of a large ballroom, but partitioned by massive wooden pylons, into open, yet private areas. Each area had an antique table and six equally antique chairs, a cocktail bar, four lush leather armchairs, and a gas-powered imitation log fireplace completing the basic comforts. An unobtrusively positioned fax machine, telephone, and computer connection linked to the newly introduced ISP system using the NSFNET were also included. A variety of bookshelves, fish tanks, and climbing vines finalised the privacy of the occupants. A minimum of two white coated attendants were also allocated to each specific area.

Ali stopped beside the entrance of Harrigan's favourite, more open and slightly smaller space, and gestured for his guests to enter. Harrigan passed through the entranceway, paused, and as the eyes of the two men met they nodded affectionately at each other.

"Welcome home, William," Ali said softly before turning towards the white coated attendant standing in the shadow of a large potted hydrangea. "Rajesh will be your attendant this evening. He hasn't been with us long, but he is extremely capable."

Sarah had waited for Harrigan just inside the area, and after Ali's disappearance, they walked together towards the two green leather lounge chairs positioned in such a way that while allowing stunning panoramic views of the Thames, the occupants were still able to face each other during conversation.

"Champagne, Miss Throgmorton?" Rajesh asked.

She turned to Harrigan who shrugged a tacit, *it's up to you* kind of answer. She looked into the smiling face and nodded. "That will be fine, thank you."

"Your usual, Chief Inspector?"

Harrigan nodded.

It was so typical of Ali's; why it was the place anybody who is anybody wanted to be a known customer. As Ali had just explained, Rajesh was a new employee, and yet he addressed Sarah as Miss, a title Ali and Sarah had only agreed on moments previously out of earshot, and he not only knew to address Harrigan as Chief Inspector, not Special Agent, he also knew "his usual".

Harrigan closed his eyes, laid his head against the soft leather and rested his arms along the top of the arms of the chair. He was happy to be back.

It was several seconds before he spoke; still with his head laid back; still with his eyes closed. "I went up to Greysbrook Manor." He paused. "I know I said I'd never visit there again and at the time I'd meant it. And up until a few weeks ago, I'd still meant it. I thought I'd put losing Margaret so violently all behind me." He opened his eyes, rolled his head to his right and looked at Sarah. "That was, until you joined the team."

She smiled, reached across the small table between the lounge chairs and briefly laid her hand on his arm. He looked towards the Thames and the party boat making its way towards Tower Bridge. "When I asked you to join us, I looked forward to seeing you. But not in any romantic way. We'd always gotten along, and we'd worked together well at Stonegate, and not for a minute did I think things would be any different between us this time. But as we were soon to find out, things were different, very different, and it was then I realised I still had some unfinished business at Greysbrook."

He fell silent as Rajesh placed their drinks and two menus on the little table between the chairs.

He took a sip of the golden Ballantine's whisky on ice. "You were there, at Greysbrook, that terrible day when that bomb took away everything I held dear to me at that time. It was you who persuaded me to lay Margaret's body on the ground and let the paramedics do what they had to do." He gave a sort of half laugh. "And it was you who stopped me from beating the life out of the bloke I'd blamed for her death. You were part of it and it was for that reason I needed to draw a line under the whole affair once and for all. I not only needed to free myself of all guilt. I had to satisfy myself our feelings for each other were not simply borne out of pity or gratitude. If I hadn't been able to achieve these things, it would always have been there, lingering between us." He turned towards her. "It's over, Sarah, the line has finally been drawn under the Greysbrook affair."

"I'm glad," she replied. There was nothing else to be said. She reached for the menu.

Rajesh brought two new drinks and took their orders.

"Does that mean I can tell my family that you and I are now going steady?" She asked somewhat light-heartedly.

"Going steady!? What are we, teenagers? I don't think people of our age go steady."

"Then maybe you'd prefer I said we were stepping out together?"

"Now you're taking the piss." He took a larger sip of Ballantine's. "I didn't tell you; I bumped into Bill Buckle at Greysbrook."

"Bill Buckle? I haven't seen him since he retired. What was he doing there? Don't tell me Betty's still dragging him around historic houses."

"I'm afraid so."

"How is he?"

"He wanted me to go up to the tea room and say hello to Betty, but I took a rain check and said I'd ring him and we'd get together for a catch up. I didn't tell him I was coming to see you, so he'll get a surprise."

'D'you think? I doubt anyone is going to be all that surprised,' she thought to herself. "Yes, he probably will," she agreed aloud.

The meal was served at the table beneath the window. They ate in elegance and sipped the Chardonnay they'd ordered with their meal. Dancing reflections of disco lights from a second passing party boat, gave life and a feeling of happiness to the blackness of the Thames.

"What do we tell Whitlock?" Sarah asked, quite seriously. "Does UNIIA have rules about fraternisation with the lower ranks?"

"Who cares?" Harrigan replied between mouthfuls of perfectly cooked medium rump steak. "If they don't like it, they can stick UNIIA up their collective Khybers; we can always come back to the Met."

And that was that. With the uncertainty of their relationship resolved, they spent the next few hours just enjoying each other.

It was almost eleven fifteen, and with their meal over and once again in the green leather lounge chairs, they prepared to have one final drink before heading home. Which home they would be heading to had not yet been discussed, but it was odds on it would be Sarah's.

"I spoke to Chief Constable Jones, yesterday," he said.

"How's he doing?" Sarah was a little surprised he hadn't mentioned it before, but he'd certainly had other things on his mind so it was probably understandable.

"It's one of those good news bad news things. The good news is he's recovering well and should make a full recovery over time. The doctors have allowed him to return to his previous position as head of the Serious National Crime and Intelligence Agency, but only on the proviso he has an assistant, which he agreed to. You met his new assistant when you were looking after Benecke during our first UNIIA case; Godfrey Windsor?"

"Yes, I remember him, and quite a hunk he was too. Had the hots for Benecke as I recall. And the bad news?"

"The bad news is he won't be returning to UNIIA."

"Bad news? Why is that bad news? Won't you be promoted to permanent head of the UNIIA team?"

"I have no idea, and to be honest, I don't really care one—"

"Excuse me, William, Miss Throgmorton, I am so very sorry to interrupt, but there's an urgent telephone call for you." Ali stood beside him, holding a portable telephone handset. "I told the caller that unless by special instruction, guests of Ali's cannot be interrupted, but he was quite insistent."

"That's okay, Ali." Harrigan reached for the handset. "Who is it, did he say?"

"He said he was Chief Constable Eian Jones, from the Serious National Crime and Intelligence Agency."

Harrigan looked at Sarah. "Speak of the devil."

***

"Sorry to drag you away, from Ali's and of course, Throgmorton," Eian Jones said apologetically.

"So you should be," Harrigan replied as he followed Jones towards the entranceway of The Sister's.

"Something going on between you two I should know about?" He called over his shoulder.

"Nope. Nothing you should know, but you might as well be the first to know that Sarah and I have decided to see each other." *'See each other?'* He asked himself. *That's almost as bad as "going steady.'*

"Surprise, surprise," Jones mumbled.

"What was that you're mumbling about?"

Jones stopped by the two dead security guards. "I said surprise, surprise. The dogs have been barking it long enough."

"The dogs have been barking what long enough?"

"Let's just say we should thank the good Lord you understand crime better than you do women." He looked down at the two bodies. "These were the two security guards-cum-doormen. It looks like they were shot in the doorway and dragged out here. The rain has washed away any evidence from the footpath, but there are traces of blood in the doorway, so hopefully forensic might still be able to find something. Let's go inside."

The ultraviolet lighting had been turned off, but the conventional lighting was minimal and with the effect of the many flashing red and blue lights from the dozen or so police vehicles outside still playing havoc with Harrigan's eyesight, it took quite some time before he was able to make some sense of what he was looking at. The one thing he didn't need his eyesight for was the immediate smell of marihuana that still hung thick in the room.

Tables and chairs lie on their sides, broken drink glasses covered much of the floor, along with what looked to be various items of drug paraphernalia. Judging by the amount of disarray, when the shooting had occurred there'd obviously been many more patrons than the handful of unsteady and glassy eyed people corralled by uniformed police on the dance floor, now being questioned by plain clothes officers.

"Most of the more conscious witnesses had fled before the police got here," Jones said as if reading Harrigan's mind. "Follow me, the bodies are this way."

One of the most often used comedic lines written into scripts of crime spoof movies is "move on, there's nothing to see here". But in reality, as Harrigan stood at the entrance of the alcove on the left side of the room, apart from the five dead bodies and eighty bullet holes shared between bloody wounds and torn red leather covering on the back of the cushioned bench seat, there really was, "nothing more to be seen here".

He turned to Jones and frowned, but as he was about to speak, Jones beat him to the punch. "You're wondering what I'm doing here, why I've called you, and why isn't this a case for the murder and major crime squad?"

"In a nutshell, yes."

There were two reasons these two men worked so well together. Firstly, they had complete trust in each other's ability, and secondly, their minds worked in sync. Well, close enough, anyway.

"We need to go somewhere else to talk, so if you've seen enough...?" His voice trailed away. Harrigan nodded. "I'll tell Godfrey I'm leaving, and meet you outside."

Jones turned towards the dance floor, and Harrigan, starting to feel the effects of the marihuana still filling the air, headed towards the front entrance.

***

Sarah picked up the telephone handset in her London apartment. "Hello? Bill?"

"Yes, it's me. Eian and I need somewhere private to talk, do you mind if we come around to your apartment?" He knew it was alright for him to go there, she was expecting him. It was really Jones he was asking about.

"That's fine, I'll put the kettle on."

Twenty minutes later, Jones and Harrigan sat in the lounge area of Sarah's open plan apartment, and as she'd expected when half filling the kettle, only Jones had a cup of tea; Harrigan was nursing a Ballantine's.

"Do you want me to leave you alone?" She asked.

"Only if you want to," Jones replied. "You're a member of the UNIIA team, so you'll find out sooner or later."

Sarah made herself a cup of tea and joined Harrigan on the two-seater lounge. Jones sat in one of the two single lounge chairs opposite.

The blinds were drawn.

"Okay, Eian, what's all this about?"

"Have either of you read Robert Ludlum's novel, The Bourne Identity?"

Sarah and Harrigan both shook their heads.

"Pity." He took a sip of tea. "I know we all agree that while the populations of all western nations expect their governments to do whatever it takes to keep them safe from aggressors, be it through large scale conflicts or single acts of terrorism, they really don't want to know the more gruesome and unpleasant aspects of how their safety is achieved. It's as though they are fearful that should they not voice their objection, they'll carry the burden of some form of vicarious guilt for the atrocity. Governments also have this emotional dilemma, but not because of any guilt factor, they are fearful of voter backlash and losing office. Governments want to stay at arm's length, so should details of any unpalatable action become known, irrespective of that action being essential for the security of the nation, they can lead the outcry of righteousness and punish those involved. And that's what Ludlum's book is really all about. An operative for an agency code named Treadstone, who falls out of favour and is hunted down before he can spill the beans. It's a great read and I recommend it."

Harrigan drained his tumbler and went to the liquor cabinet. "I'll wait until the movie comes out; if they ever make one." Desperate for Jones to get to the point but tempering his impatience with the knowledge Jones was still recovering from major brain surgery, he had no option but to suffer through this out of character pre-emptive waffle. He poured a larger than usual Ballantine's. He might have to stay quiet, but he didn't have to stay sober.

"The Sister's Basement has been well known to police for many years, I'm surprised it's still operating," Sarah commented, almost as thinking aloud.

"It's still operating, Sarah, because I want it to," Jones stated as matter of fact. "As you would be aware from your time at the Yard, there's the occasional police raid, but they're really just for appearance's sake. The Sister's is given plenty of notice of a raid so nothing too damning is ever found. We also have an agreement with the owners that ensures a sufficient number of drug users are arrested during such a raid. This gives the police hierarchy an opportunity to go on television and praise their officers, and then take most of the credit for the outstanding work the officers are doing in their fight against drugs. It doesn't do their arrest figures any harm, either."

It was time for Harrigan's two bob's worth. "And maybe even of more importance, the club is neutral territory for organised crime figures to meet and do their deals. And I'm willing to bet the chief constable here, has his own undercover people gathering information to send back to his agency and, I'm guessing, taking back information he wants passed on to the crime bosses." He turned to Jones. "Am I right?"

"Close enough."

"Any of the victims at Brewer Lane your people?"

"The couple on the left."

"I'm sorry."

"Thanks." The three law officers sat in silent reverence for several moments before Jones continued. "I said they were my people, and they were, but not from the Serious National Crime and Intelligence Agency. Not directly, anyway. They were members of a highly confidential specialist infiltration unit, which comes under my control, and whose existence is only known by a few people within the defence and intelligence industry. Godfrey Windsor is one of those people but I can't give you the identity of the others; not without a very good reason. And before you ask, Bill," he added quickly. "I can assure you there are no politicians or members of the general bureaucracy among them." He drained the last of his tea and refused Sarah's offer of a second cup. "The field agents of the unit have few rules and are capable of doing whatever needs to be done. In the interests of protection of their cover in the circles they operate, they are often involved in criminal activities, and for all intents and purposes, are criminals themselves."

"And they work for the UK government," Harrigan stated.

"Yes, but the UK Government doesn't know that. Like I said before, people want to feel safe, but are rarely willing to do whatever it takes."

"Hence the Ludlum book preamble," Harrigan commented to no-one in particular.

"Yes, and knowing how your mind works, my friend, it had nothing to do with my brain surgery."

Harrigan winced.

"Does this infiltration unit have a fancy name?" Sarah asked.

"I don't know that fancy would describe it, but it's known as Unit 29."

"Unit 29? Well, it's certainly no Treadstone; it sounds more like an address. An apartment number maybe."

"That was done deliberately. The existence of this unit must never be discovered by anyone other than those who need to know, and even some of them who need to know, don't know, so it needed as nondescript a name as possible. What is more nondescript than an apartment number? The other thing is that agents don't carry any identification or anything linking them to the unit, and more often than not, would not know the identification of any other agent sent to meet them. Or who might be working a different angle of the same target or even maybe looking for assistance in a dangerous situation. An apartment number can easily be brought into a conversation without suspicion."

Harrigan was going to make some comment about the secret handshake of the Mason's, but let it go. "So where do we come in?"

"The other two men killed inside the club were known criminals. Jimmy Qiang Yoon, UK born of Chinese parents with connections to Asian and Eastern Europe drug cartels. Muktar Ahmed Al-Yousaf, came here as the child of a refugee, and is a recognised international arms dealer, generally legitimate, but not adverse to deals under the table if they're profitable enough."

"Which they invariably are," Sarah added. "So what you're really saying is that Al-Yousaf uses his legitimate business as a front to an illegal arms trade."

Jones sat thoughtfully for several moments before responding. "Illegal is probably a little strong, Sarah. It's true that from time to time, UN member states have agreements to restrict the flow of weapons if, for example, it's known or even suspected they would be used to commit or facilitate genocide, crimes against humanity, war crimes and serious human rights violations and the like. There have been several arms embargoes or sanctions imposed by countries or organisations such as the USA, the EU and the UN over the years; Vietnam, Iran, Turkey for example, but there's no UN treaty as such, not yet anyhow. There's a growing call from Amnesty International and other Non-Government Organisations for such a treaty to be drawn up, but these things take time, especially when there's a lack of will in many countries to do so. But that being said, even if a treaty is eventually agreed, at the end of the day there will always be those who are prepared to ignore the rules."

Sarah had little experience in international matters, but she knew enough to know that history did not disagree with Eian Jones' summary of the integrity of governments.

"Al-Yousaf's customers are mainly throughout the Middle East and much of Africa, but he'll go anywhere when and if the occasion arises, embargo or no embargo. In addition to all that, my agency has long suspected that Yoon and Al-Yousaf have some kind of partnership arrangement. Not a partnership in any traditional sense, more a partnership that allows either one to promote their own business, using the other's business as a value added service."

"Meaning a drug dealer with access to an arms dealer willing to trade under the radar, is a much more attractive proposition to a major crime syndicate, even unscrupulous governments, than one without such access," Sarah summarised.

"Exactly, but we have no evidence of the suspected partnership at the moment, nothing of any consequence anyhow. That's why I had my Unit 29 people there. It took a long time for them to get close enough to Al-Yousaf and Yoon to confirm our suspicions, and were getting very close to uncovering how it was done and who were involved. But, now they've been killed, our chances of closing in on Al-Yousaf and Yoon, well, more accurately whoever takes over their operations, has been set back indefinitely. On the bright side, my agency's investigation is still on going and while ever it stays that way, it's enough to give me jurisdiction."

Harrigan stood from the lounge and talked as he walked towards the liquor cabinet once again. "Let me guess. Because agents from the Serious National Crime and Intelligence Agency do not know of, and cannot be allowed to discover, the existence of this Unit 29, which they might very well do if they dug deep enough, you can't risk putting your National Crime agents on the case. And even if you did take the chance, because of the close scrutiny the media and do-gooders like civil libertarians who prefer to protect criminals over victims place on your agency to ensure your agents play by the rules, it'd be almost impossible for you to find out who was responsible for the killings. Irrespective of the fact the people trying to ruin our nation have no rules."

Jones gave a *'that just about covers it'* shrug.

"But, if you call in UNIIA, an agency that works under different rules and doesn't give a monkey's stuff about media or do-gooders, there's a better than even chance the perpetrators will be brought to justice and probably more importantly, minimising the risk of exposing your infiltration unit."

"I couldn't've said it better myself."

"Do you think the killings had something to do with the drugs and weapons trade?" Harrigan asked.

"It's the most obvious motive we have, but there is at least one other option. It would be fair to say the Al-Yousaf arms dealership is one of the most internationally powerful arms dealing operations around at the moment, but on the Yoon drug side of things? Not so much. There's no question it's a large operation, especially in the London market, but it's still in the growing stage and has a long way to go before it gets into the top five. Our intelligence tells us Yoon's operation has recently made substantial inroads into areas north of London, areas controlled solely by Boris Akmatbayev, and there's not a snowflake's chance in hell that Akmatbayev is going to sit back and let the Yoons come in and take over. And if I'm right about the Yoons, Al-Yousaf linkup, it means that Yoon is also probably eying off more of Akmatbayev's territory in the Middle East, Africa and probably Northern Europe."

"Boris Akmatbayev, the Kyrgyzstan mobster spreading his tentacles across all Europe and into Asia?" Sarah asked rhetorically. "From what I know of Akmatbayev, he doesn't take kindly to people attempting to muscle into his territory, and the massacre style shooting at Brewer Lane is right up his alley." She looked towards Harrigan. "He'd have to be our prime suspect, surely."

It was Jones who replied. "I don't think you'll get much of an argument out of either of us that what you say has merit, Sarah. But if one of the major crime syndicates, like Akmatbayev's, had decided enough was enough and had planned to hit Yoon that night, I would've heard about it. I have Unit 29 agents in all major syndicates. The other thing that niggles at me is where it happened. There's an unwritten rule that the Sister's Basement is off limits to all gangland hits. Like we said earlier, underworld bosses need to meet from time to time, even Akmatbayev, and the Sister's is such a place. Neutral territory. A place of truce where differences, ultimatums and even threats can be argued without risk of attack from either side or other crime gangs. Calling a truce during wartime for negotiation is nothing new; it's been common practice, observed during most wars throughout the ages."

Harrigan remained leaning on the cocktail cabinet. "But whether it is or isn't a gangland related incident, it must be promoted as being gangland related so you can retain jurisdiction under your Serious National Crime's responsibility, using the control of the international world trade in drugs and under the table arms deals as the primary cause, even though it's drawing a long bow. This in turn gives you justification to bring in UNIIA."

Jones nodded agreement.

"What do we know about the other dead girl and the one sitting beside Al-Yousaf?" Harrigan asked wanting to get this over with for the evening.

"I have no idea about the dead girl sitting between Yoon and Al-Yousaf, probably just a bit of rough who picked the wrong night to pal up with Yoon. We have to assume for now that the girl sitting on the end next to Al-Yousaf, apparently fainted and fell to the floor and probably escaped unharmed. We have no leads as to her identity and don't know what happened to her. Godfrey is trying to get a description from someone there on the night, but I don't like his chances. So the bottom line is, the only witnesses we have are the patrons who were too stoned to make it to the door before the police arrived. And going by some of what I overheard while I was waiting for you, I'm not holding my breath for a breakthrough. There was also the band but they're not much better."

Harrigan looked at his watch. "We'll need to get an early start, Eian, so unless you have anything else that can't wait until morning, I think it's time we got a couple of hours shut-eye."

Jones stood from the lounge chair and began putting on his coat.

"One last thing before you leave," Harrigan said. "Have you spoken to Whitlock yet? If you have, was he receptive to putting UNIIA's potential involvement to the UN steering committee, and if he was, how long before we'll know if it's approved?"

"Immediately after being informed of the incident," Jones replied. "I spoke to someone, much higher up the ladder than I, and she spoke to someone much higher up the ladder than Whitlock, and without going into the politics of it, your involvement will be approved within the next twenty four hours at the latest. Whitlock will call you as soon as he hears something. As far as your costs, my agency will cover them while we wait for UN money to come through."

Harrigan shook his head with a slight smile. "Yes, I guess it *was* a silly question."

Jones stood with his hand on the doorknob. "There's an open ticket for Benecke and Lo waiting for them at the British Airways' New York office. Thanks for the tea, Sarah," he said with a dual purpose nod that not only supported his words of thanks, but also bade her farewell. "I'll see you later in the morning, Bill." The door closed behind him.

Harrigan took up his mobile and rang Benecke.

"So much for our two week's holiday," Sarah mumbled as she collected the cups and walked towards the sink.

Chapter Two

The meeting in Jones' Whitehall office later that morning between Jones, Godfrey Windsor, Harrigan and Sarah, provided very little additional information on the events of the previous night. As Jones had predicted, the witnesses were so stoned out of their minds, they had difficulty remembering their own names, let alone what was going on around them. The bright lights in the stage area prevented the band members from seeing anything beyond the footlights, and as far as the noise of the Berettas went, with their amplifiers playing at around one hundred and twenty decibels, it was little wonder they heard nothing out of the ordinary. The base player who'd been standing towards the front and close to the side of the stage, did say he'd heard something that could've been gunshots, but thought at the time it was just the drummer injecting his individual artistic flair.

Godfrey slid three, black, three ring binders across the table towards Harrigan. The binder on top was much thinner than the bottom two. Harrigan opened the thinner binder, inside which were a number of typed and signed witness statements, each separated by tabbed cardboard dividers.

"Those are copies of all the witness statements we collected at the club last night. I also have some of my people door-knocking the area. I'll send you a copy of those results as soon as I get them."

"Any CCTV?" Harrigan asked.

"No, unfortunately. Not in Brewer Lane. There are cameras just up the road at Piccadilly Circus and we're looking at footage from them now. If we're lucky, we might catch a glimpse of a suspicious vehicle exiting the Circus towards Brewer Lane around the time of the shootings. It's a bit of a long shot, but you never know." He paused for several moments. "I've also included mug shot photos of each victim taken at the scene and on the medical examiner's tables."

"You've been busy," Harrigan commented absently as he picked up the photos of the two women and laid them in front of him. "Which one's your agent?"

Windsor pointed to the photo on Harrigan's left. "This one. Her name's written on the back."

"Have your agents' families been notified?"

"Infiltration agents don't have family, it's a requirement of the job."

"What about Yoon and Al-Yousaf?"

"Their families have been officially notified, but they already knew of the shootings. The word spreads quickly through that community."

Harrigan picked up the second photo. "And you have no idea who this girl was?"

Windsor shook his head. "We ran it through our files, but nothing's come up so far. We're in the process of computerising all our records, but that's going to take a while so I wouldn't hold your breath."

"The girl sitting next to Al-Yousaf, the one who got away, do you know who she is yet?" Harrigan asked a little lazily as he returned the photos to the file.

"We know he had a steady girlfriend, Bethany Joseph, but we can't say for certain whether it was her there that night or not. The world of organised crime isn't famous for its monogamous lifestyle."

"Do you have a photograph of Joseph on file?"

Windsor shook his head.

Harrigan closed the binder, passed it to Sarah and reached for the next binder. He turned it around the right way.

"Those two binders contain everything we have on Yoon and Al-Yousaf," Windsor explained. "Well, not *everything*, much of it is a summary of the larger files we have downstairs. You'd need a wheelbarrow if I gave you *everything*. If there's anything you need clarified, you have full access to the complete files."

Harrigan took hold of each divider tab in turn and flicked over to each section. Personal details, arrest records, court appearances, suspected activities, family details, known associates and general. He was impressed by the professionalism of the documents. There was sufficient information to tell him what he needed to know about Yoon and Al-Yousaf, with reference points of where more detailed information or clarification could be found if required.

He closed the binder cover and having seen all he needed to know for now, didn't bother with the third. "Benecke and Lo will be here late this evening and Sarah has booked us rooms at Medwin's Royal Garter International hotel in Thistle Lane, just off Edgeware Road. We'll use our own vehicles for now, but if we need something more official I'll let you know." He looked at Jones. "What about interrogation rooms and holding cells if we need them?"

"The agency has an agreement with the Met, they'll find you space when you need it."

"Do you need one of my people to assist?" Godfrey asked.

"No, not at the moment. If we're going to maintain the appearance of independence, it's better we stay at arm's length. If we need you, we'll call."

"Understood." Godfrey paused before continuing almost too innocently. "Do you have any idea how you'll proceed from here?"

"Yes."

Godfrey sat silently, waiting for Harrigan to continue. He didn't.

"Would you care to share?" Godfrey pressed.

"No."

"*No?* That sounds a little like you don't trust us, Chief Inspector."

"Good."

Godfrey Windsor turned quickly towards Jones. Eian Jones smiled. "Don't take offence, Godfrey, it's nothing personal. The chief inspector takes the independence of UNIIA very seriously; he doesn't trust anybody. That's what makes him so good at his job."

"Of course, Sir, I was out of order," Godfrey replied before looking towards Harrigan. "Please accept my apologies, Chief Inspector."

"Forget it. Like your boss said, it's nothing personal."

***

It was a little after eleven later that morning when Sarah and Harrigan sat in Sarah's Chichester Gardens' apartment, studying the files Windsor had given them. They hadn't yet heard from Whitlock, but as Jones was still technically in charge of the UNIIA team, Harrigan didn't see any need to wait.

He closed the second binder and pushed it to the centre of the table. "Thorough these files might be, and it's obvious Yoon and Al-Yousaf wouldn't be short of enemies, but for the life of me, I can't see anything that leads us anywhere," he said.

Sarah nodded. "I agree." Given their newly established personal relationship, Sarah wasn't sure whether she should address him as *Sir* because they were discussing work, or *Bill* because they were in her private home. She chose not to use anything. "So, where do we start?"

"A good question. Notwithstanding The Sister's being a place of truce, some form of gangland dispute seems the most logical starting point, so why would Eian rule it out so quickly?"

"He didn't actually rule it out, he just thought it was unlikely," Sarah defended.

Harrigan didn't respond, choosing instead to sit in thoughtful silence and sip his coffee.

"Bill?" Sarah's one word question clearly shouted, *'for God's sake, are you going to tell me what's bothering you or not!',* and she'd clearly decided how to address him, at home at least.

"Sorry, of course, you're right, but I can't shake the feeling his lack of enthusiasm towards the gangland theory could be he believes there's a far more important line of enquiry he wants us to follow."

"It you're right why wouldn't he just come out and say it? He's on our side, remember?"

Harrigan didn't answer immediately.

"Bill? He *is* on our side; isn't he?"

"To a degree. But he's back with the Serious National Crime and Intelligence Agency, not UNIIA, and his loyalties must now lie with it. And at the end of the day he's a spook. Spooks rarely come in through the front door; there's a hidden agenda in *everything* they do."

"He *did* tell us about his Unit 29 agents and that two of the victims were his people; that doesn't sound to me like he's hiding anything."

"I'm not saying he's hiding anything, I'm suggesting there's some things he's not telling us; there's a big difference. And what did he actually tell us about his two people who were killed at the Sister's? They were gathering information. Information about what?"

"The drugs and arms trade!" She replied, a hint of exasperation entering her voice.

"Yes," he replied patiently. "But is just tracking the trade in illegal drugs and weapons across borders, a job warranting two specialist Unit 29 agents? It's bread and butter work for Christ's sake. No, for my money, their investigation was about something much bigger than that."

Sarah thought for a while. "I'm not convinced, but let's say for the minute you're right, it's then quite possible his two agents were the actual targets and the others just collateral damage?" It was one of those statement questions.

"Why not? All we know is we have five dead people, not counting the two doormen. Any *one* of the five could've been the target and what better way to throw police off track than to give us several prospective and quite legitimate targets."

"Jesus, Bill, just once, can't you take the easy route?"

"Where would the fun be in that?" He reached across the table and dragged the Yoon file back in front of him. "So, thinking caps on, and let's get started, because unless we can establish who the real target was—"

"—we'll have no chance of finding the killers," she completed.

"Okay then, what have we got? We know the girl sitting at the end of the table, the girl who fainted and fell to the floor, who we'll assume for now was the Joseph woman, wasn't the target, because if she had've been, she'd've been shot where she laid. So, we'll cross her off the target list for now. But she's certainly a witness, so we'll still need to find her."

"If she has any brains, she'll be halfway to Australia by now," Sarah mumbled under her breath.

He flipped open the cover of the file. "It says here, Qiang Yoon's brother, Fan, lives at Mallard Drive, Kingsbury Marsh, we might as well start with him.

He glanced briefly at his watch. It was twenty minutes to midday. "Benecke and Lo's flight doesn't get in until seven fifteen this evening. By the time they're through customs and get here it'll be well after nine, so we'll start without them. C'mon, let's go and see what brother Fan has to say for himself."

"I was surprised they managed to get a flight so quickly," Sarah said as she locked her apartment door.

"Would *you* argue with Benecke?"

"No, I guess not. She's one scary chick."

Five minutes later, Sarah drove her Diamond White Ford Escort out of the apartment block's secure underground car park and turned left onto Warwick Way. The traffic on the narrow streets between rows of six storied red brick apartment blocks and continuing along the tree lined Chelsea Embankment with its rows of house boats moored along the Thames, didn't ease until she'd turned into Finborough Avenue and eventually onto the A4. That is, if traffic in London could ever be described as having *eased*.

They travelled in relative silence, talking briefly again about Whitlock's possible reaction to their new personal status. Sarah wanted to bring up the matter of where they should live, but she could see Harrigan was in no mood for *that* discussion and didn't want to scare him off at this early stage. She'd smiled to herself when the thought had crossed her mind that *'courting Harrigan is a bit like a hunter stalking a skittish young deer. One wrong move and it disappears'.* Forty minutes later, as directed by Harrigan who had the A to Z, she turned right off the A4006 into Olive Grove Lane.

Mallard Drive was just over a mile on the left. She stopped beside a small parkland area opposite forty three. Kingsbury Marsh had been a small village of factory workers who'd worked for local engineering firms supplying parts to the nearby aircraft factory during the First World War. During the mid-twenties, the majority of factories had been forced to close their doors and because of the lack of blue collar jobs available, workers moved on to areas such as Birmingham and Coventry searching for jobs in the burgeoning motor vehicle industry. Not surprisingly, the area fell onto hard times. Ironically, during the Second World War, the aircraft industry once again sprung into life, followed after the war by the introduction of coachworks for luxury motor vehicles such as the Daimler. The skilled workers who came to the area, while not moneyed people by any stretch of the imagination, were certainly in the middle class bracket. The area quickly transformed into one of double storied, white semi-detached three and four bedroom houses with bay windows and pointed arch attic windows in steeply pitched red tiled hip roofs built in quiet tree lined streets.

Harrigan and Sarah sat silently and looked across at the Yoon residence. While nestling beneath the cloak of respectability covering the neighbourhood, its design varied from the neighbouring dwellings. It stood alone, stretching along the entire distance between two side streets. It was white, had a red tiled hip roof but no attics, six double windows along the top floor, and three double windows on the ground floor positioned between a small entrance way on the right side and a larger entranceway on a small verandah on the left. Both entranceways and verandah had red tiled awnings. What looked to be a four car garage was attached to the right side of the building. The two black 850i BMW's in the driveway crouching silently behind the low, immaculately trimmed hedge, created a picture of grandiose sophistication and peaceful harmony. It would be fair however, to say, the presence of the two medium to heavy weight sumo wrestler types in black suits, white shirts, black ties and extremely shiny black leather shoes, playing mahjong on the front verandah kind of shattered that peace and harmony thing.

"If one of them throws a steel rimmed bowler hat at you, don't forget to duck," Harrigan said as he opened the car door.

"If you're referring to Odd Job in *Goldfinger*," Sarah said as she got out of the car and looked at Harrigan over the turret. "He was Korean, not Chinese."

"Tom-ar-toes, Tom-ay-toes."

They walked slowly, but meaningfully towards the front driveway. There was no gate or fence as such, just a driveway entrance and exit. The neatly trimmed low hedge separated the two.

The mahjong combatants rose in unison and took a position blocking the top of the stairs leading to the front door.

"That's far enough!" The taller of the two said. "Who are you?"

Harrigan raised his badge and introduced himself and Sarah. "We'd like a word with Fan Yoon about the death of his brother."

"Fan not seeing anyone; especially police."

"We're not the police. Like I said, we're from the United—"

"Same thing. I told you. Fan not talking to police; Fan not talking to no-one. You go now or we—"

"Or you'll what?" Harrigan interrupted as he stepped forward and put his right foot on the bottom step.

Sarah looked on nervously, and anticipating the worst, put her hand into her large shoulder bag and took hold of her Glock. Standing at ninety degrees to Harrigan, she watched for movement from the second doorway entrance at the other end of the building. But it was the front door leading onto the verandah immediately in front of where they stood that opened.

"It's alright, Hung, back away," Harrigan heard a soft voice say.

Without flinching, the two giants moved away from the top of the steps and returned to their mahjong.

"You've come a long way from your earlier days at Scotland Yard, Special Agent Harrigan," the soft voice continued. "Sergeant, to Chief Inspector and now working for the UN."

Harrigan looked up at the more wiry than frail, aging Chinese man in traditional dress standing one pace from the front door. It was difficult to judge his age, elderly Chinese people always appear to be younger than they really are. He assumed from what he'd read in the files, the old man was Zhuang Yoon, head of the Yoon family, and although suspected of controlling the family's entire operation, had never been arrested.

"Should I know you?" Harrigan asked.

"No, I don't think so."

"But you know me?"

"By reputation only. I am Zhuang Yoon, Qiang's father. You put my brother away in 'eighty one, just for murdering a couple of young heroin dealers who thought they'd muscle in on our territory. He received twenty four years."

"Yoon! Of course! Ju-Long Yoon. I hope you're not waiting for an apology."

"Not at all, my brother got himself caught and has no-one else to blame but himself. Anyway, he's already served almost nine years, and being a model prisoner, having found Jesus, and working diligently helping other prisoners to reform, he'll be out in another six to twelve months. Ah, I do so love the justice system in this wonderful country.

So many people willing to help guide those who have fallen by the wayside towards rehabilitation and the pathway to model citizenship."

"Yes, but who's caring about the victims?" Harrigan asked, the bristles in his neck rising.

"Who cares about the victims? A good question," the old man mused quietly. "I'm afraid nobody really cares about *them*. Law enforcement agencies and the judiciary receive no brownie points for caring for victims. But let's not stand on the verandah, please, come inside, and bring your lovely partner with you." He stood aside, and holding the door open, gestured for his guests to enter.

Harrigan paused before entering. "Oh, and by the way, it's Chief Inspector, not Special Agent."

"As you wish, Chief Inspector," the old man replied with a slight nod of acceptance. He gestured again to the hallway. "Take the first door on the right, we'll talk in there."

As they approached the first door on the right, a smaller version of "Hung" appeared before them, and gestured he intended to frisk them before they went any further. They heard Zhuang's voice from behind as he spoke in Chinese. The man, whose name, going by the one word from Zhuang's brief conversation Harrigan had understood, was "Jian", immediately stepped to one side and allowed them to pass. He didn't follow them into the room.

With the exception of two antique dark brown, almost black cabinets of obvious Chinese heritage, three brightly coloured Chinese knotted wall hangings and a reasonably large jade model of a dragon sitting on the slightly over-sized, ebonised oval coffee table in the centre of the room, the decor was substantially of western influence. Zhuang gestured to the L-shaped, deep maroon eight seat modular sofa dressed in soft velvet-like material that looked like it belonged in a corner of the room, but wasn't. Zhuang sat in one of the matching lounge chairs. Black antimacassars with Chinese motives and red tassels covered each arm of both lounge chairs and sofa.

It wasn't until Harrigan and Sarah had taken their positions on the sofa, that Harrigan noticed the slightly built lady wearing a light blue, distinctly Chinese patterned silk dress standing inside the doorway.

"May we get you some tea?" Zhuang asked politely.

Harrigan and Sarah both refused. Zhuang didn't look at the girl as he dismissed her with a gesture of his arm. She bowed slightly, and backed out of the room, closing the door behind her.

"I'm a little surprised the United Nations Independent Investigation Agency is investigating the Brewer Lane shootings; it's a local matter, surely?" The old man said.

"Seven people, one a known arms dealer with middle eastern connections and another a known and increasingly powerful drug lord, massacred Chicago style in the heart of London looks bad on any government's CV. Not to mention the inevitable media fuelled campaign of rumour and innuendo of police corruption or worse still, speculation of a cover up by those who stride the halls of Westminster. And that's where our agency comes in; it's the reason UNIIA exists. What better way is there to avoid all that politically damaging turmoil than to call in a totally independent agency with no allegiance to anybody involved and where there's no possibility of favours being called in. It's what we do."

Zhuang nodded acceptance of Harrigan's logic. "You told Hung you wanted to speak to Fan about the death of his brother. What could Fan tell you? He wasn't there." He fell silent, and after raising his right hand, inspected his fingernails. He absently pushed down gently on the quick of each nail with his left hand thumb, and after returning his hands to his lap looked up at Harrigan. "I think it better you talk to me."

Harrigan was fully aware of the Chinese underworld community's reluctance to involve the police in their problems. They preferred to deal with the matter in their own way, and he knew arguing the toss over who he should be speaking to at this point in time would get him nowhere.

"Very well." He turned to Sarah. "Can I have those photos?"

Sarah rummaged in her shoulder bag and handed him a brown envelope. He removed the photos of Qiang from the group, and threw the photos of the other victims, politely onto the coffee table sitting between them. "Can you identify any of these people?"

The coffee table was just out of reach of both the sofa and Zhuang's lounge chair, and Zhuang was forced to sort of half-rise from his chair to collect them. It was clear from his body language, he didn't appreciate being treated as an underling, but like Harrigan, he was prepared to play the game… for a while. He studied each photo in turn and eventually flicked the two photos of Al-Yousaf back onto the coffee table. *Flicked* is probably the wrong word; it was more like dealing playing cards. "That's Muktar Ahmed Al-Yousaf, one of my son's business associates." He tidied the other photos into a neat bundle and tossed them on top of Yousaf's photos. "I don't know the others."

"Would Fan know them?" Harrigan asked innocently without the slightest hint of smugness.

"Why is it important?" Zhuang asked unnecessarily, obviously stalling for time.

"If we're to have any chance of identifying your son's killers, we need to first establish the motive. But before we can do that, we need to identify the target. So, to establish which one of the five was the target, we need to identify the victims."

This display of patience was a side of Harrigan, Sarah had never previously witnessed. She was impressed.

A few thoughtful moments passed before Zhuang reached down to a table beside his lounge chair and picked up a china bell. He shook the bell several times. Despite the vigour of his hand movements, the bell only tingled loudly at best; it certainly wasn't the noisier jangling sound you'd get from a metal bell. But, to Harrigan's surprise, it was only a matter of seconds before the door opened noiselessly and the young lady in the blue silk dress, shuffled in silently.

"Get Fan," Zhuang called over his shoulder without looking at the girl.

Once again, the girl bowed slightly and shuffled backwards from the room and closed the door.

"How long have you lived at Kingsbury Marsh?" Harrigan asked casually.

"Eighteen months."

"If memory serves, I arrested your brother on the south side of the Thames, and from what the files tell me, your business interests are much closer to the centre of the city. Why did you move? Rents get too high?"

The old man smiled. Despite being on opposite sides of the law, he took a liking to this irreverent law man. "No, the rents weren't too high, the population is spreading and we needed to grow our business accordingly."

They both knew what 'business' he was talking about, but now was not the time to raise barriers.

"The neighbours must've been excited when you moved in with your big black cars and bodyguards on the front verandah. Do they give you any trouble? And I'm of course speaking only of neighbour to neighbour type trouble, not the other kind of, well, you know what I'm talking about."

Zhuang smiled again. "I can see why Muhammad Mahmood speaks so highly of you, Chief Inspector."

The news about Mahmood's admiration of Harrigan caused Sarah's head to snap around towards the man sitting next to her, her quizzical frown seriously seeking an answer to what Zhuang had meant by saying the world's most powerful crime lord *'speaks highly of him'*.

Knowing Sarah would've picked up on Zhuang's comment, Harrigan dare not turn to face her, choosing instead to maintain contact with Zhuang.

"We have an agreement with our neighbours," Zhuang continued. "They don't interfere with our business and we won't kill their families." He gave a hearty chuckle, inferring the good humoured nature of his statement.

Notwithstanding Zhuang's display of flippancy, Harrigan knew there was nothing good humoured about it.

The door opened, probably just at the right moment. "You wanted to see me, Father?" Fan's size was not in the same league as Hung's or Jian's, but his solid, highly tuned physique, his panther like gait, and the hate and evil in his eyes, made him much more dangerous.

Zhuang introduced Harrigan and Sarah. Fan nodded disinterestedly towards them. "Why are they here, Father? Is it about Qiang?"

His father nodded.

Fan turned to Harrigan. "Thank you for coming, Chief Inspector, but we'll handle this our own way." He spoke respectfully but there was an unmistakable air of dismissiveness in his tone.

"The chief inspector isn't convinced Qiang was the main target of the killings," Zhuang explained. "To be sure who the target was, he needs to establish the identity of the other victims and I think it's in our best interests to cooperate."

Fan stood staring at Harrigan for several seconds before picking up the photos from the coffee table. "This is Muktar Al-Yousaf, a business associate. I'm guessing you know all you need to know about him?"

Harrigan nodded as he took the offered photos.

"This is Sophie, Qiang's latest squeeze. I don't know her family name, he'd only picked her up at the *Dark Knights* in Soho a couple of weeks ago. He did his nuts over her. Thought she was the dog's bollocks as you English say." He handed the two pictures of the girl who'd been sitting between Qiang and Al-Yousaf to Harrigan, and then studied the last four photos; the photos of Jones' agents. "These two I've only met a couple of times. They acted as some sort of liaison agents between Qiang and Muktar. I'm not sure where they fitted into the picture exactly, but they had connections in the right places. Managed to smooth out the rough spots."

"Rough spots? What sort of rough spots?"

"I think I've said all I'm going to say. You'll have to work out the rest for yourself."

Harrigan returned the photos to the brown envelope and handed it to Sarah. "One last thing. Who do you think might've been behind the killings?"

"We've no idea," they said almost in concert.

It was the answer Harrigan had expected. He returned his attention to Zhuang. "Really? No idea at all? You've just told us you'd moved to Kingsbury Marsh to expand the family business, and the only way that can be achieved in the illegal drug trade is to take over someone else's territory."

"Now hang on a minute!" Fan exploded. "We're not admitting anything about being in the illegal—"

"Please don't waste our time, Fan," Harrigan interrupted. "We all know what business your family is in, and that's not why we're here. Kingsbury Marsh is north of London, an area controlled by Kyrgyzstan mobster, Boris Akmatbayev, and you expect us to believe that neither of you suspect Akmatbayev could be behind the killings? That maybe he'd had enough of this young interloper trying to usurp rule over his territory and decided not only to teach him a lesson, but also to warn off anyone else in the business who might've had the same idea?" Harrigan looked at Fan. "Someone like—" Harrigan paused and stared deep into Fan's eyes. "—oh, I don't know, his *brother*, maybe?"

The closest Harrigan came to getting a reply was a disinterested shrug by Zhuang.

Harrigan stood. "Very well, then. Thank you both for your time, it's much appreciated. But let me give you a word of advice. Leave this investigation to us. We're not the local law, we can't be bought off, and we do not owe anybody, anything. There are no favours to be called in. Rest assured we will get to the truth and find out who killed your brother, and your son; so please, stay out of it."

"And if we don't?" Fan asked.

"Just remember, our agency doesn't play by the same rules as the local police, not by a long shot." He offered his hand to Sarah. She took it and stood beside him. "I think I've said all I'm going to say. You'll have to work out the rest for yourself," he mimicked. "Let's go, Special Agent." He stood aside and allowed Sarah to lead the way. "Thanks again, we'll show ourselves out."

Zhuang and Fan stood at the large bay window looking across the BMW's and watched as Harrigan and Sarah crossed the road and climbed into the Escort.

"Who does that bastard think he is?" Fan spat angrily. "Coming into our family home and warning us against avenging Qiang's death. *Nobody* orders the Yoon family around. I remained silent at the time, Father, out of respect for you and your home. But have no doubts when I say, that before this is over, Harrigan will regret disrespecting our family!"

"Be very wary of Chief Inspector Harrigan," Zhuang warned, fearful of losing his now one and only son. "He's not your every day run of the mill police officer. And if you don't believe me, he was the only police officer able to put your uncle in prison."

"I can't believe it! You're scared of him!" Fan accused.

"Not scared, just not under-estimating my opponent, and you'd be well advised to do the same."

"Bah! He's just another stupid copper," Fan said derisively as he stormed across the room and stood at the opened door looking back at his worried, stern faced father. "And he's not even a proper copper!"

The door slammed shut.

***

"Where to now?" Sarah asked as she drove slowly towards the A4006.

"It's too early to visit the Dark Knights, it doesn't open until four and there'll be no-one of interest there until after six."

She didn't need to ask about the Dark Knights, a strip club with a long history of drug related and sex crimes. She'd been called there on several occasions during her time at the Yard. "We haven't had lunch yet and we still need to book into the Royal Garter," Harrigan continued. "Let's go to my place at Finchenham, I'll get some things from home, have lunch at the *Red Lion*, after which, we can go to your place for your things and then book in.

Sarah nodded, and gunned the motor. "What did Zhuang mean when he said Muhammad Mahmood spoke highly of you? Is there something going on between you and Mahmood I should know about?"

"Not really. You know I've had dealings with Mahmood in the past, to both our mutual benefits and he's even offered me a job, twice. I refused, of course, but who knows, there might come a time when we can help each other again so I don't intend closing the door. But there's nothing *going on* between us; Zhuang only brought it up to let me know how well connected he was and to warn us to tread carefully. And I don't need to tell you, that as innocent as my connection with Mahmood is, it's information I don't broadcast. I must say though, it surprises me that was the only thing that puzzled you from our visit to the Yoons."

"It does? Then maybe you should enlighten me as to what great mystery it was I missed."

"How the hell did that young girl in the blue dress hear the tinkling of that little bell?"

She closed her eyes momentarily and gave a huge sigh, clearly enunciating a silent, *'I give up!'*

***

Lunch at the Red Lion, Harrigan's local, had been just like old times. He'd called in for a couple of pints of Bass and a catch up with publicans Roy and Sarah Knight, the first night he'd arrived back from the last case in Australia, but unfortunately, they'd gone to see Miss Saigon in Drury Lane's Theatre Royal.

He looked around the familiar surroundings; nothing had changed in the Red Lion. Sally, the Golden Labrador, laid sprawled out in front of the log fire, irrespective of the fact the fire had not yet been lit. Roy was at the bar and Sarah Knight was serving the lunch orders. He assumed the couple at the next table to be newcomers to the hotel when, after taking their orders, he heard Sarah Knight say, "Yes, I'm Sarah Knight, the publican's wife. And do you know what I always say? Once a Knight always a Knight, but once a night's enough," followed by that oh so familiar laugh that filled the room; the laugh that was more part of the decor than the beer taps themselves.

Once they'd finished lunch and promised to call in one evening when they'd have more time, Sarah and Harrigan had gone to Stonegate police station. Godfrey Windsor had rung Harrigan just after they'd left Kingsbury Marsh and said he had the statements from the door knocking detail. Harrigan had suggested he have them delivered to Superintendent Wilkinson at Stonegate. He'd pick them up there.

They say you can never go back and as they walked into Stonegate police station, the station they had both worked prior to joining UNIIA, apart from Superintendent Wilkinson and two other police constables, they knew nobody else there. Even Patricia Hedrich, personal assistant to senior police officers, including Harrigan, was absent, replaced by a young girl in her late teens, sitting at her desk painting her nails.

"Patricia?" Wilkinson had replied when Harrigan had asked about her. "You haven't heard? Patricia's husband died two and a half weeks ago; the funeral was last week. He had a massive heart attack on the bus coming home from work. It played havoc with the traffic, it's a wonder you didn't see something about it on the news."

Harrigan had explained they'd been in Australia, in Bracken Wells, a small country town in central western New South Wales, and news in Bracken Wells didn't stretch to London traffic.

"Where's Patricia now?" Harrigan had asked. "Is she at home?"

No she wasn't. Apparently after the funeral she'd gone to Ireland to visit her sister and wouldn't be back for at least another three weeks.

As sorry as Sarah had been to hear of the death of Patricia's husband, she'd felt a fleeting moment of guilt pass through her at the feeling of relief when she'd heard Patricia was away in Ireland. When she'd first gone to Stonegate, she'd soon realised, as everyone at the station had, that Harrigan and Patricia had a certain something between them, and had it not been for her marital status, their feelings for each other would almost certainly have taken their relationship to the next level. Sarah had no doubts about Harrigan's feelings towards herself, but there was still yet a long way to go, so why tempt fate?

***

It was almost five in the evening before they sat on the balcony of room 1402 at the Royal Garter, he with a tumbler of Ballantine's on ice, she a sparkling mineral water. They sat quietly, admiring the view of Marble Arch to their left, Kensington Palace to their right, Hyde Park directly in front with Knightsbridge just beyond, and Big Ben peeking through the skyline in the distance and to the left of centre. With the dry conditions and above average temperature for this time of year, not to mention that daylight saving had pushed sunset to almost three and a half hours away, there seemed no rush to get to the Dark Knights. The extra daylight meant patrons would be arriving later than normal.

"It's a beautiful view, but it's not the first floor balcony of the Royal at Bracken Wells," Harrigan said as the memories of those evenings they'd spent together just a few weeks ago almost twelve thousand miles away, flooded into his mind.

"No, it isn't," Sarah replied before adding. "And there's no smell of sheep shit, either." She still hadn't quite managed to get over the memory of spending eighty dollars at the duty free shop on a bottle of Ralph Lauren, Safari perfume, purchased solely for the purpose of exciting the man she'd grown to love, and he'd just sat there, waxing lyrical about the smell of the sheep in the two trucks parked across the road.

***

At the completion of their last case, Special Agents Angelina Benecke and David Lo's journey from Sydney airport to Benecke's 10th Avenue, Manhattan fifth floor apartment had taken close enough to twenty four hours, and despite the excitement of a city like New York, sleep was the order of the day. With the hidden secrets of the small, even sleepy, Australian country town of Bracken Wells revealed, and mysteries from the bowels of history solved, two week's leave seemed more than just reward.

Being a special agent in the United Nations International Investigation Agency was a rewarding occupation, and while their agency was only a fledgling and still in its evaluation period, they could not now imagine life without it. It was certainly no nine to five job by any stretch of the imagination, and although Harrigan was the best boss either had ever worked under, when an investigation was underway, giving anything less than one hundred percent effort just wasn't an option. Lo had once told Harrigan he was prepared to give one hundred and ten percent if necessary, to which Harrigan had replied, *"that's not possible"*.

From the very first moment when UNIIA had brought them together, Benecke and Lo shared both an unusual yet understandable relationship. They were two completely different people, and yet, in some ways, remarkably the same. She was a no-nonsense Amazonian black woman, who'd risen from the ghetto in Harlem to become a highly valued FBI agent destined for bigger things, a destiny she'd put aside when she'd joined the UNIIA team. Lo, was of Chinese European heritage and although slightly stockier than Benecke, was two inches or so shorter. He'd grown up in Hong Kong, and although an extremely talented off-road car and motorcycle rider with experience in the torturous Dakar rallies and destined for world championship honours, like Benecke, he'd put all that aside to concentrate on his Hong Kong police force and secret service career. Unfortunately, his refusal to be complicit with the unfettered, institutionalised corruption of the then Hong Kong officialdom, saw his career stall rapidly, eventually leaving him no option but to resign from the secret service, and join Hong Kong's prestigious Castle Peak private detective agency.

They were both extremely and probably equally competent in all aspects of high-powered, secretive, and in the interests of justice for the average person, sometimes boarder-line law enforcement, but Lo had a much lower keyed approach than Benecke and was more than willing for her to be the lead agent in their partnership.

The life of a UNIIA special agent left little time for any meaningful personal or intimate relationships. They were acutely aware of the pitfalls of becoming too close to your work colleagues, but the flesh has its needs. While there had been no evidence whatsoever, and it might easily be a figment of Harrigan's sometimes overly active imagination, he'd suspected for some time their relationship had developed beyond that of simple work colleagues. Not in the heart felt, swearing undying love kind of way, more of a, well, friends with benefits sort of thing. He didn't care one way or the other, as long as it didn't affect their performance in the field. And it was probably just as well he felt that way, because the answer to the enigma that was the relationship between Lo and Benecke was a secret closely guarded by them both.

Lo turned his head to his right and looked at the sleeping Benecke. He nudged her gently with his elbow. It was a little difficult to be certain, because it all happened so quickly, but Lo was sure she'd come awake a split second before his elbow had touched her. He envied Benecke. Irrespective of her surroundings, her years in the FBI had helped her develop the talent of being able to drop into a meaningful sleep for five minutes or five hours, and then come to full alertness in an instant. There was none of that rubbing eyes, yawning or stretching business, and she never looked around wonderingly and asked *"where are we?"* in that half-conscious voice, so common in all other mere mortals.

"Sorry to wake you, but the stewardesses are almost here with the dinner trolley."

Benecke looked at the flight monitor on the large screen at the front of the business class section of the British Airways, Boeing 747. The time in London was three minutes after six in the evening and they were still over the Atlantic, approaching the coast of Ireland.

"I wonder what the DCI and Sarah are up to?" She asked as she raised her tray from the armrest.

***

Harrigan and Sarah were in the back seat of a London black cab and it was just after six twenty when they entered the Dark Knights strip club. Like most of these establishments and although much more intense than at the Sister's, the lighting was well below what Harrigan would describe as normal. It was still early in strip club terms, and the lack of enthusiasm in the gyrations of the overly buxom stripper, who was closer to forty than twenty as she entertained a group of five males in their mid-twenties sitting at the table closest to her platform, clearly indicated the main events of the evening were still a long way off. Not that the five cheering and overly excited males cared about the quality of the performer, especially after her more than substantial bra landed on their table. But then, that's what tequila shots are for.

Harrigan and Sarah sat on two stools at the far end of the bar, giving them full view of the entire club.

"And what can I get you?" A voice said as the barman passed behind them with a tray of empty glasses. He placed the tray on the bar top, raised the wooden flap and entered the bar area. Harrigan wasn't given a chance to reply before the barman spoke again. "Mister 'arrigan? Is that you? It is isn't it?" He leaned closer to Harrigan and peered through the gloom. "Whatcha doin' 'ere f'gawd's sake? I 'eard you'd left London an' was workin' for some investigation mob at th' UN?"

"Hello, Billy. I hope you're staying out of trouble," Harrigan replied.

Billy Grey, an aging ex-boxer who'd obviously lost more professional fights than he'd won, glanced quickly at Sarah, moved towards Harrigan's far side and lowered his voice. "That your bit of stuff? Cor lummy, she looks a bit of orright."

"This is Special Agent Throgmorton, Billy. Sarah, this is Billy Grey, he kept me quite busy when I was at the Yard."

"Hello, Billy."

"Pleased t'meet ya, Special Agent. 'ow'd'ya like workin' f' Mister 'arrigan? 'e treatin' you orright, is 'e?" He leaned forward towards Sarah. "'e used t' give *me* some 'urry up in th' old days, I can tell ya."

"Yes, Billy, he treats me just fine. But if he doesn't, I'll give you a call." There was a smile in her voice.

Billy gave her a wink and turned back to Harrigan. "'an whatcha doin' in 'ere, Mister 'arrigan?" He asked again. He glanced quickly at the pole dancer, then to Sarah and back to Harrigan. He lowered his voice to a whisper. "It's obvious y' not 'ere for th' entertainment, if y' know what I mean."

"We're investigating last night's fatal shooting of Qiang Yoon, Muktar Al-Yousaf and three others at the Sister's Basement. We're told Yoon was a regular here?" It was another of those statement type questions.

"Mister Qiang was a reg'lar customer orright, but I can't tell you nuffin' more'n that."

"There was a girl sitting beside Muktar Al-Yousaf when the gunmen came in. She apparently fainted to the floor and escaped after the shooters had left. Her name is Bethany Joseph and we want to talk to her. Do you know where we might be able to find her?"

"I couldn't say, Mister 'arrigan. I don't know nuffin' about Mister Al-Yousaf or 'is girlfriends. 'e never come in 'ere, 'e lives somewhere up near Birmin'ham. I know 'e done bus'ness with' Mister Qiang, but that's all I can tell you."

Sarah removed the photo of Qiang's girlfriend and laid it on the bar in front of Billy. "What about this woman, Billy. What can you tell us about her?"

He glanced down almost casually at the picture of the dead girl. He didn't pick it up. "That's Sophie. Qiang's girl," he said quietly and looked at Sarah. "She dead too?"

"Yes," Sarah replied.

Billy purposefully averted his eyes from the photo and looked around nervously before turning back to Sarah. "I… I don' know nuffin' about 'er, an' even if I did, I couldn't—"

The scantily clad waitress serving the five men still mesmerised by the enchanting and surprisingly supple near naked body of the topless temptress, banged her tray on the tabletop with a force that clearly said '*Stop talking, and get my drinks!*'

"Sorry Mister 'arrigan, Miss Sarah, but I gotta serve Josie." He hurried to the other end of the bar and began filling the order, which was not all that difficult. Five pints of best lager and five shots of tequila.

Harrigan and Sarah turned their backs to the bar and scanned the darkness, watching the increasing trickle of late night revellers beginning to arrive. A strong, almost overpowering and gut wrenching smell of Aramis filled their space.

"I told you several years ago, Miguel, you're supposed to spray that bloody stuff on sparingly, not drown yourself in it." Harrigan turned to face the newcomer behind the bar. "But then, subtlety was never your strong point, was it?"

Miguel Alvarez smiled through thin lips, his pencil thin moustache rising slightly at either end as he did so. As his name might suggest, Alvarez was of Mexican heritage, but although being a second generation baby, born in the West Midlands, he spoke with a slight Mexican accent and those meeting him for the first time could easily be excused for thinking him to be a recently arrived immigrant. He was of slim build, stood five foot eight inches tall and dressed like a dandy from the nineteen twenties. His olive skin always had the appearance of continued sweating. "Eet's nice to see you too, Chief Inspector. I'd heard you'd left the Met and were now weeth some bullsheet United Nations agency?" It was more that he was seeking confirmation than asking a question.

"You heard correctly."

"Si. So do I call you Chief Inspector, or Special Agent?"

"Chief Inspector will do fine."

Alvarez then turned towards Sarah and gave her his once seen never to be forgotten nauseating grin displaying a full set of yellowing teeth, the sight of which, despite it being over four years previous when she was a Sergeant in the Vice squad and she'd first been confronted by it, still made her skin crawl. "And thee lovely Sergeant Throg... Throg—"

"Throgmorton. And it's Special Agent Throgmorton now, not Sergeant." The unmistakable tone of repugnance in her voice, almost pushed the Aramis into the background; almost.

"Very well, special agent eet is, but to me, you are a *very* special agent and steel just as beeutiful as before, and my offer to take you for a romanteec deener where we can get to know each other better is steel open." He leaned towards her slightly as he spoke, his warm anxious breath entering her personal space. She shuddered as she remembered that even his breath was sweaty.

"I told you before, Alvarez, you smelly little pervert, you make me want to vomit." She pushed the photo towards him and took an involuntary half step away from the bar. "Tell us about *her*."

He picked up the photo and studied it closely, well, drooled might be a better description. "Ah, yes, the lovlee Sophie. She was a dancer here, for a while. Beeutiful young body; beeutiful teets."

"How long had she been working here before she hooked up with Qiang Yoon?" Harrigan asked.

"Hooked up with Qiang?" He glanced quickly towards the other end of the bar before continuing. "Beelly tell you she was Qiang's girl?" It would've sounded like an innocent enough question had it not been the tone of evil accusation in each spoken word.

"No, his brother Fan told us. Billy just said her name was Sophie, he didn't mention Qiang," Harrigan lied, fearful of what might happen to Billy if this crazy cockroach thought he'd been talking out of school.

Their attention was turned away from their conversation as the roar of the increasing crowd filled the room heralding the appearance of two new, much younger, sexually charged dancers. Harrigan guessed them to be in their late teens, both with perky breasts, taut skin, a complete absence of cellulite, and wearing G strings and a well-rehearsed smile designed to give the impression they enjoyed being there. The older dancer was now standing beside the table of her five drooling admirers, and as she reached towards the centre of the table to retrieve her bra, her more than ample right breast rested on the shoulder of the youngest member of the group. She whispered into the young man's ear as she retrieved her bra. His chair skidded from the table as he rose quickly, took, no, *grabbed* the bra and with more groping than was necessary, put the straps over her shoulders, clipped it at the back and began settling her breasts comfortably into the cups. She allowed several moments to pass before reaching up and after gently taking hold of his right hand, led the eager, and, by the somewhat large and extremely obvious protrusion in the front of his trousers, overly excited young man towards the darkness of the door leading to the back rooms.

"Still running your prostitution racket on the side, I see," Harrigan said as he turned back to Alvarez.

"Prosteetution?" Alvarez replied innocently. "No, Chief Inspector, like I told you a long time ago, these girls are just dancers. What they do in their own time ees nothing to do weeth me. Ees not my beesiness."

Harrigan tapped the photo. "Tell me about the girl."

"What ees there to tell? She was a dancer who hooked up with Qiang. There ees nothing else."

With no hint of what was about to happen next and almost quicker than the human eye could see, Harrigan's left arm shot out across the bar, grabbed the front of Alvarez's shirt and pulled his upper body onto the bar top, his gold necklaces crashing loudly onto the black laminate as they fell recklessly from his open shirt. A wheezy, sort of screaming gasp rushed painfully through yellowing teeth as his ribcage slammed onto the hard surface. Harrigan didn't need to look behind him to know what was happening, his well-honed sixth sense told him that. He pulled his Glock from the shoulder holster with his right hand and pushed the barrel into his captive's left ear.

"Tell your goons to back off, or I'll blow whatever it is you use for brains out the other side of your greasy head."

Alvarez grimaced with pain as he moved his head slightly to Harrigan's left and gestured quickly with his head.

Sarah spun quickly on her heel and with her hand reaching into her shoulder bag and her back now against the bar, saw two extremely muscular and obviously very fit security guards standing threateningly near the tables four metres away, their shining shaved heads reflecting the subdued blue, violet and red lighting. The newly arrived customers at the closest table, although frightened and desperately wanting to get up and run away but just as desperately not wanting to lose such a sought after table so close to the dancers, sat in silent confusion not knowing whether to look at what was happening at the bar or at what the young dancers were doing with their four perky breasts. Sarah removed her weapon from the leather bag and took a meaningful step forward. Her actions had the desired effect on the two heavies who turned suddenly and hurried to the far side of the room.

With Sarah now one pace from the bar, Harrigan dragged the hapless Alvarez along the bar top, spilling the empty glasses Billy had put there earlier onto the floor. As they reached the opening at the end of the bar, Alvarez's feet fell to the ground and, half walking, half running and half stumbling, Harrigan propelled him towards the end cubicle against the far wall of the club. Seeing the fearsome man with a gun in one hand and the owner of the club in the other striding towards them, the three occupants of the cubicle slid frantically along the leather seat and scrambled out from behind the rectangular table. And just as well, really, because when Harrigan was still two metres from the cubicle, he swung savagely to his right and launched a now flailing Alvarez through the air, destined to land on the rectangular table, his head quickly disappearing over the far edge towards the recently vacated leather seat at the rear of the cubicle. Harrigan and Sarah stood silently as they watched his body, almost comically and in slow motion, continue its journey, eventually coming to rest leaving just one leg still lying on the tabletop.

Sarah turned and faced the room, her hand still resting on her Glock now returned to her shoulder bag. The two young dancers continued to perform their exotic duties, seemingly oblivious to what was going on around them, and definitely oblivious to the fact that all eyes were now firmly fixed on the cubicle. Which just goes to prove the fact, two law officers and one cowering club owner, beats four perky breasts every time.

"Sit up!" Harrigan ordered.

Alvarez lay still.

Harrigan reached across the table, took hold of Alvarez's shirt collar and accompanied by the tortured sound of tearing cloth, pulled him up roughly to a sitting position. "Now, tell me about the girl."

"I… I don't know what you want me to say. She was a dancer and she—"

Harrigan slapped him on the face. Not a back hander; an open handed slap. A derogatory slap. A belittling slap designed more to injure pride than inflict pain. "I think she was more than just a dancer, I think she was a plant, sent here to get close to Qiang, and I want you to tell me who it was put her in here."

"Who… who *what!*?"

Harrigan slapped him again. Harder. Twice. "Was it Boris Akmatbayev?" He spoke in lowered tone, not wanting anyone else in the club to hear the name.

A blaze of fear went through Alvarez's eyes.

"Did Akmatbayev bring Sophie to you and tell you she was going to dance in your club, and for you to keep your nose out of whatever it was she did? And if the word got out she was an Akmatbayev plant, he'd come back and cut your balls off or something equally as unpleasant?"

Alvarez looked down at the table and gave an ever so slight nod of agreement.

"And when she targeted and hooked up with Qiang, you guessed Akmatbayev was about to make an example of Qiang as a warning to anyone else contemplating trying to horn in on his area, and although this was supposed to be a Qiang stronghold, you were too scared to say anything?"

Alvarez looked up pleadingly at Harrigan. "Pleese, Meester Harrigan. We're talkeeng about Akmatbayev. The man's a monster! Hee's fuckeeng crazee!"

"Now there's the pot calling the kettle black," Sarah mumbled to no-one, louder than she'd intended.

"So it *was* Akmatbayev," Harrigan said as he stood back from the table. "Now, that wasn't so hard was it? If you'd told us that in the first place, we could've avoided all the theatrics." He looked at Sarah. "I think we have all we need for now."

"Pleese, Meester Harrigan, don't say a word about me confirming you were right about Akmatbayev; he'd keell me if he found out."

"Are you seriously asking me not to say anything to Akmatbayev because he'd kill you if I did? Where's my incentive in that?" Harrigan turned towards Sarah who was already making her way slowly towards the front door and spoke to the back of her head. "That sounds more like two birds with the one stone to me; doesn't it sound like that to you, Special Agent Throgmorton?"

He didn't hear her reply, but the nodding of her head was sufficient.

"I'll tell you what, Alvarez," Harrigan continued as he turned back to the table. "I'll make you a deal. I won't say anything to Akmatbayev, on the proviso nothing happens to Billy. Billy told us nothing, and if I hear any harm has come to Billy, and I mean, any harm at all, I'm going to assume you'd decided to teach him a lesson anyway, and I'll not only tell Akmatbayev you spilled your guts, before I do that, I'll come here and cut your balls off myself!" Harrigan thought for a few seconds and then added as an afterthought. "And even worse than that, I might even throw you under the bloody shower! And for God's sake lose that stupid accent!" He hurried after Sarah.

"How'd you know Sophie was an Akmatbayev plant?" She asked as they pulled away from the curb.

"I didn't know. But it *had* crossed my mind that with Yoon starting to move into his territory, Akmatbayev would want to find out everything he could about Yoon's operation before closing him down. The best way to get that information would be to have someone on the inside. We know the two on the end were Eain's people, and the girl who fell to the floor on the other end was with Muktar, so Sophie was the only one left. I took a shot."

Sarah continued to drive silently towards the Royal Garter, there was nothing else to be said.

***

It wasn't until ten o'clock that Harrigan and Sarah heard Benecke and Lo arrive at their rooms directly across the hallway from theirs. It was fifteen minutes after that, Benecke knocked on their door.

Sarah let the other two team members in, and after several minutes of the *"how was your flight", "yes it is warm for this time of year",* and *"bloody customs"* small talk, equally loathed by Harrigan and Benecke alike but secretly enjoyed by Sarah and Lo, Harrigan handed his visitors a glass of their preferred alcoholic beverage. Sarah refused his offer of another chardonnay; he topped up his tumbler of Ballantine's.

Benecke sipped her bourbon and coke and walked around the living area in a manner that clearly stated she hadn't missed the fact they were sharing the same room.

"Yes, Benecke, you don't need to ask. Sarah and I are, well, we're—"

"You're an item," Benecke finished for him and immediately turned and looked directly at David Lo. Lo put his tumbler of Ballantine's on the coffee table, withdrew his wallet from his back trouser pocket and handed Benecke a crisp, new, twenty pound note.

Benecke took the note and shoved it in her bra. She looked across to Harrigan, and frowned at his quizzical facial expression. "Oh, come on now, Sir, surely you didn't think for one minute that Lo and I wouldn't have a bet on how long it was going to take for you and Sarah to hook up."

Harrigan looked at Sarah and shrugged. "It looks like we were the only ones who didn't know this was going to happen," he said.

'No. It looks like you were the only one who didn't know it was going to happen is more like it!' she thought to herself as she smiled innocently and replied. "Yes, it appears we were."

"Okay, let's get down to business." Harrigan had tired of the benign chatter; there was work to do.

With the lights of London shining through the sliding glass doors leading to the balcony, they sat at the round wooden table in the centre of the living area of the open plan room. The table was sturdy enough, and highly polished, but it had a disappointing cheapness about it that spoke volumes of the tight margins hoteliers, and most other businesses for that matter, were now forced to work with in the new, 'free market' philosophy.

The other three sat quietly around the table as Harrigan brought Benecke and Lo up to date.

"And that's about it," he concluded. "We have five victims, seven if you count the doormen, but they're just collateral damage. We don't know who the shooters were or who sent them, who the target was, or the whereabouts of the girl at the table who fell to the floor and escaped unharmed and who we assume to be Bethany Joseph."

"You also have doubts about Chief Constable Jones' motive for calling us in?" Lo more probed than asked.

"More an uneasiness than doubts," Harrigan replied.

"Why?" Lo asked.

"When spooks are involved, nothing is rarely as it first seems, that's all; nothing definite. It's a gut feeling." He pushed the folder of witness statements taken from residents of Brewer Lane across the table to Lo. "Have a look at these. Tell me what you see."

He refilled his tumbler while Benecke and Lo studied the statements.

Lo eventually closed the folder and pushed it back to the centre of the table. "It's what you'd expect. Except for the two in the third floor unit almost opposite, nobody saw anything."

Harrigan sat back, folded his arms and stared across the table. It was obvious to Lo and Benecke he'd seen something they hadn't. Benecke retrieved the folder and looked again. Sarah, deciding she'd have another chardonnay after all, took the bottle from the ice bucket and refilled her glass, careful to avoid the water dripping from the bottom of the bottle from falling onto the table top.

"It's getting late." Harrigan unfolded his arms and stood from the table while Lo and Benecke continued scanning the statements. "We have an early start in the morning, so I think it's time we called it a night."

Lo and Benecke returned the statements to the folder a second time, and as Harrigan clearly wasn't about to elaborate any further, let the matter drop, downed their drinks and took their empty glasses to the kitchen area.

"We'll see you both tomorrow morning at four thirty. I want to go to Brewer Lane and interview a couple of the residents of the block opposite the Sister's before they leave for work. Once we've finished there, we'll drive up to Birmingham and visit Al-Yousaf's headquarters. I'm interested to see who's taken over his operation now Muktar is no longer with us."

They said their good nights, and Benecke and Lo returned to their respective adjoining rooms across the hallway. Harrigan closed the heavy curtains across the balcony doors, emptied the still full glass of chardonnay Sarah had left sitting on the table into the sink, turned out the lights in the living area, and walked towards the lighted bedroom.

Chapter Three

At four fifty-eight the next morning, the rented Vauxhall Senator pulled into the curb outside number 39A Brewer Lane, a heritage listed four storey sandstone apartment building directly opposite the Sister's Basement. Before finally turning in for the night, Harrigan had decided his ZX Mazda coupe and Sarah's Ford Escort were both too small for the four of them. He'd considered taking up Eian Jones' offer of the use of one of his agency's vehicles, but he still had reservations about Jones' motive for inviting them into the investigation, and had instead, arranged with the concierge to have a rental car available first thing this morning.

He pressed the button to apartment 2A on the security intercom panel, alongside which was a name tag with the neatly printed name, Welby. He stood back and as he waited, he glanced casually at the blue English Heritage plaque which read *"Admin. office of the Porters Brewery, 1709 – 1940. Brewery destroyed during the WWII German blitz of 7th Sept. 1940."*

He pressed the buzzer a second time. A click sounded through the speaker.

"Who is it?" A sleepy voice asked.

Harrigan introduced himself and at the request of the sleepy voice, raised his badge towards the camera above the row of buttons.

"Do you know what time it is? What do you want?" The sleepy voice asked with a touch of irritation.

"We need to talk to you about the statement you gave concerning the shootings at The Sister's Basement. *"*

"We've already told the previous officers we didn't see or hear anything. What else is there to talk about?"

"Mister Welby. It's early, you're tired, we're tired, and I've been very patient. But now, I'm all out of patience, and if you don't—"

He was interrupted by the sound of a buzzer followed quickly by a loud click as the front door lock opened. "Come on up, we're on the first floor."

A bland, unimaginative yet functional and undoubtedly nineteen fifties décor confronted the team as they entered the corridor running between the two front ground floor apartments. At the end was a smaller corridor running at 90 degrees across their path, reminiscent of a suburban roadway "T" intersection. Obviously the façade was all that had been preserved of the original Brewery administration building. The heavy duty grey coloured linoleum floor covering, although beginning to show the signs of wear, was clean, but without that highly polished hospital floor finish. Harrigan stopped at the crossways corridor. The two, rear ground floor apartments faced directly towards them, a narrow, elongated opaque window running almost floor to ceiling was fitted in the wall to the left, and a stairwell was located to the right. There was no lift.

The light coming from the five large circular ceiling fluorescent lights, each fitted beneath a forty inch Imperial Pattern plaster rose fitted in the corridors' ceilings, together with the light from the street lights coming through the elongated window, gave the whole area ample illumination. Harrigan turned to the right and hurried towards the stairwell.

The area at the top of the stairs replicated the area immediately below. Harrigan turned to his left and walked briskly towards apartment 2A, which he thought should've been 1A because they were on the first floor, not the second. He'd barely had time to reach the white plastic doorbell button when the door opened.

"Please, come in," the slim man with the traditional, well-barbered, college style haircut and wearing a red and black what looked to be silk, knee length dressing gown said softly as he ushered his guests passed him. "Go through to the living room!" He called a little louder as he closed the door.

The apartment was what you'd expect a two bedroom London apartment to be. A kitchen adjoining a small dining area stood immediately on the left behind the wall of the small hallway. The dining area opened up into a larger open-plan living space with double glass panelled doors at the far end leading to a tiny balcony. The bathroom, a small services room, and second bedroom were on the right. Harrigan assumed the master bedroom to be behind the closed door on the left. The apartment was tastefully decorated in retro style, with bright colours, glossy red lampshades on spindly stands, chrome legs on chairs of various design, and several Tommervik prints hanging on three walls and between what looked to Harrigan to be just square pieces of wood painted in gaudy colour.

Alan Welby introduced himself. "My, my, four of you. You must consider my partner and I very dangerous, Chief Inspector, er, *Chief Inspector?* Not *Special Agent?*"

Harrigan explained his aversion to the 'too Hollywood' title of special agent and his pride at being a chief inspector in the London Met.

"Good for you, Chief Inspector, I think you're absolutely correct; you stick to your guns," Alan replied eagerly in support. "Now, you said you had some questions?"

"Yes, I—"

Harrigan was interrupted by the sound of the door of the master bedroom opening and the appearance of a sleepy eyed young man who could easily have passed himself off as Alan Welby's twin brother. "What in the name of living Harry is going on, Alan? And… and who are all these *people?*"

"This is Geoffrey Dowling, my partner," Alan Welby explained to Harrigan before introducing the UNIIA team.

Geoffrey Dowling frowned. "*Chief Inspector?* Aren't you a special agent like the others?"

"I'll explain that later, Geoffrey," Alan Welby said softly. "The Chief Inspector and his team are here to ask us some more questions about the shooting at the club across the road."

"All *four* of them?"

"I… I said that too, Geoffrey."

"More questions!? What possible questions could you have!? We heard nothing, we saw nothing. What else is there to know?"

"Mister Welby," Harrigan said, ignoring the newcomer to whom he had taken an instant dislike. "You said in your statement, you heard nothing. Does that mean you heard nothing at all, or nothing out of the ordinary?"

"Well, um, that's a little difficult to answer absolutely truthfully. Definitely nothing out of the ordinary, but did we hear nothing at all? We have double glazing in all our front windows and the door leading to the balcony, and except for the, er… low hum I guess you'd call it, sound of traffic noise from Piccadilly Circus in the very busy times, it keeps out everything else. And to be honest, once you've lived here for a while, you don't even hear the hum; you sort of subconsciously tune it out."

They all stood in silence as Harrigan cocked his head to the left and listened to the low hum of traffic to which

Welby had referred. It was as Welby had described. He walked to the double glass panelled doors, turned the key in the lock beneath the handle on the left side door and opened the door. Even at this early hour, the immediate sounds of honking horns and rattling diesel motors of the red busses, black cabs and delivery vans as they jockeyed for position around Piccadilly Circus filled the room. He shut the door and walked back towards Welby. "I see what you mean about that double glazing. And the bedroom windows are just as effective?"

Welby nodded. "Yes, you're welcome to have a look if you want to."

"No, that won't be necessary. One last thing. You said at the time of the shooting, you were preparing to go to bed. So, where were you, *exactly*. In the bedroom, in here clearing up, maybe the kitchen, bathroom…?" His voice faded into silence.

"For God's sake, enough is enough!" Geoffrey Dowling exploded. "We were getting ready for bed! It was a weeknight and we had to get up early and prepare ourselves to go to work! We told you! We didn't hear anything, so we don't *know* when *exactly* it happened, so how the fuck are we supposed to know where we were!? And apparently it was all over in a few seconds and most of it happened inside the club." He spun on his heel. "I'm going back to bed, I've had enough of this nonsense. And if you've got any sense, Alan, you'll piss these people off and come back to bed too. We have to be up in an hour." Without another word, he strode into the main bedroom and slammed the door.

"I'm sorry, Chief Inspector, I must ask you to leave. Geoffrey can get quite angry if I don't do what he wants."

"That's okay, Mister Welby, we're finished here anyway. Thanks for your time."

With the door of apartment 2A firmly shut behind them, Harrigan walked to the apartment next door and knocked. It was a similar story. The coloured lady of around fifty years of age confirmed they too had double glazing, but as her husband was a London bus driver on morning shift, they'd been in bed at the time. He'd been asleep, she'd been reading a book.

Albert and Mary Scraggs, the retired couple in apartment 4A on the third floor had been in the dining area having their first cup of tea of the day when Harrigan had pressed the door chime. There'd been a hint of excitement in their voices as they'd invited their visitors into the apartment and insisted they all had a cup of tea and a slice of Madeira cake. The old lady in the blue fleecy dressing gown busied herself in the kitchen, while her husband quizzed Harrigan about UNIIA. "To be honest, Chief Inspector," he'd said. "I've never heard of your agency. No offence mind you." He'd then been fascinated by Benecke's FBI history, and Lo's experience in the Hong Kong secret service. His attention had then turned to Sarah. He'd looked at her for several moments and after glancing quickly towards Harrigan, leaned forward and whispered loudly. "You and the Chief Inspector stepping out together are you? If you're not, you should be, you'd make a good couple; like me and Mary." Harrigan had rolled his eyes and then slowly shaken his head.

The elderly couple's recount of the events of the previous evening had many similarities to the stories they'd heard in the previous apartments. The double glazing muffled the general sounds from the outside, and besides, they'd been watching repeats of the *Two Ronnies* on BBC1. "It's all repeats these days, isn't it?" Mary Scraggs had added. No, they had definitely heard nothing out of the ordinary. Harrigan had thanked them for their hospitality, and despite his best efforts to leave, had been given no option but to stay and listen while the elderly couple told their story of having lived there since nineteen fifty-six, that their street had a somewhat unsavoury reputation but they'd never had any trouble. They went on to explain they'd been much younger when they bought the apartment and the view from the third floor had been one of the main attractions. Unfortunately, the stairs were now a little too much, especially on shopping day. "Not that we buy a lot of groceries these days," they'd agreed in unison.

"One more to go, and then we're off to Birmingham," Harrigan called as he returned down the stairs to the second floor and apartment 3B. The door was opened by a man in clean and pressed casual clothes.

"Mister Barnaby?" Harrigan asked and showed his badge and announced who they were.

"Yes, Chief Inspector, and please, it's Asher." He stepped aside. "Come in. Come in." He nodded politely to Sarah, Lo and Benecke as they filed past him and followed Harrigan into the living area. The apartment layout was exactly as all the others. The one immediately noticeable difference, however, was the décor and furnishings. Where the other apartments had a feeling of warm homeliness about them, even the retro décor in 2A, this apartment screamed with a minimalist and obnoxious arrogance. But as minimalist as it was, none of the visitors missed the two telephones, facsimile machine, IBM PC and laser printer in the lounge area.

"Please, Chief Inspector, Special Agents, be seated and I'll get you some coffee?" It was a statement Asher Barnaby turned into a question as he waved his arm towards the Faema e61 home espresso machine taking pride of place in the kitchen.

They all declined, unwilling to rid themselves of the lingering taste of Mary Scragg's properly brewed tea (even Benecke) and homemade Madeira cake.

Their facial expressions were not foreign to Asher Barnaby, they were expressions used by almost all non, *young, upwardly-mobile professionals* when confronted by one of the growing band of the progressive young, of which he was one. "Welcome to yuppie land," Asher laughed.

"Asher!" The thirty something young owner of the slim, perfectly proportion body in the designer jogging suit and dark powder blue Nike Air Jordan III trainers chastised from the doorway of the main bedroom. "I thought we'd agreed you would stop using that dreadfully common and vulgar term." She looked towards Harrigan. "I do apologise, Chief Inspector."

"You seem to know who I am. Have we met before, Misses—"

"That's *Ms*," she interrupted sharply. "Ms Reed. Asher and I are not married, we're partners," she announced with the pride of a Germaine Greer groupie. Ignoring his unfinished question and with her outstretched arm thrust forward like some all-conquering spear of feminism, she strode towards Harrigan.

"Ms Reed," Harrigan said as he nodded politely and carefully matched the firmness of her handshake.

"It's Julia," she almost ordered as she released her hand and, after subconsciously seeking out who she assumed to be a feminist soul mate, moved towards Benecke.

"And you are Special Agen—" She caught her breath with a slight gasp as the pain caused by Benecke's vice-like grip shot through her bony fingers.

Benecke'd had no intention of sparing this person she'd recently learned the British would call a "plonker", from being knocked off her high horse. "Benecke. Special Agent Benecke."

Unwilling to lose face in front of these, *'well, they're just public servants really',* rubbing her throbbing hand was not an option. She acknowledged Lo and Sarah with a silent nod and turned to Asher. "Asher, get these people some coffee, and answer their questions, I must leave for my morning run; I'm late already." She turned to the visitors, threw them a group what only could be described as an air hostess smile, glanced a second time at her Seiko Diver deliberately ostentatious watch, and with an overly exaggerated sigh of non-appreciation at what she'd considered to be a time wasting exercise, hurried towards the front door.

"Excuse me, Ms Reed, but we need to speak to you too," Harrigan called.

Even though her back was towards them, her annoyance was obvious to all in the room. "I'm sorry, Chief Inspector," she called back without turning. "I told you, I'm late already. Asher can tell you everything you want to know." She took another step towards the door.

"I'm sorry too, Ms Reed, but it doesn't work that way. I need to talk to both of you and we can do it here, or at Scotland Yard, it's your choice."

Her second loud sigh and dramatic heave of the shoulders were clearly designed to reinforce the message to Harrigan that she did not appreciate being spoken to as a subordinate. Unfortunately for Julia Reed, messages such as that bounce off Harrigan's thick hide in much the same manner as a thrusting feminist spear does. He turned to Asher. "Okay, Mister Barnaby, this shouldn't take long. He opened the folder containing the witness statements, withdrew theirs, and handed the folder to Sarah. The two pages of the statement were stapled together in the top left corner.

"In your statement, you said you and your partner were in the front lounge area, sitting at your computer."

"Well, *I* was sitting at the computer, Julia was on the telephone," Asher clarified.

"It was getting close to eleven in the evening on a weekday," Harrigan replied. "Most people I know are either in or getting ready for bed around that time." He turned towards Julia Reed. "Not talking on the telephone."

"We're freelance journalists, Chief Inspector," Asher clarified, "and most of our work is done at night. We search for overseas news stories on the computer and talk to our contacts, seeking out stories we can sell to the local media."

"So you just plagiarise other people's work?" Benecke asked.

"No, not at all," Asher replied. "Julia and I gather facts and create our own stories."

"So, once you've gathered information about some event you consider to be of newsworthy value, you just create a story and sell it to the highest bidder?" Benecke continued.

"That's a little crude, but yes, you could say that," Asher said glancing nervously at his partner.

"So it's like one of those fiction novels the author claims to be based on fact?" The derision in Benecke's voice was clear for all to hear.

"It's tabloid journalism, Special Agent Benecke! It's about selling papers!" Julia Reed replied, still stinging inwardly from the humiliation of the handshake incident and attempting to inject a tone of sarcastic derision into her words. She almost succeeded. "Surely a woman of your experience would accept that everything reported in the tabloids isn't always as truthful as the publishers would have you believe."

Fully aware of his partner's history of getting everyone she spoke to offside, Asher Barnaby jumped in. "We could stand here all day arguing the integrity of the tabloid press, but I'm sure you have better things to do, Chief Inspector." For once, Harrigan agreed with Asher Barnaby. "Oh, and by the way, it wasn't nearly eleven, it was exactly ten forty-seven." Barnaby added.

"That's very precise, Mister Barnaby."

"Our profession is all about timing and so we're always very conscious of the time," Asher explained.

"And right at this time, I should be out running!" Julia Reed complained.

Harrigan ignored her and glanced at the pages in his hand. He paraphrased as he read. "It says here, it was ten forty-seven." He looked up at Asher and nodded briefly in recognition of the accuracy of Asher's previous comment. "You were at your computer and you heard the screeching of tyres out front. You thought nothing of it at the time, but when you heard gunfire, you got up from your computer, went to the balcony doors, opened the doors, stepped out onto the balcony and looked down towards the Sister's Basement."

"That's correct," Barnaby confirmed more for his own benefit than Harrigan's.

"And what about you, Ms Reed, did you go out to the balcony too?"

"No. I was on the telephone." The *'even a five year old could've worked that out'* statement didn't need to be spoken; it had been well and truly inferred.

He turned back to Barnaby. "From the balcony, you say you saw a large black Mercedes outside The Sister's, and two men with guns dragging the bodies of the doormen from the club entrance and onto the footpath. They then disappeared inside, leaving a third man, also with a gun, standing guard outside." Harrigan stopped talking as he turned the first page over and tucked it behind the second page. "You say you then heard what sounded like gunfire from inside the club, and approximately ten seconds later, the two shooters re-emerged from the club. The three gunmen then jumped back into the Mercedes and the vehicle sped away."

Asher Barnaby nodded silent agreement.

Julia Reed was standing behind Harrigan but he could 'feel' her shifting her weight impatiently from one leg to the other.

"Who was driving the vehicle?" Harrigan asked.

"What? Who was driving the vehicle?" Asher repeated, a sure sign he was playing for time.

"Yes. I assume the two shooters who came running from the club jumped in the back..." his voice faded, an indication he was seeking confirmation.

"Yes, that's right, they jumped in the back," Barnaby repeated.

"And the third shooter, the one on the footpath, got into the front?"

Asher gave a slight affirmative nod.

"Did he get into the passenger's side or the driver's side?"

"The passenger's side or the driver's side? I... I'm not sure. I can't remember."

"You can remember it was exactly ten forty-seven, but you can't remember whether one of the shooters got into the driver's side, which, because it's a one way street would've been almost where he was standing, or if he ran around the vehicle and got in the other side."

"Well, I... I... it all happened so quickly." He paused. "But now that you ask, he got in the—"

"It probably doesn't matter," Harrigan interrupted, purposefully indicating he had no intention of believing what Asher was about to tell him. He continued to paraphrase the rest of the statement. "It also says here you managed to identify the letter G and two other numbers from the registration plate." He folded the first page back over and handed the statement to Sarah. "A G registration means it was first registered last year, and with two other numbers and it being a black Mercedes, I'm sure it won't be long before the people at the Serious National Crime and Intelligence Agency will be able to trace it." He walked towards the balcony doors, and immediately after unlocking them and sliding them open, a tsunami-like wave of noise from the six fifteen morning traffic at Piccadilly Circus crashed into the room. "You weren't kidding; those double-glazed doors certainly keep the noise out," he commented a little too innocently as he walked onto the narrow balcony. Being less than a chair width wide, a 'Juliette Balcony' would be a more accurate description. He looked down at The Sister's and the roof of the black cab waiting outside in the breaking daylight. "Mister Barnaby, do you have a moment?" Harrigan asked, meaning, "*Come here, will you?*"

He moved to one side and Asher Barnaby joined him. "Are you absolutely certain it was a black Mercedes? It's two floors down, and looking at that black cab, you could've only seen the roof; and it was dark of course, not like it is now."

"Well, it was a little further back from where the taxi is and a Mercedes has a distinct design, especially in the grill area. It was definitely a Mercedes."

"Can you tell me the registration number of the taxi below? Just the first letter will do," Harrigan asked with a touch of, '*go on, have a go*' in his voice.

"No I can't, but like I said, the Mercedes was a little further back."

"It'd have to be thirty bloody yards further back, and there's no chance you would've been able to read any numbers or letters on the plate from up here. And from all reports, there were no other vehicles parked in the street so why would the driver stop the vehicle so far away from the front door? It doesn't make sense."

"What are you suggesting, Chief Inspector?"

"I'm suggesting that maybe you were a little confused when you gave your statement and now, instead of telling me the truth, you're trying to justify it."

Asher Barnaby stood silently, seeking a suitable reply. It was Julia Reed who came to her partner's rescue. "Yes, you're right, Chief Inspector," she called from inside the apartment. "Asher is easily flustered and not very good in these situations. The truth is, we saw the numbers as the vehicle sped away."

Harrigan turned slowly, took Asher by the arm and ushered him back into the room. He closed the doors and the apartment fell silent.

"You said *we* saw the numbers as it drove away? So you *did* go out onto the balcony, Ms Reed. I thought you just told us you were on the telephone."

"And that was true, I was. But after Asher had gone to the balcony and saw what was happening, he said something like, *"you're not going to believe what's happening at The Sister's"*. I became curious, and thought it might be a story and didn't want to miss anything. I told my contact I had to go and I would call her back." Her reply was immediate. Harrigan's many years of experience had taught him that when people are lying, and he was convinced these two were both lying, to ensure they don't contradict something they'd said earlier they invariably give a slight hesitation before answering. Julia Reed had shown no sign of such hesitation. Harrigan was impressed.

"Why didn't you say that in your statement? What's the point of lying about a thing like that?"

"It wasn't really a lie. We're busy people running a 24/7 business and being a witness can be exceedingly time consuming. We decided it best that if the police came around looking for witnesses, we'd let Asher give all the relevant details, I'd say I saw nothing, and that way I'd be left to run the business if Asher was called away to give testimony. It wasn't as if we'd held anything back, the police were given all the details."

"You said in your statements you heard a screech of brakes, which, when considering the effectiveness of the double glazing, must have been extremely loud down in the street. You weren't curious? I would have thought a noise like that would've at least been worth a quick look."

"We're very busy people," Julia Reed replied, "We don't allow ourselves time to be distracted by traffic noises."

"Yes, I agree, timing is very important," Harrigan said almost as a throwaway line. He paused just long enough to cause discomfort to the two occupants of the apartment. "And you're absolutely certain it wasn't until you heard the gunfire that you went to the window?" He asked eventually.

"Absolutely certain," Asher affirmed.

"Hmmm," Harrigan mused before staring thoughtfully at the floor.

It was Reed who broke the lengthy silence. "I'm not sure I'm completely comfortable with your line of questioning, Chief Inspector, it sounds more like you're accusing us of something."

"Accusing you? No, no accusations," he replied. "It's just that the entire shooting incident took less than thirty seconds, and like we agreed earlier, timing is everything. Anyway, enough of that, we have all we need for now, so we'll get out of your hair and let you get on with your jogging."

Julia Reed looked at her watch one more time. "I don't jog, I run, and now, because of you, it's too late… thank you very much."

***

Originally built as service roads inside the Porter's brewery, the entire Brewer Lane area was a maze of narrow circuitous cobble stone streets, running between four and five storey office blocks. Rebuilt in the nineteen fifties with a mixture of red brick and sandstone blocks and fronted with black iron railings facing non-existent footpaths, designers attempted to replicate the pre-war ambience of the old brewery. Unfortunately, the romance and poetry of the architects of previous centuries is a long forgotten ingredient in the minds of their modern day counterparts. Sadly, despite the buildings all trying desperately to inspire the locals and visitors alike, a depressing air of soullessness, forcing people to walk with heads almost bowed, shrouded the area. The only redeeming feature was the shining black with gold trim façade and hanging baskets of red geraniums of the Four Kings hotel in Amber Row.

Harrigan pulled the Senator away from the curb outside 39A Brewer Lane, turned left into Hops Lane and after negotiating several more tight corners, joined the north bound traffic on Regent Street. It wasn't until they'd travelled the length of Regent Street, eventually turning into Marylebone Road, had passed Madame Tussauds and were heading towards the A1 and the two and a half hour journey to Birmingham, that anyone said anything meaningful.

Sarah looked across at Baker Street underground railway station and then to Harrigan. "Okay, Sherlock, did you find what you were looking for?"

"You tell me," he replied to neither one of them in particular.

It was Benecke who answered. Not as a direct reply to his question but with a question that, by its own inference, indicated her thinking. "Why did Asher Barnaby and Julia Reed, the couple in apartment 3B, see and hear everything in so much detail, even down to getting a partial registration number of the vehicle, when people in identical apartments above and below them saw or heard nothing?"

"Because they are young fit journalists who were wide awake and working," Lo jumped in quickly. "The couple in 2A were getting ready for bed and from what I saw, Geoffrey Dowling rules *that* roost and even if Welby had seen or heard something out of the ordinary, he wouldn't've said anything. The bus driver's wife is in her fifties and was in bed next to her sleeping husband reading, so it's unlikely she would've got up even if she had heard something odd. And the Scraggs? They were too engrossed in the *Two Ronnies*. And let's face it, even if they had heard something, they've lived there over thirty five years and would've long lost the urge to rush to the window or doors to investigate some strange noise three floors below."

Harrigan spoke in defence of Benecke's theory. "There are eight apartments facing Brewer Lane, David. According to the witness statements, occupants of seven of those apartments said they saw or heard nothing, Reed and Barnaby say the saw and heard everything. We visited four apartments this morning because I wanted to see for myself how this could be possible. We didn't need to look at all eight apartments to satisfy ourselves they're of identical design, and that they all have very effective sound proofing. The occupants we spoke to were of varying ages and occupations so I think we have enough to assume that it's Reed and Barnaby who are the odd ones out."

It was now time for Sarah to join in the discussion. "There's no doubt about the effectiveness of that double glazing when it comes to noise reduction, but just how much noise are we talking about? I mean, I know Asher said he heard a screeching of brakes, but it was raining and I've seen no reference to skid marks outside the club so there would hardly have been much extra noise when the Mercedes pulled up outside. Sure, there could've been some extra noise, but would it have been enough to reach up to Reed and Barnaby's apartment?"

"Sarah's right, there were no skid marks," Harrigan confirmed.

"And the gun fire?" Sarah continued. "It wasn't the shoot-out at the Okay Corral and Eian Jones' people say they probably used 9mm Beretta M12's. I'm no gun expert, but how long would it take a gun like that to pump a few rounds into the doormen?"

"Beretta M12's have a cyclic rate of five hundred and fifty rounds a minute," Benecke contributed. "They also have a single shot option. Either way, it would all've been over in a second or two at the most."

"And I doubt the sounds of the shooting inside the club would've reached the street," Sarah said. "From what I remember of The Sister's when I was at the Yard, they always have live, and extremely loud bands, and local ordinance would ensure that music didn't escape into the neighbourhood." Sarah looked at Harrigan. "You think Reed and Barnaby are lying, don't you." It wasn't quite a question, but it needed an answer.

"*You're* making the case that there was virtually no noise to hear, so you tell me. And didn't anyone think it strange they knew to address me as *chief inspector* and not *special agent*? How could they know that unless they'd been briefed?"

Sarah glanced to her left and looked down absently at the traffic on the M25 London Orbital Motorway passing beneath them as Harrigan sped across the flyover. "Okay, they were lying." Her gaze returned to the road ahead. "But why? What reason could they have to lie about a thing like that, and yes, you're right about that *chief inspector* thing."

"If Godfrey Windsor can identify the owner of the Mercedes, that might throw a bit more light on the subject." Harrigan's tone clearly said he was done talking. Lo, Benecke and Sarah all took the hint.

At seven forty-five Harrigan announced it was time for breakfast and turned into the Blue Boar Services at Watford Gap. No-one argued, they were all hungry.

Having finished his traditional breakfast of crispy bacon, fried tomatoes, hash browns, little sausages and due to the absence of fried eggs, the not so traditional scrambled eggs, Harrigan was taking the last bite of his two pieces of fried bread when his mobile rang. It was Godfrey Windsor.

"Godfrey, you're up early," Harrigan said.

"Not so early, Chief Inspector, the chief doesn't see a good night's sleep as being top of the agenda. We've identified the owner of the Mercedes. It's registered to a Ms Natalya Zhestakova. Our information is she lives in a rented flat in Friedenberg House, Great Russell Street. Flat 2C."

"I trust none of your people have been around there?"

"No, Sir, we figured you'd want to do that."

"Good."

"Friedenberg House is a grand old, pale pink, four storied building directly opposite the British Museum; you can't miss it. We have her listed as being a teacher at the London College of Russian Language."

"Not the sort of person you associate with a new Mercedes."

"Especially a top of the range *S* class."

"Does she have any connection with Akmatbayev?"

"We're looking into that now."

"Have you found the car?"

"No. There're no parking facilities at Friedenberg House so we've begun a search of all nearby parking stations."

"Let me know when you find something."

"Certainly, Sir. Is there anything else?"

"No, not at the moment."

The two men rang off and Harrigan relayed the contents of his conversation to his three companions.

Benecke gave a short, derisive 'hmmph'. "So you're saying that Windsor rang you about this Natalya Zhestakova person, *before* checking whether she has any connection with Akmatbayev?"

"It appears so, yes," Harrigan replied.

"Bull shit!" Benecke sneered. "You were spot on the money, Sir, when you said you suspected this was about more than the Brewer Lane incident, there's no way he'd've rung before checking for any connection with Akmatbayev. He's already checked, he's found a connection, and is currently digging into the connection to make sure we only find what they want us to find, and if I'm wrong, I'll run buck naked down… down… whatever the main street of London's called. Damn intelligence agencies are the same the world over!"

"And you should know," Lo said with a smile, having a light-hearted dig at Benecke's FBI past.

"Jesus, you should talk," Benecke fired back with no hint of a smile either on her lips or in her voice. "You were with the fucking Hong Kong Secret Service for Christ's sake." She turned her head and stared angrily out the side window. "You wait and see. In a couple of hours, after he's quarantined any information he doesn't want us to know, he'll call back and tell you what he *does* want us to know."

"You could be right," Harrigan said. "But why get so uptight about it, we're used to people lying to us." It wasn't a question.

"I'm uptight as you call it, because I hate being used and lied to by people who are supposed to be on our side."

"Angelina," Harrigan said softly. "This is UNIIA. Nobody is on our side."

Lo looked at his watch. "Buck naked, eh? Roll on ten thirty-seven."

"In your dreams," Benecke replied.

***

The force of another seemingly relentless, open-handed yet savage slap against her already bruised face increased the ringing in her ears to a state of almost complete deafness.

"You infidel whore! You tell me you just fell to the floor when the gunmen shot my boy!?"

"I... I fainted, I... I—" the weak, trembling voice was cut short as the fierce eyed lady in the black Abaya and Niqab, allowing only her hate filled eyes to show, struck her one more time.

"You *fainted!*? After Muktar honoured you by bringing you into womanhood, you just—"

It was suddenly all too much. Battered, bloodied and having given up all hope of receiving any mercy from this brutal woman, Bethany Joseph found defiance in what she believed could possibly be her last moments on this earth. "He didn't just bring me into womanhood you vile, ignorant woman! He raped me! Not once did I invite that filthy animal to take me. Not once!"

She felt the burning tip of the dagger of fear pierce her heart as the oversized and threatening form of Ghaziyah Al-Yousaf moved one pace closer to her. The evil eyed woman leaned down until the Niqab almost touched her victim's face. "How dare you say such blasphemous things about my son. How dare you say my son *raped* you! Infidel whores cannot be raped, they are lower than a donkey mare, you stupid, worthless creature!" She stood back and out of the corner of her eye, Bethany saw the glint of steel in her tormentor's left hand. She closed her eyes and waited for death. But death didn't come.

"Ghaziyah! Ghaziyah!" The unshaven young man in his mid-twenties of Middle Eastern appearance dressed in western style shouted as he hurried into the room.

"What is it, Asim!" She replied sharply, angry at the interruption of the torturous death she had planned for the hapless Bethany Joseph.

"There're four special agents at the front door, asking for the person in charge!"

"Four *what*? What are you talking about? Are they from the police?"

"I don't think so. They said they were special agents from the United Nations International something or other agency. They have gold badges and everything."

"United Nations International Investigation Agency?" She asked.

"Yes, yes I think that's what they said."

Ghaziyah mumbled a few unintelligible words of annoyance and turned to the three young men of similar appearance to Asim standing guard over the pitiful young girl bound to the wooden chair and destined for certain execution. "Behzad," She ordered, talking directly to the young man who had tied Bethany to the chair and who had remained in a position immediately behind her. "Lock this trash in one of the rooms upstairs and make sure she doesn't make a sound. If she does, you'll both pay."

Behzad waited for Ghaziyah to leave the room before untying Bethany's bonds and taking hold of her shoulder. "Come on, whore, you heard what Ghaziyah said, don't make a sound if you know what's good for you!" He shoved her roughly through a second door leading to a stairway at the rear of the house. He didn't speak again until they were both inside a small bedroom on the first floor at the far end of the hall, the furthest point away from the front entrance. He'd made sure they hadn't been followed before closing the door.

"Why did you tell Ghaziyah, Muktar raped you?" He asked in a course whisper. "You know that's not true. Muktar took you as his companion because he respected you. He was very fond of you and you and I both know he would never have done anything to hurt you."

"I don't know, it… it was just that I knew she was going to kill me, not for what I'd done, but for what I am; a worthless infidel whore and nothing I could say was going to change that… *is* going to change that. That's why Muktar never brought me here. I guess when I realised nothing I could say would change her mind, I figured I'd give her back some of her own medicine and accuse her son of being nothing but a dirty rapist."

"Ghaziyah is from the old world, Bethany, you must try and understand she knows no better."

"You want me to understand that she only wants to kill me because she knows no better!? All I understand, Behzad, is that I want to drive a stake through her fucking heart!"

"Keep your voice down or we'll both be in trouble."

"Sorry."

He spoke as he walked towards the window. "You spent enough time with Muktar and me to know we were like brothers, and I know he would not want any harm to come to you." He stood looking purposefully at the large tree outside the window. "I have to go outside for a few minutes, a call of nature, so I want you to give me your word that while I'm gone, you won't attempt to climb out this window, down that tree and run away." He didn't turn and face her; he just paused and waited for her reply.

"I… I promise," she replied cautiously, her pulse rate quickening as her mind dared to believe escape from Ghaziyah's wrath might soon be possible.

"Good." He reached up and undid the window catch, turned and walked to the door.

"Are you saying what I think you're saying?" She ventured, desperately trying to control the nervous shiver of expectation in her voice.

He stood in the doorway. "I'm saying Muktar and I would do anything to fulfil each other's wishes, even after death. He would not want you to suffer at the hands of Ghaziyah. Muktar is dead and cannot protect you, but I can."

"But, Behzad, what about you? That crazy woman will kill you when she learns I've escaped."

But he wasn't listening, he'd already stepped into the hallway and closed the door behind him.

***

Ghaziyah Al-Yousaf walked to the still locked security door at the front of the two storey, five bedroom house standing on five acres of manicured gardens with three strategically placed copse of trees. She stared through the security mesh at the man holding a gold coloured badge. "What do you want?" She asked forcibly, purposefully injecting a tone of annoyance into her voice.

Harrigan stared unblinkingly into the two ice-cold eyes, the only part of her body this woman allowed to be seen from behind her black garb. "As I explained into

the intercom at the front security gates, we're from—"
Harrigan began.

"I know where you're from. What do you want?" She
repeated.

"We're investigating the murder of Muktar—"

"He's my son."

"Yes, we know, and we're very sorry for your loss;
please accept our condolences." Harrigan was again
demonstrating an uncharacteristic level of patience. Sarah
still couldn't decide if she admired him for it or not;
Benecke thought he should just get on with it; Lo didn't
care one way or the other. "We're trying to establish a
motive for the killings, and if you have a few moments,
we'd like to ask you a couple of questions."

"No, I don't have a few moments. I have a son to
bury and then his death to be avenged, and you can rest
assured, we don't need the likes of you or your kind for
any of that." She moved backwards and began closing the
solid wood door.

"Misses Al-Yousaf!" Harrigan said quickly. "I think
you might've misunderstood me when I asked if you had a
few moments, I wasn't giving you an option not to talk to
us, I was just being polite."

"And if I choose not to talk to you?"

"Then I'll arrest you, and we'll talk at the local police
station."

"I ignore your threats. I am a proud Muslim in a
country that hates us, and am used to being persecuted by
infidels like you. I know my rights! You need a warrant, now
get off my land!" Her voice had reached shrieking pitch
and shook with hate filled rage, all wasted on Harrigan of
course. Before he had any opportunity to respond, the door
opened wider and he saw a young man, whose appearance
left no doubt he was Muktar's brother appear behind her.

"What's going on, Mother? What's all the noise about?" He asked calmly.

"These… these *people!*" She spat the words. "They want to arrest me!"

"Go inside, Mother, I'll talk to them."

"But—!"

"Go inside! Leave this to me."

Ghaziyah Al-Yousaf threw a glare of hostility at Harrigan and disappeared into the darkness. The young man opened the security door and stepped onto the verandah. "I apologise for my mother, Muktar's death has hurt her deeply. I am Muhammad Abdul-Halim Al-Yousaf, Muktar's older brother, maybe I can be of assistance?"

Harrigan introduced himself and the team and with introductions complete, Muhammad gestured to the front steps. "Let's walk in the gardens, Chief Inspector, we'll be able to talk without interruption." He'd reached the bottom step when he spoke again, calling over his shoulder. "Why chief inspector? Aren't you a special agent like your colleagues?"

Harrigan explained his reasons as Muhammad lead them into a large octagonal gazebo nestling beneath two huge overhanging oak trees, fifty yards from the main house. They sat on the wide wooden bench seat attached to the rail and paling barrier that ran unbroken around the gazebo from the left side of the entrance to the right. "Ah, yes, the importance of titles, I understand. So, what can I do for you?"

Harrigan briefly explained what UNIIA was, and that because the shootings at The Sister's Basement might have, or at least appear to have, a political or highly sensitive national security element, they had been called in to investigate. That wasn't quite true, but he couldn't really tell him about Eian Jones' Unit 29 operatives. He'd gone on to explain that before they could start looking for the perpetrators or the people behind the shootings, they first needed to identify the prime target.

"You think Muktar might *not* have been the target?"

"We don't know one way or the other," Harrigan responded. "We know Muktar and Yoon had some kind of business arrangement, maybe even a partnership, in a business that was expanding into areas controlled by Boris Akmatbayev. It's quite possible both Muktar and Yoon were joint targets." He looked directly into the young man's eyes. "What can you tell us about their business arrangement?"

"Business arrangement?" He repeated innocently. "As far as I'm aware there wasn't one. Muktar and Qiang were just friends and on the night of the shootings, were having an evening out."

"But you did know Yoon was expanding into Akmatbayev's territory?"

Muhammad nodded. "Of course." He paused. "So you're suggesting that maybe it was Akmatbayev's men who came to the club looking for Yoon, and Muktar was an innocent victim?"

"It's possible. On the other hand, maybe, unlike yourself, Akmatbayev knew Muktar and Qiang were joining forces and they were joint targets."

"For the last time, Chief Inspector, if there had been some sort of deal going on between the two of them, we'd've known about it. Yes, Muktar was head of our organisation, but it is still a family business and Muktar would not be doing deals with the Yoons behind our backs. It would be more than his life is worth."

"An interesting choice of words, considering the circumstances." Before Muhammad had a chance to respond, Harrigan turned to Sarah who knew exactly what he wanted; she handed him the photographs.

"Do you know this girl?" Harrigan asked as he passed Muhammad the picture of Sophie.

He studied it closely and handed it back "No, I'm sorry. Who is she?"

"Qiang's girlfriend. What about these two?"

Muhammad again studied the photos, this time of Jones' people. He eventually shook his head slowly. "Sorry."

"There was another girl, sitting next to Muktar when the shooting started. We understand she fainted and fell to the floor and escaped injury. Because of where she was sitting, we assume she was with your brother. Unfortunately she disappeared from the scene before we could question her and we'd like to find her. Did Muktar have a steady girlfriend?"

"Not that I know of. He had lots of girlfriends, but he never brought them home." He leaned forward and lowered his voice. "He liked western women, Chief Inspector, and he wouldn't dare bring a western woman into the house. I mean, can you imagine how mother would've reacted to that?"

Harrigan stood and walked to the entranceway of the gazebo and stared across the lawns at the large, almost grand house. "So," he said to the open space. "You say you know nothing about your brother getting into bed with Qiang Yoon. You didn't recognise Qiang's girlfriend or the other two people at the table and you have no idea of the identity of the girl who was with Muktar on the night."

"Yes, Chief Inspector, that's sounds about right. I'm sorry I can't be of much more help."

Much more help? You haven't been any help at all you lying bastard! Harrigan kept his thoughts to himself. "This is a nice house. Expensive to buy and maintenance wouldn't be cheap, especially the gardens. The arms trade must be doing well?"

"It's a living, but most of the family money came from my father. Before we fled to England as refugees from Iraq just prior to Saddam Hussein taking charge, he'd been a senior member of the Secretariat of The Ba'ath Arab Socialist Party. His responsibilities and expertise had always been in oil production and distribution from all Iraqi oil fields. He travelled extensively to most developed countries, getting the best deals for our oil. He must've been paid very well, because when we arrived here, there were substantial funds in banks not only here, but in several countries around the world. So much so we have never wanted for anything."

Harrigan turned to face the man whose ability to maintain a continued look of innocence while lying through his teeth still amazed him. "Where's your father now?"

"He's dead; killed in a hit and run vehicle accident six years ago in London. The driver of the vehicle was never apprehended."

"Alright then, we'll probably want to talk to you again, but I think that's all we need for now. Thanks for your time and please say goodbye to your mother for me."

"I will, Chief Inspector, and sorry I couldn't have been more help. And if I hear anything about that other girl, I'll let you know."

"Much appreciated." Harrigan nodded to Sarah, Benecke and Lo who stood in unison and prepared to follow him to the Senator waiting patiently on the edge of the parking area where he had reverse parked into the cool shadow of the copse of yew trees, and immediately in front of a stunning bushy area leading into the copse that had obviously been designed by a landscape architect.

"There's no need to apologise for not being any help," Harrigan called over the turret of the vehicle. "You've been much more help than you realise."

Harrigan eased the Senator along the gravel driveway towards the large iron security gates now slowly swinging open, and turned left into Smudge Road. It was Lo who was first to speak. "You told Muhammad he'd been very helpful, what was all that about? He was about as helpful as a knife at a gunfight."

"He'll spend the next few hours going over everything he said, and wondering what it was exactly that I thought was helpful. It's always good to keep the opposition a little off balance."

Harrigan might've appeared to be a little more distracted with the traffic than usual as he turned into Wellington Street, but Sarah knew there was much more to his last comment to Muhammad than he'd just told Lo.

Lo took Harrigan's tacit reply as an invitation to continue. "He's one of the best liars I've ever come across, but did he really expect us to believe he knew nothing of the business Yoon and his brother were in? And I almost fell off the bench when he said, and with a straight face to boot, that his father must have been well paid because he had money in banks all over the world. Well paid my backside, he was on the take!"

Benecke leaned closer to Lo and whispered loudly. "I'm not shy, Lo, you can say arse."

Lo ignored her. "The bloke was selling oil to countries that can't function without it for Pete's sake! I thought the bribery and kickbacks I saw in Hong Kong were bad enough; I can't even begin to imagine the size of the kickbacks he was getting, it's no wonder he scarpered before Hussein took power."

Harrigan reduced speed as he approached the T intersection with Winson Green Road.

"What was that?" Sarah asked as a dull, thudding noise filled the car.

"It sounds like it's coming from the trunk," Benecke offered.

Being front vehicle of a line of vehicles waiting to turn at the intersection, it wasn't possible to get out and have a look. At the first break in the traffic, Harrigan drove quickly across Winson Green Road and into the visitor's carpark of Her Majesty's (Winson Green) Prison and stopped in the *no stopping* area beside the tall, oppressive outer brick wall. Benecke was first out and hurried to the rear of the vehicle. Harrigan pulled the interior release lever.

"Who in the hell are you?" Benecke asked the girl with the bruised and slightly bloodied face, probably in her early twenties, lying on the floor of the boot. The fear in her eyes even sparked a rare hint of sympathy from Benecke.

"My… my name is Bethany Joseph. I was being held captive and—"

"We're law officers, and no-one's going to hurt you." Benecke reached in slowly and took the girl's hand. "Come on, let's get you out of there and you can tell us about it later."

"Get her in the car," Harrigan said as he walked past the rear of the vehicle. "There's someone I need to talk to. I'll be back in a minute."

Benecke frowned and as she bundled the frightened girl into the rear of their vehicle, she watched him walk quickly towards a non-descript, white Mark1V Ford Escort. She had no way of knowing, but he'd noticed the Escort following them at a discreet distance in the rearview mirror since they'd left Smudge Road. As aware of, or maybe suspicious better describes his natural feeling towards vehicles that might or might not be following him, he'd managed to push his natural instincts to the back of his mind. That is, until a few moments after he'd stopped the Senator and saw it pull into a vacant space at the far end of the carpark.

After helping Bethany into the Senator next to Lo, she returned to the rear of the vehicle and watched as Harrigan spoke to the driver of the Escort. Several minutes later, he turned and walked back towards her. She didn't have a chance to ask what that was all about, he anticipated her question and answered it before she asked. "I thought he might've been following us, but he said he was some kind of social worker who worked in the prison's rehabilitation program."

"And you believed him." It was more of a sceptical statement than a question.

"That's what it says on his business card." He handed her the plain white, one colour print card. As he walked towards the driver's door, he stopped briefly beside the rear wheel and felt inside the wheel well. It was only a matter of seconds later that he placed a matchbox size black box on the turret. The magnet on the box stuck firm. He looked towards Benecke over the turret. "Social worker my arse." He looked at the driver of the escort walking towards the main entrance and then, with some difficulty, pulled the black box from the metal. "We'll catch up with him later, right now, we need to get the girl somewhere safe."

Benecke put the card in her blouse pocket.

He didn't turn on the ignition key immediately, choosing instead to stare unblinkingly into the rearview mirror, waiting for the driver of the Escort to climb the five main steps of the prison and approach the intercom beside the main entrance.

***

"What do you mean, she's *escaped*!?" Behzad felt the drops of spit on his skin and the hot breath burning his eyes as Ghaziyah Al-Yousaf screamed no more than six inches from his face, her niqab now thrown carelessly onto the floor. "Go! Go all of you! Find her! Bring her back! She must not get away, I have not yet finished with that little whore!" Four young, muscled men, all with short cropped jet black hair and dark black stubble on their faces, recently summoned to the room at the news of Bethany's escape, moved quickly towards the door. The crazy eyed woman turned back and faced the fearful Behzad, his body tensed against the ropes tying him to a heavy wooden chair now placed in the centre of the room. "Come back without her and, so help me Allah, you will all suffer the same fate awaiting this wretched dog."

Chapter Four

Eian Jones sat behind his understated polished mahogany desk in the Home Office and Foreign Affairs building in Parliament Street, Whitehall, studying the latest report titled *Serious Crime and Home Grown Terrorism in the Counties.* The Serious National Crime and Intelligence Agency was, even with the inclusion of MI5 and MI6, the most respected agency across all law enforcement agencies and the intelligence community. The high standing of his agency, was a reflection of Jones' own personal standing with the Home Secretary and most other senior members of the cabinet, including the Prime Minister. But despite such high status, Jones had purposefully avoided the usual excesses bestowed without reservation by the Civil Service on its senior bureaucrats, and his office décor was no exception. It would be untruthful to infer it wasn't several steps beyond a desk in the typing pool, but it certainly had an *everyman's* touch about it.

He looked up from the report at the sound of a knock on the door. "Come"! He called. It was Godfrey Windsor. "Come in, Godfrey, take a seat." He gestured to one of the soft, brown leather padded visitor's chair on the opposite side of the desk and closed the report. "You look worried, Godfrey, what's up?"

"I've received a call from Jay Kornick. Harrigan approached him in the car park of Winson Green Prison and asked why he was following him. He told Harrigan he hadn't been following him he'd just been going the same way and that he was a part time social worker at the prison. Kornick often uses the social worker cover story; apparently most people see social workers as harmless "do-gooders" and never question it. A bit like being a priest I suppose. Harrigan took one of his social worker business cards, apologised for the accusation and returned to the Senator."

"He actually said Harrigan *apologised*?"

"Yes."

"And Kornick thinks Harrigan bought his story?"

The hint of doubt with a splash of sarcasm in Jones' reply brought a slight frown to Windsor's forehead. "He believes so, Sir," he answered, slower than he'd intended. "He did say he'd no idea what tipped the Chief Inspector off. Granted he'd been tailing hem since they'd left their hotel early this morning, but he'd followed our standard operating procedures and had contacted two of our other agents and swapped vehicles at the Blue Boar at Watford Gap and again in Birmingham. He'd placed a tracking device on Harrigan's car when it was at Brewer Lane, so it'd been easy to remain at a discreet distance and blend in with the other traffic. Jay's very experienced in this kind of work, and it's the first time he's ever been caught out."

"This is the first time he's ever come up against Harrigan. Never forget, Godfrey, the DCI isn't like other law enforcement officers. He doesn't sit and wonder, he anticipates and takes action, and probably even more importantly, doesn't second guess his hunches. And what makes the man so annoyingly unpredictable, is he has no time for established rules and protocols and absolutely no fear of the rich and powerful; he trusts no-one and does whatever his gut tells him. That's what makes him so good at his job. Kornick have anything else to say?"

"My very word, Sir. Once they'd stopped in the car park, Harrigan didn't approach him immediately. Instead, he and who he described as a big black woman, obviously Benecke, both got out of the car and Benecke opened the boot. They said something to each other and as Harrigan began walking towards him, Benecke helped a young woman out of the boot."

"Interesting," Jones replied. "Did he give you a description of the girl?"

"Dark hair, in her twenties maybe. She was shielded behind Benecke most of the time."

"And he had no idea when or how she might've got into the boot?"

"No, Sir. The only time the vehicle had been out of his sight was when they were visiting the Al-Yousaf's place in Smudge Road, so it was probably while they were there. And he was lucky he didn't miss them as they'd left the Garter early in the morning. He'd been looking for either Throgmorton's white Escort, or Harrigan's ZX Mazda and it was only by chance he caught glimpse Harrigan in the Senator as he'd driven past."

"Kornick still on Harrigan's tail?"

"Yes, Sir. He'd had seen the reflection of the Senator in the large glass frontage of the building as it sped past towards the M1. It won't take Kornick long to close the gap and pick up the tracking device signal again."

"Well make sure he doesn't get caught a second time. Remember, it's absolutely imperative the UNIIA investigation remains completely independent, so remind Kornick he's not to get involved in Harrigan's investigation. The sole purpose of the tail is to provide backup if the UNIIA team gets into trouble they can't handle. I'm responsible for the UNIIA involvement, and while I might not know who's behind the shooting, I *do* know they're very serious people. I intend to make sure we have someone there in the background, just in case."

"Kornick's fully aware of his role, Sir, but I'll remind him again."

"Good." Jones sat quietly for several minutes. "You know, Godfrey, having just said we must not interfere, I would dearly love to find out that girl's identity." Jones suspected it was most probably Bethany Joseph, but he knew her by name only. He had no picture of her and could find no evidence she even existed. It was just a name, and probably just a made up name at that. "If we can find out where Harrigan is taking her and get her photo, we could run it through our database."

"Do you think she's the girl who fainted the night of the shooting?"

"Do you think she isn't?"

Godfrey shook his head. "No, Sir, not really, and as she was in the boot she was obviously hiding from somebody. Maybe the DCI will take her to the Royal Garter? I'll tell our man there to take a photo if he gets a chance."

"Harrigan won't take her to the Garter, he doesn't trust hotel rooms; he thinks they're all bugged."

"*Is* his room bugged, Sir?"

"Not by us, but who knows what the other agencies have done. They're not overly pleased that we have jurisdiction, let alone that I brought in Harrigan. No, he'll want to keep her hidden somewhere well out of reach, at least until he has all the information he needs from her."

"What about his own home in Finchenham, or maybe Throgmorton's London apartment?"

"I doubt it, those addresses are too easily traced, but have someone watch them, just in case. And have the person outside Harrigan's house keep an eye on the Red Lion just a few doors up the road."

"What about the Stonegate police station?"

"A bit too obvious; but there's an old police sergeant he used to work with, Bill Buckle, retired now and lives somewhere in Stantonthorpe. Have someone there too."

"Ali's?" Windsor tried one more time.

"No, that's Harrigan's private retreat and he likes to keep work well away from there if he can. Let's keep an eye on the places we've just discussed and keep our fingers crossed."

"The tracking device will eventually tell us, anyway. I'll tell Kornick to let us know as soon as Harrigan's destination becomes clear." Windsor stood quickly and hurried towards the door.

Jones sat silently until the sound of the closing door filtered through the room. He rose slowly and walked to the window behind his desk. "Where are you heading, Bill?" He mused aloud as he looked across the rooftops of the white stoned buildings of Whitehall and at the barge, dutifully ploughing its way slowly up the Thames. "Where are you taking that girl?"

***

Harrigan turned right out of the car park and drove past the main entrance of the prison. The man from the Escort was standing facing the intercom with his back to them. Harrigan slowed slightly, giving the man ample time to see them pass in the reflection of the large glass frontage before speeding off towards the M6 which ultimately leads to the M1 and London. At the Hockley Roundabout, he wound down his window, drove into the left lane and alongside an articulated lorry with the words, *Château Aurelien – Bordeaux* written beneath a picture of a beautiful smiling, red lipped woman pouring a tempting glass of red wine emblazoned along its entire length. Holding the little black box with the magnet to the front, he reached out towards the side of the lorry. His hand was almost against the lorry when the hungry magnet suddenly tore the little black box from his grasp and attached itself to the metal coping of the lorry's tray. Unaware of the goose chase he was about to lead, the lorry driver continued around the roundabout and towards the M6. With the tracking device now on its way to France, Harrigan immediately left the roundabout, turned into Hunters Road, and guided by Sarah as she used the A to Z, sped towards Birmingham Airport.

***

"Hello? Kornick?" Windsor said as he answered his mobile. "What was that?... You've picked up their signal? Good work! Where are they... on the M6 and heading towards the M1? Great! Now don't forget, stay well out of Harrigan's sight. Keep your distance and just follow the signal. Call me when you get some idea of where they might be heading... yes, it does look like they're heading for London, but we need to know *where* exactly." He rang off, smiled, and dialled Eian Jones' extension number on the inter-office telephone.

***

It was five minutes after midday, when, having parked the Senator in the Birmingham Airport long term car park and hiring a dark blue 1989 Mk III Ford Granada from Hertz rent a car, Harrigan purposefully avoided the M6 and travelled southwards along the A45. With most of Harrigan's concentration having been on losing the tail and ensuring they didn't collect another, there'd been little conversation since Bethany had joined them. Benecke and Lo had explained who they were and that they had been given the task of investigating the killings at The Sister's, but apart from that, Sarah's directions from the A to Z had virtually been the only words spoken. Satisfied they were once again on their own, Harrigan relaxed and glanced at the pale, confused, Bethany Joseph in the rear view mirror.

"The Farmhouse Lodge, a hotel cum golf course complex is just a little way down the road," he explained. "It serves great meals and has plenty of secluded hide-a-ways. You'll be able to tell us your story with no risk of being overheard."

Bethany didn't reply verbally. She simply looked at him in the rearview mirror and nodded her head.

This wasn't the first time Harrigan and Sarah had been to the Farmhouse Lodge, they'd stopped here when they were on the trail of Margaret's killer. Sarah was a little surprised Harrigan had chosen the complex to question Bethany. She had no doubt his love for her was real and would prove to be everlasting, but she was also under no illusion that the raw and gaping emotional wound inflicted on him by the brutal death of the woman he was to have married, had yet to be completely healed.

The buildings of the Farmhouse Lodge, or simply, the Lodge, as the locals called it, were a mixture of the old and new. In the early seventies, the current owner's father had retired from the land and handed the reins of the very successful sheep and cattle farm to his only son, a farm that had been in the family for seven generations. But like so many of the new generation, farming seemed old hat and not "cool", and the entire farming complex had been transformed into a hotel with accommodation, and an eighteen hole golf course. Despite his father's misgivings, the venture had been extremely successful and now offered one of the largest number of four and five star rooms across rural England. The golf course was designed by world champion and highly respected golfer, Arthur Oscarsen, and celebrates the reputation of being the best private golf course in the country. But despite its high status, the course still retains its common heritage and offers its splendour to non-members during the non-tournament periods. If there was a down side, it was that because of the A45 being a dual carriage way, the entrance and exit were only accessible to traffic heading north. Coming from the North, Harrigan had no option but to continue past the complex, complete a U-turn at the Coventry exit roundabout and drive back one mile to the entrance. Despite there being ample parking spaces in the front car park, Harrigan drove behind the building and parked the Grenada in the rear car park and out of sight of traffic on the A45.

The rear entrance of the original farmhouse building, which now housed the traditional English hotel and restaurant, was by no measure as grand as the front entrance, but it was still grand enough, in a rustic sort of way.

They were met by John Buckingham, the owner of the Lodge, who led them down a flight of stone stairs and into a stone walled room suitably dressed in the décor of its history of once being the wine cellar of the old farmhouse. Flickering shadows from the original, but now electrified, oil lamps covering dusty wine bottles on rickety looking wooden shelves draped with imitation spider webs, completed the scene.

"Here we are, Chief Inspector, you won't be disturbed in here."

"Thank you, John, much appreciated," Harrigan replied.

"I'll have a waiter take your order and your meals will be brought down shortly."

"Thanks again, oh, and please," he added quickly, "don't go crook at the manageress, she was only doing her job. Unfortunately, I also have to do mine, and to do that, we needed somewhere private."

"It's all good, Chief Inspector, but I'll give her your message."

With their drink orders taken and their meals still some little time away, Harrigan looked across the heavy wooden plank table at the still drawn but freshened up Bethany Joseph. "Alright, Bethany, you have the floor. Tell us how and why you came to be stowed away in the boot of our car." His voice had more of a tone of warm invitation than one of expectation.

"Where… where are you taking me?" She replied nervously, clearly more concerned about her immediate future than answering the question asked.

"I'm not sure, yet," he replied honestly. "You tell me what I want to know, and then we'll decide where we go from there."

She gave a slight nod of agreement, and continued softly, and understandably in the circumstances, with some trepidation. "I… I'm not sure where to begin, I… um—"

"Start from the beginning." Immediately recognising the simplistic ridiculousness of what he'd just said, Harrigan continued hurriedly. "It's easier if you start with something you're familiar with and work up to it. Tell us a little about yourself; where you were born, your parents, your work. Take your time, and don't worry, the rest will come."

Bethany gave a little sigh but remained silent.

"Okay, let's start with your age. How old are you, twenty? Twenty one?" He cued.

"Just turned nineteen," she replied with a slight hint of a smile. Somehow, the fact that Harrigan thought she was a little older than she was, pleased her and helped calm her nerves, which of course, was Harrigan's objective of adding a couple of years to his estimate. "I was born on the twenty first of April, nineteen seventy one, in a two bedroom apartment off Hackney Road in East London. It was nothing flash mind you, but compared to many in the area, it was top of the tree." She paused and took a large sip of her green ginger wine. "My mother wasn't a beautiful woman, not in the traditional sense of the word, but she had an animal sexuality about her that men found irresistible. Before I came along, from what I gathered from gossip I'd heard over the years, my mother used to have many men callers, but I don't ever remember anyone refer to her as a slag, or even a prostitute. It seems she only sold her favours to men she deemed to be worthy of her. It was almost like the other wives and mothers had a respect for the way she used the desires of men to pay her way. I remember overhearing my friend Elsie's mother saying once, *"At least she don't give it away. Them men, always sniffin' around, an' prob'ly married at that; why shouldn't they 'ave t'pay? Good on 'er, I say."* Anyway, her alcohol intake slowly increased and eventually, and probably inevitably given her life choices, she began to use cocaine. She was never a crack head, more a social user, but maybe it was because of the effects of a cocktail of cocaine and alcohol dulling her memory that she occasionally forgot to use protection or take the pill. I don't know the exact details, but she had one of those lapses nine months before I was born. And I know it had to be a lapse, she'd never made secret of the fact she'd resented having me right from the start. It cramped her style. It seems that once there is a child in the house, men callers are less generous with their time and money. It was more, *wham! bam! thank you M'am*, than a playful evening's romp. But just after my sixth birthday things changed. One night she brought home a well-dressed man in his early thirties, wearing a full but well-trimmed black beard, manicured finger nails and the shiniest brown shoes I'd ever seen. She introduced him to me as David. I immediately knew this was different because until that night, she'd always made me go into and stay in my room before she'd ever allowed a man into our apartment. This

David was different too. He smiled, nodded politely and said, *"It's very nice to meet you, Bethany."* I remember his voice was soft and somehow comforting. David became a regular visitor. He often stayed overnight during the week but was never there on weekends. There were also times he wouldn't call around for several weeks, but he always eventually returned. Mother told me he had a job that took him away a lot, and to be honest, I didn't care at the time because he'd been very generous not only to mother, but to me too. It was around six months later David moved us into an apartment in the better area of East End. Life was good for the next eight months, until one night in May, just after my seventh birthday, mother came into my room and sat on my bed. She told me about all the nice things David had done, and was doing for us, our new apartment, our new clothes, presents, the money he gave us, he even gave me pocket money. She then said that if we wanted to keep getting all these nice things, we must be nice to him. I didn't know what she was talking about at first, I'd always been nice to him, but the more she spoke, saying things like she wanted me to be nice to him the same way she was nice to him, I began to understand. Like I said before, I'd always known she'd resented having me, but to her credit had always fulfilled her obligations as far as I was concerned, and despite my misgivings, I felt I owed her and I told her that if she wanted me to be nice to David, I would be. Mother called out to him softly, and told him to come into my room and with my mother sitting on side of my bed, the years of me bestowing sexual favours on the man who paid our bills began. But there was never any intercourse!" She said quickly. "It was fondling and, masturbation and… and… well, I don't need to say more, but please, you must understand, never once did David have intercourse with me. He would never have done that."

Sarah couldn't help feeling sadness at the way, despite everything this man had done to her, and she to him, she still felt a need to defend him.

"How long did this go on?" Benecke asked.

"Until I was almost seventeen, when I left home."

"Seventeen!?" Benecke exploded. "You stayed there until you were *seventeen!?*"

"Almost seventeen," Bethany replied defensively.

"What happened that made you decide to leave home?" Sarah asked sympathetically after glowering at Benecke, clearly indicating her disapproval of Benecke's somewhat accusive tone.

"I'd met a boy at school. He was a couple of years older than me and had a car, and one day, well early evening really, we… we did it. I was excited and when I got home, I told mother. She was a little shocked, and said nothing at first, but what I didn't realise was that David was in the next room, I thought he'd gone away. He burst into the kitchen and began shouting and abusing me. He called me a slut and an ungrateful little bitch and then walked angrily towards me and hit me. Not with his fist, his open hand, but it was a hard and violent slap. I turned to my mother for help but her demeanour had changed as soon as David had entered the room. She too began shouting at me, and repeated David's accusations and then, for the first time ever, she hit me as well. I burst into tears and ran to my room. There was no lock on my door, so I pulled a chest of drawers in front of it and sat on the bed.

David and my mother began banging on the door, demanding I open it immediately, but I sat silent. The banging and shouting eventually stopped and my mother began apologising, saying she was sorry, that she hadn't meant it and if I would come out, we could talk about it. I ignored her."

"And that's when you left?" Sarah asked.

"Not that night. I left the next day. David had gone to work and mother had a doctor's appointment. She came to my door after David had gone and begged me to come out so we could talk. I refused, so she said we'd talk when she came back from the doctor's. I heard the door shut and I went to the window and looked down at the car park two stories below. I watched as she walked to her car and drove away. I hurried from my room, went to the toilet, I was busting, and ran to the kitchen. Mother had always worked for cash and fearful that if she'd put her money in a bank the tax man might discover her banking records, she kept her money at home in a small fireproof safe in her wardrobe, but it was locked and I didn't have a key. She did however, also keep what she called *everyday money*, in an old biscuit tin at the back of the food cupboard. I grabbed the tin and there was just over two thousand pounds in it. With the money I'd saved, I had almost three thousand pounds. I also had a suitcase under my bed that I'd used on a recent holiday mother and I had taken in France. I'd spent a lot of time during the night, carefully, and quietly, packing everything I was going to need, you know, clothes, toiletries, make up, that sort of thing, and all the jewellery David had bought me. I also went into mother's bedroom and grabbed her jewellery as well. Because of our holiday, I also had my passport and birth certificate. I looked around the apartment one last time and left. I've never seen or spoken to mother or David again."

"Do you know if they tried to find you?" Harrigan asked.

"I don't know."

"Would you be able to identify this David person if you saw him again?"

"If he still has his beard, yes, I think so, but I never saw him without it, so if he's shaved it off, no, not by his *face*, anyway."

"Not by his *face*? What does that mean?" Harrigan asked.

Bethany blushed slightly. "Well, he had an odd shaped... foreskin. It had no underneath part which gave it a kind of eyeshade appearance. A birth defect of some kind. I'd recognise *that* if I saw it again."

Even Benecke had to smile at that.

Mostly, when a person's mobile telephone rings mid conversation, it's a cause of much annoyance, but on this occasion, the sound of the ringing of Harrigan's mobile as it filled the small area, brought almost blesséd relief from the heavy atmosphere that had developed as Bethany told her story. He looked at his phone, and stood quickly. "I have to take this."

He hurried up the stone stairs, into the car park and raised the phone to his ear. "Harrigan."

"Well, Chief Inspector what can I say? You were right. UN members certainly see UNIIA in a different role than you and I do." Nelson Whitlock's voice had a definite tone of resignation as it filtered through the small speaker in Harrigan's mobile. "How this shooting in London qualifies as a case to be investigated by your team and is not a matter for the British authorities I have no idea, but quite obviously someone high up in the British government can see a public relations downside in them being involved. But, who am I to argue? I have my orders, so good luck!"

"Thank you, Sir." Harrigan wasn't an *"I told you so"* type of person.

"I've sent your leather pouches with letters of authority, local contacts etcetera to your hotel by special courier, you should get them in the morning. One other thing before

I go, Chief Constable Jones has officially retired as head of the UNIIA team and the steering committee have agreed with his recommendation that you be promoted to that position. And before you give me one of your smart alecky comments, I'm not in the mood, so please, just say you'll accept the position and let me get off the line."

"I'll accept it, for now, but before you go, Sir, you sound like you might be contemplating doing something stupid like resigning from your post as Under Secretary for the UN Office of International Investigation?" His comment ended up as a half question.

"You're very observant, Chief Inspector, and yes, you're right. I've been a bureaucrat all my life and am used to taking instructions from elected representatives, irrespective of their political persuasions or how self-serving their instructions might be. But UNIIA is different. I genuinely believed in UNIIA's potential of bringing justice to those without privilege but, as you said right from the start, the UN sees it as little more than a PR exercise, and I'm afraid, for me, that's a deal breaker."

"Sir, I also said it doesn't matter what the UN members' agenda is, as long as *we* don't forget why we're doing this is all that counts. I know you and I don't see eye to eye on many things—"

"To put it lightly" Whitlock thought.

"—but I firmly believe you are genuine in your desire to ensure UNIIA is given every opportunity to achieve the positive results you and I know it can. I urge you not to do anything rash. I'm not in the business of telling other people how to run their lives, but I'd ask you to think about it carefully, I think the effectiveness of UNIIA would be greatly diminished if you resigned."

"Thank you, Chief Inspector, that's very kind of you to say so."

"It has nothing to do with me being kind, Sir, I just don't welcome the prospect of having to break in another Under Secretary."

Whitlock could not help but smile as he shook his head slowly. He was about to replace the handset to its cradle when he heard Harrigan's voice calling loudly.

"Sir! Before you go!"

Whitlock raised the handset back to his ear. "Yes, Chief Inspector?"

"There's something else you need to know. It's a personal matter."

"Is this about you and Special Agent Throgmorton?"

"You *know* about Sarah and me?"

"The Chief Constable let it slip, but I didn't need him to tell me, it was only ever going to be just a matter of time."

"It was!?"

"Of course. You might be a great detective, but you know nothing about women."

"And you're okay with it?"

"Okay with what?"

"Two government agents having a close personal relationship."

"Why wouldn't I be? This isn't the FBI or CIA. As you've reminded me on more than one occasion, UNIIA lives in the real world, not some Hollywood movie."

The line went dead.

He returned his mobile to his inside pocket and walked back inside the hotel.

Their meals and a fresh round of drinks had been delivered while he'd been away. They hadn't waited for his return and having ordered only a light lunch, Sarah and Bethany were almost finished.

He retook his seat. "Alright then, where were we?" He asked, picking up his steak knife and fork.

"Bethany was talking about deformed foreskins," Benecke offered offhandedly.

"Ignore Agent Benecke, Bethany," Sarah said with a touch of the maternal. "Tell us what happened after you left home."

The young woman spoke without interruption for almost ten minutes. She'd left London immediately and had taken up casual work in the provinces; tending bar, waitressing, anything she could find. She hadn't known what David did for a living but he'd obviously had a good job and probably had contacts in many of the right places. Not wanting him or her mother to find her, she hadn't stayed in one place too long and only took cash in hand work.

Harrigan decided he'd heard enough of her earlier life. "How'd you get mixed up with Al-Yousaf?" He urged.

"I first met him on my eighteenth birthday. I was waitressing in a restaurant just outside Birmingham, and when the restaurant closed, some of the girls I worked with took me into Birmingham City and The Black Dragster nightclub in Gasworks Bridge Road. Blacks, as all the locals call it, is basically a men's club with female strippers and pole dancers, many of which also provide additional services on request. I didn't know it until we'd arrived, but my waitress friends all worked there."

"If they worked at the strip club, which I assume paid fairly well, why would they need to take on a second job waitressing?" Lo asked.

"For appearances more than anything. To have a job waitressing gave them and air of legitimacy, especially with their parents. And besides, unless you performed special services for the clients, the pay as a dancer wasn't all that great."

"Did you work as a dancer?" Sarah asked, purposefully avoiding asking her about any involvement in the special services part of the job.

"Just once. On that first night. I can't be sure how it happened, probably because of the outrageous number of shots we'd all consumed including, flatliners, purple nipples and something called a girl scout cookie. But I do remember one of my friends persuading the owner of the club to get me up on stage. I'd been past caring by that time and obliged. I remember stripping down to my panties, and although my lack of experience must've been absolutely obvious, the clientele didn't object to my lack of professionalism and I received a standing ovation. And, I might add, more than one request for special services."

Benecke shifted her gaze from Bethany's face and nodded directly at her more than ample bosom. "Forgive me if I don't look surprised," she remarked with complimentary light-heartedness.

"And that was the only time you ever danced at the club?" Harrigan asked, seeking confirmation of his understanding of her previous statement.

"Yes. And I wouldn't have done it then if I hadn't been drunk." She took another large sip of her green ginger wine. "Anyway, after I dressed and before I'd had a chance to return to my friends, I was taken to a table in a private alcove and introduced to the man sitting between four very serious looking men of similar appearance, all with extremely short haircuts, shaved at each side, thick black moustaches and black stubbled faces, and two scantily dressed girls, obviously well affected by either too much alcohol or drugs. I never found out which."

"Al-Yousaf was the man in the middle." Harrigan stated, trying to hurry her along.

"Yes. Two of the men on one end stood up and I was ushered into the space next to Muktar. Once the two men had returned to their seats I was trapped and feared the worse. I knew if any of them wanted to grope me, even sexually assault me, no-one would come to my assistance. But it never happened. Muktar treated me with utmost respect. Sure, he put his arm around my shoulders and pulled me slightly towards him, but it was more an action of display than one of affection. And the man sitting on the other side of me, who I later learned to be named Behzad and who was Muktar's closest adviser, also kept as discreet a distance as was possible in such a small space. Muktar did say he thought I was an extremely beautiful woman, and particularly admired my—" she interrupted herself as she looked directly at Benecke "—perfectly formed breasts, but that was it; that was the extent of any reference to my sexuality. He was the perfect gentleman. At the end of the evening, well it was actually early morning, I rode with him in the back of his limo to my apartment, and after saying goodnight, he asked if we could meet again the next evening. I agreed, and that was it."

"Not even a good night kiss?" Sarah asked.

"Not even a good night kiss." She returned her gaze to Harrigan. "And that, Chief Inspector, is how our relationship began."

"Did you ever become lovers?" Harrigan asked.

"No. I was more of a constant companion than a lover, going with him to posh restaurants and nightclubs, mainly the Dragster, but sometimes to the Sister's when he had a meeting with Yoon. The evenings were always very enjoyable, and of course there were times of hugging and kissing, but never anything overly passionate. He said he respected me too much for that and we would wait until we were married before things went any further. And besides, apart from Behzad who was never far away, there was always one or two bodyguards hanging around in the background which always served to kill the moment."

"If you spent your evenings with Muktar, does that mean you gave up your waitressing job at the restaurant?"

"No, I transferred to the lunch period. Not as much money, but I didn't mind."

"Were you aware Muktar was an international arms dealer with some very suspect clients?"

"No. I knew what ever business he was in couldn't have been totally lawful, he had far too much money to throw around for that. But to be honest, I enjoyed the attention, the high life and the lavish gifts he gave me, so I didn't ask, and he didn't tell. And before any business was discussed, whether it be with his cohorts or outsiders, I made myself scarce."

"If there were always bodyguards hanging around, where were they on the night of the shooting?" Lo asked.

"I can't tell you exactly; sitting somewhere on the other side of the room probably, like they always did when we visited that club. It was supposed to be a safe haven. Personal security, for all sides, was much more relaxed there." She paused, frowned, and looked at Lo. "That was the whole point of the place!" A tone of *I can't believe you asked that question* rang clearly through her words.

"What do you remember of the night?" Harrigan asked.

"Yoon and Muktar had finished their business talk, I'd returned to the table and we were just sitting around, having drinks and a few laughs. Suddenly, two gunmen, both dressed in black and holding automatic weapons, appeared out of the darkness and opened fire. Their sudden appearance startled me and I fainted and fell to the floor just before the shooting started. Five seconds later, the two gunmen had disappeared as quickly as they had appeared. It took quite a few moments before people began realising what had happened, the screaming started and most patrons ran for the exits. The next thing I remember was Behzad and Muhammad—"

"Muhammad? Muktar's elder brother?" Harrigan asked.

"Yes, he was one of Muktar's bodyguards. Anyway, they were standing by the table and then, seeing what had happened, they grabbed me from the floor and we all hurried out the back door to Muktar's car. Once we were all in the back of the vehicle, the driver of the car who as usual had been waiting ready for a quick getaway just in case, sped down the back alley and didn't stop until we'd reached the Al-Yousaf stronghold at Birmingham."

"Had you been to the Al-Yousaf stronghold before?" Harrigan asked.

"No. Muktar's mother lives there and he'd explained she is old world Islam and would not approve of him marrying an infidel. And believe me, as soon as we'd arrived, I realised he hadn't been lying." Bethany went on to tell how she'd been tied to a chair and abused by the crazy woman in black, of how she'd feared for her life, and the events leading to her escape after Harrigan and his team had arrived.

"So this Behzad, he saved your life?"

"Yes. I climbed out the window, saw your car reversed up close to the hedge running around the copse of trees and ran as fast as I could towards it, hoping no-one saw me. Luckily you had all their attention, and just as luckily you'd not locked your vehicle. I popped the boot, climbed in, and you know the rest."

"Behzad took a big risk letting you escape, from what you've said about Muktar's mother, she won't take too kindly to him leaving you alone with an opened window. Why do you think he took that risk?" Harrigan probed.

"I told you, he said it was what Muktar would've wanted."

"Hmmm," Harrigan replied.

It was then the waiter entered with a new round of drinks. "On the house, compliments of John Buckingham," he said with a smile.

***

"You're *where*? On the A2 south of London heading towards *Dover*!?" Godfrey Windsor asked with the touch of the unbelievable in his voice. "What?... yes, close the gap. Let me know as soon as you see them... no, I'll stay on the line." Several silent minutes passed. "Yes, I'm still here... you've found the tracking device?... it's where!?... on a lorry heading for France!? For God's sake, Kornick, how'd that happen!?... yes, Harrigan is more cunning than we've given him credit for... what do I want you to do? There's not much you can do. Just get the device off the lorry and get back here." He slammed the handset of his desk telephone into its cradle.

Windsor's office door opened and Eian Jones stood in the doorway. "What's all the noise about, Godfrey? It's not like you to raise your voice." He entered the room, closed the door and sat opposite Windsor. "Don't tell me, it's Harrigan, right?"

Chapter Five

The first thing to strike newcomers to Briefing Room C on the first floor of the Cabinet Office Building in Whitehall, was the absolute "brownness" of it. The claustrophobic impact of the teak wood panelling reaching three quarters of the way towards the dark brown ceiling, was mercifully breeched by the much lighter pastel brown top quarter section of the wall between the picture rail and the elaborate cornice. Twelve dark brown leather conference chairs stood like sentinels around the oak, boat shaped conference table complete with cherry wood inlay centre. The dark wood parquetry flooring mimicked the colour of the ceiling. The soft cove-lighting running around the room almost succeeded in its task of giving the top section of the walls a slight hint of life. But it was the artificial fluorescent ceiling skylight running the full length of the table that gave the room illumination. While recognising its own efficiency in the supply of light, it undeniably, even belligerently, boasted with pride the re-enforcement its aesthetic appearance gave to the lack of imagination and sense of boredom that filled the room. And it was no coincidence the dullness of the room was also greatly enhanced by the six occupants sitting at the far end of the table beneath a cloak of their own self-importance.

Sir John Fitzwilliam, Second Permanent Secretary at the Ministry of Defence, and Chair of the Joint Intelligence Committee, held position at the head of the table. Admiral Sir Jason Collins, GCB OM CGM, Chief of the Secret Intelligence Service or MI6, filled the first chair on the left side. A distinctly agitated Dame Joan Hamilton-Westbrook, Director-General of the National Security Intelligence

Agency or MI5 occupied the next chair along. Directly opposite Collins and Hamilton-Westbrook respectfully, were Sir Anthony Alcock, KCMG, Permanent Secretary and Director-General of Government Communications Headquarters and Sir Lindsay Springburn, Chief of Defence Intelligence Staff.

The final member of this elite sextet, Lady Elizabeth Mandeville-Fookes, Baroness of Upper Fifthwhistle and Permanent Under-Secretary of State for Foreign Affairs sat at the head of the table to Sir John Fitzwilliam's right.

"Thank you for coming, I know what busy people you are."

"Just get on with it, John," Dame Joan Hamilton-Westbrook interrupted. "We all know how busy we are." She glanced quickly around the gathering. "And if this meeting is important enough to warrant calling us together so urgently, where's Eian Jones? He's a committee member, and I would've thought the head of the Serious National Crime and Intelligence Agency would be here. Especially knowing how highly the Prime Minister regards *that* agency." She leaned back into the brown leather chair and continued under her breath. "The Lord only knows why."

Her last comment brought a leathery smile to the other five faces around the table.

"He's not here, Joan, because it's him and that damn UNIIA crowd called in to investigate the shootings at Brewer Lane I want to discuss."

"The *Massacre at Brewer Lane* the media are calling it," she continued. "Damn media, nothing but sensationalist rabble if you ask me. And why is UNIIA investigating the shootings anyway? Surely it's a police matter. But either way, what does it have to do with any of us?"

"If you give Sir John the opportunity to speak, Joan, there's a good chance we'll find out." Lady Elizabeth's gender and position in the Foreign Office, made her the single person around the table who could not only say that to Dame Joan, but for the words to also have an impact.

Sir John was far too polite to directly acknowledge his appreciation of Lady Elizabeth in bringing Dame Joan to heel, but as he began to speak, his tonal implication was unmistakable. "As you have all undoubtedly observed, our confidential minute secretary is a second absentee."

Their complete disinterest in people they deem to be below their own station in society, meant they hadn't noticed. But they did now.

Sir John continued. "Taking into account the current government's platform of complete transparency, it's essential I make it clear that the absence of a minute secretary, or any documented evidence this meeting has occurred, *and* the desire of the chair that all matters discussed are not to be repeated outside this room, are all to be seen strictly as good intelligence practices taken in the interest of national security and does not imply this meeting is in anyway a clandestine or secretive meeting."

"Then how would you describe it?" Dame Joan asked.

"It's simply an informal gathering of persons with a common interest in national security, called to discuss with complete confidentiality, recent actions taken by this committee that might have severe repercussions on the reputation of everyone here today, should those decisions not be viewed within the context of world events at the time of the decision."

"Okay, I understand," Dame Joan said. "We're covering our arses and it's a clandestine meeting."

The flippancy in Joan's sarcastic but light-hearted comment, bypassed the others in the room. Serious and silent heads nodded in understanding as pens were returned to inside coat pockets and handbags. Leather bound notepads closed.

"Very well then." Sir John grabbed the edge of the table with hands placed six inches from both sides of his body. A gesture, kinesics experts would interpret as offering inclusive openness. "Joan, your comment the Brewer Lane shootings were a police matter almost answered your question about Jones' absence. Of *course* the shootings are a police matter." He fell silent for several moments before continuing slowly and with a hint of suspicion. "That is, unless someone *here* was responsible?" He carefully eyed each one of his colleagues, deliberately pausing longer at Admiral Sir Jason Collins and Dame Joan Hamilton-Westbrook. If anyone in the room did have any involvement in the shootings it would most likely have been MI5 or MI6. Or perhaps both working together. Even the artificial skylight was forced to give a few extra, and even a little cheeky, fluorescent flickers as the clouds of well-rehearsed innocence above each attendee battled for supremacy as they raced towards the ceiling.

"I have no intention of wasting anyone's time attempting to establish why Eian Jones sought approval for UNIIA to have jurisdiction, it's happened, and we must live with it. Our task now is to ensure UNIIA's investigation stays locked strictly onto the shootings, and not be allowed to stray beyond its jurisdiction."

"Especially the shipments of arms we are currently sending to the Kajmanistan insurgent Muslim rebels in the Middle East?" Lady Elizabeth's comment was more a statement of confirmation than a question.

"In a nutshell, yes. Nobody took these rebels seriously at the start, but their progress in gaining and holding substantial regions across oil rich areas in the Middle East has been quite spectacular."

Sir Lindsay Springburn chose to expand the point. "Our on the ground intelligence across the Middle East reports that although most of the unrest is Middle Eastern countries fighting themselves, there's a definite divide between countries that support the West and those who do not. That's nothing new. What has changed, is that maintaining the West's access to oil through diplomatic means is becoming more tenuous by the day. The tricky part is not only knowing who is friendly, but more importantly, how long they will stay that way before they jump ship; Middle Eastern rulers are not known for their loyalty. And when we throw the increase in rebel fighters into the mix, fighters whose popularity is growing with the locals at an alarming rate, our access to oil is becoming increasingly fragile."

"Thank you, Lindsay," Sir John said, retaking the helm. "Which brings us back to the arms shipments to the Kajmanistan rebels. Without going over too much old ground, we agreed the uncertain future caused by the moving footprint in the Middle East, left us with no option but to ensure we have a foot in both camps. The UK will of course, continue its support of the US, siding with Saddam Hussein and the Saudi's. But it's imperative we keep some favour with countries not so acceptant of the West. Because of this resolve, we created a fictitious company to deal with the Al-Yousaf arms dealership for the ordering of small arms from Littlewood's. Arms delivered to our contacts in Urbadistan for distribution. To ensure the contents of the containers remain confidential, using claims ranging between national security, diplomatic immunity and humanitarian reasons, we also secured agreement the containers will remain sealed throughout the entire journey. And finally, I'm sure I don't need to remind you of our commitment for each of our departments to allocate funds through miscellaneous accounts to finance the entire operation."

It was Lady Elizabeth who brought up the elephant in the room. "I've gone along with this arms to rebels program to date. But these rebels are proving to be equally as murderous and ruthless as the current dictatorships. I feel obligated to ask if these are the kind of people we should continue to support? Albeit somewhat restricted and at arm's length."

Lady Elizabeth's questioning of their involvement in what was becoming a human rights disaster in the Middle East, was not unexpected and Sir John was well prepared with a response. "I'm sure we all share your concerns, Elizabeth, but our foremost concern and duty must be to protect our own. To do that, access to oil is essential." He paused. "But it's not only about oil. The Middle East is also a strategically important military location, and to have access to the area for a military base is also of enormous importance."

"You seem to be putting a lot of faith in the word of these, *Arabs*, Sir John." It was obvious from Lady Elizabeth's use of his title and the manner in which she spat the word *Arabs*, she was far from convinced. "Have you ever considered what might happen if these people have a change of heart? If the weapons we are partly responsible for putting in their hands are used against us?" She turned her attention to Lindsay Springburn. "Lindsay, what does your intelligence tell you about that new group in Afghanistan. The Taliban? From what I hear *they're* no friends of the West."

Springburn smiled dismissively. "They're just another branch of Muslim radicals with some far-fetched notion of forcing old world Sharia law on the local population. I don't like their chances. I mean, who in their right mind would want to live under Sharia Law? I give them six months at the most."

Sir John gave a slight, almost patronising laugh. "So there, you see my dear? Your fears are unfounded. The conflict in the Middle East is all about Muslim against Muslim, Shite against Sunni, Abu Bakr versus Ali, Sharia law, and all the rest of that malarkey. They have no interest in attacking the West, they have enough to fight about between themselves. Believe me, Elizabeth, the Taliban is a non-issue."

"Can we get back to the subject?" Admiral Collins asked a little impatiently.

"Certainly, Admiral. Despite the absolute necessity to continue the arms supply, there are those in the socialist left media, even some on the conservative side, who would salivate with joy if they got even the slightest whiff of the program. And that is why we're here today; to guarantee we are all cognisant of the absolute necessity that the UNIIA investigation is kept on course." He glanced broadly at his colleagues and frowned. "By the looks on some of your faces, I get the feeling some of you don't see that to be much of a big deal, so let me explain. To ensure UNIIA's independence, it has been given almost unfettered investigative powers, free from any political, local enforcement agency or commercial interference. Including I might add, it cannot be removed by any party from an approved investigation. That would be interpreted as political interference. I say *almost*, because there are two exemptions to that rule. National Security of the host nation must always be maintained, and, UNIIA's jurisdiction remains solely within the boundaries of the matter being investigated. It cannot move beyond those boundaries, and it's up to us to make certain it doesn't."

"I'm sure we can do that," Dame Joan said optimistically, maybe even a little dismissively.

"Don't be too sure, Joan. UNIIA is led by a Detective Chief Inspector Harrigan, and—"

"Detective chief inspector? I thought he'd be a special agent."

"He is," Sir John replied.

"Then what's all this detective chief inspector nonsense?"

"Harrigan's on indefinite unpaid leave from the London Met, on attachment to UNIIA. But he only agreed to join UNIIA on the proviso that although officially he will hold the position of Senior UNIIA Special Agent, he is to be commonly addressed by his preferred DCI title."

"Why?" Joan persisted.

"Something about him thinking special agent sounds a little girlie and much too Hollywood."

Dame Joan looked thoughtful for several seconds. "You know, I think I agree with him. He sounds like a man I'd like to have on my team."

"He was offered a very senior position in the intelligence community some time back; he refused. But the title thing does give an idea of the type of person we're dealing with. He's not one to care too much about the rules. He has no respect for persons of position or wealth and believes more in justice than the letter of the law."

"*Definitely* a man I want on my team." Joan iterated enthusiastically.

"Be careful what you wish for, Joan, he also believes in equal justice for the masses, not just for those of influence."

"Oh, does he? Maybe I'll pass," she mumbled.

"I thought you might," Sir John said with a smile.

"We all agreed Jones wouldn't support the rebels' arms deal, that's why we kept it from him," Sir Lindsay interrupted, trying to bring this meeting to a conclusion. "But he's no fool and I'm certain he knows something is afoot. It would come as no surprise to me that Jones brought UNIIA and this Harrigan chap in to investigate the Brewer Lane shootings, hoping that during the course of his investigation, Harrigan will stumble onto whatever it is he suspects is happening. And I also believe there is no doubt that if Harrigan does uncover the arms deal, Jones wouldn't hesitate to let the cat out of the bag."

"UNIIA has responsibilities when it comes to the national security of the country they are visiting, but considering Harrigan's reputation, yes, Lindsay, I think you're right. And need I remind any of you, if the truth is ever known, it will be us, and us alone who'll suffer the consequences."

An apprehensive silence fell across the room.

"So," Sir John continued eventually, having allowed enough time to pass to ensure they felt the full weight of their own concerns. "If we a're to keep this Harrigan chap on the straight and narrow, we must pool our resources. We need to know where he is, what he's doing, what he's planning, everyone he talks to. If we discover any indication he's getting too close, we must take whatever steps are necessary to stop him. Lay false trails, give him false information, give him someone, anyone, to blame for the shootings, I don't care. Nothing is off the table. We must be prepared to do whatever it takes to prevent him, and his team, from learning the truth. And if that fails, stop them disseminating the truth."

"When you say 'whatever it takes', what do you mean, *exactly*?" As head of MI6 with 00 operatives under his control, Admiral Sir Jason Collins needed absolute clarification of Sir John's intent.

"I mean, whatever it takes," Sir John replied with a hint of menace.

"Tell me, John," Lady Elizabeth asked soberly. "Is the P M aware of your, whatever it takes, plan?"

"Plan?" Sir John replied innocently as he sat up and turned quizzically towards the woman beside him. "What plan? You seem to be forgetting, dear lady, this meeting never took place. And besides, there are some things a Minister does not need to know, *especially* a Prime Minister." He lifted his bulky figure and air of self-importance from the brown leather chair. "And let me remind you all, one more time. If this ever gets out, no-one, and I mean *no-one,* will come to our defence. This is on our heads, and our heads alone." He turned and led the way towards the door.

A very concerned and extremely thoughtful Lady Elizabeth Mandeville-Fookes, was the last to leave.

***

Their luncheon plates, cutlery and drink glasses now cleared, Lo, Sarah and Harrigan sat together in the private hideaway at the Lodge, enjoying the smell of freshly brewed coffee. Harrigan had never quite made up his mind which he enjoyed most; the smell of freshly brewed coffee or newly cut grass. Bethany had needed to go to the ladies, and with her FBI personal security background, Benecke had been the natural nomination for the role of Bethany's guardian.

"Do you think Bethany's in danger, Sir?" Lo asked.

"I don't think there's any doubt about it," Harrigan replied. "But we won't know the exact level of danger and from whom it might come, until we decide how much of what she's told us we believe."

"You think she's lying?" Sarah's question was not so much to state the obvious, but more as encouragement for Harrigan to share his thoughts and not lapse into one of his extremely annoying thoughtful silences.

"I think most of the stuff about her early life and that David arsehole molesting her is true enough, but on the night of the shooting? For someone who supposedly fainted, she certainly remembered a lot of detail."

"*Supposedly* fainted?" Sarah failed to disguise the hint of scepticism in her voice.

"Well think about it. It was dark inside the club. Suddenly, two men in black appeared out of the gloom and started shooting. The whole event only lasted a few seconds; she barely had time to faint, let alone faint and fall to the floor."

Sarah thought for several seconds before responding. "If she'd had prior knowledge of the shooting, she could've watched the entrance door and as soon as the shooters entered the club, prepared to throw herself to the floor seconds before they began firing."

"It's more believable than *her* story. If she had been in her seat when they raised their guns, she'd be dead. And even by some wild stretch of the imagination she *is* telling the truth, why didn't the shooters get her on the way down? Given the Beretta's firing rate, they would have had plenty of time."

"That certainly adds strength to the prior knowledge theory. Maybe she's a mole for some opposition arms or drug dealer? Boris Akmatbayev, maybe?" Sarah was warming to the hypothesis.

"We can't dismiss the idea. If Jones had two of his people at the table, it's quite possible there could be other players in that same game," Harrigan supported.

"If she was a plant, why did she go to Birmingham with Muhammad and Behzad? She must've known that wasn't going to work out too well," she continued.

"The way she tells it, she didn't have a choice. Maybe she'd planned that once Muktar's bodyguards realised Muktar was dead they would just scarper out the back to the waiting car before the police arrived. Once they'd gone, she'd just disappear with the rest of the patrons. It didn't occur to her they would waste time checking if his girlfriend was still alive, pick her up from the floor and take her with them."

"Playing the devil's advocate," Sarah said. "If she did know there was to be a shooting, why was she there in the first place?"

"It was probably the only way to guarantee Muktar would be there that night. If he'd suddenly changed his mind for whatever reason and not gone to the Sister's, whoever's behind the shootings would've needed to know. And if we're right, they'll be waiting to hear from her at this very moment." Harrigan took a sip of coffee. "And getting back to your earlier question, David, now that both Muktar and Yoon are confirmed dead, it's quite possible she's no longer any use to those who sent her there and they're only waiting to find her location to tie up loose ends."

"And the Al-Yousaf clan aren't going to be overly happy she's escaped either," Lo said.

"Yep," Harrigan agreed. "And so until we are able to sort fact from fiction, Benecke will stay close to her. Keeping her safe and also making sure she contacts no-one."

Lo decided it was time to move the conversation along. "I still wonder why Muhammad and Behzad took the risk of wasting time grabbing Bethany before they left the Sister's. Could they have taken her as some form of sacrificial lamb to throw to his mother, hoping she'd take her anger out on her and leave *them* alone? But then, if that had been their motive, you'd hardly think Behzad would've then risked his own life by allowing her to escape."

"Yes, I wondered about that too, and to be honest, I haven't been able to come up with an answer. Not yet, anyway." Harrigan drained the last of his coffee, returned the cup to its waiting saucer and pushed it into the centre of the table.

"*I* have a theory," Sarah said almost smugly.

"Then go on, let's hear it," Harrigan replied, a little irritated she hadn't come out with it immediately instead of going through all that timewasting *I have a theory* bull shit.

"Well, supposing—" she stopped abruptly. "Hang on, I think I hear Bethany and Benecke coming back, I'll tell you later."

"Okay, where to from here?" Benecke asked once she and her charge had retaken their seats.

"I've a couple of telephone calls to make," Harrigan said as he slid out from his seat. "Wait here and have another cup of coffee and I'll let you know what's happening when I come back."

He hurried to the front foyer of the hotel and after closing the door of the public telephone box in the far corner, dialled the first telephone number. After a brief conversation he terminated the call and dialled a number in Northern Ireland.

"'ello?"

"Good afternoon. My name's Bill Harrigan, I'm looking for Patricia Hedrich. I've been told she's staying with you."

"An' jest who would ye be bein' exactly?"

"I used to work with her at Stonegate police station. I was an Inspector there."

"An' what would you be callin' y'self again?"

"Bill Harrigan. Detective Chief Inspector Harrigan."

"Oh, you're *that* 'arrigan, why were you not sayin' that in th' first place? I'll be getting 'er."

It was almost three minutes before Patricia picked up the telephone. "Bill? I mean, Sir, is that *really* you?" A tone of pleading expectancy filled her voice.

"Yes, Patricia, it's me, and *Bill* is fine. Wilkinson told me your sad news, I'm sorry."

"Thank you, it was very sudden, but life must go on. Where are you, are you in Ireland?"

"No, in the UK. I need a favour."

"You only have to ask," she replied willingly.

He gave her no details other than he needed a place to hide someone for a few days, and as she was in Ireland and her house was empty, and that the house could not be connected to him, he wondered if she would let him use it.

"Of course, anything you want." She went on to explain about the alarm system, and the keys to her car were on a hook in the kitchen. The neighbour had the spare key to the front door. She said she'd contact her as soon as their call was over and ask her to look out for him. If the neighbour had to go out, she'd put it under the front door mat. "Will I see you, Bill? Maybe we could get together for a drink. Or maybe two?" Her tone was soft, inviting. She'd loved her husband, but from the first time she and Harrigan had met, there'd always been something there. A small something. Something akin to the flame of a tiny pilot light, flickering almost unseen as it waited for the moment when it will be called upon to ignite the flammable gas of supressed desire.

There was no doubt of the intent of her invitation. Loathe as he was to give Patricia any more pain the death of her husband had forced upon her, he had no option but to tell her of his new relationship with Sarah.

"When you say you and Throgmorton are *together*, does that mean you're engaged to be married?"

"Engaged!? No, we're *together*... you know, we're—"

"There's no need to explain any further, Bill, I understand." There was a notable crispness of optimism about her answer.

They said their goodbyes. Harrigan dialled a second number from his small address book and tried to push Patricia's last comments to the back of his mind. But try as he might, he couldn't shake the uneasy feeling that Patricia's understanding about his and Sarah's relationship, was more of a, *"then nothing's final",* than one of *,"I wish you and Sarah a happy future together".*

***

Behzad Abu al Khayr Moustafa sat motionless in the hard wooden chair previously occupied by Bethany Joseph, his legs and arms bound tightly with rope cutting into his flesh. With hope of life now drained from his soul, the emptiness in his eyes gave them a ghostlike appearance. In contrast, blood red fury blazed through the narrow opening in the full faced covering of the black robed figure of hatred standing immediately in front of him. Even the glint of light from the razor sharp blade of the pointed, double edged, thirty six inch sword as it touched his naked chest, failed to stir any emotion. Seventeen seconds of tense stillness inched its way through time. Then, with the strength of the Great Satan filling her arms, Ghaziyah Al-Yousaf leaned forward, pushing the instrument of death slowly, meaningfully, through his bloodied skin. Following its deadly path through his ribcage, pausing not even for a second, it plunged into his heart, silencing the vital organ for eternity. Watched on by a smiling Muhammad Al-Yousaf and three others standing behind the bound man, with blood dripping with victorious celebration, the blade left Behzad's lifeless body and passed between the wooden slats at the back of the chair. Its forward motion eventually ceased as the hilt came to rest against the flesh of its victim's bare chest.

Ghaziyah Al-Yousaf threw her head back and emitted a chilling high-pitched ululation as she invited the warm comfort of revenge to flow through her body. Revenge satisfied by the death of the man she'd deemed to be a traitor to her beloved Muktar Ahmed. Revenge paid in full. She turned and without another sound, left the room.

Muhammad was the first to speak. "Alright, you three, get this mess cleaned up, and be quick about it. I have a business to run; contracts to fill."

"*You* have a business to run?" Asim questioned. "It was agreed a long time ago that if anything ever happened to Muktar, *I* would be—"

His words were cut short as the force of Muhammad's backhander knocked his head sidewards, causing blood to spurt immediately from his split lip.

Anger filled Asim's face, defiance flaming the anger in his eyes. He opened his mouth to speak, but Muhammad was in no mood to enter into any debate as to who was now in control. He walked to the front of the wooden chair, pulled the sword from Behzad's body and without any warning, hurled the sword spear like towards the man who had dare question his authority. His aim was perfect. The sword entered Asim's left eye, passed through his brain, wedging itself momentarily into the back of the skull causing the hilt of the weapon to vibrate. For several sickening moments, Asim stood motionless, his wide open lifeless right eye appearing to stare at the diminishing vibration of the sword's handle. With the weight of the protruding weapon eventually tilting the head forward, the sword slipped back out of the eye socket and crashed noisily to the tiled floor. The seemingly everlasting echo of the crashing sword, was accompanied moments later by the dull thud of Asim's body as it fell to its final resting place on the cold surface.

"Anyone else have any questions about who's in charge?" Muhammad asked picking up the fallen sword.

Two heads shook vigorously,

"Okay then. Faysal, you start clearing up this mess. Aneeq, you get in touch with the others, tell them to call off the search for that stupid girl and get back here. We have work to do."

***

The trip to Patricia's house in Southgate Ponds, four miles from his old police station in the outskirts of London was taken mostly in silence. Harrigan hadn't mentioned who owned the house or the address. It hadn't been difficult for Bethany Joseph to pick up on the cloud of suspicion hovering over her and she'd asked if she was under police protection or some sort of house arrest. Harrigan had replied it was a little bit of both, but until he'd had time to decide how much of her story he believed, it was probably more house arrest than protection.

He'd no intention of allowing Bethany to know the address of where she would be held. At the junction of the M25 London ring road he explained she would now be blindfolded. Pursuant to her objection, having been given the option of the blindfold and a comfortable home, or a holding cell at Scotland Yard, she'd reluctantly chosen the blindfold. Patricia's home was a double storied, semi-detached cottage with a garage attached to the left side wall. As he'd pulled into the driveway, the next door neighbour had come to the side fence with the key. After a few simple words of greeting, he waited until she'd returned to her own home before unlocking the front door, turning off the alarm system, and beckoning the others to come inside.

With no street numbers or street name visible, the blindfold had been removed and Bethany walked in single file between Benecke and Sarah. Lo brought up the rear and closed the door. He almost bumped into Sarah as she stopped suddenly and picked up a photograph from the sideboard and studied it closely.

"Nice looking couple," he said looking over her shoulder.

"Yes, aren't they," Sarah replied through clenched teeth and banged the frame down much too hard on the sideboard top.

The alarm system covered all doors, windows, and could isolate the ground and first floors. More than adequate for her protection. Harrigan doubted she was much of a flight risk. If she was genuine, she'd *want* protection. On the other hand, if she was associated with the shooters, she'd want to stay and report back to her cohorts as the investigation developed. It was only her ability to discover her whereabouts and contact someone outside he wanted to avoid.

The disconnection of the home telephone, the quality alarm system and Benecke's experience, meant that forty five minutes after their arrival, Harrigan, Sarah and Lo were back in the Granada heading towards the Royal Garter. It was agreed Sarah and Lo would get off at Friedenberg house and investigate the Natalya Zhestakova connection.

Sarah was the first to speak. "That's Patricia Hedrich's house." It wasn't a question or even a statement. It was an undeniable accusation. Even Harrigan recognised the iciness.

"Er, yes, it is," he replied giving her a quick, '*why, is that a problem?*' glance.

"You telephoned her from the Farmhouse Lodge." Her tone hadn't softened.

"Yes. I rang Bill Buckle, got the number, rang her, explained the problem and asked if we could use her house while she was away." He tried to sound as reasonable as possible.

"And?"

"And what?"

"Was there anything else?"

"I asked her how she was, that I was sorry to hear about her husband and we'd catch up and have a drink when she got back."

Lo sunk down in the back seat and stared out the window. He knew nothing of Harrigan and this Patricia's background, but even he knew what Sarah was about to say.

"You'd catch up and have a drink!?"

"For God's sake! She's an old workmate of both of ours, she's just lost her husband, and she's letting us use her house; it's the least we can do."

Sarah stared quietly at the stationary late afternoon traffic in front of them, a surge of uncertainty flooding through her brain. *'What's wrong with you woman?'* She scolded herself. *'He's right! But why do I feel so jealous? Am I that unsure of our relationship? Is the hierarchy is right regarding people in our business becoming attached to each other Maybe this is all a mistake.'*

It was then, as if he could read her mind, she felt his hand take hers and give it a little squeeze. It was a kind, loving, understanding squeeze. It was a *Patricia is only a friend,* squeeze. She squeezed back, smiled and watched the rear of the red bus in front move forward.

And then, as is their way, Harrigan's mobile telephone rang, shattering the mood completely.

"Hello?... Lew? Did you find anything?... in all three rooms, eh?... high end quality?... yes, you're probably right, governments are the only ones who can afford them… no, don't remove them, I just wanted to verify my suspicions… thanks, Lew, I'll be in touch." He returned his telephone to his pocket. "That was Lew Canning," he explained, anticipating the question he knew one of his passengers would ask. "He's a private detective I helped out of a scrape when I was at the Yard. I called him from the Farmhouse Lodge and asked him to sweep our rooms at the Royal Garter for bugs."

"Helped him out of a scrape?" Sarah asked, more interested in Harrigan's personal history with this Lew Caning than the bugs thing.

"It's a long story. He got himself into trouble helping a young woman being threatened by her rich married lover. I managed to not only keep him out of jail but to also hang on to his licence."

It was Lo who was interested in the bugs. "It sounded like he found some devices?"

"In all three rooms. Top end of the range; the types used by UK intelligence agencies. MI5, MI6, and all that mob."

"And you told him not to remove them?" Lo asked half the question. He didn't need to ask, the *why* part, he knew that would be part of the answer.

"Yes. If we take them out, whoever put them in will know we're onto them and would more than likely replace them with something a little more sophisticated. If we leave them in, we can feed them whatever information we want them to hear. If it is one or all of the intelligence agencies, they're so full of themselves and over confident in their ability, we'll be able to send them all over the country, sniffing out non-existent clues, while we get on with the job at hand."

"You're a cunning bastard," Lo said irreverently.

"I do my best," Harrigan replied and turned to Sarah. "Getting back to the Farmhouse Lodge. Now would be a good time to hear your theory about why Behzad risked his life by letting Bethany escape."

She hesitated. "I'm not sure about it now. The more I've thought about it, the more ridiculous it sounds."

"Don't second guess yourself, Sarah. You had a theory, so let's hear it," Harrigan encouraged, albeit somewhat forcibly.

"Very well." She paused momentarily. "Supposing Behzad and Muktar were lovers, and Bethany was only there for appearances to throw others off the scent? Rock Hudson did it. Elton John did it. Why wouldn't an arms dealer do it? I mean, let's face it, who's going to take a gay arms dealer seriously? Not that there's anything wrong with that of course."

"Of course," he replied returning her smile. "But it's certainly an interesting theory. She *did* tell us he said he was helping her because it was what Muktar would have wanted."

"It's quite possible it had been *Muhammad* who'd wanted to take Bethany back to Birmingham, and Behzad'd had no option but to go along with it," Lo reasoned. "It's also equally possible that after seeing the man he loved shot when he was supposed to be protecting him, he was filled with guilt and regret. Maybe he thought allowing Bethany to escape, the girl Muktar had chosen to hide their secret, somehow helped repay Muktar for his failure to protect him."

"Enough to risk the wrath of Muktar's mother?" Sarah countered. "Because if you're right and Muhammad *was* the one behind the move to take Bethany to Birmingham to use as some sort of sacrificial lamb, Behzad would've known that letting her escape would've had dire consequences. Which, if we can believe what Bethany said about the mother, would almost certainly've included the possibility of death."

"Maybe that's what he wanted. It wouldn't be the first time someone has forced another person to kill them. Death by cop for example," Lo replied.

"He lets the girl escape to ease the guilt and then allows himself to be killed to join his loved one on the other side?" Harrigan summarised. "It's possible, but to be honest, it does have a touch of Agatha Christie about it. Anyway, we're getting a little ahead of ourselves, we don't know if Behzad's dead yet." Nothing more was said until he'd negotiated the traffic chaos around the Euston Road interchange and turned into Gower Street. "You know, Sarah," he continued eventually. "The more I think about your gay idea and about them using Bethany as a front, the more I think you might be onto something. It certainly explains why he never had sex with her."

Harrigan was forced to stop the vehicle at the pedestrian crossing near the British Museum gates and wait for a group of tourists to cross the road and make a bee line for the Museum Tavern. Friedenberg House was only two minutes walk from there, so Lo and Sarah grabbed the opportunity, hopping out of the car and joining the last of the group of sightseers.

Harrigan thought it almost certain that whoever had bugged their rooms would probably have someone in the street on the lookout for the Vauxhall Senator, so the odds were in his favour that his entry into the carpark in the Granada would go unnoticed. He also assumed they would probably have someone sitting in the foyer behind a large newspaper trying not to look like a person sitting behind a large newspaper. He decided the fire stairs were the best option to reach the Seamed Stocking bar on the second floor. He ordered a double Ballantine's, went to the public telephone booth hidden behind a six foot tall fibreglass model of a lady's shapely leg dressed in a black meshed seamed stocking attached to a garter belt and dialled a number. "Hello, Eian? It's Bill. We need to talk, now. I'm in the Seamed Stocking bar."

"Give me twenty minutes," Jones' voice replied. "Oh, and I was about to call you just before you called me. Godfrey Windsor said that apart from Akmatbayev owning the Russian language school Natalya Zhestakova works at, he can find no other connection. I told him I'd pass the message on."

Harrigan hung up without reply. He gave a slight smile at the thought of Lo's disappointment when he hears he won't be seeing Benecke run naked down Whitehall. Not that Harrigan thought for a minute they hadn't already seen each other naked. He took a quick sip of the golden liquid, sought out a table in the darkest corner of the room and once seated, again raised the tumbler to his lips. This time, it was not for any quick sip.

***

"'oo is it?" Lo and Sarah heard a woman's voice with the distinct raspy sound of a smoker ask through the speaker of the security panel beside the front door of Friedenberg House.

"Special Agents Lo and Throgmorton M'am, we're here to speak with Natalya Zhestakova." Lo spoke slowly and clearly.

"Special agents? Wha'cha mean, special agents? 'oo you work for?"

"The United Nations International Investigation Agency, we're—"

"Never 'eard of it." There was a short thoughtful pause. "You sellin' somefink?" She asked suspiciously before adding with blatant accusation. "You're not a coupla of them Je'ovah's Witnesses, are you?"

Sarah stepped forward.

"No, Madam, we're not Jehovah's Witnesses." Her voice was soft, but firm. "It's true I'm a special agent, but I am also a Detective Inspector with the London Met."

"The London Met? Why didn'cha say so the first time!? I ain't got all day. And I ain't no madam!" Her last few words were almost obliterated by the sound of the loud click of the door lock.

As their eyes slowly adjusted to the dim light in the hallway, a man passed them on his way to the front door. "Good afternoon," he offered in a low guttural mumble, a strong smell of a cigarette smoker filling the area.

"Good afternoon," Sarah replied. It was several seconds later before they could begin to make out the shape of the slightly built, undernourished woman leaning in the doorframe of the first doorway to the right. Her untidy grey hair complemented the wisping smoke spiralling from the burning Woodbine in the side of her mouth. Her flimsy and extremely tired frock, and her stained well-worn pink slippers complete with the side cut out of the left foot slipper making way for what looked to be a very painful bunion, completed the picture of one of London's forgotten poor.

"You said you're from the Met; you with the Yard?" She removed the smoking cigarette from her mouth, tilted her head backwards and carelessly blew the smoke into the air. Lo watched with admiration as she returned the cigarette to her mouth without disturbing the half inch long ash on the end of the cigarette.

"I used to be, before I transferred to Stonegate," Sarah replied.

"You know a Detective Sergeant 'arrigan? 'e's at the Yard."

"He's my boss. He's a Detective Chief Inspector now."

"An' so 'e should be. You tell 'im 'azel Spinks 'as been true to 'er word, and ain't stole nuffink since 'e helped 'er out all them years ago. I work proper now."

"I'll tell him, Hazel, I promise," Sarah said with a smile.

"Don't you forget!" She ordered. Much to Lo's disappointment, the long ash from her cigarette suddenly dropped onto her frock. She looked downwards, brushed the ash onto the floor and trod it into the carpet. She frowned at Sarah's look of disapproval. "Keeps out the moffs," she explained as if instructing a young child. She turned towards Lo. "You said you was 'ere to talk to the Russian woman in 2C?"

"Natalya Zhestakova, yes; do you know if she's home?" Lo asked politely.

"I dunno, I don't get paid to watch the comin's an' goin's of thems what live 'ere young fella." She paused as she put her hand in the pocket of her apron. "If she ain't 'ome, I suppose you'll be wantin' to look in 'er apartment. You'll be needin' this." She held out a single door key. "Slide it under my door on your way out. I've just run an 'ot bath, an' I don't want you knockin' on my door, disturbin' me." She dropped the key into Sarah's outstretched hand, stepped back into her room and closed the door. The sound of two security bolts sliding into position echoed through the hall.

As they walked up the stairs, signs of the building's years of neglect were difficult to miss. It was clean. But the worn carpets, faded paintwork peeling in places where slight cracks in the wall appeared, the occasional blown fluorescent tube and more than several cracked window panels, gave the building a feeling of shame as it remembered its glory days when serving as residence of the multi-millionaire industrialist, Samuel Friedenberg.

They knocked on the door. There was no reply. Sarah knocked again. "Miss Zhestakova! It's the police, we need to speak with you." After their experience with Hazel Spinks, Sarah figured it was easier to say they were from the police, and then identify themselves as UNIIA agents once the door opened.

But it didn't open. And it didn't open after the third knock, either. Lo and Sarah looked at each other and after nodding silent agreement, Sarah inserted the key in the lock and was forced to jiggle it a little before it yielded. To the sound of squeaking hinges, the door swung open. The security chain rattled as it hung loosely from its fitting.

The interior was typical of most single bedroom London apartments. A small but sufficient kitchen dining area sat immediately to the left. A breakfast bar and two chromed stools separated the area from what property agents would call a cosy living space. There was no television in the living area and apart from a large glass topped coffee table, the furnishings were limited to a two seater, fabric covered sofa and one matching lounge chair. Both had seen much better days. The large window in the living area offered a view overlooking the British Museum. The bedroom and ensuite bathroom were to the right. During the building's heyday, this entire floor had been one large ballroom cum entertainment area, complete with overly large chandeliers hanging from long chains, various life-sized portraits of the master of the house in ornate gilt frames, and matching grandiose accompaniments. The conversion into four small apartments thirty three years previous, had made absolute financial sense. The conversion had not included the installation of a false ceiling, and the ultra-high ceiling of the original room in the context of a small apartment, gave it's dimensions a sense of, well, *ridiculousness* probably best described it.

"Hello! Miss Zhestakova? Are you here? It's the police!" Sarah called loudly and then stood in silence waiting for a response. The apartment remained silent. "Miss Zhestakova!?" She repeated and waited again. Still nothing.

She nodded at Lo and moved towards the bedroom. Lo walked to the breakfast bar and briefly picked up the black leather purse lying on the bar top. "This looks like her everyday purse, so if she's not here, she won't be too far away," he said casually, not really caring if Sarah heard him or not. It was just one of those things you say. He then followed Sarah into the bedroom, and, like the rest of the apartment, the furnishings were sparse and definitely not of the quality you'd expect of a person who owns an S class Mercedes.

"I'll check the ensuite." Lo slid open the wooden door and entered the larger than he'd expected ensuite. It was less than five seconds later when he reappeared momentarily in the doorway. "Sarah, I think you should see this."

Sarah could only see Lo's back as he bent over the bath. She was almost beside him when Natalya Zhestakova's lifeless body, lying naked, face up in the full bath came into view. The complete stillness of the body, left little doubt she was dead. Lo reached his hand into the water and checked her neck for a pulse, just in case. He turned to Sarah and shook his head.

Sarah took a few paces back. "That water on the floor. Did you just do that when you checked for a pulse?" She asked.

"No," he replied. "It was already there." He stood upright. "Whatever happened here, happened very recently."

Sarah glanced quickly around the white tiled room. "An accident?"

"Could be," Lo replied. "The water feels very oily, probably from that bath oil bottle on the end of the bath, and from what I could see, it looks like she has a nasty head wound on the back of her skull. She wouldn't be the first person to slip getting into a bath, knock herself unconscious and drown."

Sarah used the tip of her biro to raise the lid on the cane washing basket against the wall between the hand basin and the bath. "Hmm. A couple of pieces of underwear on top," she said softly, but not particularly to Lo. She walked back to the bedroom. Natalya's street clothes were lying on the bed. Not folded, but still laid carefully. Her black leather high heeled shoes, one standing, one lying on its side, rested on the floor at the foot of the bed.

"What do *you* think?" Lo asked.

"It certainly looks innocent enough. She came home, put her purse on the breakfast bar, came into the bedroom, kicked off her shoes and undressed. She went into the bathroom, ran a bath, tipped in the bath oil, took off her underwear, dropped it in the washing basket, stepped into the bath, slipped, and *wham!*" Sarah summarised.

Lo nodded in agreement. "And there's no sign of anyone else being here."

"It certainly looks that way," she replied distantly.

"But?" Lo asked. Sarah's tone definitely had an implied *but* in it.

"The security chain wasn't fastened."

"Maybe she intended to fasten it after she'd put her purse on the breakfast bar, and after putting away a few groceries just forgot."

"Possible. But does a woman living alone, enter her apartment, do whatever, walk into the bedroom and undress without fastening the security chain?"

"You're the woman around here, you tell me."

"I don't think she does. I think there's something in a woman's psyche, especially a woman living on her own in a big city that would force her to make sure she'd fastened the security chain before doing anything else."

"Okay, for the sake of the argument, suppose I agree that because the safety chain wasn't fastened it means she was murdered and didn't just slip in the bath. How did the murderer get in the front door of the building? It's a secure building."

"It's an old building with a security system using yesterday's technology. If Natalya *was* murdered, it has all the hallmarks of being a professional job and I don't think a professional would have much problem with the security system. But it's more likely he, or she, came in with her. A friend maybe, or at least someone she knew well enough to trust. Someone she felt safe with."

"How many people do you know have professional killers as friends?" It was a reasonable question.

"Professional killers don't walk around with signs on their backs, or hand out business cards. Any one of us could have a friend in the business." It was an equally reasonable answer.

"Touché." Lo frowned. "You know, it's quite possible the man who passed us as we came in could've been the murderer. If she *was* murdered that is," he qualified quickly.

"It's possible. He also had that strong distinctive smell of a cigarette smoker. When we came into the apartment I smelled it again, but dismissed it as being left over from the hall."

"I thought the same thing," Lo admitted.

Sarah removed her mobile telephone from her shoulder bag. "It's time I rang the boss."

***

Harrigan glanced at the black and white clock on the far wall and the hands in the form of a shapely woman's legs, continuing the Seamed Stockings bar theme. It was five twenty. He sat quietly, his mind blank, watching the small bar fill with hotel guests eagerly anticipating the first taste of their favourite tipple after their day's activities. He raised his second Ballantine's to his lips. "Damn" he whispered as he felt the vibration of his mobile in his coat pocket. He returned the tumbler to the table top.

"Harrigan."

"Sir, it's Sarah, we've found Natalya."

"She been of any help?"

"I'm afraid not. She's dead."

Harrigan regathered the tumbler and sipped his Ballantine's as Sarah told him what they'd found and their thoughts on what might or might not've been the cause of death.

"What's your gut feeling?" He asked after she'd fallen silent. "Was she murdered or did she slip?"

"I think she was murdered, but the ever cautious Lo can't get passed a fifty-fifty chance either way."

"And you're certain you couldn't identify the man in the hall if you saw him again?"

"Absolutely certain, Sir. Our eyes were still adjusting to the light. From his shadowy outline, I'm reasonably confident he was wearing an overcoat with the collar turned up, and some sort of trilby hat pulled forward protecting his face. He also had that strong odour of a cigarette smoker, probably foreign cigarettes, but that's about it. It could've been Humphrey Bogart for all I know."

"What about the landlady?"

"She keeps herself to herself. Oh, and she asked me, well more accurately, *told* me to give you a message."

"What message?"

"She said to tell you that, 'azel Spinks 'as been true to 'er word, and ain't stole nuffink since 'e helped 'er out all them years ago. That she works proper now," Sarah repeated in her best cockney accent.

"Hazel Spinks," he said and paused briefly. "Now *there's* a blast from the past."

"Care to explain?"

"It's a long story, she was just someone down on her luck who I didn't think belonged in jail. And great accent by the way."

"Thanks, you big softy." It wasn't something one would normally say to a boss, but their relationship allowed a few privileges. "What do you want us to do?" She asked, getting her mind back on the job.

"Treat it as murder until forensics tell us otherwise."

Having not yet received their leather pouches from Whitlock with the local UNIIA contacts, Sarah's next question was predictable. "I'll contact the Yard and get them to send someone?"

"No, don't do that!" His reply was a little more emphatic than she'd been expecting. "Well, not directly, anyway," he continued, softening his tone. "Contact your Uncle Charles and ask *him* to arrange it."

"Ask Uncle Charles!? Are you serious!? Police Commissioners don't go around arranging forensics to visit crime scenes. That's what the lower ranks are for! You know, people like, well, *us*!"

"And tell him to instruct forensics this is highly confidential and to report only to me, or you, it doesn't matter which," he continued, completely ignoring her objections.

"But—"

"There're no buts, Sarah. My gut tells me this case is about more than protecting the identity of Jones' Unit 29 people; much more." Eian Jones appeared in the doorway and looked around the room. He nodded to Harrigan and headed for the bar. "I'm not sure what it is just yet," Harrigan continued, "but I intend to find out very shortly. I have to go." As he removed the telephone from his ear, he heard Sarah's fading voice calling his name. "Sir, wait! Bill! I can't just ask Uncle Char—"

He pushed the button with the red motive and returned the mobile to his coat pocket.

Jones placed a tumbler of Ballantine's in front of Harrigan, took a sip of his own gin and tonic and sat down. "Okay, Bill, what's so urgent it's got your knickers in such a knot?"

"What's this case really about, Eian? And before you answer, I'm not in the mood to be fucked around and have no time for any more of your bullshit. Just give me the truth."

"The truth?" Jones replied innocently. "I told you, Unit 29 is a highly—"

"And I told you not to fuck me around. I've no doubt there's some element of truth in the Unit 29 story. But there's more to why you were so keen to have us on this investigation than protecting the identity of Unit 29 and I need to know what it is. And I need to know now."

"Bill, I have no idea what you're talking about," Jones replied earnestly.

Jones's response to Harrigan's demands wasn't unexpected. He knew from the outset that just throwing a few expletives around and issuing demands for the truth wasn't going to have much effect on a man of Eian Jones' calibre, but he needed to lay down some ground rules; set the parameters of his expectations. Now that had been done, he began to lay out his case for more information. He leaned forward and rested his arms on the table in such a manner that invited Jones to do the same. He then continued in hushed tones. "I first became suspicious when I read the witness statements from the building opposite the Sister's. I wondered why the occupants in all the units except for one saw and heard absolutely nothing, and yet the occupants in the one unit who did see something, saw *everything*. Even a partial registration number of the shooter's vehicle as it drove away."

Jones opened his mouth to say that some people are more observant than others, but Harrigan didn't give him a chance.

"We visited a few of the *identical* apartments and spoke to the occupants. The two who saw everything were very convincing in their claim to be freelance journalists. But they are no more journalists than you or I. They had been put there to watch the Sister's."

"Are you suggesting you think they're my people?"

Harrigan ignored the question. He took a large gulp of Ballantine's and continued. "After we'd left Brewer Lane, I noticed a suspicious vehicle following us. The driver was quite skilled in trying to appear as just another vehicle travelling the motorway. Unfortunately, for him, he portrayed several tell-tale repetitive characteristics in his driving."

"Such as?"

"Such as always keeping three cars between us until I sped up. When I did that, he'd always allow me to get almost out of sight before catching up again and regaining his three vehicle buffer. Tailing someone unnoticed is not as easy as they make it out to be on the TV. We stopped for breakfast at the Watford Gap Blue Boar services, and after we'd left, I didn't see the car again and thought I'd been mistaken. But it wasn't long before I saw a different car displaying the same driving techniques and realised he must have changed cars at Watford Gap. Having access to different vehicles along the route meant the driver was working for a large, well run organisation, probably with experience in this type of operation."

Harrigan paused, giving Jones the opportunity to take a shortcut through this entire process and maybe admit the driver was one of his agents. But no such luck. Jones remained silent, and with the sound of ice cubes tinkling gently against the glass, took another sip from his G & T.

"Anyway," Harrigan continued. "It wasn't until after we'd visited the Al-Yousaf clan, stopped in the prison carpark and found a girl hiding in the boot of our car, I had a chance to front the driver. He gave me some cock and bull story about being a social worker visiting the jail, which I knew was bullshit because he'd been on our tail since we'd left London. I figured he must have followed us from the Garter, and if he was some kind of spook, he more than likely took the opportunity to fix a tracking device to our car while we were visiting witnesses in Brewer Lane. I found the magnetic tracking device inside the rear wheel well, and after we'd left the prison carpark, attached it to a truck that looked like it was on its way to Dover heading back to France. We changed cars at Birmingham airport, and while having lunch, I called an acquaintance and asked him to check our hotel rooms for bugs."

"Lew Canning?"

Harrigan nodded.

"A good man, and knows how to keep schtum. So you still have your paranoia about people bugging your hotel room?" Jones said light-heartedly.

"Scoff if you want, but this time, I was right. He found bugs in all our rooms."

"Well it wasn't me," Jones replied a little defensively.

"I know."

"You know?"

"Why would you? You've just admitted knowing how I feel about people bugging hotel rooms, so why would you bother? You know I'd find them."

"Did Canning remove them?"

Still unsure of the role Jones had in what he'd convinced himself was a much bigger game than he'd been led to believe, Harrigan didn't answer immediately. But, it was Jones who'd brought him in, in the first place, and he had no doubt that before this case was over he'd need Jones' resources. He had little option but to trust him. "No. I told him to leave them there. While ever those responsible believe I haven't found them, I can send whatever message I like and keep them chasing shadows. Not that you spooks need much encouragement in the chasing shadows department."

Jones just smiled. "The girl hiding in your boot, have you identified her?"

"You know, Eian, when I first mentioned her, you gave no reaction. A person hiding in the boot of a car is not an everyday occurrence. I would've expected, if not a comment, at least a frown, or a raised eyebrow. But there was nothing. It was almost as if you already knew about it. And if you *did* already know about the girl in the boot, that can only mean the bloke tailing me was one of yours." It was a statement that required a response.

Jones considered carefully before answering. "Yes, alright, he was one of mine, but it's not what you think. Another drink?"

Harrigan drained the tumbler and pushed it to the centre of the table. Jones indicated to the blonde haired waitress in the short black skirt, white blouse, black bow tie and black meshed stockings, who immediately glided across the room.

"Gin and tonic and Ballantine's on ice."

"Yes, Sir."

"Make the Ballantine's a double," Harrigan added.

She smiled at Harrigan, turned and walked towards the bar. Harrigan noticed the stocking seam running down the back of her left leg was off centre. He looked back at Jones and issued him a silent *"well, go on then, let's hear about why you had a man on my tail"* invitation.

Jones sighed. "Everything I told you about the absolute necessity of keeping the existence of Unit 29 from being discovered, by *anybody*, was true, and that hasn't changed. But you're suspicions about there being something else are well founded, well, I think they are anyway. As head of the Serious National Crime and Intelligence Agency, I'm a member of the Joint Intelligence Agency Committee, a group of—"

"Yes. I know who they are," Harrigan interrupted.

"I have no proof of what I'm about to tell you, but I have a gut feeling they're up to something, and something they want to keep from me. If I'm right and they *are* keeping me out of the loop, whatever it is has to be something very big, very suspect, and something I would not approve of and I want to find out what it is."

"And you think it's tied up with the shootings at The Sister's?"

"I don't know. But something doesn't smell right about those shootings. If it was gang related, why The Sister's? In my experience, I've always found organised crime syndicates to stay loyal to their own code of ethics, and The Sister's was off limits. If we assume it was not gang related, who else has a big enough organisation to pull off something like that?"

"A government agency," Harrigan answered the obviously rhetorical question. "And is that all you have? A gut feeling?"

"Not quite. Just before I called you at Ali's and asked you to come to the crime scene, I'd received a call from Jason Collins, head of MI6. He asked me if there was anything his agency could do to help. Now why would he do that? MI6 is the last agency to be involved in a shooting on home soil."

"So you brought us in to sniff around and see what we can come up with." It wasn't a question.

"Got it in one."

Harrigan leaned back in his chair and looked thoughtfully around the room, his eyes eventually coming to rest on the crooked seam on the left leg of their waitress still waiting at the bar. After several silent moments, he turned back to Jones. "To be clear, you want us to hunt around for some kind of clandestine government operation you don't agree with, which might have some link to the Brewer Lane killings?"

Jones gave a noncommittal shrug of semi-agreement.

"And would I be right to assume that anyone who sticks their nose in where it doesn't belong could get it cut off?"

Jones nodded.

"Does Godfrey know of your suspicions?"

"No."

"You don't trust him?"

"No, it's nothing like that; I'd trust him with my life. It's just that, well, if I told him of my suspicions, he might, you know, I'm still recovering from brain surgery and I thought he might, well, he—"

"Might think you were still off your trolley?"

"Yes."

"And why do you think I wouldn't?"

"Because, Bill, you wouldn't care and would help me anyway." He paused for a few moments. "I know I should've told you when we were at Sarah's. Because if I am right, God only knows what those crazy MI5 and MI6 bastards would do if they suspected you were looking to link them to the shootings. That's why I had a man follow you. I didn't send Kornick to *spy* on you, he was there to protect your back."

"And a bloody lot of use he was. He fell at the first hurdle." He reached for his Ballantine's but the table top was still empty. *"Damn it,"* he cussed under his breath. "Where's that bloody waitress!?"

"Right here, Sir, behind you." He could almost feel the caress of the velvet in her whispered voice. She reached over his shoulder allowing her more than ample breasts to brush his left cheek before twisting slightly, coming to rest with the full view of her low cut blouse dangerously close to his line of sight. The faint odour of Calvin Klein's Obsession for Women, synonymous with commercial eroticism and society's current perfume of choice invaded his sensory organs. It was also a vital accessory in any genuine temptress's arsenal. And thus began Harrigan's battle of mind, denying all natural instinct and keeping the correct thinking brain in control. She lowered his Ballantine's gently over her now only partly covered breasts and placed the tumbler in front of him. "I believe you ordered a—" She leaned forward just a little more. "— *double*?"

Not daring to turn his head to the left, or God forbid downwards, he stared directly at Jones who was obviously enjoying his discomfort. "Y...Yes, thank you," he replied almost meekly.

He felt her body press a little harder against him as she reached across and placed the gin and tonic in front of Jones. "Would you like me to charge it to your room, Sir?" She asked Harrigan, not Jones, who'd ordered the drinks, albeit from a different waitress. "If you'd care to give me your room number, I'll personally make sure everything is taken care of." She stood slowly, her pencil poised upright with eager anticipation over a small notepad. Jones threw a twenty pound note onto her tray. "This one's mine. Keep the change."

The smile quickly disappeared from her face as she nodded a mechanical acknowledgment of the tip and hurried away.

"How quickly things change," Jones said with a glint in his eye. "That's the first time I've seen a couple of tits get the better of you, and you're not even married yet."

Harrigan ignored the jibe and stared seriously across the table. "Call your men off, Eian. If I see someone tailing us, I need to know they're the enemy, not one of your nursemaids."

Jones took out his mobile and called Godfrey Windsor. Several minutes later he returned his mobile to his coat pocket. "All done. From now on you're on your own. But for God's sake, Bill, call me if you get into trouble. I have people in some of the most unlikely places, so there'll always be someone close by." He took a sip of his gin and tonic. "Getting back to your stowaway, do you know who she is?"

"She calls herself Bethany Joseph."

"My agents killed on the night of the shooting, reported a girl called Bethany Joseph as being Al-Yousaf's girlfriend, but I've never seen her picture," Jones said. Harrigan reached into his side pocket and took out Benecke's small digital camera. He pressed the power button on the top and waited a few seconds for it to warm up. It took several more seconds before he found the photo of the girl Benecke had taken through the half-opened bathroom door earlier that day. "This is her."

It was clear from Jones' expression he recognised her immediately. "*This* is the girl you found hiding in your boot? The girl you assume to be the same girl who fainted the night of the shooting?"

"You *know* her?"

"I don't *know* her, but I know who she is; I've seen her several times at David Littlewood's office. She's his private secretary."

"*The* David Littlewood?"

"Yes, *the* David Littlewood. One of the most powerful and respected men in the country, maybe even Western Europe. He has all the right contacts and not a man to cross swords with. But I don't know her as Bethany Joseph. *I* know her as Connie West." Jones pressed the power button and with the screen now blank, slowly handed the camera back to Harrigan. "Jesus, Bill, Littlewood's one of the largest weapons and weapons systems designers and manufactures in Western Europe. The Al-Yousaf operation is one of his biggest private customers. But if West *was* the girl sitting with Al-Yousaf the night of the shooting, it can only mean Littlewood suspected something and saw the necessity to have a spy in the Al-Yousaf camp."

"There's no *if* about it, Eian, she's the girl. But industrial espionage is nothing new, it could be Littlewood was just protecting his own interests. Making sure Al-Yousaf stayed loyal to his product."

"Maybe, but it could be Littlewood suspected Al-Yousaf was somehow involved with the Yoon drug trade and wanted part of the action." Jones leaned away from the table, tilted his head back, emptied his gin and tonic in one swallow and turned his head, looking for the waitress. She was nowhere to be seen.

"May I take your order, Sir?" A young waiter asked.

An obviously disappointed Eian Jones looked up at the man. "Where's the waitress?" Jones more demanded than asked.

"On a break, Sir."

"It's my shout," Harrigan interrupted and gave the young man the order. Once again alone, Harrigan continued. "You didn't *really* think the waitress was flirting with me when she stuck her tits in my face and pressed hard against me, did you? She was plainly up to something, and with her task completed, has now returned to whereever she came from."

"Okay, I'll bite. What was she up to?"

"She was either identifying me to someone else, or—" he felt in his two side coat pockets but found nothing. He then reached into the coat's top pocket, the pocket no-one's ever used since 'kerchiefs went out of fashion. He smiled and slowly removed a small round metal object slightly smaller than a ten pence coin. After examining it closely, he slid it across towards Jones. "Here, this is more up your alley. What is it? The latest model listening device?"

Jones turned the small object over in his fingers several times, scrutinising it with a look of almost disbelief. He closed his hand and held the object out of sight while the waiter delivered the drinks and Harrigan signed the chit, charging it to his room.

"No, not a listening device, a GPS tracking device. Global Positioning System," he explained to a puzzled Harrigan. "It uses satellites in space to track things. I saw a prototype of a much larger version at a top secret briefing with the US military about twelve months ago." He studied it closely one last time. "I had no idea they'd come this far with it; just look how small it is! And what surprises me even more is that the yanks have given whoever is behind putting this thing in your pocket, access to the system. Unless it was the yanks themselves." He took another sizeable sip from his glass. "You're not going to like what I'm about to say, Bill, but my mind's made up so please, don't make a scene." He took a second sip. "If the yanks are involved in any of this, or more likely, someone with enough grunt to have access to this device, it means something much bigger and definitely more dangerous than I ever imagined is going on. I have no intention of putting you or your team at any more risk. UNIIA will be pulled off the investigation into the shootings until I have more information. Sorry, Bill. I'll set the wheels in motion immediately."

Harrigan didn't cause a scene, he simply smiled and took a large swallow of golden liquid. "You can't."

"I *can't?*"

"No. You seem to have forgotten, probably conveniently, that once UNIIA has been given a case, it's nigh impossible to take them off it. It was a condition *you* insisted on during the creation of UNIIA. You were adamant that if UNIIA was removed from a case because the investigation wasn't going the way it was supposed to be going undermined its core purpose; independence. Sorry, old friend, hoisted by your own petard I believe the saying goes." He held out his hand, gesturing for Jones to return the device. Jones sat rigid. Harrigan beckoned with his fingers several more times, this time more forcibly. After a few tense moments, Jones sighed and reluctantly dropped the device into Harrigan's palm. Harrigan nodded and returned it to his top coat pocket.

As concerned and regretful for involving Harrigan's team as Jones was, he knew it was fruitless to pursue the matter and changed the subject. "Where's Sarah and the others?" He asked, attempting to inject a tone of semi-disinterested conversation into his voice. He did it pretty well, too.

"Benecke's looking after Bethany, or Connie, whichever you prefer, and Sarah and Lo followed up with Natalya Zhestakova."

"And what did Zhestakova have to say for herself?"

"I thought you wanted to stay at arm's length?"

"I do, but I'm concerned, for all of you. I should never have involved you."

"Why not? It's what we do. As for the Russian woman, I'm afraid I can't tell you what she said."

Jones gave a tacit nod of understanding.

"No, you don't understand. I can't tell you, because she's dead."

"She's dead? How?"

"It looks like she probably slipped in the bath, banged her head and drowned, but I'll wait for the autopsy results before I decide."

"You have some doubt it was an accident?" It came out as a question.

"Could be, but until forensic tells us differently, we're treating it as murder." Harrigan swallowed the last of his Ballantine's and stood from the table. "I'll be in touch."

Without another word passing between them, Harrigan strode quickly towards the entrance to the stairway leading back to the car park. Out of the corner of his eye, he saw two, well-built, extremely physically fit men with college haircuts, almost identical grey suits and dark ties, prepare to rise from the shadowy table in the corner closest to the bar.

The stairs in the bare concrete stairwell leading down to the three parking levels below, were in two sections between each floor running at one hundred and eighty degrees to each other with a landing at the bottom of each section. The heavy blue metal doors leading into the carpark on each second landing, were fitted with strong, but relatively slow self-closing mechanisms. With the exception of two *courier delivery only* spaces alongside the reserved handicapped parking area against the back wall closest to the lift, parking level one was for hotel guests only. Levels two and three were for public parking consisting mostly of permanent prepaid spaces used by commuters to central London. An automatic payment machine for casual parkers was on the second level.

Hurrying purposefully down the first flight of stairs, he heard the sound of the door at the top of the stairwell open. He opened the door to parking level one, but didn't enter. Instead, he continued quickly down the first section of stairs leading to parking level two. With Glock in hand and back pressed hard against the wall, he listened to the approaching footsteps he assumed belonged to the two men he'd seen at the table near the bar.

"Look. There! The door leading to the guest parking area; it's still closing," he heard one voice say.

"I can see it! I'm not blind!"

Harrigan heard the door to level one opening again followed by the sound of scuffling feet entering the car park. He retraced his steps to the now closed blue door, and opened it as quietly as he could.

"Can you see him?" He heard the man crouching low against the left side wall ask.

"No."

"He can't have gone far. I'll go straight ahead." He waved his hand, his gun hand, to the left. "You go that way."

"Or," Harrigan said. "You could just turn around."

The two men spun on their heels, an expression of stunned shock and surprise etched into their features as they stared into the barrel of Harrigan's raised weapon. Instinctively, the tall man began raising his Walther PPK/S, which, as he was to soon learn, was probably not the wisest decision he'd ever made.

Not having been blessed with the *ask questions first* gene, Harrigan's Glock coughed twice. The tightly grouped projectiles tore into the man's right shoulder, forcing him to spin heavily against the grey cement block wall, drop the Walther PPK/S and grasp at his wounded shoulder as he fell to the ground.

Ignoring any threat to himself, the shorter man dropped to one knee beside his fallen partner. "Errol, Errol, are you okay!? Errol, talk to me."

'Errol? What sort of name is that for a man with a gun?' Harrigan thought.

The kneeling man looked up at Harrigan. "What the fuck are you doing!?" He shouted. He glanced back at the grimacing Errol before turning once again towards Harrigan, still standing unmoved, the Glock still aimed, ready for any unfavourable reaction the kneeling man might be contemplating. "We're with the Secret Intelligence Service, Special Operations, you can't just…" he stumbled for words. "This is London for Christ's sake! You… you can't—"

"I can't what?" Harrigan asked. "In my jungle, the man with the gun makes the rules, so stop talking, slowly remove Errol's ID from his pocket, and slide it to me across the floor. When you've done that, very carefully take *your* weapon from its holster and lay it next to his, and then also slide *your* ID across the floor. You will then sit on the ground with your hands on your head, facing the wall."

"This man's just been shot! I need—"

"You need to do exactly as I've told you, or you'll join him." Harrigan's icy stare and chilling tone removed any doubt in the man's mind that the man with the Glock was deadly serious. Two minutes later all tasks had been completed.

Harrigan re-holstered his Glock, picked up the PPK/S's and put one in each of his side coat pockets. He then read the names on the ID's. "Errol Jenkins and Campbell Gregory," he read aloud, not attempting to hide his loathing for people with last names as first names and first names as last names. "SIS operatives. SIS, that's MI6, isn't it?"

"Yes! And you're in deep doody, Harrigan!" Campbell Gregory said defiantly to the wall from his sitting position. Which, in reality, with his hands still on his head gave his tone of defiance more a sense of childish stupidity than anything else.

First a man with a gun named Errol, and now 'doody'? Who are these clowns?' Harrigan thought. "Hmmm, MI6? Now unless I'm mistaken," he half mused, "MI6 is an *external* agency with authority to deal with matters beyond UK borders only, not chase citizens around London hotel carparks with guns in their hands, so I doubt it's *me* who's going to be in the shit." Harrigan put the ID's in his pocket, "I'll tell you what I'll do, Gregory. Your mate's lost a fair amount of blood and right now isn't looking too good. If you carry him to my car over there, I'll drop you off at the closest hospital."

Without another word, Harrigan walked towards the Granada. The little toot of the horn and the flashing indicators lighting the area around the vehicle after he'd pressed the unlock button on the little black remote-control thingy, spurred Gregory Campbell into action. He was almost at the vehicle with the now only half-conscious

Errol when the car park door flew open and a uniformed man with ACME Security Services emblazoned on his blue uniform shirt appeared.

"Hey, you there! Stop! What's going on!?"

"Secret Service!" Harrigan shouted holding up one of the ID cards across the turret of his vehicle. "Special Operations! Top Secret! If you mention this to anyone, you'll be sent to prison under the Official Secrets Act!" Even Harrigan had trouble keeping a straight face.

The guard stood thoughtfully for less than a second before hurriedly disappearing behind the closing door.

***

"You're where!?" Admiral Sir Jason Collins exclaimed more loudly than he'd intended into his mobile telephone causing a sea of disapproving raised eyebrows to turn his way. "Wait on, I'll go outside." He rose quickly from his chair, looked apologetically towards the other nine diners seated around table three at the one thousand pound a head fund raising event for the Minister of Defence. After manoeuvring his way through a maze of white linen tablecloths, hallmarked silver cutlery, bone china, Veuve Clicquot Yellow Label Brut Champagne, bow ties and diamond jewellery, he hurried towards the entrance doors as quickly as protocol allowed.

With his face turned to the wall in the far corner of the reception area of the Westminster Grand Ballroom, he spoke in a hoarse whisper. "Okay now. Did you say you were at London Central Hospital?"

He listened silently as Campbell Gregory, the man on the other end of the telephone, gave a brief report on the events in the car park.

"What do you mean, Jenkins's been shot!?" Collins spluttered, briefly displaying a chink in the armour of his trademark calmness. "How!? Who!?... Harrigan? *Harrigan* shot him!? Damn it man, how could you let that happen?... what do you mean, it wasn't your fault, of course it was your fault, you're the senior operative... did you just ask if we're going to report Harrigan?" Collins paused briefly and then continued on quickly without giving Gregory a chance to reply. "I can't believe you'd ask such a thing. *No,* of course we're not going to report Harrigan!... Because Harrigan's a UNIIA agent and has a right to carry a weapon *and* he has a right to use it. And in case it's slipped your mind, he also has a right to investigate crime committed inside the UK. How do you suggest we explain away *you* being there!?... what!?... for God's sake, this isn't the time to be arguing the rights and wrongs of the UNIIA process. Just get Jenkins patched up and have him moved to one of our own facilities. And make sure the hospital understands the shooting is a matter of National Security and they're not to report or even mention the incident to anyone. And Gregory, make sure when you leave the hospital you leave nothing that might indicate Jenkins has been there. I'll arrange the necessary paperwork re-enforcing the hospital's obligations to comply on matters of National Security to be sent to them in due course." He didn't wait for Campbell Gregory to reply. He rang off and returned to the table

Chapter Six

Having decided to share a much more pleasurable activity in their room than going down for an early breakfast, Harrigan and Sarah arrived in the restaurant as Lo sat waiting patiently reading the morning paper. His breakfast dishes had been removed by a waitress who was much cheerier than she had a right to be at seven thirty in the morning. He returned his third cup of coffee to its saucer. Sarah walked directly to the continental breakfast area; Harrigan, the Bain Marie. Sarah had been several spoonsful of muesli into her breakfast before Harrigan made his way to the table with his plate of little sausages, grilled tomatoes, hash browns, mushrooms, bacon, fried egg and two slices of fried bread.

It had been just after eight fifteen the previous evening when Harrigan, after dropping the two MI6 operatives outside the London Central Hospital, had returned to the Royal Garter. Campbell Gregory had spent the entire journey to the hospital, complaining about outsiders being brought in to do local agencies' work, and that Harrigan hadn't heard the last of the shooting of his partner.

Gregory's constant whining had put Harrigan in an anything but a *Seamed Stocking* bar mood, and he chose instead the more serene surrounds of *Albert's Basement* on the Lower Ground floor. Albert's Basement had a calming, old-worldly, royal décor, with coronation crown motives in all the right places and a mostly rich but subdued red and gold colour scheme. Soft to the touch velvet-like dark maroon wallpaper with more fleur-de-lis than was necessary covered all four walls. Gold coloured tassels hung on most things that moved, and three, half-sized statues of famous Knights of the Garter completed the picture. Dominating the entire scene were two gilt framed portraits of Queen Victoria. Ironically, given the room's title, there were no portraits of Prince Albert.

He had not been in a Ballantine's mood either and leaving the bar area with a pint of the locally brewed Prince Consort traditional bitter ale in his hand, he'd found the most secluded table available and sunk down slowly into the softness of the maroon faux velvet covering of one of the four high backed chairs. He'd next telephoned Benecke, warned her to take extra care of her charge, said he'd be there early in the morning and returned his mobile to his inside coat pocket. He'd afforded himself the luxury of a few quiet moments for the events of the day to clear from his mind before raising the pint of Prince Consort expectantly to his lips. He took a long, well deserved draught of the room temperature, almost gasless liquid, and allowed it to flow gently down his throat. It was disgusting.

Sarah and Lo had returned to the hotel two hours later, at ten minutes before ten. They'd spent less than fifteen minutes in a short debriefing session and after agreeing to fill in the gaps over breakfast, the trio had retired to their rooms.

Harrigan picked up a crispy hash brown with his fingers, wiped it along the tomato sauce caressing the pile of little sausages and took a careful bite. "Did you have much trouble convincing your Uncle to contact forensics?" He asked Sarah.

"Surprisingly no. There was no doubt he'd been caught off guard, but all he said was, *"for all his faults, Harrigan usually knows what he's doing"*, and agreed to *"get on with it immediately."* Harrigan smiled and began to make short work of the rest of the last hash brown. "Before you start feeling too pleased with yourself, Uncle Charles then gave me a right tongue lashing for not telling him we were together, that he didn't appreciate having to hear it from Wilkinson, and he expects us to join him for Sunday lunch. My parents will also be there. And in case you're interested, I was also in trouble for not telling *them* either."

"*This* Sunday?" Harrigan asked, the thought that maybe she'd meant some Sunday in the far distant future uppermost in his mind.

"*This* Sunday. And by the way, thanks for being so sympathetic towards me copping it from Uncle Charles." The only thing missing was a pout.

Like most men, Harrigan's understanding of the workings of a woman's mind was sparse at best. But he did know that anything he said about the matter would be wrong, so changed the subject. "What time did forensic say they'd get back to you?" He asked them collectively.

"They didn't," Lo said, feeling Sarah still needed a little time to get over Harrigan's lack of understanding of her feelings. "But to be honest, I'm not holding my breath for anything too much. *If* it was murder, and I'm still far from convinced it *was* murder, the killer was extremely professional, and I doubt would've left anything behind. That being said, if we accept Sarah's theory about the high priority a woman in London would put on ensuring the safety chain was in place, the hanging security chain does suggest someone else had been with her and when leaving the apartment, closed the door behind them. If that is what occurred, then murder is well and truly back in the picture."

The discussion moved onto the man who had passed them in the hallway, and it was agreed by both Lo and Sarah, that apart from being able to say he was a smoker because of the smell of smoke in his clothes, there had been no other clue as to his identity. It was then Harrigan's turn. He expanded on the details of his discussion with Eian Jones, and of his phone call to Benecke. They waited silently while the waitress filled their coffee cups and Harrigan masterfully filled his fork with half a little sausage, a small slice of bacon and a corner of crispy fried bread, put it in his mouth and returned the empty fork to the plate. He leaned back and wiped his mouth with the white linen serviette. "Oh yes, and I shot an MI6 operative in the carpark of the hotel."

The sound of two coffee cups being slammed into their saucers, caused other diners to look across to their table and see two wide eyed faces staring open-mouthed at the third person.

"What?" He asked innocently. "I didn't *kill* him for Christ's sake, I shot him in the shoulder." He finished the last of his fried bread and pushed his empty plate towards the centre of the table, and told them of the waitress and the GPS tracking device. "When I left Jones," he continued, "not wanting to let anyone who might've been watching the foyer know that I'd been at the hotel for some considerable time, I intended to go back down to the car park, and then catch the lift to my room."

"Why bother? The tracking device in your pocket clearly indicated you'd already been sprung," Lo reasoned.

"True, but sprung by whom? There's more than one agency interested in what we're doing, and I figured we would have a better chance to discover their identity if I acted as if I didn't know it was there. Anyway, as I left, I had noticed two very suspicious characters rise from their table and suspected I was about to have company." He went on in some detail as to the events leading up to the shooting, the shooting itself, him discovering they were MI6 Special Operations operatives and what he believed to be Gregory's empty threat that he hadn't '*heard the last of it*'.

"You sound very confident," Sarah remarked, referring to his almost offhanded dismissal of what she thought to be Gregory's quite reasonable threat. "Sure, they're not MI5, but just because MI6 deals in foreign intelligence, that doesn't stop them investigating any foreign threat on UK soil," she reasoned.

"True, and Gregory knows that as well. So tell me, when I challenged his authority, why didn't he argue that point?"

"Because you'd just shot his partner and he wanted to get him to hospital, not stand around discussing the rights and wrongs of it all." There was a little impatience in her voice.

"Maybe, but I don't think so."

"Of course you don't." Sarah's tone wasn't quite one of exasperation, it was more one of *"what's the point of arguing?"*

"No, Sarah, I don't," he replied matter of factually. "And, if, as you say, MI6's basic responsibilities lay with *foreign* intelligence, why are they so interested in our investigation? An investigation into an event we were told right at the beginning was little more than a local shooting?" He didn't wait for her answer. "I'll tell you why, because like I told Jones and he eventually had to agree, this case has always been much bigger than that! And *that*, Sarah, is why no more will be said about me shooting one of their operatives because if they took it any further, they'd have to explain why they were following me in the first place. Their explanation would include mention of UNIIA, opening the door for us to widen our investigation. And that's the last thing they want. They also wouldn't want an, *'MI6 cowboy operatives in London car park shootout,'* headline splashed across all media."

Sarah had little option but to accept his explanation. "So where to from here?" She asked coldly.

"When we started the case, we agreed that if we were to discover who was behind the shooting, we needed to establish who the specific target was, and up to a point, that's still true. But knowing what we know now, it's no longer quite as simple as that."

"Because even once we've identified who the target or targets were, there is more than one person or group of people with motive to kill them?" Sarah asked almost rhetorically.

Harrigan nodded agreement. "Sarah, I want you and David to keep on Zhestakova. We need to know more about her background. Where she's from, how long she's been in the UK and her financial status, you know the sort of thing. Hopefully, when you pay a visit to the school she taught at, you will be able to establish a link between her and Akmatbayev. And get the local police onto finding that bloody Mercedes. And one last thing, keep on to forensics and establish one way or the other if her death was accidental or murder. Lastly, we might not know who is behind the shooting, but we do know we are dealing with some extremely dangerous characters. Watch your backs. Do not split up under any circumstances. And I mean *any* circumstances, you got that?"

They nodded. "What about you, Sir?" Lo asked.

"I think we can assume with a high degree of certainty that Connie wasn't the target. I'm not buying the theory that once the shooters had reached the table she fainted and fell to the floor out of harm's way; that's bullshit."

"If West *did* have time to duck out the way," Lo mused aloud. "It's more evidence she's associated with whoever's behind the shooting, was expecting it to happen and was prepared for it and the fainting story is a cover to throw investigators off the scent."

"And that would explain why they didn't shoot her when she was on the floor under the table," Sarah added.

"It's a definite possibility," Harrigan said. "And that's why I'm going back to Patricia's house and see if Benecke and I can get the truth out of her." He finished his cold coffee. "Any questions?"

"Yes," Lo said. "There'll undoubtedly be people watching the hotel, how do you plan we get out of here unnoticed?"

"I have two new rental vehicles being delivered to the carpark in—" he looked at his watch, "—twenty minutes time. I've specifically asked that the vehicles are delivered by one male and one female driver. When we're ready, they'll take the Granada away, and with the Granada's slightly tinted windows, hopefully those watching will assume it's you and Sarah and follow them."

"Why would they assume it was David and me?" Sarah asked. "We don't need a car to get around London."

"Because that's what we're going to tell them." He paused just long enough for the penny to drop and to ensure Sarah didn't have a follow-up question. "Okay, if we all know what we have to do, let's go up to our room and when we're up there, just follow my lead."

Harrigan opened the door to his and Sarah's room and allowed his two companions to enter first. He closed the door and walked to the centre of the room. "Alright everyone," he began loudly enough to ensure his voice carried to the bugs, but not so loud as to arouse suspicion. "We have a busy day ahead. As we agreed before, David, I want you and Sarah to take the Granada and go to where Benecke is keeping Bethany until we need her to testify about the shootings at Brewer Lane. Remember, Bethany was there at the time and is our only witness. Without her, we'll have Buckley's chance of getting to the bottom of what happened and might just as well pack up now and get back to New York."

"We'll be careful," Lo said earnestly.

"Good, and make sure you're not followed."

"What about you, Sir?" Sarah asked the pre-rehearsed question for the benefit of the bugs.

"I have a ten fifteen meeting with a senior person from Century House, in Westminster Bridge Road. He called and said he had some vital information for me."

"Century House? Isn't that where MI6 have their headquarters?" Sarah asked.

"Yes, but we're not meeting there, he gave me another location. So, unless there's anything else?" Neither answered. "Okay, let's get started. Good luck."

Twenty minutes later, the two rental car drivers exited the car park in the Granada, with instructions as prearranged by Harrigan when ordering the two new vehicles, to drive directly out of London towards Brighton for forty five minutes before turning back and returning to their depot.

In the meantime, Harrigan, Sarah and Lo had been forced to wait several anxious moments in the car park before a woman in her mid-twenties or thereabouts, stepped from the carpark lift and walked swiftly to her silver Audi. She wore the latest fashion trendy businesswoman's two-piece business suit complete with collar and tie and carried a suitcase, garment bag and briefcase. About to close the boot of the Audi, Sarah approached her and explained she was a visitor to London and asked directions to the M25. The woman, more than willing to air her knowledge, failed to notice Sarah flick the GPS device, dropped into Harrigan's top pocket the previous evening, into the boot and coming to rest behind the suitcase.

Ten minutes later, with Sarah and Lo sitting cramped in the back of the rental Opel Kadett Combo van, Harrigan drove from the carpark towards the London Museum.

"I'm sorry, Sir, but I must ask," Lo began tentatively. "Where're the two guns and ID's you took from the MI6 operatives? They're going to want them back."

"I unloaded the weapons and sent them by priority courier to Jason Collins, at MI6 headquarters. I also enclosed the IDs, and of course, an appropriate note."

Lo and Sarah could only imagine what was written in the 'appropriate note'.

***

According to the hands of the replica Victoria Station pendulum clock hanging obediently on the wall in Admiral Sir Jason Collins' office, it was fifteen minutes after nine. This was the exact time Lo and Sarah were climbing unceremoniously from the rear of the Combo at the corner of Bloomsbury and Great Russell Streets, and the telephone on the Admiral's desk gave a single ring. He rested his Parker Duofold fountain pen on the monogrammed note pad and pressed the intercom button with more pressure than was necessary. He disliked being interrupted, especially when writing to his daughter in Canada.

"Yes, Cynthia." There was no warmth in his voice.

"I'm sorry to disturb you, Sir Jason, but I have a security man from the front desk with me who has an urgent parcel addressed to you. He says he needs to deliver it to you personally."

"Nonsense. I am in the middle of something extremely important and cannot be interrupted. Just sign for it and I'll look at it in a few minutes."

"I told him that, Sir, but he's *very* insistent. He said it's something you will want to see, and he cannot let the package out of his sight."

Collins returned his Parker to the front groove of the solid silver desk tidy and closed the red leather desk compendium. "Damn the man! Very well, send him in." He leaned back in his executive Chippendale chair and placed his hands on the polished mahogany wood of the chair's arms.

Having spent most of his working life in the Navy, Jason Collins gave an involuntary wince at the sight of the overweight security guard. His uniform shirt was clean, but sparsely ironed with its two bottom buttons straining as best as possible to keep from popping open. In contrast with his shoes, his black trousers had a shine only a trip to the cleaners could remedy. He carried a package about the size of a shoe box.

"I'm terribly sorry to be so insistent on delivering the package personally, Sir Jason, but after I'd opened it for inspection, I figured you would not want its contents broadcast throughout the building."

'At least he's polite' Collins thought as he sat forward. "Well, go on man, what's so special about this particular package?"

The security guard removed a rigid cardboard box from its delivery envelope, placed it on the desk in front of Sir Jason and raised the lid.

Collins leaned forward and looked at the contents. His face lost all colour as he sat paralysed for much longer than he'd intended. Eventually, he managed to slowly raise his head, look momentarily into the face of the security guard and then quickly back to the box. He reached forward with both hands, pulled the box towards himself and closed the lid.

"Good work, er, what was your name?"

"Conroy, Sir Jason. Jason Conroy."

"Jason, eh? A good name lad, a good name. You did the right thing bringing it to me, and Conroy, this must remain between us. Is that understood?"

"Of course, Sir."

"Good man."

There were no words of farewell, but the dismissive tone in Collins' last two words, coupled with his apparent lack of recognition there was still someone else in the room as he re-opened the box, told Conroy his seventy five seconds of fame were over.

The Admiral picked up the handwritten note. *"Collins. I thought you'd probably want these back, and don't panic, they're not loaded. And a word of advice. If you send any more of your pussies after me or any of my people, guns and ID cards won't be the only thing to be returned in a box. Harrigan."*

He rested his arms on the desktop and stared at the note he now held with both hands. "Collins? He addresses me as… *Collins*!?" He said aloud to the empty room. "Good God, even the Prime Minister addresses me as Admiral." He snatched up the telephone handpiece of his private line and dialled a number. Chase Roper, the senior MI6 operative in charge of tracking the UNIIA team, answered the ringing of his mobile after two rings. "Good morning, Sir."

"Do you still have Harrigan and his people under surveillance?"

"I have two agents on Lo and Throgmorton's tail at this very moment, Sir. They are travelling towards Brighton to an unknown location where Benecke is holding the girl who escaped the night of the shooting, and—"

"We need to get that girl; we don't know how much she knows, but whatever it is, we need to get her away from Harrigan before she talks."

"If she hasn't talked already," Roper added solemnly.

"God forbid. And Roper, once you have her, under no circumstances must Harrigan's people suspect it is us who've taken her. Is that understood?"

"Yes, Sir."

"And what about Harrigan? What's he up to?"

"All we know is he has a meeting at ten fifteen this morning with a senior person from Century House in Westminster Bridge Road."

"*This* building!? He is meeting with someone from this building!?"

"Yes, Sir. We don't know who this man he's meeting works for, and he didn't give a name, but he did say it was a man and he has vital information."

"So it's possible it could be one of *our* people?"

"It's possible. We don't know."

"Do you know where the meeting is to take place?"

"No, Sir. We do know it's not at Century House, but he didn't say where."

"Do you at least know where Harrigan is now? I trust you have someone tailing him?"

"He's a hard man to keep track of. We had people outside the Hotel carpark, but he must have switched cars, and—"

"You have *lost* him!?"

"No, Sir, we know exactly where he is. Luckily, he's wearing the same jacket he was last night, and according to the GPS tracking device we slipped into the top pocket of the jacket, he's currently travelling towards Heathrow."

"Good work. Keep on to it, and in the meantime, I'll set some enquires in motion at this end and see if I can identify who might be on their way to the airport."

"Yes, Sir."

Collins rang off and dialled a second number.

"Joan? It's Jason. We need to talk. Meet me in our usual place in an hour."

The line went dead. Dame Joan Hamilton-Westbrook, Director General of MI5, didn't take offence at the abruptness of the call. The least said on the telephone, be it a private line or not, the better.

***

"Nice wheels," Benecke said as she opened the front door and looked out at the Combo parked in the driveway.

"Thanks," Harrigan replied, pushing past her and leaving her to close the door as he walked towards the kitchen. "Where's Bethany?" Harrigan hadn't told Benecke the Connie West story.

"In the downstairs loo. There's no window in that loo and I can see down the hallway to the back door from here. She's not going to get away."

"Good, I need to talk to her."

Benecke followed him into the kitchen and opened the brown paper bag from the local takeaway he had placed on the kitchen table.

"I didn't know what food was in the house and thought you might need something for breakfast." He filled the kettle.

Benecke shuddered at the assortment of hash browns, flapjacks with maple syrup, and egg and bacon muffins lurking evilly inside the innocent looking brown paper bag, each waiting impatiently to attack her cholesterol level and dress size. But there being little else in the house, it would have to do. It was another two and a half minutes before Connie West joined them.

She stared coldly at Harrigan. "How long before I'm allowed to leave?" It was more a badly worded demand than a question.

"That depends," Harrigan replied unhelpfully.

"It depends on what exactly?"

"How long it'll take for you to stop lying to us."

Benecke showed no reaction to the directness of his question; she had been expecting it. In fact, she thought it was well overdue.

"*Lying?* What possible motive could I have for lying to you? You saved my life for God's sake! Everything I've told you is the absolute truth; *everything*." The tone of pleading innocence she managed to inject into her words impressed Harrigan.

"You told us that after you met Muktar, you continued working as a waitress?" It was one of those statement questions.

"Yes. I moved to the lunch time shift."

"You see, that's where I have a problem. I showed your picture to a friend of mine—"

"Picture!?" She exclaimed. "What picture? How'd you get my picture?"

He reached into his pocket and removed Benecke's camera. "With this." He returned the camera to Benecke.

"You can't take my picture without my knowledge! I know my rights! That's an invasion of my privacy and I demand you delete it immediately!"

"And my friend told me—" Harrigan continued, ignoring her outburst, "—that you actually worked for Littlewood's Armaments, one of Europe's largest weapons and weapons systems design and manufacturing companies."

"*What!?* What do you mean, I work for Littlewood's Armaments? That's ridiculous! I told you, I'm a *waitress*!" She raised her arm, held her left hand palm up in front of her as if holding a notepad, and positioned an imaginary pen above it in her right. "May I take your order, Sir?" She parodied. "Shepard's pie with a side of vegetables? Is that all? Two cruise missiles as well? Of course. Would you like assault rifles with that?" She clasped her hands together and placed them on the table in front of her. "For crying out loud, you can't be serious!"

Harrigan fought hard to curb a smile desperately attempting to dance across his lips. He had always admired a person who could prevent any re-action to an unexpected revelation from revealing itself, it was not an easy thing to do; there was always a 'tell' of some sort. But there had been no tell. She was good; very good. Maybe a little *too* good.

"You tell me if I'm serious or not...Connie." He paused briefly. "It is *Connie*, isn't it?"

"C... Connie?" It had been an ever so slight stammer, but he hadn't missed it, and she knew he hadn't. Benecke, although just finishing the last of the flapjacks, had not missed it either. After a small sigh of resignation and with head bowed, she sat silently for several moments. "Alright, yes, my real name *is* Connie. Not Constance, just Connie." Her admission of deceit carried no hint of guilt.

It is no secret that any good lie always has an element of truth within it, and Bethany's story, well, Connie's story now, had been no different. The recount of her early life and the sexual favours required to be performed on who she now confirmed to be David Littlewood, had been true. Walking out and never seeing either of them again however had been a half lie. It was true she'd never seen her mother again. Not that the chance to do so had offered itself. David had explained her mother died suddenly from a brain aneurysm four months after she'd walked out. Meeting Littlewood again had never been intended, but life has a way of getting in the way of best intentions. While working for minimum wage in a hairdressing salon in Birmingham, washing people's hair, sweeping up, that sort of thing, one of the clients reading a magazine made comment about an article she was reading. The article featured an extremely beautiful socialite wife of a wealthy businessman, living in luxury in a chalet in the French Alps. Her name was Anastasia Littlewood. It had been a marriage of convenience. She'd wanted money and a luxurious lifestyle, he'd needed a beautiful wife by his side at events where protocol demanded it. Except for those occasions, she and her husband, David, rarely saw each other. *"The perfect marriage,"* the client had said with a laugh and showed Connie the photograph of the husband. Photographs of the camera shy Littlewood are rare. This one was taken without his knowledge by an anti-war protester outside his German munitions factory.

"I recognised him immediately, even without his beard," Connie said.

"So, you lied about not recognising him without his beard, and that foreskin thing," Benecke accused.

"Well, I lied about the beard." She paused, everyone grateful for the slight comic relief. "Later, when discussing his wife, and their loveless and childless marriage, he'd explained that while enjoying the trimmings of wealth, the absence of love and intimacy in his life, had created a constant emptiness; an unhappiness within him."

"And this is why a man of his status took up with a prostitute and her daughter in an East End flat," Benecke completed for her.

"Yes."

"And how'd you come to work for him?" Harrigan asked, trying to move the conversation along.

"When I'd learned who he was, I was down on my luck and thought that if he can afford to keep a trophy wife in outrageous luxury, surely he'd be able to see me right."

"You intended to blackmail him?" Harrigan asked.

"No, I don't think so. Well… maybe. I never thought of it like that. I needed money, he had plenty and he wouldn't have wanted the media to get hold of my story. So, yes, now that you ask, I suppose it was blackmail. But it never came to that. When I arrived at his London head office building in Horseferry Road, the girl at the front reception desk refused to let me in at first, but as soon as he heard my name and that I was waiting downstairs, I was taken to him immediately."

"How'd you feel when you first saw him?" Benecke asked as she placed a cup of tea in front of Connie and Harrigan and re-joined them at the table.

"Surprisingly, I felt very little. I had what I was going to say all worked out in my mind. Go in, ask for money and then leave; simple. But it's never as simple as you think of it in your mind, is it?" The question was more to herself than the others at the table. "His private secretary ushered me into his huge office and as soon as I was inside, she left the office and closed the door firmly behind me. As much as I tried, my well-rehearsed words would not come. I just stood there, frozen, memories, dreadful memories, flooding through my mind. He hurried towards me. *"Connie,"* he said, *"Connie, how wonderful to see you. Where have you been?"* I remember he spoke quickly, and when he reached me, he put his arms around me and pulled me towards him. I felt my body stiffen; so did he. He released me immediately and took a pace backward. *"I'm, I'm so sorry, please, forgive me. That was very insensitive, considering that… well, let's not go there."* Without saying another word, he turned swiftly, walked to the coat rack in the far corner of his office to the right of his obscenely oversized mahogany desk, removed his wallet from the tailored suit coat and handed me a wad of notes. *"Here, take this,"* he said forcibly, leaving me no room to refuse. *"Buy yourself some new clothes, have your hair done and we'll have dinner at Du Mauriers. We'll be able to talk there in private."* She paused long enough to take a long slow sip of her tea before continuing. "He asked for my address so his driver could pick me up. I refused his offer of a driver, told him I'd meet him there, and left his office. When I arrived at the luxurious Du Mauriers, he was waiting for me in one of three private dining areas."

"And you still had no real feeling of hatred for the man who you'd been forced to sexually satisfy, albeit without actual intercourse?" Benecke asked, still unable to grasp such a concept. If it had been her, she would have cut his heart out. But then, she would never have allowed herself to get into the situation in the first place. Even at seven years of age.

"Not at first. I didn't like him, obviously, but I was more interested in getting a meal ticket from him—," she paused and glanced at Harrigan, "—blackmailing him, than worrying about the past. My feelings towards him changed twenty minutes later when, over our aperitifs, he told me that what happened in the flat, the acts I'd been expected to perform, had not been his idea. It had been my mother's. The miserable little worm told me that because of her lifestyle before they'd met, normal foreplay no longer gave her the sexual stimulus she'd needed to be fully satisfied. She needed something more. He told me she'd said that just the thought of her daughter satisfying him excited her and she would like to try it. When asked if he would try it, he said he reluctantly agreed. And that's how it all started. He said he'd always felt guilty about it but admitted he'd enjoyed it. Well, he'd have to say that wouldn't he? There was no way he could deny it. He repeated he'd only agreed to go along with it because he hadn't wanted to disappoint my mother and pleaded for my forgiveness. It was then a wave of uncontrolled hatred towards him flooded through me. How dare he try and justify his actions by shifting the blame onto my mother? I didn't care if what he said was true or not; my mother was dead and he should've said nothing. He should've kept his mouth shut and taken the blame like a man! It was then I decided I needed more than just money. I wanted to destroy him."

"Why didn't you just report him to the police?" Benecke asked.

"And tell them what!? That someone as well connected as David Littlewood had forced me, a poor nobody on minimum wage, to sexually gratify him for ten years because that's what my dead mother asked him to do? And no, there weren't any witnesses to support my story so they would just have to trust I was telling them the truth? Sorry, Special Agent Benecke, in my world it doesn't work like that, and I decided if I was to have my revenge, I had to do it another way. I learned early in life that playing by the rules does not allow anyone to become as rich and powerful as he is, and somewhere there would be skeletons he wanted kept hidden. What I needed to do was come up with a way to get close enough to him to find his skeletons and enough proof so the authorities would have to believe me. And without giving him any more of the other," she added quickly.

"And the best way was to wangle yourself a job in his business," Harrigan said, uncharacteristically stating the obvious.

"It didn't take any wangling. We'd been talking less than fifteen minutes when he said I deserved better than minimum wage and offered me a position at his company. A position that came with a six figure salary and an all-expenses paid flat in London. I was under no illusion that part of the offer was payoff for my silence but what the hell, it was the best offer I'd ever had. Before I agreed, I made it perfectly clear that there wasn't to be any of the previous, because there'd be none of that, and he assured me that was not part of the package. And to be fair, since that agreement, he's never once even hinted at anything untoward."

"You agreed to take the position without even knowing what was involved?" Benecke choked back the words, *'you stupid girl!'*

"My official role would be as his personal assistant, which of course I wasn't, that's Crystal's job. During the meal, he explained one of his customers, a Muktar Al-Yousaf, had a client who regularly purchased weapons for shipment to the Middle East. It's a very lucrative contract, but recently he'd become concerned about a close relationship Muktar had developed with a Qiang Yoon, head of a known illegal drug family. He had no proof, but didn't want to risk losing the weapons contract and needed someone on the inside of Muktar's operation. Or better still, someone who could get close to him on a personal basis to keep their eyes and ears open and report back."

"So just hours after your reconciliation with this man, he wanted to pimp you out to Al-Yousaf so you could spy on him?" Benecke asked.

"Yes."

"And you took up the offer?"

"Of course. What better way was there to dig up a few skeletons?"

"Did you learn anything of significance about Al-Yousaf and Yoon?" Harrigan asked.

"Not anything *I* thought was of any real significance. I could verify they were is business together, how many times they met, where they met, anyone else who might meet with them, that sort of thing."

"And that story about meeting him while you were waitressing was also a lie?" Benecke verified.

"Partly. I was working with David. It was he who told me where to find Muktar. But the part about going with my friends and being taken to Muktar's table after my dancing performance was true."

"Tell me about the night of the shooting, and don't give me that fainting story because neither I, nor Special Agent Benecke, believe a word of it."

"I was sitting at the end, next to Muktar, just like I always did. The band was too loud for me to hear what Yoon and Muktar were saying, so I sat, like I often did, with my back turned away from the bright lights over the bandstand and stared into the gloom. Once your eyes are used to the darkness, it's surprising how much you can see, and believe me, it's amazing what some of the patrons get up to when they think no-one's watching. But that night was different. I suddenly saw the figures of two men wearing long overcoats in the entrance doorway as they stood silhouetted against the outside streetlights and alarm bells started to ring in my head."

"Why?" Benecke asked.

"Because there should've been a third silhouette. At that time of the evening, males without female partners, are not allowed to enter. Because there were no females with the two men, one of the guards should have entered with them to make sure they were joining friends already in the club and not trying to pick up unaccompanied women. My fears heightened as I watched the two black figures stride quickly through the club and in the direction of our table. They didn't wait for their eyes to adjust to the light, they knew exactly where they were going and that they had a specific purpose for being there. I'd been hanging around with Muktar and Yoon long enough to know the dangers associated with their types of businesses, and so, before the gunmen reached our table and had a chance to see me, I slid quietly beneath the table. As I did so, I vaguely saw two sets of black shoes stop in front of the table and then heard the muffled gunfire. It wasn't all that loud and what with the noise of the band it would've been difficult for most people in the club to hear. I suddenly felt Muktar's feet kicking me as the bullets entered his body, and then seconds later, it was all over. The shooting stopped, the two sets of shoes disappeared and I began to climb out of my hiding place. The first thing I saw was Behzad and Muhammad rushing towards the table. Behzad felt for a pulse in Muktar's neck.

"He's dead," Behzad announced as he looked up at Muhammad.

Muhammad didn't reply directly, he just grabbed at my shoulder, pulled me to my feet and started dragging me towards the back door, and, well, you know the rest."

Harrigan looked across to Benecke who gave a *"she could be telling the truth"* kind of shrug. Harrigan agreed silently and pushed the empty teacup and saucer to one side and stood quickly.

"So what now, Chief Inspector?" Connie asked.

"A good question." He picked up the cup and saucer and took it to the kitchen. "The first thing we have to do is get you to a safe place." His raised voice was forced to carry over the sounds of the running tap and placement of the rinsed crockery on the stainless steel draining board.

He re-entered the room. "You do realise the danger you're in, don't you?"

She looked up at him questioningly.

"The Al-Yousaf clan would like to get hold of you, and the Yoons wouldn't want you running loose with information about their dealings with Muktar, either," he explained patiently.

"But I don't know anything more than the authorities already know."

"The Yoons don't know that. And besides, both mobs will already have new leaders who will want to start with a clean slate. They won't want any loose ends, and Connie, in case you don't already realise it, you're a loose end." He retook his seat. "And then there's David Littlewood, he stands to lose the most if you tell what you know about the association between Al-Yousaf and Yoon, not to mention the sexual offences."

"David wouldn't hurt me."

"Don't bet on it," Harrigan warned. "The man's a reptile and don't think for one minute he intends letting someone who could bring his empire crashing down around him run around on the loose." He looked at Benecke. "But she can't stay here. You two gather up your things and I'll make a couple of telephone calls."

Thirty minutes later, in the deserted carpark of the Western Rovers football club's home ground, Harrigan stopped the Combo beside the black Ford Granada. The ex-SAS man in the grey suit opened the rear door of the waiting vehicle. Connie West scrambled from the back of the Combo and climbed into the rear seat and fitted her seat belt.

"I'll keep in touch," Harrigan said to her. He stood and looked at the stern, emotionless face of Eian Jones' agent. "Godfrey Windsor given you your orders?" He asked.

"Yes, Sir."

"Good."

Harrigan climbed back into the Combo and watched the black Granada speed towards the exit gate.

"I thought Eian Jones wanted to stay at arm's length?" Benecke asked.

"I guess it all depends how long your arms are." He turned the ignition key and the 1.3 litre petrol motor whimpered into life. "I think it's time we had a talk to Littlewood."

"Not before I have a shower and change into some clean clothes," Benecke asserted in a tone that left Harrigan with no option but to head for the Royal Garter.

"We might as well have lunch while we're there," he replied.

**

The Cornelia Refugium, or The Cornelia as it is now more commonly known, opened its doors in 1823, and holds the distinction of being London's first female-only member's club. The Cornelia Refugium was never a political statement or meeting place for women dissatisfied with their standing in society. It was simply a place where women of well to do means could meet in private, be pampered, and indulge in the luxuries enjoyed by women of substance. A place where women were able to celebrate the joys of their own womanhood away from any male interference or often hostile disapproval from the growing suffragette movements and women of lesser means. And it would be true to say that in contrast to the increasing number of ladies-only clubs appearing in London in modern times, *The Cornelia* fiercely fought to maintain its philosophy of being more pro-woman than anti-male. The original *Cornelia Refugium* occupied the top floor of a late 16th century British Baroque style three storey building in Boadicea Square, an address, which, while it undeniably could not've been more suitable, came about by sheer coincidence. *The Cornelia* of today owns the entire building. The top floor remains strictly off limits to male visitors, maintaining the original purpose of female sanctuary. The second floor restaurant, bar and lounge area is open to accompanied male visitors, although with some minor restriction on hours. In response to the increase of women members travelling to London for overnight business meetings, in 1979, *the Cornelia* board changed the ground floor usage of a little used casual bar area and gymnasium. The bar was simply closed. The Gymnasium relocated into the basement area. In their place were built combination self-contained office suites suitable for private meetings with clients and separate semi-luxury bed-sit type overnight accommodation. Innovative design and the large footprint of the Cornelia building which covered a small city block, allowed eight suites to be made available for rent. Not surprisingly, the suites were in great demand. With the exception of some slight modinisation, the reception foyer immediately inside the main entrance doors had been left mainly untouched. To cater for the demand, the bylaws were amended to include rule 110, limiting the use of the suites to members visiting London for business purposes only and rule 110 (a) that unless prior agreement had been made, a maximum limit of three nights stay at any one time applied. Rule 110 (b) stated the rental will be at the discretion of the board. Suite 3 was the only exception to rule 110. Lady Emily Louise, foundation member and driving force behind the creation of *The Cornelia*, was a Rothesbury-Worthington, and ancestor of Dame Joan Hamilton-Westbrook. At the drafting of the original constitution, Lady Emily inserted a clause granting the title, *President Indéfinītus,* onto herself, a title to be passed to the next surviving direct female relative. A subclause giving the *President indéfinītus* power of veto over all board decisions had also been included. Over the last one hundred and fifty years, governance laws relating to corporations, associations and not-for-profit organisations have transformed the position of *President Indēfinītus* into little more than that of a figurehead. But respect for the tradition of the position, coupled with the prospect of any member who might consider objecting to the continuace of the position suffering 'adverse considerations' regarding her membership, has resulted in the *President Indēfinītus* retaining access to more "favourable considerations" than could be expected by others. When the amendments to the bylaws relating to the office suites were being drafted, it was the unnanimous decision of the board that the *President Indēfinītus* be allocated the suite of her choice for her sole use and rule 110 does not apply. A situation from which the casual observer might reasonably conclude that 'hierarchal privilege', for which male dominated institutions are much maligned, is actually gender neutral.

It was five minutes after eleven when Dame Hamilton-Westbrook opened the door of Suite 3. "Sir Jason, please, come in," she invited warmly. Collins thanked the receptionist for escorting him across the seventeen paces of the marbled floor reception area and pressed a five pound note into her hand. He knew the rules, he'd been there before.

At the sound of the closing door, he turned towards his hostess and they enjoyed the intimacy of a warm, affectionate hug completed by a full lipped kiss that lasted slightly longer than just a friendly kiss, but shorter and less passionate than one shared between lovers in a binding, adulterous, clandestine relationship. If there can be such a thing as a binding yet adulterous clandestine relationship.

"Sit down. I'll make us a drink," Joan said with familiarity. With equal familiarity, Jason Collins hung his coat on the coat rack and went directly to his usual chair. Joan handed him a Glen Fiddich on ice, sat in the second medium sized, unpretentious but still soft leather armchair, took a sip of her gin and tonic and placed her tumbler on the glass topped coffee table between them. She leaned back and crossed her shapely legs, displaying more than was modest of her smooth, perfectly tanned skin.

"Alright, Jason, why are we here? Is it something to do with the Brewer Lane shootings?"

"I'm worried about this Harrigan chap, I think I've underestimated him."

"So you underestimated him. If I remember correctly, at our meeting yesterday, you were confident that if he became unmanageable you would silence him; *do whatever it takes* I think the expression was."

"Well… well maybe that's… maybe it's not going to be as easy as I first thought." His voice was quiet, uneasy.

"Jason, I've never seen you like this; what's happened?"

"He shot one of my men. And in the Royal Garter carpark for God's sake!"

She laughed and regathered her gin and tonic, showing no sign of embarassment as the front of her low cut dress fell open. "Good for him!" She raised her glass in a toast. "Here's to Chief Inspector Harrigan!" She took a long draught.

"This is no laughing matter, Joan!" His raised voice of rebuke was out of character from the normal controlled response those around him have come to expect.

"My, my, he *has* got you rattled," she mused. "I'd like to meet this Harrigan."

"Hold onto that thought."

She frowned, returned the tumbler to the coffee table and laid back into her chair. "I'm sorry, Jason. Go on."

"As I said yesterday, it's imperative we keep the UNIIA investigation limited to the shootings at Brewer Lane and not let it spread any further. To do that, we need to know what they're up to. But keeping this man under survellience is proving almost impossible, even Eian Jones' man had trouble. I learned late last night, Harrigan sent one of Jones' best men tailing him to Dover on a wild goose chase."

"Why would *Jones* have a man following him?"

"We have no idea and right now, we can't waste time chasing it up." He took a nervous sip of his Glen Fiddich. "We don't know how he discovered we'd bugged their rooms at the Royal Garter, but he did, and this morning he sent our people off on wild goose chases of their own. Consequently, right at this moment, we have absolutely no idea where Harrigan or any of his people are. And worse still, he has the girl who witnessed the shooting in his possession in an unknown location. We don't know if she has any information about our protection of Al-Yousaf's shipments, or if she has any intention of telling him, but we can't take the risk. We need to get her out of his clutches before it's too late, if it's not already."

"That's big talk for someone who has no idea where they're hiding her. And the more I hear about this Harrigan chap you won't find her until he wants you too." She finished the gin and tonic and covered her unneccesarily exposed flesh. "What are you going to do?"

"Well, first up, I'm going to stand down all survellience. We're not only wasting our time, if Harrigan can be convinced he's no longer under survellience, he might get careless."

"I wouldn't hold my breath waiting for *that* to happen, he doesn't sound like the *might get careless* type." She went to the small bar, poured herself another gin and tonic, turned and leaned against the bar, her silky tight fitting frock accentuating her sensuality. "And anyway, if this man is half as smart as you seem to think he is, the act of suddenly dropping all survellience will almost certainly arouse his suspicions. And if he links your survellience to the Brewer Lane incident, it will open the door for him to investigate the *who and why* questions regarding the survellience and undoubtably lead him directly to us." She thought silently for a few seconds before continuing. "We have access to increasingly sophisticted electronic, even satellite survellience options from the US military. Why not ask *them* for help?"

"It would create too many awkward questions. And the last thing we need is for the Americans to learn we're helping supply weapons to the very people they're fighting; the shit would really hit the fan if that happened. Using their GPS tracking devices is one thing; asking for direct assistance is another. No, Joan, we need something much more subtle. We need a spy in his camp. Someone who can get close enough to him to know when he is straying too far from his charter. Someone we can use to send snippets of information to lead him away from our connection with the Al-Yousaf family."

"Someone to get close to him? Just how *close* are you suggesting, Jason?" Her question was somewhat redundant; she was certain she already knew the answer.

He rose from the leather armchair and walked slowly, deliberately, towards her. After ridding himself of his empty tumbler, he placed his hands either side of her on the edge of the bar top, leaned into her and stared directly into her eyes. "Desperate times call for desperate measures, my darling, and we need someone prepared to get *really* close." The pause was just long enough. "As close as two people can get."

"Are you asking me to prostitute myself for Queen and Country, Sir Jason?" There was a tone of flirtatious sillyness in her voice.

"*Prostitute* is a little strong. You wouldn't be getting paid for it." Silly questions deserved silly answers.

"Oh, well, that's alright then."

He prepared to push his body into hers, but she quickly placed her hands on his chest. "I'm sorry, Sir Jason, but now you're my pimp, our relationship has taken on a more businesslike appearance. Besides, I have preparations to make." She moved skillfully away and began tidying the liquor bar. "You do know Special Agent Sarah Throgmorton is his steady love?"

"Are you saying you are doubting your ability to arouse a man's—"

She looked sidewards and then purposefully down to his front trouser area. Several seconds passed before she raised her eyes slowly. "No, Jason, it's quite obvious I am more than capable of doing that." Any other man might've blushed a little, but not Jason Collins. He just smiled, albeit somewhat boyishly. "What I'm saying," she continued. "Is I don't think Harrigan is the type to go behind his woman's back. But, you never know, I could be wrong." A discernible hint of hope coloured her response.

Dame Joan arranged for Wilhelmina, the receptionist, to escort her visitor across the foyer to the front entrance, which left him another five pounds lighter, and then picked up the ivory white telephone handset and dialled her beautician.

"Hello… Andrea?... I need an urgent appointment… yes, the full treatment… oh yes! I definitely need *that* done… three o'clock? I'll see you then."

Chapter Seven

David Littlewood had met Muhammad Abdul-Halim Al-Yousaf casually during meetings with his now deceased brother. Subsquently, the belligerent attitude displayed by the visitor sitting across the highly polished mahogany desk in his Horseferry Road office came as no surprise.

Littlewood rested his forearms along the padded arms of his chair, and leaned back slowly. "So just to be clear. You're saying I *knew* about your brother and Qiang Yoon smuggling drugs bound for the Middle East, Russia and parts of Europe, in the shipping containers bound for Urbadistan?"

Muhammad Al-Yousaf nodded.

"And unless I allow the smuggling operation to continue, the weapons contract will be cancelled, and the police will be informed of the operation and of my supposed involvement?" It was true Littlewood did have strong suspicions about the drugs, but he'd needed more information. That's why he'd used Connie to get close to Muktar, a detail he wasn't about to share with his extremely unpleasant visitor. Muhammad wouldn't take kindly to the news he'd had a spy in the Al-Yousaf camp.

Muhammad somewhat lazily slid his chair slightly away from the table and crossed his legs. "No, I'm saying much more than that. Qiang Yoon was a careful man, shipping only limited amounts of heroin. His approach was to suss out the opposition and get a toe hold. A sort of market research if you like. But Fan isn't Qiang, he's like me, a man of action who intends to flood those markets with the next big thing in illicit drugs; Crystal Methamphetamine, or Ice. Ice is cheap and easy to make and Fan isn't about to sit back and let that bloody Rusky get the run on him."

"By that bloody Rusky you mean Boris Akmatbayev?"

"Yes, Akmatbayev. He won't know what's hit him."

"If we assume for the moment I agree to allow this *Ice* to be shipped in my containers, what's in it for me?"

Muhammad shrugged. "It's not what's in it if you agree, it's what's in it for you if you don't."

"And I suppose you'll be getting a sizeable kickback from the Yoons?"

A second casual shrug accompanied by an equally casual *"of course"* motion of his head crossed the desk.

"Well let me give you some advise," Littlewood advised, the tone of any civility now noticeably absent. "Don't start counting your money too soon, because, you little thug, I didn't get to where I am today by giving in to everyone who threatened me. You can tell your mate Fan Yoon to go fuck himself. Now get out of my—" The jangling of the telephone brought Littlewood's abuse to a sudden halt. He snatched up the handset. "What is it, Crystal! I told you I wasn't to be interrupted!... W*ho's* waiting to see me?... Chief Inspector Harrigan!?... No, ask him to wait, I'll be a couple of minutes. I'll buzz you." He stood urgently, slammed the handset into its cradle and speaking in a hoarse whisper, gestured to his frowning visitor. "Quickly, go into my private washroom, and stay quiet. I don't think it wise to let Harrigan know you're here."

Al-Yousaf hurried through the door on the left side of the office and closed it quietly. Littlewood pressed the intercom button. "Crystal, show the Chief Inspector in would you?" He asked in his most welcoming voice.

David Littlewood was not what Harrigan had expected. Rich and powerful men invariably carry an air of self-importance, a bearing of superiority, and an expectation of privilege. And most telling of all, while attempting to ooze humility, were burdened with a need to be noticed. Littlewood's suit appeared to be more *off-the-rack* than tailor-made Armani or Saville Row. There was neither the almost mandatory distinctly styled hair with a touch of grey at each temple, or smooth European tan. He hadn't gone to the other side of the spectrum either, like wearing blue jeans to board meetings. He was ordinary looking. A man who would not look out of place riding the tube train or catching a Number 38 bus to Hackney. A wolf in sheep's clothing. A man of which to be very, very wary.

"Chief Inspector Harrigan," he said with an open, welcoming and almost cheery smile as he pulled the low backed semi circular padded leather visitor's chair on the right, away from the desk. "Please, make yourself comfortable. I apologise for the delay, damn mobile telephones, more of a hinderence than a help. Would you care for tea, coffee?"

Harrigan shook his head and purposefully moved to the chair on the left. Benecke took the one on the right.

"I've heard a lot about you, Chief Inspector," Littlewood said as he returned to his side of the desk.

"You have?"

Littlewood drained the last of the coffee he'd poured several minutes previous, and refilled his cup. He continued speaking as he did so. "Well, only from what I read in the newspapers. I know you prefer 'chief inspector' over 'special agent' because you think special agent is a little too Hollywood. I think most people would agree with you. Of your love hate relationship with people from the fourth estate. Quite understandable, considering their reporting of your successes always appear to be written in a left handed sort of way."

"Then you'd also be aware of my aversion to small talk."

"Er, well, of course." He glanced towards Benecke. "And you must be Special Agent Benecke?"

Benecke's experience as an FBI profiler clearly told her small talk was not part of Littlewood's normal character, and was most probably induced by some level of discomfort of them being there. She'd never been one to ease the discomfort of others. "Yes, I'm the black one."

"Oh, Special Agent," Littlewood replied quickly, "I didn't mean any offence, I just—"

"Offence?" Benecke interrupted, feigning indignity. "Why would I take *offence*?"

Not willing to continue conversation with a person he saw as nothing more than an underling, he turned back to Harrigan. "And what have we done to warrant a visit from UNIIA?"

"You know about the shootings at the Sister's Basement in Brewer Lane?"

"What I've read in the newspapers or seen on TV. *That's* why you're here?"

"Yes. Just gathering background. Nothing too specific."

"I fail to see how I can be of any assistance."

"Tell us about your association with Muktar Al-Yousaf."

"He was a customer. He purchased our product. I assume he bought groceries from Sainsbury's as well. Will you be visiting them too?"

Harrigan was pleased Littlewood had gone on the defensive. "Muktar Al-Yousaf was an international arms dealer with customers who, I suspect, are not as reputable as the rest of the world would like." The hint of accusation in Harrigan's tone wasn't lost on Littlewood.

"I don't know what you're trying to imply, Chief Inspector, but let me make something very clear. My company sells weapons and weapons systems to many arms dealers and governments and I'm not a confidenté or have a close personal relationship with any of them. We are diligent in our compliance with all regulatory requirements, including sanctions, embargoes, and political factors that might apply from time to time. To be perfectly frank, I find your veiled accusation quite offensive."

Harrigan would've been disappointed if he hadn't taken offence. "I understand your company designs and manufactures the whole gambit of weapons and weapon systems?"

"Conventional weapons only. Not nuclear."

"What range of weapons were you supplying Al-Yousaf?"

"Arms dealers are just middlemen. They establish a customer's needs and then find the best product. Over the years we've supplied a wide range of products to Al-Yousaf. But small arms mainly. I can have a printout of their order history sent to you if it would help. It'll take a while."

"No, that won't be necessary." Harrigan sat silently before moving on. "Let's get back to Brewer Lane."

"I told you, I only know what I've learned through the media."

"Nothing more?"

"What more could there possibly be?"

"So you can't think of any connection between the shootings and your company's dealings with Al-Yousaf?"

Littlewood's growing impatience was obvious. "I'm sorry, Chief Inspector, but this line of questioning is becoming a little tedious." He pushed his chair away from the desk. "So, if there's nothing else?"

Harrigan shook his head and turned towards Benecke. "You have anything, Special Agent?" It was a simple question with no hint of previous rehearsal.

"Just one thing, Sir," Benecke responded, right on cue. She looked at Littlewood. "Muktar had a girlfriend, a Bethany Joseph. Did you ever meet her?"

"Bethany Joseph?" He repeated, frowning in deep thought. "No, I don't think I ever did."

"We thought you might've met her during a business luncheon with Muktar, or maybe even a dinner meeting?" It ended up as a half question.

Harrigan rose slightly as if preparing to leave and then quickly retook his seat. "What about Connie West?"

"Connie West?" As the blood drained quickly from his face, he fought valiantly to supress the involuntary glance in the direction of his private wash room desperately attempting to rise to the surface. He was successful, too, and except for the effort taken showing briefly across his face, to the average observer his demeanour remained unchanged. He glanced at his Rolex. "It's time I took my regular break from the office; keeps the mind fresh. There's a little place around the corner I guarantee serves London's best espresso coffee and pastries." He rose quickly and without giving Harrigan or Benecke a chance to refuse his offer, walked swiftly into the reception area. "Crystal, I'm taking our guests to Mario's, I shouldn't be too long. While I'm out, would you contact Muhammad Al-Yousaf and tell him it's urgent we talk and could we arrange to meet tomorrow."

"Certainly, Sir," she replied without the slightest acknowledgement she knew exactly what he was asking.

Littlewood stepped into the sunlight in Horseferry Road. "Mario's is just around the corner of the next block; it's not far." He urged them to follow, turned and hurried away.

"I'd prefer something a little stronger," Harrigan called to Littlewood's back. "That pub across the street looks more like my cup of tea, metaphorically speaking of course. Come along, Benecke."

A protesting David Littlewood had little option but to rejoin them. Once across the road, Harrigan didn't enter *The Rose and Thistle* immediately. He leaned against the red brick wall between the two large picture windows with black, high gloss painted wooden frames, and stared back in the direction from which they'd just come.

Benecke reached for the brass door handle. Harrigan took her arm. "Hang on, there's something I need to see first, it won't take more than a couple of minutes."

Littlewood moved his more than substantial figure in front of Harrigan, blocking his view of the front entrance of his office building across the road. "Chief Inspector, I've been very patient, but I am a busy man, and unless you—"

Harrigan placed his left hand on Littlewood's shoulder, and with a vice-like grip, forced him to turn. He then raised his right hand and pointed to a man stepping onto the footpath directly opposite them. "That man coming out of your office building," Harrigan whispered over Littlewood's shoulder. "That looks like Muhammad Al-Yousaf to me. What do you think, Special Agent Benecke?" He asked raising his voice. "Does that look like Muhammad Al-Yousaf to you?"

"It sure looks like him to me, Sir." Benecke replied.

He turned Littlewood towards him. "So, *David*, how do you explain that?" He managed to inject just the right amount of disrespect into the man's given name.

Littlewood looked at Harrigan, then Benecke, and finally across to the disappearing Muhammad Al-Yousaf.

"Well?" Harrigan pushed.

"Let's have that drink," Littlewood replied.

The Rose and Thistle, or *the Thistle* as the locals call it, was a typical, traditional English pub, with plenty of dark wood, old paintings and antiquities displayed throughout and a row of tankards hanging above the bar. High-backed wooden cubicles with padded leather bench seats hugged the three walls beyond the front bar area, and there was not quite enough lighting throughout the entire hotel. With the exception of the cubicle at the far end on the left, occupied by a lone, timid little man with thin framed glasses, hunched shoulders, tired creased suit, and nursing a half pint of best bitter, all the cubicles were full. Littlewood stopped at the timid little man's cubicle and banged the silver knob of his ebony walking cane on the table. Harrigan couldn't explain why he'd not noticed the cane before then.

"I need this table. Go away," Littlewood demanded.

"Yes, Mister Littlewood. Of course, Mister Littlewood. I'm sorry, Mister Littlewood." And with those sad little words, from the sad little man, he quickly vacated the cubicle and hastened into the smoke filled area of the front bar.

"Who was that?" Benecke asked.

"One of my bookkeeper's. No-one of any consequence." He slid into the now vacant seat.

Benecke, knowing Harrigan's preference for the end seat, was first to slide in opposite Littlewood.

"You're a formidable opponent, Chief Inspector, I like that," Littlewood complimented. "My organisation is always on the lookout for someone of your ability. I could offer you a package you couldn't refuse."

"Thanks, but I think I'll pass."

Like most pubs there was no table service. But again, like in most pubs, David Littlewood was the exception that proved the rule. As ordinary looking as Littlewood was, there were very few Londoners who didn't recognise him, and no service industry business dared ignore a person of Littlewood's standing. Not if they wanted to continue in business that is. There was no need for him to summon a straff member, a female bar attendant in her mid twenties appeared the moment they were settled. She wore a forced smile that did absolutely nothing to soften her hard features.

"The Chief Inspector will have a double Ballantine's on ice, and Special Agent Benecke will have a....?"

"Bourbon and coke," Benecke said.

"And I'll have my usual."

"A double Weston on ice," the bar attendent offered and hurried away.

"Do you like Irish whisky, Chief Inspector?"

"What's his name?" Harrigan asked ignoring the question.

"Whose name?"

"The timid little man of no consequence."

"I have no idea. He's one of my part time bookkeepers. I think it could be Timothy something or other. I don't know, and neither do I care. He does work for my company and I pay him for doing it. What else is there to know?"

Harrigan's contempt for the man opposite jumped three notches. "You were about to explain why Muhammad Al-Yousaf was hiding in your washroom. He *was* in your washroom?"

Littlewood shrugged a carefree '*so I lied*' response, his growing dislike for the irreverant and disrespectful commoner clear in his eyes.

"What was the point of denying he was there?" Harrigan persisted. "You had to know we were already aware of your connection with the Al-Yousaf family and we would eventually be talking to whoever had taken over the family business. I would've thought there'd been more brownie points in inviting us to sit around the table with both of you, than hiding him in your bloody washroom!"

"It was a spur of the moment thing. You have a fierce reputation and at the time, keeping Muhammad out of the picture seemed to be the best option until I'd had a chance to, well—"

"Suss me out?"

"I think that's a fair assessment."

They all leaned back as the drinks were served. Littlewood threw a twenty pound note on the tray and waited for the change the more than astute bar attendant had brought with her. He offered no tip. Harrigan looked up apologetically at the bar attendant who threw a smile in his direction that said, *"don't worry about it, Sir, the tight arsed bastard never tips."*

"Tell me about your business operation. When Al-Yousaf or whoever, comes to you with an order, walk me through the process."

"I fail to see how that might assist your investigation."

"Niether do I, but tell me anyway."

"Very well, but there's very lttle to tell. With the exception of the destination country to make sure it's not covered by some arms embargo or sanction by our Government or one of its allies, it's like any other supplier or manufacturer. An order is received, the goods are picked or a work docket is created for the factory floor, and once the order is ready to go, it's packed ready for despatch."

He took a large swallow of his Weston's.

"What about security?"

"All our design, manufacturing and storage areas are secure facilities, not only from possible robbery but also from our opposition. Weapon design is a very competitive business."

"How are your goods shipped?" Harrigan asked.

"It depends on the product. Larger weapons are disassembled and components shipped separately. Smaller weapons like assault rifles, handguns, ammunition and accessories are usually shipped by container, again often with some degree of disassembly. Once the order has been loaded into a container, the container is sealed and not opened until it reaches its destination."

"What about customs?"

"We have varying arrangements dependant on the particular order. You'll understand I can say no more."

"National Security?"

"Something like that."

Harrigan let the matter drop. The vagueness of his answers told him everything he needed to know.

He barely had time to return his empty tumbler to the table before the bar attendant brought a repeat order. Littlewood reached for his wallet; Harrigan beat him to it, threw a twenty pound note on the tray and waved his hand in the international manner that said *"that's okay, keep the change"*.

"Thank you, Sir," she replied loudly, and returned to the bar. The true meaning behind the tipping melodrama performed by Harrigan and the bar attendant wasn't lost on Littlewood, but it was water off a duck's back. People of his ilk might have a need to be noticed, but they don't care if they're liked.

Littlewood drank half of his Weston's. "I hope I've been able to help, but like I said, I'm a busy man, and can spare you no more time."

"You know, I've been thinking about why Muhammad might've been hiding in your washroom like some mongrel dog and I couldn't come up with a satisfactory answer. But then I thought, maybe I have it the wrong way around. Maybe you weren't keeping him from us, as much as keeping us from him. Do you know what made me think that?" He paused long enough to make Littlewood think he had to answer, but short enough not to give him time to do it. "When I asked about Bethany Joseph, you gave no reaction other that quietly denying any knowledge of her. Which, by the way, we know was a lie. But the moment we asked about Connie West, you immediately came up with an excuse to get us out of your office. Why would you do that? Quite simply, if we happened to mention Connie West, a person who is on your payroll and Bethany Joseph were the same person, it wouldn't take him long to connect the dots. And there was no telling how that crazy bastard would react. Granted, you didn't know at the time if we knew West and Joseph was the same person, but you couldn't take the risk."

Littlewood calmly regathered his Weston's. "I have no idea what you're talking about."

"Before you start telling any more porkies, did I forget to mention we have Connie in protective custody? She's told us everything." Harrigan leaned forward and with icy hatred in his eyes, lowered his voice and spoke with an evil tone that even sent a chill down Benecke's spine. "And when I say everything, I mean, *everything*, you filthy, lowlife pervert."

Littlewood raised his Weston's to his lips, drained the tumbler and returned it to the centre of the table. "It's becoming apparent you have little understanding of just how far my influence reaches. If you did, you would choose your words much more carefully. I can make or break governments, and it would take me just one telephone call to rid the world of troublemaking liars like you—" he glanced quickly at Benecke "—and you, unless you're very careful." He turned back to Harrigan. "I could in fact, make your whole team and the entire UNIIA experiment disappear into the ether. So tread carefully, Chief Inspector, tread very carefully indeed."

He went to slide out of the seat but Harrigan grabbed his arm.

"Remove your hand from me immediately!" He demanded.

Harrigan tightened his already vice-like grip. "Now you listen to *me* very carefully. I don't know if you had any involvement in the Brewer Lane murders, but rest assured that if you did, I'll prove it. But irrespective of the outcome of *that* investigation, as soon as it's over, I intend bringing Connie out of hiding and she'll tell the world of how she was sexually abused by you. She was seven years of age for God's sake!" Harrigan released the man's arm and threw it violently away from him. Littlewood scrambled urgently to his feet. "Be warned, you bloody parasite," Harrigan continued. "You'd better start getting your house in order, because either way, I'm coming after you. Now, get out of my sight."

Littlewood spun angrily on his heels and strode violently towards the Horseferry Road exit, using his ebony cane to knock aside anyone in his path. Ignoring the screech of tyres, blaring horns, words of abuse hurled his way and the danger facing any pedestrian who chooses to force some imaginary right of way when crossing a busy London street, it was less than ninety seconds later when he strode past Crystal Beers. He shouted he was not to be interrupted and entered his office. After placing his cane in the cane stand behind his desk, he thumped down heavily into his substantial chair, unlocked and opened the large bottom drawer on his right and removed a black telephone. He dialled a number. At the cessation of the ringing sound in the earpiece, he didn't wait for the voice at the other end to answer; he was in no mood for niceties. "I want Harrigan off the Brewer Lane case and off my back, and I don't care how you do it."

"David, what's—"

"And I want him thrown out of the London Met."

"What!? Even I can't—"

"You can and you will, or so help me you'll be next!" About to terminate the call, he suddenly added one final demand. "And while you're at it, he has Connie West and I need to talk to her urgently, so find her!" He slammed the handset into its cradle, replaced the telephone roughly back into the bottom drawer, closed and locked it and returned the key to the fob pocket of his waistcoat.

"Call *me* a parasite will you?" He muttered as he stood at the window looking down to the street below and at Harrigan and Benecke as they hailed a black cab. "Well, mister high and mighty special agent, get ready to have the life-blood sucked out of you."

***

"Thanks, driver," Harrigan said mechanically after paying the fare through the driver's window. He and Benecke were only two paces from the entrance door of the Royal Garter when they heard a heavily accented voice behind them.

"Chief Inspector Harrigan. You come viz me. My boss vant to talk."

They turned in unison and were equally taken aback by the massive gorilla-like figure with the shaved head staring at them through unblinking and emotionless eyes.

"And who might your boss be?" Harrigan asked. Not that he really needed to, he was fairly certain what the answer was going to be.

"You soon meet him. No more talk, you follow me." He turned and walked towards the black stretched Mercedes limousine parked alongside the unbroken yellow curbside line twenty yards beyond the hotel entrance. Harrigan and Benecke followed. Once at the Mercedes, gorilla-man raised his right arm hanging down almost to his knee, opened the rear door and ushered them in. Due to the darkened windows, they were not aware of the person inside until they'd entered.

"Chief Inspector Harrigan and the beautiful Angelina Benecke. Thank you for agreeing to speak viz me." Boris Akmatbayev spoke in the typical Russian low pitch monotone voice with rolling *r*'s and elongated sylables. Despite his annoying habit of sometimes pronouncing his 'w's' and 'th's' correctly and sometimes not, he spoke in clear, reasonably well constructed English. The rear cabin of the vehicle, separated from the driver's compartment by an electronically operated glass panel, boasted four genuine leather armchairs, cocktail cabinet and table, and was luxurious to the extreme. "I trust Igor treated you with respect?"

Assuming Igor to be the gorilla about to open the driver's door, Harrigan nodded. They felt the vehicle rock as Igor climbed into the driver's seat.

"We'll drive while we talk." Boris Akmatbayev opened the cocktail cabinet, and put three perfectly formed ice cubes into three Bohemian cut crystal tumblers. He poured a liberal amount of Jack Daniels Bourbon and a limited splash of coke into one of the tumblers and handed it to Benecke. Next came a bottle of Ballantine's forty year old finest scotch whisky, this time pouring *more* than a liberal amount over ice into the second tumbler. "I've been told you're a Ballantine's man, Chief Inspector."

"Not *forty* year old Ballantine's I'm not," Harrigan replied a little too quickly, failing to hide his excited expectation. "At over five thousand pounds a bottle, it's a little out of my pay range."

Boris smiled. "And they say crime doesn't pay." He gave a guttural chuckle and filled his own tumbler with the comparatively inexpensive five times distilled, Kazakhstan,

Snow Queen Vodka. "How is your investigation into Brewer Lane shootings going?"

"Slowly." Harrigan had no intention of volunteering any information until he had a better feel for Akmatbayev's motives for the meeting.

"Have you decided who target was yet?"

Harrigan sipped the liquid gold and allowed it to line his throat with soft velvet. He was surprised at the smoothness of Igor's driving. Despite the stop start of the afternoon traffic, there was no discernable change in speed movement. "That's an interesting question," Harrigan replied.

"Interesting? I vould say more obvious than interesting. There were five people at table, not *all* could be target."

Harrigan was having some difficulty concentrating on the conversation. He'd already decided that drinking forty year old Ballantine's was the most exciting and satisfying experience he'd ever had; on his own that is. "We're still looking," he replied honestly._"Yoon or Al-Yousaf, or maybe both appear to be the logical targets." He took another sip and placed the tumbler on the small imitation woodgrain table. "*You* didn't have them shot, did you?"

Even Benecke was taken by surprise at the directness of the question.

"Did I have them shot?" Akmatbayev repeated calmly. "Why do you ask me this question?"

"Well, off the top of my head, because Yoon has made considerable inroads into your north London drug territory, and if what my gut tells me is correct, with Al-Yousaf's assistance, has already begun serious infiltration of your stronghold in the Middle East. I'm sure you've had people killed for much less."

Benecke braced herself, ready to respond to any adverse reaction Akmatbayev may have had to Harrigan's more of an accusation, than probing question. But her apprehension proved to be unfounded. Boris's reaction was to give a hearty laugh.

"I like you, Chief Inspector, you say vat you think!" He drained his tumbler in one swallow and refilled it with the Snow Queen. This time he didn't bother with the ice. "And of course, you're right, I did have every intention of eliminating them, unfortunately, someone beat me to it."

"Unfortunately?" Harrigan asked.

"Yes. I vas vaiting to find out the identities of *everyone* who vas involved in the plot to take over my territories, not just the two leaders; then I could eliminate *all* of them. But now, because of their untimely elimination, I'll have to start over. And considering the turmoil and political maneuvering happening in my homeland at moment, my need to be close to action and ensure my business interests are not adversily affected is essential. These shootings have come at most inconvenient time."

"The two remaining brothers, Fan Yoon and Muhammad Al-Yousaf, will most likely take charge, so nothing has really changed," Harrigan commented, explaining the obvious.

Boris just shrugged. "Then maybe I vill get to kill a Yoon and an Al-Yousaf after all. We'll just have to vait and see." He raised his vodka, cried *"Na zdorovie"* loudly, and drained the glass.

Harrigan didn't know if it was the forty year old Ballantine's casting some sort of spell over him, but despite everything he knew about this brutal man, there was something about him he liked. Probably his blatant honesty about who and what he was and his absolute disregard for who and what he and Benecke were. Or for that matter, what they thought of him.

"And besides," Boris continued, after taking a mouthful of his replenished Snow Queen. "My beautiful Sophie vas also killed. I vould never have had her killed."

"Sophie? The girl sitting between Yoon and Al-Yousaf? She was one of *your* people?" Harrigan asked as if hearing it for the first time. He could easily have said he already knew of his association with Sophie and given up Miguel Alvarez as the informant, but he might need Alvarez again before this investigation was over.

"Of course. How else vas I going to find out who needed to be disposed of?"

"How long had she been with Yoon?"

"Not long, she'd only seen him a couple of times, but she vas getting closer."

"Did she find out anything useful?" Harrigan asked.

"Nothing I didn't already know."

"What about the others at the table? The couple at the end near Yoon, and Al-Yousaf's girlfriend who fainted, fell to the floor. What can you tell us about them?"

"Fainted? I don't believe zat. I think maybe she vas like my Sophie; a spy for someone. Maybe Littlewood."

"David Littlewood?" Harrigan feigned silent thoughtfulness for several seconds. "Why David Littlewood?" He eventually asked as innocently as possible.

"Because he supplies guns for Al-Yousaf," Akmaybayev replied with a *'and you call yourself a detective'* sarcastic intonation.

"If she *was* a spy, of course," Harrigan countered.

"Of course." The Russian drained his tumbler and reached for the Snow Queen one more time. "If she wasn't, I don't know why she stayed with Al-Yousaf for so long. Because from what I've heard from my people, she wasn't *real* girlfriend. Not a girlfriend like you and your Special

Agent Throgmorton. Sure, they held hands and kiss a little, but not in vay lover's do."

"You're very well informed, Mister Akmatbayev." There was a tone of unmistakable annoyance at his and Sarah's relationship being brought into the conversation.

"Oh come now, my dear Chief Inspector, don't be so sensitive. In my business, it's essential I know everyzing about all my opponents… on *both* sides of law." He leaned forward, dropped one more piece of ice into Harrigan's tumbler and refilled it, this time almost to the top. Harrigan was about to refuse, but what the hell, he'll probably never get to drink the stuff again.

"What about the couple at the other end of the table, the ones sitting near Qiang?"

"Oh, now they were *definitely*, how you say in English… moles?"

"Really?" Harrigan tried to sound surprised. "Moles for whom?"

"I don't know, but probably some government spooky spooky agency. MI5, MI6, Secret Service. they might even have been some of your old boss's people, you know, from Serious National Crimes Agency?"

"What makes you think they were government people?" Harrigan asked. "Were they *that* obvious?" Not that he was all that interested how he knew, he just thought he might learn something worth passing on to Eian Jones.

"On contrary, they were not obvious at all. But no matter what Al-Yousaf wanted from government, they always managed to be able to arrange it. On its own, zat is not so difficult to believe; is no secret what right amount of cash can achieve. But like you, Detective Chief Inspector, I trust no-one and suspect everyone."

"If you're right and all Yoon and Al-Yousaf's associates around the table *were* spies or moles of some sort, surely Al-Yousaf or Yoon would've twigged onto at least *one* of them." Harrigan just couldn't believe Yoon and Al-Yousaf had been that stupid.

"Not really. Well, the government couple maybe, but not the girls. Most men trust voman. They have no warning bell inside brain that says, *beware of voman, she might be lying*. And anyway, even if they did have little warning voice, sight of pretty young voman makes man's second brain kick into gear and take charge, and from zat moment on, is no contest. Most men like to think voman is talking to them because they fancy them, not because they vant to do harm. A young, beautiful, sexy and intelligent voman, capable of acting, as they say, the *'dumb blonde''*, is man's natural and most dangerous predator."

There being no argument Harrigan could launch against Akmatbayev's last observation, he looked at Benecke, laid back into the soft leather and raised the tumbler to his lips.

Benecke took over the running, and true to form was all business from the start. "What can you tell us about Natalya Zhestakova?"

"Zhestakova? Not much. I know she works in our Russian language college near London Museum. And I only know zat because she was at door welcoming guests at college family orientation function two days ago. I saw her name badge. I visit there as part of duties as responsible citizen." There was no doubting the tongue-in-cheek nature of his last sentence. "Why you ask?"

"She's been found in her flat." The cause of her death had not yet been officially determined, but 'murdered' seemed the right terminology for the occasion.

"Murdered?" He replied with a hint of surprise in his otherwise emotionless response. "That's very sad." He sat thoughtfully for several moments. "Surely murder of simple language teacher is matter for local police. Why is your agency interested in Zhestakova's death?"

"Because the car used in the Brewer Lane shooting was registered in her name."

Benecke couldn't decide whether it was anger or shock that passed through the Russian mobster's staring eyes. He raised his glass slowly to his humourless mouth, and without moving his chilling, even threatening stare from her, slowly tipped the tumbler until its entire contents had been emptied.

She stared back, equally coldly, drained her Jack Daniels and rested the empty tumbler on her knee.

"It might've been stolen," he offered as he casually refilled his tumbler.

"There's no record of the car being reported stolen."

Akmatbayev persisted with the stolen theory. "There's no long term on-street parking around most of London, so maybe car is permanently parked in parking station somewhere. She lives around corner from college and maybe only uses it occasionally. Maybe she didn't know it had been stolen."

"It's possible," she agreed. "But I think a better question would be, how can a simple language teacher afford the latest model S Class Mercedes? I would've thought a car like that is more likely to belong to a person of affluence, like, oh, I don't know, a Russian mobster?"

He admired this strong, intelligent, fearless woman. He liked strong, intelligent, fearless women and to Benecke's disappointment, failed to rise to her bait. He gave a suggestive and shameless chuckle. "There are many ways a beautiful voman, a beautiful Russian voman, can earn money, Special Agent Benecke." He leaned closer to her and lowered his voice. "As could a beautiful black American voman. I can give you name and contact number if you are interested." He leaned back with a roguish smile.

"Thanks, but I think I'll pass." She sensed Harrigan tense angrily and prepare to defend her honour for what he considered to be a totally inappropriate comment. Denying him the opportunity to vent his anger she continued quickly. "Do you smoke, Mister Akmatbayev?"

"Do I Smoke? Yes, sometimes, but never in car! Smoke gets into air-conditioning and Igor would never let me hear end of it."

"Where were you yesterday afternoon, around five, five thirty?"

"Yesterday afternoon? I was with Russian ambassador from just after midday until early evening. We were finalising details of discussions I will have with President Gorbachev when I return to Moscow day after tomorrow. USSR is teetering on edge of bankruptcy and when it falls, I need to be ready." He leaned forward once more, took her glass and began replenishing it.

"Why are we here, Mister Akmatbayev?" She asked bluntly. "Why are we driving around London in your luxury vehicle drinking Jack Daniels and forty year old Ballantine's. What's your angle?"

He handed her the Jack Daniels. "*Angle?* There is no *angle*. But there *is* a reason. I'm leaving for Moscow day after tomorrow and could be away for quite some time. I just wanted to meet with your detective chief inspector face to face before I left. Like I explained, in my business I need to know everything there is about my opponents. And I mean, *everything*. I'd heard your boss is a fierce opponent and I needed to see for myself."

"And now you've met him, what did you decide?"

"Oh, reports were not exaggerated, he is fierce opponent. An opponent worthy of his reputation; as are you."

Harrigan wasn't all that sure he appreciated being talked about as if he wasn't there, and he didn't believe for a moment that meeting him was the only reason for the tété a tété. But, on the other hand, it's amazing how much peace of mind three quick glasses of forty year old Ballantine's can produce.

Igor drew the large vehicle to a silent and motionless stop in the Porte-corchere of the Royal Garter. It was only a matter of a few seconds before the concierge opened the rear passenger door.

They said their polite good-byes, and while exiting the vehicle, Benecke suddenly checked her forward motion, and slowly lowered herself back into the inviting leather. "Oh, there *was* something else."

"Oh? And what vould that be?"

"If you only knew of Natalya Zhestakova because you read her name badge a couple of days ago at a college family orientation function, how did you know she, and I quote your exact words; 'lives around corner from college"?

"How did I know?" He repeated. The following, overly lengthy pause gave Benecke the answer.

"Good bye, Mister Akmatbayev."

Chapter Eight

"An' jus' 'ow long is it b'fore I can rent out that room again, eh?" Hazel Spinks asked, any sympathy she might've had for her deceased tenant quite obviously now a thing of the past. "Th' owner 'spects me t' keep all th' rooms full! I'll be gettin' th' sack a'fore long!"

"I'm sorry, Hazel," Sarah explained patiently. "We're working as quickly as possible, but forensic science takes time."

"Bah! Forensic this, an' science that; it's not like th' old days when we 'ad proper coppers not young over educated upstarts. In them days, coppers was coppers and weren't afraid t' use their own brains. You ask Mister 'arrigan, 'e'll tell you!"

"I'm sure he would." Sarah opened her notebook. "If you'd like to give me the owner's phone number, I'll call him and explain the situation."

"It ain't an 'im, it's an 'er, an' a right bitch she is too. Not the sort that'll want t' be talkin' to th' likes of you. And who's gonna pay to clean up th' flat after you lot 'ave finished? Eh? Tell me that?"

Having decided any further effort to placate Hazel Spinks was simply casting seed upon barren ground, Sarah decided to move on. As if reading her mind, Hazel continued. "I'll get th' key."

Lo hurried up the stairs, taking two at a time, removed the police tape from across the doorway of the apartment and slid the key into the lock.

There was no need for discussion, they both knew what they were looking for. Invoices or receipts identifying the parking station where the Mercedes used in the shootings might be located. Financial records, personal letters from family, or where her clothes and other items had been bought. Anything that could help trace her past.

It took less than thirty minutes to thoroughly search the apartment and her belongings. They looked behind the one painting on the wall, inspected underneath and the back of all drawers for any document that might've been hidden. They found nothing. The bedroom was just as disappointing. They stripped the covers from the thin mattress, removed pillowcases, and searched the small wardrobe. The few clothes hanging in the wardrobe, undergarments and folded jumpers and blouses in the drawers all bore labels of London retailers, mostly Marks and Spencers. Inspection of more exotic places such as under the lid of the toilet cistern, the hollow curtain rods and curtains that might have had pockets sewn in them all drew a blank. They emptied the contents of the sugar and coffee canisters, the only two canisters in the kitchen. Apart from a smattering of basics, the food cupboard held only a small number of tinned products, mostly baked beans and spaghetti. The freezer including the ice trays was empty, and apart from the opened half-pint carton of milk and a half empty container of *I can't believe it's not butter*, the bottom refrigerator section contained little else. With the exception of two coffee mugs, there was only enough crockery and cutlery for one person. Forensic had taken her purse and as there was also no passport, forensic had probably taken that too.

Sarah walked to a cup hook screwed into the wall near the refrigerator and removed a small bunch of keys. She recognised the key to the apartment, what looked to be a locker key and one other door key. "I wonder what door this fits," she half mumbled to herself.

Lo glanced over to the key and just shrugged.

They stood silently and gave the apartment a last 'once over' sweeping glance before moving into the hallway, closing the door and replacing the tape.

"From what we found in the kitchen, she either eats like a sparrow or she eats out," Sarah said. "Before we visit the language college, I think we should have a chat to some of the nearby eateries, they might know her."

"Sounds like a plan," Lo replied.

***

Three generous tumblers of forty year old Ballantine's in less than forty five minutes had taken its toll on Harrigan's usually resilient constitution. "I need a shower and freshen up," he said as he and Benecke climbed the steps of the Royal Garter. "But first, I need a coffee." They veered away from the lifts and towards the hotel coffee lounge on the far right.

The coffee lounge was full. They were about to turn away when Benecke spoke. "There's a couple leaving now. We'll grab that table." They had barely had time to sit, before the waiter cleared the other couple's cups, wiped the table with a cloth that was a little too damp, and took their order. "I wonder how Lo and Sarah got on today." Harrigan was thinking aloud more than asking a question.

"There they are now, coming through the doorway." Not prone to stating the obvious, it must be assumed Benecke too, was thinking aloud.

Sarah was talking into her mobile telephone as they arrived at the table and filled the two empty chairs.

"Sarah's talking to forensic," Lo whispered.

Harrigan and Benecke nodded in understanding and listened silently to Sarah's side of the conversation.

"You found nothing to indicate foul play?... I see. What about the head wound?... it was consistent with a fall? So, you're saying it was an accident." She listened quietly for several moments. "Yes, I suppose it could have happened that way… yes, that is our job. Thanks very much. Send a copy of the report over to us would you?… The Royal Garter, that's right. Thanks again, 'bye." She returned her mobile to her black leather shoulder bag.

Assuming they had all heard her side of the telephone conversation, Sarah filled in the gaps. "That was the Medical Examiner, she said the wound is more consistent with the back of her head hitting the bath than blunt force trauma caused by a blow to the head. They'd also found fine particles of blood and hair on the top edge of the bath, and while it looks like it might've just been an accident, she couldn't definitively rule out foul play. There was no bruising around the forehead area, but it's possible someone could've used something like a rolled up towel around her forehead to smash her head against the top edge of the bath. She then reminded me it was our job to determine what actually happened, not hers."

The conversation stalled as Sarah and Lo gave the waiter their order.

"Anything else?" Harrigan asked.

"There'd been little food in the apartment, so we canvassed several restaurants around the area. The owner of one of them said Zhestakova was a regular customer, eating there most evenings."

"Alone?" Benecke asked.

"Always. Until about two weeks ago. Since then, a man has joined her on several occasions. He wasn't able to give us much of a description, explaining that years as a restaurateur had taught him to mind his own business when it comes to who's dining with whom. Especially when a couple enters separately and sit at the most secluded table in the room."

The waiter returned with both orders. Sarah thanked the waiter and picked up her skinny latte. Lo took over the commentary.

"He gave us a general description. A large man, had a shaved head, could've been Russian, but didn't hear him speak. One interesting detail was he always wore an overcoat and a trilby hat when he entered the restaurant and by the smell of his overcoat, was also a heavy smoker."

"Your man in the hallway?" Harrigan asked.

"Sounds a lot like it," Lo replied. "Also, Natalya usually came to the restaurant around seven thirty in the evening and never had the appearance of coming to the restaurant straight from work. It was as if she'd always gone home and freshened up before coming out to dine."

"So put all that together," Sarah resumed, "and there's little doubt he was our man in the hallway. They'd dined together regularly before her death so he would've known her routine of going home and having a bath before going out to eat. It's highly likely he'd become close enough to her to gain her trust, so maybe on the afternoon she died, he met her after work and went with her to her flat to wait while she had a bath before dining. It's also possible they'd decided to skip the dining part and stay home for a little bit of the other. That would better explain why he went with her to her flat, and not meet her at the restaurant. But either way, he certainly had opportunity to kill her the way the M.E. suggested, and on his way out, closed the door of the apartment leaving the security chain hanging."

"It certainly fits, but even if you're right, does it connect her death to the shootings? I don't think it does," Harrigan asked and answered. "If we could identify the man and connect him with Akmatbayev then we might have something, but just being Russian, and let's assume for now he was, as was she, *and* she taught in a Russian language college, he could easily have been a student."

"No-one of that description was a student," Lo countered. "We asked."

"Then maybe a relative of a student," Harrigan persisted a little impatiently. "It doesn't matter. The point is, she mixed with the Russian community, so he could be *anyone*. And what do you think the odds are of getting a positive identification of a man from the Russian community described as being large, heavily built, is a heavy smoker and wears a large overcoat? Jesus, you could take your pick."

After several moments of silent reflection, it was Lo who eventually summarised what they were all thinking. "So, unless we can find something more substantial than the Mercedes used in the shooting being registered in her name, or are able to connect the man with Akmatbayev, we have little choice than to accept the police position her death was an accident and move on."

"We do have that unknown door key," Sarah reminded. "Unfortunately, it has no markings on it to give us a starting point, so realistically, right now it's of little use. We'll try it in every door associated with the case, of course, but unless you believe in miracles..." Her voice faded away, leaving the others to complete the sentence in their own minds.

Recognising the long and varied individual and collective law enforcement experience of the group, Harrigan quickly dismissed the 'miracles' theory and returned to the Mercedes. "Up to this point, we've assumed Natalya knew the vehicle was in her name, am I right?"

They all nodded.

"What if she *didn't* know? Suppose it was done *without* her knowledge?"

"*Without* her knowledge?" Sarah repeated. "You cannot be serious."

"Of course I'm serious. I'm not suggesting someone just picked her name out of the 'phone book, I'm suggesting she was targeted specifically. Her nationality and employment at the college, makes her the ideal person to be used to throw suspicion on to Akmatbayev." Not one of his colleagues had the courage to roll their eyes in disbelief, but their facial expressions clearly indicated what they were thinking. Harrigan continued doggedly. "And if that *is* what occurred, it means the decision to lay the blame at Akmatbayev's feet was part of the plan *before* the shooting, not as part of a scheme to misdirect us to Akmatbayev when we were unexpectedly brought in to investigate. Find who was able to set this up, and we find our killer, or killers."

"If you're right, and I'm not suggesting you are," Sarah quickly qualified. "Whoever's behind it would have to be someone with a lot of pull; they'd need false ID documents to start with."

"It also throw's one hell of a doubt over Akmatbayev's involvement in not only the girl's murder, but also Brewer Lane." Benecke paused as their eyes all turned in her direction. "I mean, why would Akmatbayev go to all this trouble just to throw suspicion on himself? It doesn't make sense. And if he *isn't* responsible," Benecke continued to reason, "whoever set this up has gone into a lot of detail, right down to the man in the hallway. Maybe he wasn't Russian at all, just dressed up to look like one. Another mis-direction."

Lo returned his coffee cup to the saucer. "I hate to be the one to pour cold water on all this, but the Mercedes was also registered at her *address*, so she *must've* known about it; she'd get the letters from the MOT."

"Maybe, maybe not," Harrigan argued. "It's not an unusual practice in these old majestic buildings now converted to apartments, that traditional practices aimed at preserving an old worldly, more relaxed atmosphere continue to operate. One such practice is the mail being delivered to the caretaker and then distributed by the caretaker to the apartments."

"So, if Hazel Spinks received all the mail, she could hold back any MOT letters addressed to Natalya and pass them on to whoever's behind this whole plan?" Lo was warming to Harrigan's theory.

"Yes. For a fee," Harrigan replied. "The Hazel Spinks I remember would jump at the opportunity."

They sat in silence getting things straight in their minds. It sounded like something out of a penny-dreadful crime story, and all three of his team clearly had their doubts, but none of them could come up with a decent argument against it. "It also gives a good motive for killing Zhestakova," Harrigan added. "She couldn't be left alive to testify she had no idea the vehicle was registered in her name and that she'd never received any mail." He watched in silence while, trying their best to not display their scepticism, they digested all the possibilities presented by this new concept.

He leaned forward and spoke directly to Sarah. "The bunch of keys you found in the apartment, do you have them?"

Sarah nodded, retrieved them from her purse and handed them to Harrigan. He studied them for less than fifteen seconds before throwing them into the centre of the table. "There's no car key."

An almost suffocating silence fell over the group as three pairs of eyes searched the bunch of keys.

"She could've lent the car to someone else," Sarah suggested.

"It's possible, but if it *is* her car, and as Akmatbayev suggested, she earned the money to buy it laying on her back, would she be the kind of person who'd lend the vehicle to somebody? I don't think so."

"If she's prepared to take money from someone to use her body, why wouldn't she take money to let someone use her car?" The ever-practical Benecke reasoned. "And honestly, Sir," she added. "Laying on her *back*? It's obvious you know very little about the tricks of the trade of high-class prostitution."

Her comment brought smiles all around, easing the tension that had been building between them.

"If someone went to all the trouble to set her up, would they forget to leave the car key?" Lo reasoned.

"All good points," Harrigan agreed. "But we have to start somewhere, and my gut tells me the vehicle is not hers, and for whatever reason she was just a pawn in a much bigger game. And the missing car key? Let's hope, like the unfastened door chain, it was one of the things that goes wrong no matter how grandiose the plan."

"Is Akmatbayev still our prime suspect?" Sarah asked, knowing that to argue against Harrigan's gut would be a futile exercise.

"He's certainly the most obvious," Harrigan replied. "But Benecke's point is a good one. If he *was* behind the Brewer Lane shootings, why would he go to so much trouble creating this Zhestakova thing just to incriminate *himself*? And there's something else. Benecke and I have just spent the last twenty odd minutes with Akmatbayev. I can't put my finger on it, but the little voice in the back of my head is still telling me there's more to this than a drug lord protecting his territory." He told Sarah and Lo of his and Benecke's meeting with Akmatbayev, of him openly admitting he would've eventually killed Yoon, and probably Al-Yousaf, and of Sophie recently getting close to Yoon to gather information, information he had not yet received. "So yes, he admitted he was *going* to kill them, but not before Sophie had discovered all he needed to know; and I think I believe him."

"He told you he was returning to Moscow, the day after tomorrow, Sunday. Do we want to let him go and if not, can we stop him?" Lo half asked, half suggested.

"On what grounds? There's no evidence he's done anything wrong. I'd *like* to keep him around, if for no other reason than at the moment we have little else, but even UNIIA has its restrictions. Not to mention his diplomatic immunity."

"Then let's go through it. If it wasn't Akmatbayev, who else can we put in the frame?" Sarah asked. "Littlewood?"

"Littlewood had Connie West gathering information, and like Akmatbayev and Sophie, he still needed her services. It's difficult to imagine he'd do anything too drastic until he had everything he was looking for. And before anyone asks, if Yoon or Al-Yousaf wanted to kill each other or suspected Jones' people and had decided to do away with them, it's hardly likely they'd do it at the Sister's and get themselves killed at the same time."

"What about the two brothers who'll take over the family businesses? It wouldn't be the first time siblings have been murdered in the name of power," Sarah continued.

"That's a good thought, Sarah," Harrigan agreed. "And it needn't necessarily have been *both* brothers; just one brother could've been behind it." He finished his coffee. "Benecke, you and Lo start looking into that tomorrow. Right now, I'm going to have a shower and fresh—" the ringing of his mobile caused him to pause. "Hello?... Joan who?... Hamilton-Westbrook from the National Security Intelligence Agency? What can I do for you

M'am?... What, *now*!?... Well, yes, if it's urgent, we'll come right over… you want me to come alone? I can assure you, my people... very well, if you insist. Give me an hour… yes, I know The Cornelia." He returned the phone to his inside coat pocket. "That's interesting. Dame Joan Hamilton-Westbrook of MI5 wants to talk to me, in private."

***

It was a little after five forty-five when Harrigan entered the foyer of the Cornelian Refugium and approached the smartly dressed, attractive, full bosomed young receptionist.

"Good afternoon. Chief Inspector Harrigan, to see Dame Joan Hamilton-Westbrook."

"Yes, Chief Inspector, Dame Joan is expecting you. I'll let her know you're here."

Wilhelmina Abbamonte barely had time to reach for the in-house telephone before the sound of Suite 3's opening door echoed through the foyer. "It's alright, Wilhelmina," Dame Joan called before turning her gaze towards Harrigan. Her clinging silk dress caressed her slim, well toned body, allowing its plunging neckline to unashamedly display acres of velvet smooth, golden tanned skin. The long opened slit in the skirt had been pushed aside by her slightly bent right leg. A warm glow filled her body as she watched the look of naked approval cross her visitor's face.

"Please, Chief Inspector?" There'd been no requirement for any further soft words of welcome. The inviting nod and the sight of the clinging fabric against her firm buttocks as she turned and disappeared into her suite, was enough to send Harrigan scurrying across the polished floor.

Akmatbayev's generosity earlier that day, had led to Harrigan's decision during the journey across London to resist any temptation to partake in any further alcohol consumption until at least tomorrow. Unfortunately, the vision of the beautiful sirenesque figure standing in the centre of the room, fondling rather than holding a tumbler of golden liquid in her outstretched hand, disintegrates resistance to temptation like fire on wood in a tinder factory.

He moved more quickly towards her than he knew he ought, and as he took the tumbler from her slender hand, felt her brief, flirtatious resistance.

"Thank you for coming so promptly, Chief Inspector." She moved to the two-seat sofa, sat slowly and crossed her legs. The slit in the skirt once again performed its task.

She looked casually at the vacant seat beside her, but Harrigan, determined, this time at least, to be strong, gripped the tumbler in his right hand almost tightly enough to shatter the glass, and sat in the single armchair opposite. "It's my pleasure, Dame Joan."

She issued a throaty chuckle. "You can forget that *Dame* business, Chief Inspector, call me Joan."

"Joan," he said as if correcting himself.

"And what do I call you, Chief Inspector; *William?*"

"Only if you want to sound like my mother," he replied good-humouredly.

"Well, that wipes *William* off the table," she replied quickly and equally good-humouredly.

"My friends call me Bill."

She thought silently for a moment and reached for the Dublin crystal highball glass of Sipsmith London Dry gin and tonic, with lime, not lemon, resting on the small table to the left of the sofa. "No, I think I'll remain with Chief Inspector, it has a certain air of being a cut above the rest, garnished with a comforting warm charm feel about it. Nothing like that brassy, almost department store, special agent thing." She was letting him know she'd done her homework. The seductive ring she'd majestically injected into, 'Chief Inspector', took him back to Washington, DC and Samantha Cox. Lieutenant Samantha Cox of the Washington MPD to give her full title. He'd always believed he'd never again hear the words, Chief Inspector, uttered with such bare skinned lust. He was wrong.

He took a larger gulp of Ballantine's than he had intended. "You said on the telephone you needed to see me urgently?" It wasn't only a question, it was also an announcement the time had come to get down to business; investigative business that is, not monkey.

She leaned further into the back of the sofa, uncrossed her legs, placed her right foot on the floor and crossed her left leg over her right, closing the hip length slit in the skirt. She slowly laid her right arm across the exposed bare skin of her cleavage, her slender neck now held lightly between thumb and forefinger. The shop was closed, for now, anyway.

The coldness in her voice, re-enforced the mood change. "I cannot deny, when I first learned you and your people had been given the investigation into the Brewer Lane shootings, I was angry. *Quite* angry in fact, and, I suggest, reasonably so considering the victims were a home-grown drug dealer and an arms dealer, a *reputable* arms dealer, murdered on home soil. Try as I might, I could see no possible justification for bringing it under your jurisdiction. Along with most of our law enforcement agencies, I believed it was an investigation better suited for Scotland Yard, with assistance from my agency as required. I'm sure you can understand how I felt?"

He nodded. "It's not the first time I've heard that speech, or something similar. It comes with the territory."

"Yes, I suppose it does." She sipped her Sipsmith's and Tonic, gently prodding the ice cubes with her finger as she lowered the glass. She returned her right hand to her naked chest. "Do *you* have any idea why UNIIA was asked to investigate the shootings? Is there something more I should know? Within your own confidences, of course." As talented as she was, she was unable to give the question that throwaway innocent feel aimed for.

"My job is to investigate without fear, favour, or influence from any third person or organisation, not question the whys or wherefores of being given the task." He wasn't about to go down *that* path. He changed the subject. "You asked if I understood how you felt, past tense; does that mean you've had a change of heart?"

"I wouldn't go that far. More an acceptance of the reality, rather than a change of heart."

"If you can't beat them, join them?"

"Something like that, yes."

"And you've called me here to offer your assistance and the use of your agency's resources?"

'Among other things' she whispered to herself, more as a verbal thought than an actual whisper. "You're getting a little ahead of me, but generally, yes, you could say that."

"Thank you, it's appreciated and if the need arises we'll be more than willing to take advantage of your offer." It was his turn for a 'pause for effect'. "But why the urgency? You could have spoken to me about this tomorrow. Why tonight? And why here, in your private apartment and not in your office?" He had a fair idea of the answer to the last part of his question but was interested in hearing her version.

The first part of her answer came a little more violently than he'd expected. "You shot a 00 operative in the car park of your hotel for Christ's sake, did you really think that would go unnoticed!? Jurisdiction or no jurisdiction and irrespective of any provocation you thought you might've had, you can't just go around shooting operatives of the UK intelligence community without questions being asked." She purposefully stopped herself and allowed several calming seconds to pass before continuing in the more normal, modal register. "I'm a person who likes to be one step ahead and when someone from Number 10 eventually asks what I'm doing about you shooting one of our people, and they will ask, I will need a reasonable response. I want to be able to tell them you and I have come to an understanding and are now working together to solve the mystery of the shootings as expeditiously and incident free as possible. And more importantly, without the involvement of the media."

As feasible and logical as it sounded, especially the bit about the media, Harrigan had his own idea of why he was there and could see no reason to move away from his tried and true basic instinct of trusting no-one until trust had been proven. But now wasn't the time to argue.

"Fair enough," he replied rather blandly.

She once again, raised her glass from the small table beside the sofa and took an ineffective, even disinterested sip. "How's the investigation going?" She asked casually.

He admired the manner in which she was able to make the question sound more like a topic of general, inconsequential conversation than probing interrogation. On reflection, maybe 'admired' is a little weak; 'respected' is probably closer to the mark.

'Admit it Harrigan, she's almost as good as you are,' he thought. *'Almost.'*

"It's difficult," he replied.

"Difficult?" She failed to mask her surprise at his choice of words. "That wasn't the answer I was expecting. What do you mean, difficult?"

"You spoke earlier of a home-grown drug dealer and an arms dealer being the victims of the shooting, but they weren't the only victim. There were four other people at the table. Three were killed and one managed to escape unharmed, which in itself, is a mystery."

"You cannot be serious. A couple of confidantes and a girlfriend sitting between them. What could be *difficult* about that? Just three people at the wrong place at the wrong time." He sat silently, his face almost without expression. She frowned and returned her glass to the table before continuing. "Surely you're not suggesting one or more of *those* people were the target and Yoon and Al-Yousaf were the innocent bystanders!?"

"I'm not suggesting anything, I'm just being thorough."

Despite her resentment at the less than subtle inference that his thoroughness was far more substantial than hers, it served to help her appreciate the depth of her visitor's ability. She nodded tacit approval of his barb. "But you *would* admit that Yoon and Al-Yousaf were the most likely targets?" She'd almost fallen into the silence that occurs in conversation when waiting for the other person to respond, when, in a sudden effort to negate his earlier criticism of her thoroughness, she continued speaking. "I should probably clarify that a little. Obviously, *both* men need not've been the target. It's quite possible either one of them could've been the main target, the second one was just a bonus."

He smiled. An opponent on the defensive is almost certainly in the weakest position. "Obviously." He had no intention of leading the conversation at this point. When your opponent is in a hole, always give them opportunity to keep digging. His hostess didn't disappoint.

"This girl who supposedly escaped uninjured, what do you know about her? Her identity? Was she Al-Yousaf's girlfriend? Where she is now?"

"We know very little," he lied. "She appears to have disappeared without trace. But I'm certain we'll find her eventually." He sipped his drink and waited silently. Waiting for his beautiful sparring partner to get to the *real* reason he was there.

"You do know that Qiang Yoon is expanding his illicit drug business into areas north of London that are currently held exclusively by the Russian mobster, Boris Akmatbayev?"

'And there it is! At last we've come to the direction she wants the investigation to go. All I need to find out now is why, and the identity of the person whose idea it was for her to invite him into her most private hideaway. Bringing the fly to the spider.' He kept his thoughts firmly locked away.

"Yes," he replied simply, knowing that to tug on the line too quickly invariably resulted in the fish dropping the bait.

"Would I be right in assuming he's your number one suspect?"

"I don't know about number one, but yes, he's up there."

"Anything I can do to help?"

"No, not at the moment."

"Do you know he's planning to leave the country on Sunday? I can stop him if it would help."

"Yes, I do, I had a long conversation with him this afternoon." He drank the last of his Ballantine's. Maintaining her current closed shop persona, she stood immediately, took his empty tumbler and walked to the small bar.

"And you're comfortable with that? Him returning to Moscow?" She spoke to the ice bucket. "It'll be nigh impossible to get him back if he decides not to return of his own accord." She returned the refreshed tumbler and retook her seat.

"I'll get him back if I need to," he replied confidently.

"Of course you will," she said, giving a slight 'silly me' giggle. "I'd almost forgotten about your association with Asif Mahmood." Her reference to the world's most feared and powerful underworld character surprised Harrigan. Not surprised she knew about it; surprised she *admitted* knowing about it. "Oh come now, what's that look on your face all about? The UK has the best Intelligence community in the world. Don't tell me you thought we wouldn't know about your, as some would say, *inappropriate* dealings with Mahmood over the last couple of years?"

"I'd've been more surprised if you hadn't known. But I'm curious, are *you* one of those people who believe my past dealings were, as you so quaintly put it, inappropriate?"

"In my job, Chief Inspector, I can't afford any dalliance in the world of the politically correct. I'm expected to get results despite the self-righteous nonsense the media likes to pedal to the growing multitudes of gullible minds. Not to mention the self-interest driven platitudes offered to the masses by those within the political arena or the results demanded by both the people and our Lords and Masters. Results rarely able to be achieved without bending the odd rule or two. Is your association with Mahmood bending the rule too far? I am not certain. It depends I suppose."

"On what?"

"The flexibility of the rule and the results expected to be achieved."

He liked the sound of her response, but now he needed to decide whether it was a genuine response from the heart, or a response solely for his benefit.

Sensing his doubts about her sincerity, she moved on quickly. "To get back on topic, we've been trying to put Akmatbayev behind bars for a long time. But a man of such wealth and influence, irrespective of how he achieved such a position, is almost Teflon coated." She removed her right hand from her chest area and used her left arm to retrieve her Dublin crystal. Reaching out much further than was necessary, she encouraged the deep opening of her dress to immodestly expose more of her perfectly formed breasts than was proper. "What I'm saying is, if you need help to put this man away, my agency is at your service. We'll do whatever is necessary, Bill, whatever is necessary." She'd thought she'd experiment with the shortened version of his given name, just in case, but as she'd feared, it lacked the penthouse ring she needed for stimulation and vowed never to do it again.

With the motive of her invitation being to steer his investigation along a certain route now confirmed, any doubts he might have had that there was much more to the shootings than just a gangland war had now dissipated completely. It was time to broaden the boundaries of their conversation. "Was it your lot who bugged our rooms at the Royal Garter?"

"No, that was MI6." He was surprised by her honesty. "Jason Collins, my opposite number in MI6, is a little too fond of all that electronic bugging and tracking stuff. But there is some good news on that front. He told me this afternoon that he'd arranged for his men to remove the bugs immediately."

"Oh, why?" He asked innocently.

"Why did he tell me or why did he have the bugs removed?"

"The bugs thing."

"He didn't say." It was her time to lie, but she needn't have bothered, Harrigan didn't believe for a second she didn't know. It also disappointed him a little; it was such a stupid thing to lie about.

She stood once more, this time the slit in her dress returning to its earlier risqué ways. "I'll leave you alone for a few minutes, Chief Inspector. I need to freshen up a little."

She returned five minutes later looking even more radiant than when they had first met. He drained his glass, rose from his chair and placed the empty tumbler on the coffee table in the centre of the room. "If there's nothing more, I'll say good evening."

Without any seemingly visible movement, she was suddenly standing in front of him; close to him. *Very* close to him. She took his left hand, and feeling no resistance, raised it slowly and held it against her firm right breast. She closed her eyes and placed her lips lightly on his. He felt the movement of her lips on his as she whispered softly. "Just one thing more, Chief Inspector." Her lips remained against his, open apart wider and longer than would normally be needed, before placing her left hand behind his head and pulling downwards until his lips rested gently against the anxious, willing golden skin between the plunging neckline.

She felt his left hand squeeze her excited breast, and with his lips urged on by the subtle smell of vanilla and almonds clinging to the perfumed body, he reached his right arm around her and pulled against the nakedness of her backless dress. She pressed herself into him, feeling his own, unmistakable excitement.

"Don't be angry," he said softly, his lips moving against her moistening skin, "But I need to know who asked you to talk to me."

Her body stiffened, but only briefly. Her resentment towards his less than tactful and untimely question having been quickly pushed aside by her almost uncontrollable desire. "I… I don't know what you mean," she breathed.

"Joan, I beg you, if I am to quench our thirst for each other, I need to know who—"

"It was Admiral Collins, Jason Collins, it was one of his men you shot; he suggested it. But I was going to ask you to come anyway," she added hurriedly, pulling his head harder against her heaving chest, desperately trying to reclaim the mood.

She felt his left hand relax and leave her breast. His right hand moved to his side, his lips left her naked skin.

He straightened and took her by the shoulders. "I'm sorry, Joan. There's no doubt that you know I'm in a steady relationship, and as beautiful and sensual as you are, I must leave before I do something I regret."

She stood erect and slapped his face with her right hand. "You bastard!" She screamed. "You fucking bastard!" She slapped him again; harder than before. "Get out! Get out, *now!*"

He stood motionless for longer than he can remember, and then, to her surprise, he didn't turn and leave immediately, instead, he leaned forward, held her softly and kissed her gently on the lips. "I am truly sorry, Joan. I wish it were another time, maybe even just six months earlier. You are indeed a beautiful and most desirable woman. A woman no man could ever forget." He turned quickly and closed the door quietly behind him.

She stood silently, and not completely understanding how or why, allowed his last words to melt away the anger she felt by his rejection. Unfortunately, his words did nothing for her raised libido or her desire for satisfaction. If anything, they'd made it worse. She sighed heavily. "Oh, what the hell!" She walked to her front door. "Wilhelmina!"

She called across the empty foyer. "Get Julia down from the bar upstairs to relieve you will you, I need you in my suite for an hour or so. And the quicker the better."

"Yes, Dame Joan, right away." Wilhelmina knew what was to be required of her, after all, it wasn't as if it would be the first time.

***

"Here he comes now," Sarah said as Harrigan entered the restaurant.

"Have you ordered?" He asked, taking the seat opposite Sarah.

"Fifteen minutes ago," she replied. "We weren't sure how long you were going to be." There was an undeniable hint of suspicion in her voice. She indicated to the waiter they needed a menu.

He didn't feel particularly hungry, not for what was on the menu that is. The physical arousal he had experienced, driven by Dame Joan's unashamed passionate advances and her firm, anxious, yielding sweet smelling body, might well have at last subsided, but there'd been no diminishing of his inner desires. He gave a more than casual glance at his watch, it was seven forty.

"Is there something else you have to do tonight?" Sarah asked, a slight frown creasing her brow.

'You have no idea, but we're in mixed company' he thought, impatient to take her to their room. "I'm expecting a call from Lew Canning, that's all."

"The bug sweeping guy?" Benecke asked.

In between reading the menu and ordering a medium to rare 400 gram, fully matured grain fed Black Angus rib eye with red wine jus, Harrigan outlined in detail the conversation he'd had with Dame Joan Hamilton-Westbrook. He especially emphasised her efforts to steer the investigation towards Akmatbayev and her offer to prevent him leaving the country. And to a lesser extent, that MI6 have realised that bugging our room had been a bad idea and have supposedly removed them from their rooms. He'd also learned it had been Collins' idea for the meeting, wisely omitting any reference as to how the latter information had been gleaned.

With perfect timing, as he finished the last of the ribeye his mobile rang. "Lew?" He asked, not leaving the table and ignoring the disapproving stares of other diners. "You have?... And the rooms are clean?... Great, thanks Lew." He hung up, mouthed a general apology to the room, ending with the words *"Police business"*.

He pushed his plate aside, took Sarah's hand and stood more quickly than was normal. "Come with me, Sarah, I need to see you; privately."

She stood, apologised to Benecke and Lo, and tomorrow being Saturday arranged to meet for breakfast at eight thirty. Still holding Harrigan's hand, she followed him towards the lifts matching what only could be described as his indecent haste.

Benecke looked at Lo. "The DCI *did* say our rooms were clean too, didn't he?"

"That's how I heard it," Lo replied.

"Then I think I'll retire to my room too." She placed her serviette on the table. "What about you, Lo?" She asked.

He placed his serviette on top of hers. "I think that sounds like a good idea."

As they stood together, Benecke picked up the serviettes and moved them more towards the centre of the table. Lo watched silently as she rearranged the serviettes; hers was now on top.

Chapter Nine

Admiral Sir Jason Collins sat on the terrace of his and his wife's London twelfth floor penthouse apartment, complete with uninterrupted distant, but not *too* distant, views of the busy Thames. He sipped his first cup of tea of the day from his translucent Campbellware bone china tea cup. It was appoaching eight thirty when he absently picked up the unopened copy of the Times from the far side of the marble top iron cast table and read the date; Saturday Fifth May 1990. He sighed, returned the still unopened newspaper to the table and gazed silently at the tourist vessels loaded with early bird tourists as they left their moorings along the bank of the Thames, joining other working craft already cutting temporary scars into the dark water.

"Cheer up, Darling, it might never happen," Lady Annabelle Collins, his wife of thirty years this coming Thursday said in a tone that turned the flippant, almost playful statement into a threat; a tone he'd grown quite used to over the years. Being an agreed marriage between a titled family and a family with wealth, common in the upper classes, theirs had never been an overly romantic relationship. They'd always had separate bedrooms, and only came together occasionally for what she viewed to be her obligatory duty.

"Care to share?" She asked casually, a deliberate air of the disinterested clearly visible. She poured a cup of black tea with lemon, sat at the opposite end of the table and picked up the now disgarded Times. She was a handsome woman and he'd often wondered if the circumstances of their marriage limited her frigidness towards him alone, and if she'd had, or maybe still has, lovers beyond the marital home. In a strange way, he hoped she had. Thinking of her with other lovers somehow made her more desirable. It also eased his occasional feeling, not of guilt but the more simple wrong doing for his taking of other women. Prostitutes mainly, it was safer that way, no personal involvement, just a release of desires and thank you very much. Although there was *one* prostitute, from many years ago he'd never forgotten. Not that she'd been anything special, but she'd undoubtedly had a certain something about her and unlike the others, they'd developed, although not a permanent arrangement, a lengthy period of regular assignations. He remembered it was through her he'd met David Littlewood who by chance was also partaking of her pleasures. Well, to say that's how he and Littlewood had met was not quite true. They'd both attended the same exclusive *Knights College* during their early years, but had never been close friends and not surprisingly had lost touch until she'd brought them together again.

Why someone of Littlewood's position and wealth, not to mention his beautiful wife, had eventually taken the woman on as a mistress had always been a source of contemptuous amusement for Collins. He'd even moved her and her daughter, who Collins had never met, to a better location in the East End. *She was a whore for God's sake!*

The sound of Jason Collins' derisive chuckle caused Lady Annabelle to throw a momentary glare of disapproval towards the opposite end of the table.

The reminicence of Littlewood and his whore, brought him back to his earlier thoughts. He'd received a telephone call from a highly agitated Littlewood late yesterday explaining he had something he'd needed to discuss urgently. They'd arranged to meet after seven for drinks at *Du Mauriers*.

It was clear from the moment he'd arrived at *Du Mauriers*, Littlewood's agitation had not shown any signs of subsidence. But like many persons of influence and power, their agitation drove them not into a state of irrationality, but into thoughtful vengeance against the creator or creators of the agitation. He hadn't known at the time who might be the creator of Littlewood's state of mind, but what he'd heard about DCI Harrigan, he'd had no doubt that Harrigan was more than capable of ruffling feathers. Littlewood's opening sentence had confirmed his suspicions. Collins remembered their opening conversation word for word.

"I had a visit from that Chief Inspector Harrigan this afternoon, Jason, and he left me feeling very uncomfortable. Very uncomfortable indeed. Have you met him?"

"No."

"Then maybe you should. Take it from me, he's a dangerous man, very dangerous, and unless we take immediate action to neutralise him, the newspaper headlines will have our agreements all over the front page quicker than you can say, you can't throw me in jail."

"I told you on the telephone, David, I'm on to it. At this very moment, Joan will be working her magic and Harrigan will only have eyes for Akmatbayev."

"You underestimate Harrigan, Jason, he won't be sidetracked by that nymphomaniac. And even if you do manage to lay a trail good enough to force him to arrest Akmatbayev, he won't stop there. He knows there's something else and he'll keep digging until he finds it."

"He won't be able to. UNIIA's jurisdiction boundaries are very limited, and—"

"Jurisdiction!? Harrigan's not the kind who cares about jurisdiction!"

"Then we'll buy him off. Everyone has his price."

Littlewood had then leaned back into his chair, shaking his head in despair. "You really don't understand the man, do you. He's not the sort you can just buy off, at any price. That's one of the things that makes him dangerous."

"One of the things?"

"Yes. He also possesses a complete lack of respect or fear of the ruling classes or those in authority which makes it impossible for us to intimidate or bully him in any way, and, maybe his most dangerous trait, is his belief in equal justice for all."

"Equal justice for all, eh? Now, that is a problem."

It had been about that time, Collins had begun to realise how cheaply he'd taken Harrigan. But it also gave him cause to wonder about Littlewood's excellerated level of concern. He had little doubt that the truth about the 'guns to the rebels' operation could be kept from Harrigan, after all, they'd been successful against several snooping journalists in the past. *'Did Harrigan have something else on Littlewood?'* he'd wondered. *'Some dark secret Littlewood was desperate to be kept hidden?'*

Littlewood had continued, interrupting Collins' private thoughts. "But his justice-for-all policy and his pride in being a lawman of the people, is also his greatest weakness. Exploit it man! Get some dirt on him. Show the world he is not as squeeky clean as he'd have us believe!"

"I'm not sure he has any dirt to find."

"Then make some up! Christ, do I have to do all you're thinking for you?"

"I'll see what I can do," he'd replied.

And that'd been the end of their meeting. Collins had finished his drink, and driven home.

Sleep had eluded him for several hours. It was all right for Littlewood to say make some up, and under normal circumstances he'd have had no problems; but this was

Harrigan! He ran through several plans he'd used in the past but discounted them all. About to give up for the night, a glimmer of hope appeared. "Yes," he'd said aloud. "That might just work!"

Annabelle mechanically turned the page of the Times. "Jason?" She urged. "I know something's bothering you; what is it?"

"It's that Harrigan from UNIIA, he refuses to, well, I can't tell you. Official Secrets Act and all that, but I can say he's a right pain in the arse." He stood abruptly from his balcony chair. "I have to make a telephone call." Without looking at, or offering a farewell nod towards his wife, he disappeared swiftly into the apartment.

Having had no use for their apartment's third bedroom, it had been converted into a private study area he used solely for MI6 business. It was sparsely decorated, with the main piece of furniture being a medium sized, but quality rosewood desk complete with the traditional accessories behind which waited a large, high backed leather chair. There were two telephones. One an extension of the house phone, and the second, a secure line installed through his intelligence agency. A small wood-grained filing cabinet stood to attention against the rear wall to his right. There was no visitor's chair and apart from a smallish but exceptionally comfortable soft leather lounge chair on the far left beneath a modest bookcase, that was it. One noticeable absence was the almost obligatory silver framed photograph of the desk owner's spouse, usually positioned to the person's right.

He sat behind his desk and reached for the secure telephone. He startled slightly as it rang beneath his hovering hand.

"Collins."

"Jason, it's Joan."

"How'd you go with Harrigan? Did your womanly charms convince him to see things our way?"

"I steered him towards Akmatbayev as you asked, and although he showed interest, he didn't take the bait as well as we'd thought he might."

"Did you offer to stop Akmatbayev leaving the country?"

"Of course. He wasn't interested."

"And your womanly charms?"

"There's even less good news on that front. Unfortunately, for me anyway. Unlike you, *darling,* he's one of the few men in the world whose head brain is more powerful that his penis brain."

"Of course it is," he replied, not trying to disguise the sarcasm. "Does he know I asked you to invite him over?"

"No," she lied. "We'd just got to first base when he suddenly pulled away and scampered back to that Throgmorton woman."

"Poor Joan, you should've called; you know I would have been only too pleased to come over."

"That wasn't necessary, I managed."

"And how *is* Wilhelmina?"

"Before you go throwing smart arse statements like that around, Jason, you should remember I not only know all *your* dirty little secrets, I also have Annabelle's telephone number."

"I was joking," he replied in that slightly embarrassing tone men use when they realise they'd stepped over the line.

"I wasn't."

And he believed her! It was time to change the subject. "So it's unlikely you'll be meeting him again, privately I mean?"

"More than unlikely; I'd say it was a definite."

"Oh well, thanks for giving it a go, it was worth a shot." He paused for several moments before announcing more brightly than she was expecting. "It looks like it's time to start the ball rolling on plan B."

He was part way through his *"Let's not leave it too long before we see each other again"* speech when he heard the sound of the disengagement of Joan's telephone.

He shrugged, replaced the handset momentarily and dialled a new number.

"Chase Roper," the voice at the other end of the telephone announced.

"Chase, Admiral Collins."

"Good morning, Sir," he replied obediently.

"Do we still have the bullets Harrigan shot into Jenkins' shoulder?"

"Yes, Sir, locked away in our secure evidence locker. Considering that as far as records go, the shooting didn't occur, I was intending to destroy them, but wanted to check with you first."

"Don't destroy them, just keep them under lock and key."

"Yes, Sir." Roper had been around MI6 long enough to know not to ask questions.

"Any sign of Connie West?"

"No, Sir, we're watching her known haunts, but she could be anywhere. Unless she comes out of hiding or Harrigan gives her up, I don't like our chances."

"Well, keep onto it, and if you do find her, bring her in immediately."

"Yes, Sir."

Without any message of farewell, the two men rang off simultaneously.

***

Without exception, despite a shared look of tiredness around their eyes, all four UNIIA agents had displayed a definite spring in their step as they'd entered the restaurant for breakfast. There'd also been an unusual lack of conversation as Sarah, Benecke and Lo devoured breakfasts of Harriganesque proportions.

With plates cleared amd coffee cups drained, laden with remorse and the discomfort of their out-of-character overly large, greasy breakfast, Benecke and Lo left for Birmingham and the Al-Yousaf stronghold. The standard 1.4 litre Vauxhall Astra, delivered to the hotel during the night as a replacement vehicle for the Combo, was about two sizes too small for Benecke who was forced to hunch down a little, making driving anything but a pleasure. Lo had offered to drive but her sudden fierce glance made him wish he hadn't.

In contrast, Harrigan and Sarah sped towards Kingsbury Marsh in the comfort and familiar surrounds of Sarah's Xr3i Diamond White Ford Escort. They'd been in the vehicle less than ten minutes when Harrigan's telephone rang.

"Harrigan…who?…oh, Godfrey, yes, how's Connie getting along?… she's what!? How the *hell* did that happen!?… when?… sometime between nine last night and nine thirty this morning? That's great, over twelve hours, she could be anywhere in Europe by now. Is it possible she was taken?… there's no sign of forced entry, so your men believe she's just run off?… I see… yes, I'm sure you are. Just let me know as soon as you find her." He pressed the little red button and dropped the telephone heavily into his inside coat pocket. Sarah was positive she heard the sound of several stitches of the pocket lining give way. "Connie West's fucking disappeared!" He announced angrily. "Bloody morons! I told them, don't let her out of your sight. Fair dinkum, if you don't do things yourself…" He allowed his voice to trail away.

"Why would someone who knows their life is in danger, escape from protective custody?"

"Because they have somewhere else to go they think is safer. Or maybe they have someone else they trust more than us. Who knows? But we can't worry about it now, we've lost a witness, but we do have everything on tape; all we can do is hope Winsor's people find her before someone else does."

***

"You wanted to see me, Father?" Fan Yoon asked as he closed the door of the front room used during Harrigan and Sarah's visit three days previous.

Zhuang Yoon sat silently in his favoured lounge chair, raised his arm from the black antimacassar with red tassels, and gestured towards the L-shaped deep maroon sofa on the opposite side of the jade and ebonised coffee table.

Fan walked obediently to the sofa and sat slowly. His father's choice of the grey Zhongshan or Mao suit over his preferred Manchu style dress, a style that despite offering a high degree of comfort and freedom had fallen out of fashion in Chinese circles, told Fan he'd been summoned to discuss the family business.

"You have not yet reported to me the results of your talks with Muhammad Al-Yousaf." Zhuang knew there'd been no contact with the Al-Yousaf family, but there should've been, and to rebuke Fan for not reporting on a meeting that should've happened but hasn't, put his son on the defensive.

"I have not yet spoken to Al-Yousaf, Father."

"Oh? And why not?" His soft tone was politely neutral; neither friendly nor unfriendly.

"Respect for Qiang. His funeral is Monday. I'll arrange to meet with Al-Yousaf after that."

"Respect for Qiang? Now is not the time you should be lying to me, Fan. You had no love or respect for your brother when he was alive, especially after he was promoted over you to run the business following the disappearance of Zhang Wan Fok. And don't believe, even for one moment, you've been promoted now because I have confidence in your ability. You've been promoted because you are now my only son. So tread very carefully, Fan, you're on probation, and if you lie to me one more time, or I find you have held something back or give me any other cause to doubt your loyalty to the family, you will be dealt with swiftly."

The Yoon family first came to prominence in the mid fourteenth century after the role it played in bringing about the collapse of the Mongol led Yuan dynasty and the subsequent installation of the Ming Dynasty. During the next two hundred and fifty years, the family amassed its fortune, carrying out the more unpleasant tasks that must be performed if those in power are to maintain their dominance over those of lower status. In later years, the family's influence with the ruling classes diminished and it was forced to venture into more obvious illegal activities. But, as many such families of ill-gotten wealth and influence have over the centuries, by that time, the Yoon family had developed an air of almost reverent respectability, resulting in any illegality seen more as, *something those types of families do*, than as something more serious deserving punishment. Since the early nineteen hundreds, careful management, keeping a low profile and understanding how the minds of those of influence can be manipulated, the family had been left in peace by both the law enforcement and underworld communities alike. But things were changing. The world was developing into an ever increasingly violent dog eat dog world, where respect for others, irrespective of their achievements and past status meant nothing. Modern technology, easy access to weapons, explosives and drugs, coupled with the growing mentality that if you want what the other person has you just take it, has meant a change in direction for the Yoon family. Eight years ago, Zhuang had accepted his advancing age and decided it was time to step aside from the day to day running of the business. Neither of his sons were old enough to take over the transition of the business into the new world, and he employed the services of Zhang Wan Fok, a long term acquaintance and person once tipped for the top job in the now feared Triad organisation.

Fok had done the job well. With so many new players coming and going from what he'd considered peripheral businesses such as prostitution, Fok persuaded Zhuang that the cost of maintaining their position in those businesses was hard to justify and they would be better concentrating all their efforts on the more profitable and rapidly growing trafficking of illegal drugs. It was a good decision and in less than two years, the Yoons controlled the entire London drug trade and most areas south.

It had been in November, nineteen hundred and eighty-seven when, no longer satisfied with his most generous remuneration package, Fok had approached Zhuang and demanded a doubling of his share of the profits.

"It's because of me the profits have soared, and it's only reasonable I get a more equitable share," he'd reasoned.

Unfortunately for Fok, Zhuang hadn't viewed it the same way. "We have an agreement, Fok, and part of that agreement is you are to increase our profits, and I agree, you've done your job well. But that's what you're being paid for; and being paid handsomely."

"Are you refusing my request?"

"Of course."

"And that's your final word?"

"That's my final word." He'd turned his back to his visitor and stood staring out the front bay window. "And Fok, remember, no-one is indispensable." He'd paused for several seconds before continuing. "I'm willing to forget this ridiculousness, this time, but I don't want to hear any of it again. Now, get out of my sight and get back to work."

Fok had walked angrily across the room and stood at the open doorway. "Then don't say you haven't been warned."

Two hours after that conversation, it was reported Zhang Wan Fok had mysteriously disappeared. The police investigation, albeit somewhat lacklustre, had found no trace of him and the investigation now languishes somewhere in Scotland Yard's cold case files.

"Alright, Father, yes, I did resent Qiang. When Fok disappeared, *I* should have been his successor, not Qiang! You have always underestimated my abilities, and very soon I will prove it to you! And this time, Father, you will not stand in my way!" His voice rose in volume as his speech quickened.

Zhuang had agonised for many days before breaking with tradition and promoting Qiang over his elder brother. Each brother had their own individual strengths. Qiang had a good business brain, but lacked the ruthlessness required, whereas Fan was a poor businessman with no concept of the political game essential to successfully negotiate a way through the maze of corrupt politicians, bureaucrats, and rival gangs, but had ruthlessness to spare. Unfortunately, he was also an unpredictable hot head and prone to action before thought. All traits that give advantage to their enemies both in government and the rival underworld and could bring their reign over all their territories to a swift and probably violent end. But against that, although Qiang's drive and expansionist program had been extremely profitable and raised the family's standing in underworld ratings, the family was now reaching into Akmatbayev's territories, and a person with Fan's qualities was probably more suitable to deal with a man of Akmatbayev's reputation for violence than Qiang.

"Is that some kind of veiled threat?" The old man responded. "Be warned my son, I will not be threatened. Zhang Wan Fok threatened me and was dealt with. You will do well to remember that irrespective of me being your father, you will be dealt with in the same manner."

Fan Yoon jumped quickly to his feet and stood looking down at his father across the ebonised coffee table, a derisive sneer covering his face. "*You're* going to deal with *me*!? Do you hear yourself old man? Do have any idea how stupid you sound!? It's time you took a good look at yourself. Weak and feeble, spending most of your life sitting in that soft chair, watching old black and white movies, and issuing orders like some crazy, syphilitic minded despot who still believes he has the authority to rule. Well, let me set you straight. *I'm* in charge now. *I* give the orders, and *I* will decide what you need to know and when you need to know it. So sit there in your chair old man and stay out of my way or it will be *you*, not *me*, who'll be swiftly dealt with. Do you understand!?"

Zhuang pushed down on the arms of his chair as he rose slowly and stood directly opposite his only son, their faces barely twelve inches apart. In contrast to his son's wild, hateful even evil eyes, Zhuang's expression was calm, or better still, maybe placid would be more accurate. Suddenly, with no indication of what he was about to do, his right arm jerked upwards and he slapped Fan's left cheek with his open hand.

"Speak to me like that one more time and I will kill you." He spoke with quiet, chilling monotone, a tone that has put fear into many men. But not Fan. Not his angry son standing defiantly before him, the hate in his eyes burning brightly.

Zhuang raised his right arm once again, quicker, harder than before, but Fan was ready this time and with an air of superiority, caught the arm in mid-air and slowly tightened his grip on the thin, bony arm, blocking the blood running up to the fingers. It was several seconds later a quizzical frown formed across the young man's forehead. The old man's stare was not one of fear or pain, but of the cat who'd caught the mouse. Fan's heart beat faster as he felt something sharp against his throat. Without tilting his head, he moved his eyes down to his bottom right and caught a glimpse of the 8" double edged dagger pressing into his skin, deep enough to cause an indentation, but not deep enough to draw blood. He heard his father's voice.

"And *that's* why I chose Qiang over you. You allow your temper to control you. This leaves you vulnerable. Anger makes a person single minded, fixing all their attention to a single action, blinding them from the other dangers surrounding them. You were so intent on showing me how tough you were you saw only my right hand, leaving yourself open for attack from the left. This time it didn't cost you your life; next time, it will."

Fan released the old man's arm and without moving his neck, slowly lowered his head. "I'm sorry, Father."

"Learn this lesson well, my son, and carry it through to every aspect of your life, especially your business life. Be aware of all your enemies, remain calm and think before you act; don't give your enemy the upper hand."

"Yes, Father."

"Very well, we'll talk no more of this."

As the tension slowly eased, Fan relaxed, but then suddenly flinched as he felt the knife pierce his skin and open a 2" gash running down the side of his throat. "This scar will remind you of what you've learned today and of the consequences should you fail my expectations."

Fan left the room and went to the main bathroom to stem the bleeding and dress the wound. Zhuang had barely returned to his chair before he heard a knock on the door. "Come!" He called.

"That policeman and his lady sidekick are here again, they want to see you," the voice said from the doorway.

"Show them in, Hung," he replied.

Zhuang remained seated in his soft lounge chair, his back to the door. "We meet again, Detective Chief Inspector, and so soon," he called over his shoulder and gestured for them to enter and retake their seat on the sofa. "May I offer you tea?"

"No, we don't intend to stay, we only have a few more questions," Harrigan replied.

As Zhuang waited for them to be seated, he moved the little china bell aside and picked up a diary-like notebook from the small table to his left and began writing. It was nearly twenty seconds after they'd taken their positions that he closed the book, and returned it to the table. He raised his head slowly and looked at them silently for a further five seconds. "Ask your questions," he invited in a tone that begged the question, *"what are you waiting for?"*

"Last time we were here, your son told us Qiang and Muktar were business associates; we need to know a little more about that business."

"I have very generously given you access to my time. Please don't insult me asking questions to which, as we both know, you already have the answers."

"Not all the answers. It's true, we know your family are in the drug trafficking business, mainly in London, Southern England and moving North, and the Al-Yousafs are international arms dealers. What we are seeking is the link that ties the two together."

Zhuang sat silently, staring thoughtfully into Harrigan's eyes, searching for a clue as to what this very astute law officer knew or didn't know. Harrigan's eyes gave nothing away. "I'm not sure I understand what you're asking, Chief Inspector."

"Then I'll lay it out more clearly. I think, and this is purely speculation at this stage, that Qiang was not only moving into Akmatbayev's territories in the UK, but also internationally and he and Muktar had an arrangement where drugs would be hidden in arms shipments destined for international markets."

"I apologise in advance for my forthcoming rudeness, Chief Inspector, but such ridiculous speculation is not worthy of your reputation."

"As your own pleas of innocence are not worthy of yours."

Zhuang Yoon raised his eyebrows inviting Harrigan to continue.

"I know Boris Akmatbayev suspects the same thing and be assured his suspicions are much further down the line than mere speculation."

Zhuang's reaction was slight, but it was there. "I would be very interested to hear how you could possibly know what Akmatbayev is thinking."

"That's easy, I met with him yesterday. We had an interesting drive around London in the back of his Mercedes drinking forty year old scotch and swapping thoughts."

Zhuang's outward calmness belied the anxiety growing inside him as he desperately, and unsuccessfully, tried to find something, anything, in Harrigan's eyes that would give him a clue as to where he was going with this line of questioning. "Would you like to share anything else Mister Akmatbayev supposedly told you?" He'd tried to inject an air of derision into the question. He failed.

"Well, since you've asked, he also told me that once he's established the identity of all those involved in your family's intended takeover of his territory, he's going to kill them all. He'd already intended to kill Qiang and Muktar himself, but unfortunately someone beat him to it."

"Unfortunately?"

"Yes. He still needed them alive, for the moment, because he hadn't had time to identify everyone. He also said that Sophie, Qiang's new girlfriend, was working for him, gathering information and was a valuable asset."

"And you believed him?"

"Yes."

"You don't think he was behind the killings." It was a statement, not a question.

"No." It was of course, a lie. Harrigan hadn't decided one way or the other, but telling a suspect that you've ruled out someone else, increases the pressure on the remaining suspects.

"I find it interesting you have ruled out the most obvious suspect, just because he told you he didn't do it. Who else could it be?"

"A jealous brother springs to mind. Maybe Fan saw an opportunity to get rid of Qiang and take over the business. He obviously resents his younger brother being in control. It's just a thought," he added casually as he stood from the sofa. "Thank you for your time, Mister Yoon. We'll show ourselves out."

Harrigan stopped at the doorway and spoke to the back of Zhuang's chair. "Oh, I forgot to tell you. We've located Muktar's girlfriend, the one who escaped the shooting. She tells an interesting story, especially about your son's and Muktar's relationship." In fact, she'd known little about their relationship, but he wasn't about to tell old man Yoon that.

They'd reached the front door when they heard the tinkling of the little bell and Zhuang's voice thunder up the hallway.

"Get Fan in here! Now!"

Harrigan clicked his seat belt in place but didn't remove his hand from the locking device. "You know, if we're right about Natalya's name being used without her knowledge and Hazel *was* involved with passing on the mail, with Natalya now out of the picture, Hazel's the only link to the perpetrators. Being a loose end puts her in considerable danger. We need to get over to her right away. We need to find out about this mail thing, anyway."

The urgency in his voice was underlined by the slamming of the accelerator against the floor.

***

The opening fifteen minutes of the conversation between Benecke, Lo and Muhammad Al-Yousaf had been along similar lines as Harrigan's conversation with Zhuang Yoon, including the drugs in arms shipments, Akmatbayev's intention to kill all those directly or indirectly involved with the attack on his empire, and Sophie being an Akmatbayev informant. Predictably, Muhammad protested his innocence of any knowledge of what they were talking about. He also angrily denied any suggestion he'd had any part of killing his brother so he could take over the business.

"The girl you call Bethany Joseph, you brought her here after the shooting, is that correct?" Benecke asked.

Muhammad's reply was not immediate. He'd paused for several moments, half tempted to deny any knowledge of what had happened to her. But conscious of the fact there could easily have been witnesses who'd seen them leave together, he took the safest option. "Yes."

"Why?"

"Why did I bring her here?" He asked purely as a delaying tactic; he needed time to think.

"Yes."

"She was my brother's girlfriend. He wouldn't have wanted me to just leave her there."

It was Benecke's turn to pause. "Can we talk to her?" She asked eventually.

"She's not here. She only stayed a little while to gather her thoughts and then left."

"She wasn't held against her will, and manage to eventually escape?"

He was visibly shocked at Benecke's question. "What, um, makes you think that?"

Benecke explained about finding Bethany in the boot, well, she said trunk, of their vehicle, and the story she told of being tied, assaulted and her escape.

"She's lying."

"Then maybe we could talk to Amir or Behzad? They could clear things up."

"They're not here either. They've left us."

"*Left* you? What does *left* you mean exactly?" There was no doubting the inference in Benecke's question but Al-Yousaf wasn't about to take the bait.

"I'm not sure what you are asking, Special Agent. They were loyal to my brother and when he was killed, they decided it was time to move on." He paused. "They left us."

"And you had no problem with two people who knew everything about your business just walking out the door?"

"Of course not, why would I? We're a legitimate business; we have nothing to hide."

The problem with fishing expeditions, and that's what their visit to the Al-Yousafs had been, is that sometimes you don't catch anything and must be satisfied with hoping you've thrown enough burley out to attract the fish for next time. And there was no doubt in either agent's mind that there would be a next time. They said their farewells and returned to the Vauxhall Astra. Reluctantly, Benecke let Lo drive; there was more room to spread out in the passenger's seat.

"Did you believe his story about allowing Behzad and Amir to just say goodbye and walk away?" Lo asked as he turned onto Smudge Road.

"Do you believe I'm still a virgin?"

Lo smiled.

***

A surge of numbing apprehension overtook Harrigan and Sarah as she forced her way into the almost stationary traffic on Great Russell Street and saw the flashing lights on three police vehicles and one ambulance opposite the British Museum. The no parking area outside the museum, gave the four police officers in bright yellow jackets blessed relief as they patiently directed less patient drivers into one lane. Sarah stopped the Escort in the blocked lane behind the first stationary police car.

There was an immediate knocking on her window by a police constable in his late thirties. "You can't stop there, Miss. Keep moving!" He ordered with all the authority he could muster. Sarah held up her UNIIA badge, which did nothing more than bring a frown to his face. As Harrigan opened his door and alighted from the vehicle, the constable instinctively stood up straight and looked across the turret.

"Excuse me, Sir, you'll have to get back in the— oh! Chief Inspector Harrigan. I'm sorry, Sir. I didn't recognise you."

Harrigan wasn't one to seek fame and preferred to keep a low profile, but sometimes being the most recognised police officer in the London Met, probably the entire British police force, did sometimes have its advantages. "That's fine, Constable. What's happened?"

The sound of Sarah's closing door followed them to the footpath. "I'm not entirely sure, Sir. At first report, a woman in Friedenberg House, that's the pink building, slipped in the bath, banged her head and drowned. But for some reason, Inspector Russell from homicide seems to think there's more to it than that. I have my doubts to be honest, but the Inspector has only recently come to the Yard from up north in the Lakes District, and it could just be a matter of a country copper trying to make a name for himself in the big smoke. You know how it works, Sir."

Harrigan had seen many police officers like this one. Content to be a constable, with never having any ambition for promotion. They come to work, do their shift and go home and enjoy their family life, content to stand back and be entertained by the spectacle of those desperately trying to climb the greasy pole, grasping at every opportunity to add another commendation to their CV. Harrigan had always considered these constables to be the backbone of the force. Officers everyday people turned to in time of trouble; the officers they trusted. But, in any regimented organisation, there must be a modicum of respect for rank or the whole thing collapses.

"I'll pretend I didn't hear that last part, Constable," he said with a definite hint of lightheartedness.

"Yes, Sir. Thank you, Sir."

"Did you say Inspector Russell came from The Lakes District?" Sarah asked a little too eagerly.

"Yes, M'am."

"Do you know Inspector Russell's Christian name?"

"I'm not certain, M'am. I think it might be John, but I could be wrong. Why, do you know him?"

'Do I know him? He's seen me naked for God's sake!' They'd originally met on the first case she'd worked at Stonegate. After resisting his persistent advances for longer than she dared to remember, she had eventually weakened and enjoyed a perfect evening meal at the upmarket, *Una Serata Innamorata* Italian restaurant. But the night hadn't ended there. What followed was a long, lingering night of, well, maybe that's best left that to the reader's imagination, before being interrupted by a telephone call from Harrigan. She flushed, and purposefully avoided looking at Harrigan.

"John Russell?" Harrigan turned to Sarah. "Isn't he the chap who—?"

"Yes, he is! Let's drop it, shall we!?" She snapped.

He smiled mischievously and squeezed her hand softly. "I'm only teasing. C'mon, let's go inside."

Mercifully for Sarah, the news of her and Harrigan's relationship had already spread through the corridors of the Yard. "Sarah, Chief Inspector, it's good to see you again," Russell said with unmistakable genuineness as they approached him in Hazel Spinks's front room. "And I believe congratulations are in order."

Harrigan frowned.

"On being a couple!" He explained enthusiastically.

"News travels fast," Harrigan said.

"You might be with UNIIA, Sir, but you're still one of us, and your insistence on being addressed as chief inspector and not some poncy special agent, doesn't hurt your reputation either."

"*I'm* a special agent!" Sarah said defensively, more by way of snuffing out any remaining thoughts of their previous sexual relationship by establishing her role in UNIIA, than caring about her title.

Russell took the hint and changed the subject. "If you don't mind me asking, Sir, how did you hear about Hazel Spinks's death?"

"We didn't," Harrigan replied. "Hazel was part of our investigation into the Brewer Lane shootings and we needed to ask her a few more questions." It was close enough to the truth. "Can you tell us what happened?"

"The local boys received a call from one of the residents, concerned that something had happened to Spinks because her mail hadn't been delivered to her room. Apparently there's an arrangement where Spinks collects the mail from the postman, or from the inside doormat if she's not here when the postie arrives, and distributes it around the building. Don't ask me why they don't use the letter boxes on the outside wall, it's just what happens. Anyway, after the resident had knocked several times on Spinks's door and received no reply, because Spinks rarely, if ever, was away from her apartment in the afternoon, she became concerned and telephoned the police. Two uniformed officers came around and couldn't raise Spinks either. They were unsure about breaking down the door with such flimsy evidence something was amiss, they contacted the Yard. Luckily, the call was put through to me."

"Luckily?" Sarah asked.

"Yes, because, although I hadn't been involved, I was aware of the investigation into Natalya Zhestakova's death in the flat upstairs, an incident the Yard has put down to misadventure. Having had the opportunity to see how you both operate a few months ago, I figured you'd probably have your doubts about that. When I heard the initial report of another death in the same building, I decided to have a look at the scene myself. After the locksmith opened the door, I went directly to the bathroom. I found her drowned in the bath with a wound to the back of her head, similar to Zhestakova. That's when the alarm bells rang. I know people do slip in the bath, and they do sometimes drown, but it's not an everyday occurrence, let alone in two units in the same building a couple of days apart. I became concerned the Yard would be tempted to put this down as misadventure as well and thought you should know about it. I was about to contact you when you arrived."

"You said a locksmith opened the door," Sarah said, feeling much more at ease with John Russell's clear acceptance of her relationship with Harrigan. "Does that mean the security chain was not attached?"

"Yes, and not only the security chain." He walked to the front door of the apartment and closed it. "You see there's two slide bolts as well; one at the top, one at the bottom; neither were in the locked position."

"Where's Hazel's body?" Harrigan asked.

"On the way to the morgue."

Harrigan took out his notepad and began writing. "I want her examined by the UNIIA medical officer. I also want our own forensic team who investigated the Zhestakova death to go over this flat." He handed Russell the paper with names and contact details. He'd also added his mobile number at the bottom. "Do you want me to clear it with your boss?"

"No, Sir, I don't think the Guv'nor will mind, not when he knows it's you who's asking. If I get stuck I'll call." Russell took the note, read it quickly and put it in his pocket.

Harrigan gave the room one last cursory glance and turned to Sarah. "I've seen all I want to see. Let's get out of here."

After manoeuvring the Escort into the traffic, thanks to the police constable stopping the line of approaching cars. "Are these accidents that look like murders, or murders that look like accidents?" she asked

"I think they're murders, made to look like accidents, that look like murders."

"I should've known better than to ask."

There was little else to be accomplished before Monday morning, so before returning to the Royal Garter, Harrigan and Sarah took the opportunity to call into their respective homes and collect fresh clothes and other personal necessities. Benecke and Lo were already well and truly settled comfortably in the Seamed Stocking lounge by the time they returned.

***

The evening at the Seamed Stocking had passed uneventfully, and determined to leave their current case at the door, the UNIIA team's conversation had been filled mostly reminiscing about their past adventures. It had been a few minutes to midnight when Sarah, having prepared their clothes for tomorrow's luncheon at her Uncle Charles' house, retrieved the little chocolate mints the maid had left on their pillows, ate them both and climbed into bed. Harrigan had begun preparing to join her when his mobile telephone rang.

"Hello?"

"Chief Inspector Harrigan?" A male voice he didn't recognise asked.

"Who wants to know?"

"That's not important. If you want to know where to find Bethany Joseph, meet me near the bandstand in Tudor Castle Gardens in thirty minutes. Don't be late and come alone." The phone went dead.

"Who was that?" Sarah asked.

Harrigan repeated the details of the call and walked to the wardrobe to retrieve his coat. "The Gardens are only a short walk from here; I shouldn't be too long."

"I'll get dressed," she said, throwing back the bedclothes.

"I'm a big boy, you stay there and catch up on your beauty sleep. Not that you need it," he added quickly.

She didn't argue and with a smile on her lips, her head disappeared under the blankets.

Chapter Ten

The smell of coffee brewing, gently woke Sarah from a deep sleep.

"What time is it?" She asked.

"Just after seven."

"I didn't hear you come back last night. You should've woken me."

"You looked so peaceful, and besides, there was nothing to tell you; whoever telephoned didn't show."

"They didn't? That's odd." She swung her legs out of bed.

Her tone clearly invited him to espouse his theory of why he thought the caller hadn't shown. He remained silent; he wasn't sure himself yet. "Coffee?" He asked.

"I'll have a shower first."

He took his stronger than usual long black coffee onto the balcony and sat thoughtfully for a full twenty minutes. *"It wasn't because they'd been delayed getting there, you waited over one and a half hours,"* the little voice in his head reasoned. *"So that leaves only two real options; either they'd changed their mind at the last minute, or—"* the little voice fell silent as his thoughts developed a second, and to his mind more plausible answer. He finished the last of the now tepid coffee. "Yes, I think that's much more likely," he said aloud.

"Did you say something?" Sarah called from inside the apartment. She was fully dressed and standing beside the coffee percolator.

"Just talking to myself." He re-entered the apartment, placed his empty coffee cup in the sink and headed for the bedroom. He opened the larger of the two wardrobes and pressed four numbers into the keypad of the small security safe used by guests to store their valuables. He removed their Glocks and returned to the living area. The smell of coffee wafted in from the balcony. "I've got your gun from the safe!" he called.

"Thanks. Just leave it in there, I'll put it in my bag when we've finished our coffee. I made you a second cup."

He placed the dark grey weapon on the dining table beside her black leather shoulder bag and accepted her unspoken invitation to join her.

***

The Journey via the A3 to Fincock House, Sir Charles Reeces' home in Cottcombe-over-Fincock, took exactly forty seven minutes. The Reece estate had been in the family since 1559. The architecture of the two storey Elizabethan house standing at the end of the red gravel driveway within the shadows of four giant oak trees, although consistent with the last phase of the Tudor period, had a clear European Renaissance influence, and for many centuries had been referred to by village commoners as the 'big house'. Much to the disappointment of village residents during the early years when a Manor House, usually built on lands granted to a nobleman for services to king and country and historically the main residence of the Lord of the Manor, gave a village an air of nobility and patriotic presence, Fincock House had never attained such high status. But Manor House or not, it was the cause of much joy and celebration when the land had been purchased by Sir Edward Cecil Reece, Lord Chief Justice of England, Queen's Bench, and a magnificent home built overlooking the village centre. Local folklore has it that Edward Cecil Reece, then a senior justice in the Court of Pleas, had become a close confidant of Elizabeth 1st during her almost twelve months house arrest at Woodstock at the hands of her half-sister, Mary Queen of Scots. Following Elizabeth's accession to the throne, Edward was elevated to Lord Chief Justice of England, Queen's Bench, partly for his support during her incarceration, and partly, and maybe more importantly, because he was a Protestant. After creating the legal pathway towards the establishment of an England Protestant church, Elizabeth offered to grant him a large parcel of land which included the village of Cottcombe-over-Fincock. Anxious that his position as Lord Chief Justice might be compromised by such a gift, he chose instead, to purchase, notwithstanding for a minimum price, a 100 acre parcel of land just beyond and overlooking the village.

Sure, it wasn't a Manor House with a Lord of the Manor ensuring prosperity for the surrounding area, but it was close enough for the locals. And anyway, if you said "the big house" with enough respectful tone, strangers would assume it was a Manor House anyway.

But it was now 1990, and while the house still stood proudly behind large glossy black iron gates, centuries of death duties, maintenance costs and a reduction of the once obscene income enjoyed by families of influence in years gone by, much of the acreage had been sold off in smaller parcels. The big house now languished a little sadly on the remaining five acres.

Harrigan stopped the Mazda behind a 1956, two tone green Armstrong Siddeley Sapphire 346 four door limousine, standing majestically, and opposite, the front entrance of the house.

"It's father's," Sarah offered, knowing Harrigan's fondness of early model motor vehicles.

"It's beautiful," he whispered in almost hallowed tones. "It must be worth a small fortune."

In contrast to the tone of Harrigan's last spoken words, *her* reply flowed freely with rank disinterest. "I believe it is, but Daddy didn't buy it, it was grandfather's." She opened her door, clearly indicating she had no desire to continue the conversation. *'What is it with men and old cars?'* she asked herself.

The first fifteen minutes following the formal introductions were both pleasant and awkward. Sarah's parents, Ballard and Charlene Throgmorton held pride of place on the pleasant side. The awkward side of the equation consisted of the several moments taken to decide how Sir Charles and Harrigan were to address each other. They eventually decided "Chief Inspector" and "Sir" were probably the most suitable; for now, anyway.

At Charles's insistence, the group settled in the high ceilinged drawing room dressed with period décor. In fact, from what Harrigan had seen since driving through the glossy black iron gates and entering the foyer of the Grade II heritage listed building, the entire house, gardens, and décor including furniture and accessories gave a feeling of stepping back in time. As a pre-luncheon aperitif, Millicent, Charles's live in cook-cum-maid-cum-housekeeper since his wife Adele had passed away three years previous, served chilled Valdespino's Fino Inocente dry sherry in small thin stemmed hand cut crystal glasses. "Luncheon will be served in twenty minutes," she announced before silently exiting the room.

In most people's lives, meeting your prospective spouse's parents, ranks in the top five moments of high anxiety and dread, and despite his bravado, Harrigan was no different. It was two thirty before the meal was over and despite his earlier misgivings, had to admit to himself that the last one and a half hours had been much less stressful than anticipated; almost pleasant if he was honest. Not that he'd enjoyed the small talk or the persistence of Sarah's parents to keep returning the conversation to his early years in the Australian outback as the son of a country copper, but oh, the meal; now that was something else. Pea and Ham soup, roast lamb with all the trimmings including the best crackling and Yorkshire puddings he'd tasted since his mother had died, rounded off with apple crumble and custard. *"Yes, I'd love a second helping, thank you."*

A few seconds before that moment had arrived when the meal is finished, the conversation has run its course and diners were uncertain of what should happen next, Millicent entered and announced coffee and tea had been served in the drawing room.

"You three go ahead," Charles said as they rose in almost perfect synchronization. "I need a couple of minutes alone with the Chief Inspector." He took Harrigan's arm firmly and ushered him towards the rear glass doors. "We'll talk on the rear patio." It wasn't an invitation.

Sir Charles closed the patio doors behind him and approached Harrigan admiring the small acreage from behind the concrete balustrade. "My brother is a very successful man in his field, Chief Inspector, you couldn't find a more able barrister. Unfortunately the same cannot be said for most other aspects of his life, especially when it comes to Sarah. He could never say no to her, and if I hadn't assumed the role of a disciplinary parent, Sarah would not be where she is today. Not that I agree with her current position at UNIIA, but that's only a temporary diversion."

"Temporary diversion? Did Sarah tell you that, Sir?" Harrigan asked, showing more concern in his voice than he'd wanted.

"Not in so many words, but even you must realise Sarah has the ability to become the UK's first female

Police Commissioner. I know it, she knows it. And make no mistake, I intend to wield whatever influence I have over her and ensure she comes to her senses, gives up this UNIIA nonsense and gets back to the task of climbing the promotional ladder to its top rung."

Harrigan sighed with bored impatience. "Why don't you cut the waffle and just say what it is you want to say, or do you want me to say it for you?" He didn't waste time waiting for Reece to respond. "You don't approve of our engagement and want me to break it off and get out of her life. Is that about it?"

"In essence, yes." Charles placed both hands on the balustrade, leaned forward heavily and gazed into the distance. "You know I have a high regard for your ability as an investigator; you get results. Your clean-up record is second to none. But your absolute disrespect of authority and tradition, and your disregard of the law—" he paused momentarily. "maybe *disregard* is a little harsh; it's more of an *end justifying the means* attitude. Whatever you choose to call it, it's not something I want Sarah exposed to one minute longer than I can help."

"You're forgetting Sarah joined UNIIA *before* we became what the younger generation call, an item. So even if I did end our relationship, I don't think—"

"For God's sake, Chief Inspector," Charles interrupted, his voice raised more with frustration than anger. "For such a smart investigator you know nothing about women. Sarah had eyes for you from the first moment she met you at Stonegate; long before she joined UNIIA!"

"You know, Sir, you're not the first person to tell me that."

"Excuse me, Sir," Millicent said urgently as she entered the patio. "I'm sorry to interrupt, but there's someone at the front door asking for you."

Reece turned quickly towards his housekeeper, the dark cloud crossing his face clearly indicating his disapproval at being interrupted.

"I think you should come, Sir," Millicent insisted, not giving Sir Charles an opportunity to voice his objection.

He sighed heavily and turned back to Harrigan. "Wait here."

Under normal circumstances, such an arrogant order would've ignited Harrigan's dislike of authoritarianism and forced him to automatically walk back inside the house. But not this time. Not because Sir Charles was the Police Commissioner but because he was Sarah's Uncle. He turned and stared at the twenty metre high Beech hedge surrounding the boundary of the property. The hedge had obviously been trimmed mechanically, and like the grassy areas, while tidy, could in no way be described as manicured. The acreage had three small stands of yew trees, with traditional gardens, fish ponds and water fountains, all noticeable by their absence. Quite clearly a Police Commissioner's salary didn't run to a full time gardener.

"I thought you might need this," a voice sounded from behind him. He hadn't heard Millicent enter the patio.

He turned and a grateful smile immediately crossed his face as he saw the small bottle of Bass Lager standing beside a typically English pint glass. "Thank you, Millicent, you're an Angel."

She accepted his compliment with a smile and polite nod of her head.

It was another three minutes before Sir Charles returned; he wasn't alone. "Sir Jason Collins, Chief of the Secret Intelligence Service is here to speak with you, Chief Inspector. Sir Jason tells me you haven't met."

"There's been correspondence, but that's correct, we haven't met face to face." He didn't think it appropriate at this time to explain the situation surrounding the shooting of Errol Jenkins, his returning of the two MI6 operatives' guns to Collins, and his none too subtle warning of the consequences should any of Collins' people harass him or his people again.

"Alright, Jason," Charles said as he turned towards Collins. "He's all yours."

"Thank you, Charles. Good afternoon, Chief Inspector, I'm sorry to interrupt your Sunday afternoon, but this matter can't wait."

Harrigan simply gave a disinterested, *well get on with it then* shrug.

"I'd like to talk to you about Connie West, or Bethany Joseph if you prefer. I believe she's part of your investigation?"

Harrigan nodded.

"I'm informed you've had her hidden away down the south coast?"

Had her hidden away? Harrigan kept his thoughts to himself and nodded again, but this time more cautiously.

"Is she still in your possession?" Collins continued.

"That's need to know, and as far as I'm concerned, your name isn't on the list of those who need to know."

"Maybe, maybe not, but I have information that might change that."

Harrigan sighed, drained his glass and returned it to the table. "Look, Collins. You've obviously come here to say something, so why don't you stop pissing about and get to the fucking point."

"Please, Chief Inspector, I don't appreciate that kind of language in my home," Sir Charles interrupted. "And remember who you're talking to. Show some respect!"

"It's alright, Charles, the chief inspector is right, I should get to the point." He stood silently for more than twenty seconds, trying unsuccessfully to hold Harrigan's stare. "The point is, following an anonymous tip-off in the early hours this morning, two of my people went to the Tudor Castle Gardens, a block from your hotel."

"I know where it is," Harrigan snapped. He had no idea what was coming next, but whatever it was, he knew it wouldn't be *good* news.

"And as explained by the mystery caller, they discovered Ms Joseph's body with a single gunshot to the head." Collins walked slowly to the patio's outdoor setting, pulled out a large cane chair and with purposeful deliberation, sat down and leaned his arms on the table. "Can you shed any light on who might've murdered her, Chief Inspector?"

Knowing Collins would've already sought out witnesses such as the night porter and drivers of taxis on the rank outside the hotel who'd testify he'd left the hotel shortly after midnight and returned an hour and a half or so later, he gave a detailed recount of the events following his own anonymous midnight telephone call.

"So you admit being in the Tudor Castle Gardens around the time of the murder?"

"I admit being in the gardens between twenty minutes after twelve and one forty-five, but right now, that's not important. What I want to know is why MI6 is investigating Connie's murder and not the local police? Better still, as she is part of a current UNIIA investigation, UNIIA has jurisdiction and we should have been contacted immediately. You had no right to become involved."

"MI6 is investigating because she's been working for my agency long before *your* agency came onto the scene. I think that gives us precedence."

"She was an MI6 operative?" Despite his best efforts, an annoying tone of surprise filled his words.

"Not an operative, no. She was a civilian who'd agreed to infiltrate the Al-Yousaf, Yoon, Littlewood, Akmatbayev group and keep us informed of their movements."

"Really. And just why would she agree to do that?"

"To quote your earlier statement, Chief Inspector, that's need to know."

Under normal circumstances, Harrigan would've argued UNIIA not only needed to know, but had a right to know, but that could wait for another time. "How'd she get involved with your lot in the first place? Who made the first contact, her or you?"

"She did." Collins paused, deciding how much information he was willing to pass on to Harrigan. "We'd long held suspicions of a possible connection between the four groups' operations but were getting nowhere. Then out of the blue my office received a telephone call from Connie, or Bethany as she'd then introduced herself, saying she had information in which we might be interested."

"When she first contacted you, you knew she worked for Littlewood?"

"Not until our first face to face meeting, no."

"Why did she contact MI6 and not the police?"

"Littlewood sold arms to foreign countries and she figured that would be beyond the reach of the local police."

"What was her motive?" Harrigan asked, far from convinced of the truthfulness of what he was being told.

"A few months after commencing employment as Littlewood's secretary, she'd begun having concerns that some of Littlewood's weapons transactions were not as Kosher as they should've been. As a concerned citizen, and a fear she might be seen as an accessory of some kind, she'd decided to bring it to our attention."

"And you believed her?"

"Whether I believed her or not wasn't relevant. Our investigation was going nowhere and I needed to get someone on the inside. Coincidentally, our first meeting was in the Tudor Castle Gardens bandstand close to where we found her body. It only took a few minutes before she made it quite evident she was more than willing to oblige."

"And you didn't find that suspicious?" Harrigan asked.

Lack of understanding of Harrigan's question caused a frown to cross Collins' brow. Harrigan responded with a smile best described as one of derisive disbelief.

"You find something amusing, Chief Inspector?"

"You spooks, you're so busy looking under rocks you can't see what's in front of your face!"

"What *are* you talking about?"

"You didn't know she was also passing information back to Littlewood?"

Collins' years of experience in the art of deception, manipulative negotiation and, as Harrigan would put it, *all that other secret service bull shit*, had taught him to mask the sudden anger exploding inside him. But despite this skill, it didn't fool Harrigan. "If the truth was known," Harrigan added, "it was probably Littlewood who put her up to calling you in the first place."

A lengthy period of combative silence drifted across the balustrade, consuming all the previously unnoticed sounds of nature. It was Harrigan who broke the silence. "Getting back to the present, why did you drive all the way out here just to tell me of Connie's murder? You could've telephoned and saved us all a lot of trouble."

Collins turned to Sir Charles Reece. "I don't like to ask, Charles, but would you give us a few minutes privacy?"

"Sir Charles stays," Harrigan stated firmly, denying Reece any opportunity to respond. "I have no secrets from the commissioner."

Their conversation was interrupted by the sound of Reece almost choking at Harrigan's 'no secrets' declaration. Several seconds passed before he regained his composure. "I'm sorry," he spluttered quickly. "Something got caught in my throat. Please, carry on."

Collins continued. "Very well, Chief Inspector, if that's what you want. Once the identity of the body had been established, I contacted the local police, explained we had jurisdiction and would be using our own medical examiner and forensic team. During a preliminary examination of the body, the medical examiner removed a single 9 millimetre bullet from her brain, and declared that as the cause of death. A full autopsy will be done tomorrow, but I doubt anything will change."

"As fascinating as you might find all that, Jason," Charles Reece remarked somewhat coldly. "It doesn't explain why you interrupted my Sunday afternoon family gathering. For God's sake man, get on with it!"

Collins answered as if answering Reece, but his unblinking accusatory stare was firmly fixed on Harrigan. "Our forensic people compared that bullet with one of the bullets the chief inspector shot into Errol Jenkins' shoulder in his hotel car park."

"What!?" Sir Charles exploded. "In the name of all who's mighty, who is this Errol Jenkins chap?" He turned to Harrigan. "Chief Inspector?" There was a clear, "*would you care to explain?*" question in his voice.

"He's nobody; an MI6 operative," Harrigan explained offhandedly.

"You… you shot an MI6 operative in the car park of your hotel!? What in the blue blazes—"

"It's okay, Sir," Harrigan re-enforced. "It was self-defence and no one died; I'll explain later." He turned to Collins. "You were saying?"

"The bullets were a perfect match."

"They… they were a perfect match?" Harrigan said weakly. "That… that's not possible. There must be some mistake."

Charles Reece was taken by surprise at Harrigan's uncharacteristic nervous reaction. He thought that guilty or not, Harrigan was made of sterner stuff.

"Forensic doesn't lie, and forensic tells us the bullet that killed Jervis, came from your gun."

"But… but," Harrigan turned to Reece. "Sir, isn't there something you can do?" He pleaded.

Disappointed at Harrigan's immediate capitulation, Reece's attitude towards Harrigan hardened. "I'm afraid not, Chief Inspector, and rest assured that you might have immunity under your UNIIA title, but by the living Harry I can strip you of your association with the London Met!"

"But, Sir!"

It was Collins who offered the solution. "Look, I want to be fair in all this. Do you have your weapon with you, Chief Inspector?"

"Yes," he replied warily.

"Then I suggest you hand it over to me right now. I'll have forensic fire a test bullet for comparison purposes, and that'll establish the fact beyond doubt." He paused before adding quickly. "One way or the other."

"I don't think so," Harrigan replied. "I know I'm innocent and that's all I need to know."

Charles Reece took a step towards Harrigan. "Well *I* want to know, one way or another. Give Sir Jason your weapon, now."

"But, Sir, I don't—"

"Now, Chief Inspector!" A red faced Charles Reece ordered angrily.

"You can accompany me if you want, and bring Sir Charles as a witness," Collins added with an air of genuine conciliation. "And just to make sure there's no funny business, you can witness the entire process."

"That sounds fair to me," Charles said. He turned to Harrigan. "Hand Sir Jason your weapon."

"But—"

"Hand him your weapon damn it, or I'll arrest you myself!"

Reluctantly Harrigan removed the Glock from his shoulder holster and handed it to a gloating Admiral Sir Jason Collins.

Sarah entered the hallway as the trio approached the front door. "What's going on out here? What's with all the shouting?" She demanded.

"Sir Jason thinks I shot Connie West last night in Tudor Castle Gardens."

"West's *dead*?"

"I'm afraid so."

"The Tudor Castle Gardens?" She glanced quickly at Collins and then back to Harrigan. "Isn't that where the caller said to meet—" she paused and stood silent for several seconds as her brain processed the information. "And Admiral Collins thinks you—"

She didn't have time to complete her question. "Tell me about that telephone call, Sarah," Collins interrupted.

She looked quickly at Harrigan, seeking instruction; he nodded. She took hold of Harrigan's arm and quietly related the events surrounding the midnight telephone call.

Collins stood silently for longer than was necessary as he analyzed her every word. "So, you heard the caller tell the DCI to meet him in the Gardens?"

"Well, no, I couldn't hear the caller, but—"

"So you don't really know what the caller said. You're only telling me what the DCI told you." It was a sort of a question.

"Well, er, yes, I suppose, but—"

"Why didn't you go with him?"

"I offered, but I was in bed and Bill said the Gardens were just down the road, he was a big boy, and not to bother."

"You're saying he wanted to go alone?"

"No, I didn't say that. Don't start putting words—"

"Didn't you find that a little suspicious?" Collins interrupted again, denying Sarah the opportunity to gather her thoughts.

"Suspicious? The caller said to come alone and my partner told me to stay in bed in the warm. No, I didn't find it in the least bit suspicious. Why would I?"

"Come now, Sarah, do you really expect me to believe that after the telephone rang just after midnight and the DCI told you the person who telephoned didn't identify himself, or maybe it was herself, who supposedly tells the DCI to go immediately to the Tudor Castle Gardens and to come alone you didn't at least find it a little suspicious? Especially after you offered to accompany him and he told you to stay in bed?"

Jason Collins had been a family friend for many years and had virtually seen her grow up. He'd almost become one of those friend of the family 'uncles'. But friend of the family uncle or not, she'd had enough of his belligerence. It was time to attack. "Admiral, I find your tone and your constant interruptions offensive, extremely bad manners, not to mention ungentlemanly. It's bad enough you use your family connection to come here unannounced on a Sunday afternoon and interrupt a private family gathering.

But to treat me like a common murder suspect and then have the gall to accuse me of some level of untruthfulness is beyond the pale and I cannot begin to tell you how disgusted I am regarding your actions."

"Sarah, I apologise, but I do have a job to do."

"I think under the circumstances, Admiral, I prefer you address me as Special Agent Throgmorton."

Jason Collins looked to Charles Reece for support but his hopes faded immediately as he recognised the look of pride on the commissioner's face. Gently taking Sarah's arm and guiding her towards the drawing room and out of earshot, Harrigan broke the impasse. "What are you doing!?" She demanded in a hoarse whisper. "I was just getting started!"

"You can finish Collins off another time. Right now, there're a couple of things I need you to do. Akmatbayev said he was leaving the country today. If he hasn't already gone, I want you to stop him, take him to our hotel room, and hold him there until I get this Collins bullshit out the way. And, Sarah, it's absolutely essential nobody knows we have him. I don't care how you do it, that's your problem."

"Thanks a lot," she replied, a sarcastic smile fleeting passed her lips.

"There is *one* person who might be able to help. She's a member of the Joint Intelligence Committee and Eian Jones has often spoken highly of her. If we are to stop Akmatbayev, we might have to trust her."

"Who?"

"Lady Elizabeth Mandeville-Fookes. She's the baroness of somewhere or other."

"Upper Fifthwhistle and Permanent Under-Secretary for Foreign Affairs. I have her number; she's a not too distant relation of Daddy's."

"Of course she is, I might have known," he remarked matter-of-factly. "See if you can persuade her to use her influence and find out if Akmatbayev is still in the country. If he is, she'll also probably know where to find him. Once you grab him and get him quietly tucked away, I should be back to the hotel by that time. Also, contact Eian Jones and find out exactly how Connie West escaped. I need every detail, no matter how insignificant it might sound."

"What if you don't get back to the hotel? You do realise Collins has a plan to fit you up for Connie's murder, and he sounds confident enough to make it stick."

He winked. "Let me worry about Collins." He handed her the keys to the Mazda.

She kissed him lightly on the cheek and disappeared into the drawing room to say her goodbyes. Harrigan rejoined the two men waiting by the front door. "Alright, gentlemen, let's get this over and done with shall we?"

Harrigan travelled with Collins and his driver, Sir Charles Reece, followed in his own vehicle.

***

It was eleven minutes after two when, not wanting her telephone calls to be overheard by Millicent or her parents, Sarah waited until she'd driven the Mazda through the big iron gates of the Reece residence before dialling. Steering with only one hand, she held the phone to her ear.

The telephone at the other end, rang three times. "Good afternoon, Lady Elizabeth Mandeville-Fookes' residence. May I ask who's calling?"

"Camila, it's Sarah Throgmorton, I need to speak with Lady Elizabeth." Sarah couldn't remember a time when Camila Aguado hadn't been with Elizabeth, be it as a companion, maid, cook, housekeeper and every position in between, even for many years before she'd married

Lord Mandeville-Fookes. *'How long ago was that? It must be over twenty years'*. She also couldn't remember a time when Camila's appearance had changed. She could see her now in her thoughts; her greying hair worn in a tight bun, a physique of homely plumpness, and an infectious smile that filled every room.

"Sarah, my love, what a nice surprise, I'll get her ladyship." Camila had always been a person of little words, a trait worn as a badge of honour by those in service, proudly reinforcing their status in the household as the keeper of stability within the lives of their betters.

"Sarah, how delightful to hear from you, it's been far too long," Lady Elizabeth gushed.

"And it's lovely to talk with you, Elizabeth." During her early years, Sarah had always addressed Elizabeth as Auntie Elizabeth. But in her teens the 'Auntie' had slowly disappeared and it simply became Elizabeth, with the exception being in formal company and speaking to Camila it was always, as it should be, Lady Elizabeth.

"Congratulations on landing that dishy DCI Harrigan, quite a catch. I suppose I don't need to tell you he has ruffled a few feathers around the corridors of power."

"Yes, he has a habit of doing that."

"Good for him. We all need a rocket up our collective arses from time to time." The tone of refined flippancy left her voice. "Am I right to assume this isn't a social call?"

"I wish I could say it was a social call, but you're correct, I need a favour." Sarah explained the situation in short, sharp statements of fact. Akmatbayev intends leaving for Russia some time that day. If he hasn't already left, Harrigan wants to stop him. He has no idea how, when or where he intends to leave. She also stressed this is solely a UNIIA operation with no involvement of the UK government or any of its agencies.

"And you want to know if I can find out if Akmatbayev has already left the country, and if not, when and from where he intends to leave?"

"Yes."

"Hmm. Your man wants to prevent Akmatbayev from leaving the country does he? Now that's what I call a real feather ruffler, in more ways than one."

"Can you help us?"

"Of course I can, Dear. Give me your number and I'll call back shortly. And, Sarah, this must be our secret. No one outside your team can ever know I helped you."

"Our lips are sealed."

The phone went dead. Sarah dialled a second number.

***

Listening to Benecke and Lo discussing their morning's experience in the Petticoat Lane markets and watching them enjoying the majesty of the Tower Bridge as they cruised along the Thames, their fellow travellers would not've thought of them as anything but two simple tourists sharing the magic that is London.

The ringing sound of Benecke's mobile telephone shattered the moment.

"Benecke."

"Benecke, it's Sarah. Meet me at the hotel in thirty minutes. Harrigan's in trouble."

Benecke returned her phone to her shoulder bag and began walking towards the wheelhouse. "We have to get off," she said, answering Lo's silent look of questioning. The wheelhouse door was locked. Holding her badge against the glass she knocked loudly. All eyes and most cameras shifted from the Tower Bridge and looked towards the wheelhouse. The captain glanced quickly at the badge, and returning his eyes to the front, reached behind himself and unlocked the door. Benecke entered and stood directly behind the man at the helm; there was no room for Lo.

She introduced herself. "My partner and I must get to the shore immediately." It was a demand, not a request.

"I'm sorry, special agent," he said, not taking his eyes from the river ahead. "As much as I'd like t' oblige, I 'ave a timetable t' stick to and I ain't auth'rised t' vary it in any way. 'specially dockin' at a unauth'rised pier."

Still standing behind the man at the wheel, Benecke reached up between his legs and grabbed his testicles with a large powerful hand. She leaned forward and whispered into his left ear. "I'll see your timetable and raise you two testicles."

"Yes, M'am." His reply came via a weak, kind of squeaky voice as he began turning the wheel to the port side and Blackfriars Pier.

***

Collins, Reece and Harrigan, watched closely as Erika Petersson, MI6's forensic munitions specialist, fired Harrigan's Glock into the water tank and then carefully removed the bullet. With earmuffs jettisoned and at Collins' invitation, Harrigan took the offered evidence bag into which the bullet had been dropped. With Reece in tow, he followed Erika Petersson through the large wooden doors into the next door laboratory. She stopped at a comparison microscope situated halfway along the bench running the full length of the right side wall.

Petersson stood directly in front of the microscope and spoke to the wall in front of her. "I have already placed two bullets in the microscope. The one on the left came from the body of a woman shot last night in Tower Castle Gardens. The second bullet on the right, was supplied by Admiral Collins earlier today. I don't know the origin of the bullet, but I'm informed it came from the MI6 evidence locker room. I should explain both bullets were supplied in properly sealed evidence bags and in accordance with SOP's."

"The Commissioner and the Chief Inspector are aware of the origin of the second bullet," Collins explained a little too eagerly. "What did you conclude from your examination of the bullets?"

She turned away from the bench. "They were fired from the same gun, Sir, and going by the distinctive polygonal markings, almost certainly from a Glock."

Collins waved his hand in the direction of the microscope. "Inspector?"

Harrigan took three steps forward and looked into the microscope. "Yep, they're identical alright."

Reece also inspected the two bullet comparison but made no comment.

At Collins' instruction, Petersson took the evidence bag from Harrigan and replaced the right side bullet in the microscope with the bullet she'd retrieved from the water tank.

She'd bent forward to begin her examination when Collins suddenly interrupted her. "Wait outside for a few minutes, please Erika."

"Outside, Sir?" She stood erect and looked quizzically at her superior.

"Yes, Erika, outside." He waited until an obviously irritated Petersson had closed the door. "Before we complete the comparison of these two bullets, Chief Inspector, I need you to verify your satisfaction with the process to date, and ensure you understand the ramifications should the bullet just fired from your weapon, matches the one taken from Jervis's body."

Harrigan nodded slowly. "I understand."

"Very well then. One thing I must ask before Erika completes the comparison, is you put your unfavourable feelings towards me aside and consider the consequences should the two bullets match."

"You mean about me being arrested for murder?"

"For starters," Collins replied almost flippantly. "But it goes a lot deeper than that. I would also suggest that your agency would suffer irreversible condemnation. The public are a fickle bunch, and even those most loyal to your cause would not accept the murder of an innocent young lady in a public park."

"Innocent?" Harrigan asked sarcastically.

"She would be by the time my people had finished with her CV."

Harrigan knew he wasn't bluffing, but now wasn't the time to get sidetracked on minutia.

Collins continued. "And then there's the backlash to a government who agreed to invite you here instead of using local law enforcement in what is clearly a local matter. I won't even mention the fact you are still a member of the London Met."

"If you have a point to make, Jason, please make it," Charles Reece demanded, well and truly over the tiresome word games the other two men were playing.

"His point is very clear, Sir," Harrigan replied, denying Collins any opportunity to respond. "He's saying that if I confess to murdering Connie West, he would arrange for the investigation into her death to be buried in the archives. In return, I would wrap up the Brewer Lane investigation with the conclusion the murders were arranged by Akmatbayev, who, having now left the country and bound for the USSR, would never be held accountable for the crime. He might even want us to pin West's murder on Akmatbayev as well."

Reece's furrowed brow clearly indicated his confusion. "Are you seriously suggesting that today's palaver is because of some inconsequential jurisdictional dispute?"

"No, Sir. Sure, jurisdiction is part of it, but only a minor part. I believe, or at least highly suspect, that MI6 or MI5 or maybe the entire intelligence community as they like to call themselves, are running some type of clandestine or maybe even illegal activity they want kept secret. A secret that might come to light during our Brewer Lane investigation, something that must not be allowed to happen. That is why whoever is responsible for this activity, need us to wrap up the investigation before we stumble across whatever it is they are trying to hide. How am I doing, Collins?"

"How the intelligence agencies operate is not open for discussion. The only issue you need to concern yourself with is whether you want this whole Connie West matter to go away so you and your agency can continue your work. Or we call Petersson back in and verify it was your gun that killed West, you go to jail for murder and the discredited UNIIA disbanded. It's your call."

Reece sighed heavily. "My God, Jason, you people are unbelievable." He sighed again and after taking Harrigan's elbow, moved to the far side of the laboratory. He spoke in hushed tones. "You do understand don't you, that as Police Commissioner, I can't be seen to have had any part of the deal Jason is offering you. And should the truth ever get out, I'll have no option but to protect the integrity of the position of Police Commissioner and publicly deny any knowledge of it and pursue anyone who said differently. I'd expect your support on that."

"Of course, Sir. You have my word."

"But really, Bill—"

Bill?

"—even *you* have to admit it's a good offer. Everyone wins."

"Not everyone, Sir. Yes, the government, some senior civil servants, and if Akmatbayev isn't responsible, then the real killer or killers definitely win, but UNIIA doesn't; UNIIA loses. UNIIA's sole purpose is to investigate without fear or favour. Its strength is its absolute independence, and you can't have true independence without unwavering integrity. I'm sorry, Sir, but like you, I am bound to preserve my agency's integrity."

"Well, Chief Inspector, what's it to be?" They heard Collins call across the room. "Do we have a deal or do I call Petersson back?"

"Thanks for the offer, Collins, but I must refuse." He walked back to the man from MI6. "Call your girl in and let's get this thing over. I'll take my chances. And, Commissioner, look on the bright side, if the bullets match and I am locked away, Sarah'll be able to return to the task of becoming London's first female police commissioner."

Reece gave a rare hint of a smile followed by a slight, *"well you said it, not me"* nod of his head.

Harrigan stared unblinkingly at Collins. "Well, are you going to call her back or will I?"

Chapter Eleven

Sarah had been driving into the Royal Garter carpark when Lady Elizabeth telephoned. Akmatbayev was still in the country and was due to take off in his private jet from the Cobbler's Last corporate airport at five forty-five that afternoon. Sarah had thanked her and promised not to be a stranger.

"And bring your Chief Inspector Harrigan with you," Lady Elizabeth had replied. "I just have to meet a man who could resist the pleasures of Dame Joan Hamilton-Westbrook." She'd paused briefly before continuing. "You are sure he's not gay, aren't you?"

"Oh yes, Auntie Elizabeth, I can assure you he's definitely not gay." There'd been an unmistakable saucy smile in her voice.

She walked into the lobby and immediately saw the waiting Benecke and Lo sitting in one of the four large, soft, genuine leather guest lounges.

"What's happened to the DCI?" Benecke asked urgently as she and Lo approached Sarah who remained standing near the carpark entrance door.

"I'll explain in the car." They followed Sarah back to the carpark and with Harrigan's Mazda not designed with Benecke's long legs in mind, they sped away in the rented Vauxhall Carlton.

One caveat in the development approval for the Cobbler's Last airfield back in nineteen sixty-nine, was the establishment of a half mile deep forest buffer zone, separating the airfield and the surrounding planned housing development. With the passing of the years, the forest of common English oak trees, beech, ash and complimenting exotic wellingtonia, sweet chestnut and Japanese cedar, was now a thick woodland used by many of the local residents seeking solace from the rush and bustle of working life in London. The woodland also gave hiding to their Vauxhall as they waited out of sight for the appearance of Akmatbayev's Mercedes.

"He should be arriving any time now," Lo said unnecessarily from the rear seat. Benecke knew the Mercedes and Akmatbayev's driver from the other night, so it had been logical she'd take the front passenger's seat and watch vehicular movement in Runway Lane, the long private road running east west towards the airfield entrance. Sarah had positioned the vehicle close to the sharp bend to the left at the top of the lane. The entrance to the airfield stood on the right three hundred yards further on. The actual entrance gateway and security checkpoint was well set back and out of sight from their vantage point.

It was five o'clock when a long black vehicle turned into Runway Lane.

Benecke sat forward. "This could be it," she said more to herself than the other occupants. "It's... it's the right model... the registration number is... is... that's it!"

Sarah started the motor, and as the Mercedes slowed to a walking pace and prepared to negotiate the sharp left turn, the Carlton burst out violently from the thick woodland and blocked its pathway. Benecke and Lo jumped from the vehicle, and with his badge held high and Glock trained menacingly towards the vehicle's windscreen, Lo positioned himself immediately in front of the braking Mercedes. Benecke moved to the right side of the road. As the vehicle drew to a halt, with her long shapely legs astride, she stood adjacent to the driver. Her weapon glared with excited anticipation, eager to spew forth its deadly load towards the huge man in the driver's seat.

"We meet again, Igor," she said through the now opened driver's door window. "Would you step out from the vehicle please?"

"You tell man in front to move or I move him myself, wiz car," he replied in a deep guttural and humourless voice.

She took two paces towards the vehicle and with her eager second generation Glock 17 now only inches from Igor's face, jerked it up and down. "Just get out of the vehicle." The calmness in Benecke's tone in no way minimised the threat in her voice.

He sighed loudly and with head bowed, turned off the motor, pulled on the hand brake and slowly reached for the door handle. Benecke casually transferred her weight to her right foot and prepared to step away from the door. It was a casualness she immediately regretted. With a sudden turn of speed belying his gorilla like physique, Igor flung the door open, knocking her staggering back. She tried desperately to regain her balance, but the big Russian moved too quickly and seconds after feeling the full force of his hairy fist smash into her jaw, she fell to the ground. A dark blanket of semi consciousness hovered above her.

Ignoring the sharp stabbing pains throughout his body and the smell of his own burning flesh caused by the barrage of 9mm lead spitting from Lo's weapon, a barrage of lead that would've felled any other man, the half man half ape figure reached down and with one enormous hand, grabbed Benecke's throat. He dragged her from the ground and holding her high in the air, denied her life giving breath. Hanging like a rag doll, Benecke desperately fought to maintain consciousness. With her lungs almost bursting, and in a frantic attempt to clear her foggy brain and plan a counter offence, she kicked her legs like some broken wind-up toy doll. It was all to no avail. Eventually, totally exhausted and left with no other option, she began preparing herself for the end.

Suddenly and without any warning, the blurry figure of Lo passed across her line of sight as it flew through the air. A surge of adrenaline filled her body and although her foggy vision prevented her seeing exactly what happened next, when recounting the incident later that night, she'd said it was a little like one of those soccer players who leap into the air and while horizontal, swing their leg with unbelievable force and crash the innocent soccer ball into the back of the net. *"And the sound of the toe of Lo's right shoe crashing against that bastard's temple, isn't something I'll forget in a hurry, either,"* she'd added.

Seconds after the vice-like grip of the massive hairy hand released its hold on her throat, like a wounded tigress, Benecke instinctively landed in a crouching position beside the prone Russian, ready to pounce upon her aggressor should he begin to stir. But there was no movement. Igor lay motionless like a fallen giant oak.

Lo searched the unconscious body and removed two, Russian made Makarov pistols from shoulder holsters on both sides of his victim's body. Satisfied Igor was no longer a threat, he turned quickly towards Benecke and kneeled beside her.

"You okay?" He asked simply.

She nodded. "I'm fine, thanks to you. I owe you one. Maybe I owe you two," she added, a non-too subtle glint filling her eyes.

They smiled knowingly towards each other.

"How touching," a throaty, almost rasping Russian voice said from behind them.

Lo and Benecke stiffened, turned slightly, and looked up into Akmatbayev's cold, dull eyes. The sound of the pump action loading a cartridge into the chamber of the shotgun pointing unwaveringly towards them, echoed through the eerily stillness of the surrounding woodland.

"I'm sorry to have to do zis, but I have important meeting in Moscow and have no time for diplomatic niceties."

"And neither do I." It was Akmatbayev's turn to hear an unexpected voice from behind.

"Vell, vell, vell, the very special agent Sarah Throgmorton if I am not mistaken."

"You're not mistaken. Now, lower the weapon."

He gave a short laugh. "I don't think so. You British are too domesticated to shoot man in back, especially one with diplomatic immunity."

Akmatbayev's adult life had been saturated with death and brutality. Not only during his time spent in the Russian military as a young officer, but more importantly during his treacherous climb through the ranks of the Russian mafia. It wasn't the first time he'd been in this situation, and he felt no threat from Throgmorton. He quickly ran his next moves through his agile mind. His one big advantage was the two agents on the ground in front of him. Throgmorton would do nothing to risk their lives and if he suddenly dropped to a crouching position before springing to his right, they would be directly in her firing line. Anxious not to shoot her two companions, Throgmorton would pause long enough for him to turn as he sprang and fired his weapon towards her. He would then have time to dispose of Lo and Benecke. He readied the shotgun.

Boxing experts will explain to new fighters the importance of developing skills to assist them recognise when their opponent is about to strike. This can only be achieved by paying attention to the *whole* of their opponent's body. Not just the eyes, or arms or chest; the whole body. Focus too much on the leaf and you miss the tree. Focus on the tree, and you miss the forest. Sarah's warning came from a slight contraction of Akmatbayev's right arm triceps muscle as his grip tightened around the shotgun.

The pain and shock felt when a 9mm bullet passes through the outer fleshy part of a human shoulder is, to say the least, intense. Sarah had to admit to herself a level of admiration for Akmatbayev, when, after her bullet ripped a gaping, bloody opening in his right shoulder, he just stood unflinching, seemingly oblivious to the pain. But oblivious to the pain or not, it *had* given him a second's pause to reconsider his next move. It wasn't so much the bullet wound itself that gave him pause, or even the fact Throgmorton had actually fired her weapon. It was the fact she'd been prepared to fire first and ask questions later.

"Now, lower your weapon," Sarah repeated.

He stood there defiantly, making no effort to lower the KS-23.

Sarah's second bullet passed through the exact same location as the first. This time Akmatbayev couldn't hide his pain.

"The next one goes through your—"

"Okay!" The wounded Russian replied as he bent slowly and placed the shotgun carefully on the ground.

"Now, put your hands on your head and turn around slowly." Sarah was taking no chances.

Akmatbayev obeyed, the pain in his right shoulder now obvious.

Lo frisked Akmatbayev and found no hidden weapons. Benecke secured the shotgun.

"Okay, Mister Akmatbayev, you can lower your arms."

He lowered his arms and looked directly at Sarah. "Vat is this all about? I have diplomatic immunity. You have no authority to harass or detain me or my driver!"

"DCI Harrigan wants to talk to you before you leave the country," Sarah stated, ignoring Akmatbayev's question.

"Does he now. Vell I have very important meeting in Moscow. As much as I'd like to oblige your DCI, I have no option but to refuse."

"The DCI has taught me much about law enforcement," Sarah replied calmly. "And one of the first things he taught me was the person with the gun does the talking and the person without the gun does the listening. So, let me tell you what's about to happen."

Sarah spent almost four minutes laying out the plan. He would wait with her in the Vauxhall while Benecke drove the Mercedes to the airport entrance. Lo would sit in the rear with the still unconscious Igor lying at his feet. The security guard would only see Lo's silhouette through the dark tinted glass. Once at his waiting private jet, Benecke would give the pilot a note written by Akmatbayev telling him to take off as planned and wait at another private airfield until contacted with new orders. *"I assume you have some private unauthorised airfield you can use?"* She'd asked. Akmatbayev had nodded a tacit *"of course"*. Benecke and Lo would load Igor onto the plane and then they'd all return to the Royal Garter. The Mercedes would be parked in the Garter's guest parking area, next to the Vauxhall; there's no CCTV in the car park, and anyway, there are other stretch limousines there, coming and going, so it wouldn't look out of place. To minimize the risk of being recognized, they would take the back stairs to Harrigan's room and wait for Harrigan. Once Harrigan had the answers to all his questions, Akmatbayev would be free to continue his journey to Moscow.

"I need doctor to treat my shoulder."

"They're flesh wounds you Jessy," Sarah replied unsympathetically. "We'll stop at a pharmacy on the way and pick up some aspirin and band aids."

Akmatbayev had never been one to waste energy on futile argument. "Very well, but there is one thing I must insist on."

"Oh? And what would that be?" Sarah asked as they moved towards her vehicle.

"You tell no-one, and I mean *no-one*, that I rode in a… *Vauxhall.*"

***

Erica Petersson raised her eyes from the comparison microscope, again stared directly at the wall in front of her, before returning her attention to the instrument.

"Well?" Jason Collins asked impatiently.

Petersson affected some minor refocusing of the instrument below her and stared at the magnified bullets for several tense filled seconds. She eventually moved away from the counter, paused briefly, turned with that air of deliberate authority used by those within the scientific community when addressing mere mortals, and stared at Collins. "They're not a match."

"What!?" Collins almost shouted.

"They're not a match," she repeated. "The bullets are from two different firearms."

Collins strode fiercely towards Petersson, physically pushed her to one side and stared into the microscope, desperately trying to see something that wasn't there. He placed his hands on the edge of the stainless steel countertop, slowly pushed his body away and looked down towards the floor. "You've swapped weapons, haven't you?" There'd been no need for him to address the comment.

"Excuse me, Sir," Erica Petersson's voice interrupted. "If you have no further need of me, I have—"

"Yes, yes, go!" Collins snapped.

Harrigan waited for the forensic specialist to leave the room before answering Collins' question. "Swapped weapons?" His tone carried just enough innocent indignation. "Are you serious? You come to the Commissioner's private residence during a Sunday family luncheon without invitation or warning. You then make some outlandish accusation about me shooting Connie West, a witness I needed alive, and, at the Commissioner's insistence, immediately relieved me of my weapon. And now you have the audacity to suggest that during that time I somehow ditched my own weapon and found another to replace it? Give me a break, I'm not bloody Houdini!"

Collins remained silent.

"I believe we're finished here," Sir Charles announced, his displeasure at what he saw as a wasted afternoon clearly apparent.

"Before we go, Sir, there's just one more thing. If you don't mind," Harrigan said.

"Oh?" Reece asked with a slight touch of impatience.

"I still have the Brewer Lane shootings to investigate, and my people will quite likely have the need for further dealings with Collins' department. It would be easier for everyone if there was no bad blood between us."

Charles Reece frowned; he'd never known Harrigan to concern himself about creating bad blood with anyone. *"The blighter's up to something"* he told himself as a nervous knot tightened in his stomach. *"Oh well, in for a penny..."* He gave Harrigan a silent, cautious nod of approval.

Harrigan turned towards Collins. "Sir Jason, I don't want the Commissioner and I to leave here today, without removing any doubt what so ever as to the validity of your forensic test. So, in case there *has* been a mix up somewhere, I'd like the same test to be run using the *second* bullet I fired into Errol's shoulder and compare *that* one as well. Just to make doubly sure."

"Are you sure you know what you're doing?" Reece asked hurriedly, anxious Harrigan was about to play one card too many.

"Absolutely sure, Sir."

"Okay, it's your funeral." Reece turned to Collins. "You heard the man, Jason, let's have a look at that second bullet and settle this thing once and for all."

Sir Jason Collins didn't move.

"Jason?"

Still no reaction.

"Is there a problem?" Reece asked.

Collins took a step closer to Reece and lowered his tone. "I don't have the second bullet." He glanced quickly at Harrigan, took hold of Charles Reece's elbow and moved several paces to the left. He spoke in a whisper. "It was disposed of with all the other evidence relating to the incident in the car park."

"You disposed of evidence? Jason, you astound me!" Reece replied, his reprimand unmistakable.

"Charles, please keep your voice down." He ushered Reece one step further away from Harrigan. "I have no doubt you realise my operatives were acting well beyond their jurisdiction when they confronted Harrigan in the car park; especially with guns drawn. If the media ever got a whiff of what happened there would be calls for another damn judicial inquiry into the whole department and we'd end up having our hands tied even further behind our backs. It's hard enough now to do our job, keeping the UK safe. I decided the best line of action was to destroy all evidence of the incident. Operative notes and reports, hospital records, everything except for that one bullet in the microscope. Not standard operating procedure, but sometimes in the interest of national security these things need to be done."

"If you were so desperate to destroy all traces of the incident, why keep even one bullet?" Reece interrogated.

"I almost didn't. But Harrigan's reputation and unorthodox manner in which he conducts himself is hardly a secret. And it would be impossible to trace a lone bullet back to the shooting in the car park. Putting those two things together, I thought having a bullet I knew came from Harrigan's Glock might prove extremely useful in the future." He again glanced quickly at Harrigan and leaned a little closer to Reece, lowering his voice once again. "And it looks like I've been proved right."

"I don't know anything about you being proven right, Jason," Reece replied in normal tone as he moved back towards Harrigan. "All you've proved so far is that you have two bullets that match and one that doesn't."

"Sir Jason has proved much more than that, Sir," Harrigan interrupted

"He has?" Reece invited Harrigan to explain.

"*I* knew I didn't shoot West, so it was simply not possible that a bullet from my gun could've killed her."

Collins gave a slight snigger of disbelief. "We only have your word for that."

"Let him finish, Jason," Reece demanded.

"Thank you, Sir." Harrigan turned towards Collins. "Like I said, I know I didn't shoot the girl, so when you produced one bullet you claimed came from Errol's shoulder, and then a matching bullet you said was retrieved from West's body, I knew you were lying. The bullets you showed us had to be the two from Errol's shoulder."

"And that is why you asked Sir Jason to get the other bullet?" It was more of a statement verifying Reece's own assumptions than a simple question.

Harrigan nodded. "Yes. How could there be another bullet in the evidence locker when both bullets I'd fired into Errol's shoulder were sitting in the microscope? It wasn't possible, so the only conclusion I could reach was Collins had hatched some half-baked plan to establish my guilt in the West murder." Harrigan looked at Collins. "And to be honest, if, with Commissioner Reece a witness, the bullet from my gun *had* proved to be a match to the two you already had, together with falsified statements from members of whatever intelligence agency establishing some bull shit motive, and witness statements putting me at, or at least near, the scene of the crime at the time of the murder, I would've been hard pressed to establish my innocence. Lucky for me the bullet from my weapon didn't match."

"Lucky!?" Collins almost shouted. "I don't know how you did it, but using your own logic, can you explain that if the bullets in the microscope both came from Errol's shoulder, as you say, and I'm not saying they did, why didn't they match the bullet from your weapon we fired today? If anyone needs proof you've changed weapons, there it is! Believe me, Harrigan, this isn't over; not by any stretch of the imagination."

"For God's sake, Collins, give it a rest; the cat's out of the bag." Harrigan had just about reached the end of his patience. It'd been fun up to this point, but now he needed a Ballantine's. "Today's theatrics were a set up right from the start which became obvious as soon as you offered me a way out. I mean, why go through all this charade to prove I murdered West and then, just before presenting the final piece of proof, offer me a way out? It didn't make sense. This was never about West's murder. You used her death as a means to set your ridiculous plan into action. It was always about UNIIA and the Brewer

Lane investigation. Your plan was to either blackmail me to accept your deal, blame Akmatbayev and move on. If I refused your deal, you'd go through with your threat to accuse me of murder, produce the murder bullet and the bullet from the gun fired today, and along with all the other fabricated evidence and witnesses, I'd be locked up and UNIIA would be disbanded. You would then have one of the local authorities investigate the shootings and produce the pre-arranged result you wanted."

"Is this true, Jason?" Reece asked.

"Of course not! Charles, you more than anyone should know how Harrigan works. He twists the facts, says anything, will *do* anything, to avoid suspicion being levelled against him, and up until now he's been successful. But not anymore, not now MI6 is involved. I'll have his guts for garters." Collins turned sharply and began to walk towards the exit doors. He stopped suddenly, turned and walked slowly back. "Tell me, Charles, why don't you ask your man here what motive could I possibly have to get UNIIA off the investigation that would force me to perpetuate this so called charade; these theatrics?" Collins' voice dripped with sarcasm.

Reece looked towards Harrigan, hoping desperately he had a plausible reply. "Well, Chief Inspector?"

"Right from the start, Collins has had his people tailing me and my team; he even had our hotel rooms bugged. Why? Why would MI6 be interested in what we were doing? And why arrange to have the sensual Dame Joan Hamilton-Westbrook lure me into her private quarters in the *Cornelian Refugium*... do you know about the *Cornelian Refugium,* Sir*?*" Harrigan interrupted himself to ask Sir Charles.

Charles Reece nodded just a little too quickly. "Yes, yes, carry on, Chief Inspector."

"...to lure me into her private quarters," Harrigan continued, "for the sole purpose of using her sensuality to convince me Akmatbayev was the guilty party. Why? Why, I asked myself, would Sir Jason Collins be pimping the beautiful Dame Joan over something he theoretically has no interest in?"

"And what did you conclude?" The sarcasm in Collins' voice continued to dribble down his chin.

"Well, having ruled out jurisdiction, the only other possibility I could come up with was that you personally, or your agency, have some direct, or indirect connection with the Brewer Lane shootings. I have difficulty believing even *your* agency would be involved in the actual shootings, especially on UK soil, so my gut tells me it's most likely about some highly contentious clandestine operation running in the background you are desperate to keep hidden and are afraid we might stumble upon during our investigation."

"Oh come now, Charles, surely you can't be buying this malarkey," Collins almost pleaded.

But Harrigan hadn't finished. "And as Dame Joan was a willing participant in the sex-capade at *Cornelian Refugium*, it must be assumed she too knows the answer. And taking my conjecture one step further, considering the Joint Intelligence Committee connection between you and Dame Joan, I'll bet London to a brick on the entire Committee has a hand in it too. Or at the very least, are aware of what's going on." It was important Collins didn't suspect Eian Jones had told Harrigan of his concerns. He continued angrily. "And it must be big because Eian Jones is on that committee and he hasn't said a dicky bird. You can rest assured he'll be my next port of call and it won't be pretty; he'll need more brain surgery by the time I've finished with him."

An ugly silence filled the space between the three men.

"Jones can't tell you anything," Collins mumbled eventually, unable to disguise the defeat in his voice. "He might suspect something is afoot, but nothing more. He'd never sanction our actions so we've kept it from him."

"Are you saying that DCI Harrigan's conclusions are correct?" Reece asked.

"Yes, I suppose I am, more or less. I can't reveal the details of course, but he has the gist of it."

"You do realise the situation you have placed me in, don't you?" Reece continued. "Over the last hour, I have witnessed your attempted blackmailing of Harrigan using a trumped up murder charge as the bait, the tampering with evidence, obstruction of justice, and that's before I learned you have some clandestine operation doing heaven's knows what, an operation unknown to the Prime Minister and therefore without Prime Ministerial sanction. My God, Jason, I'm the bloody Police Commissioner for Christ's sake, not one of your lackeys. Why did you have to bring me here?! What the eye doesn't see etcetera. But now I *have* seen I'm duty bound to report it." Reece turned and began walking aimlessly around the laboratory.

"Why?" Harrigan asked simply.

Reece turned and walked angrily back to Harrigan. "Why?" He repeated, spittle bursting forth from his mouth barely inches from Harrigan's face. "Why!? Are you seriously asking why I have to report it?"

"Yes, why do you have to report it?" Harrigan's tone was calm and relaxed. "What harm has been done? And really, what have you actually witnessed? That Collins has two matching bullets we know came from his operative's shoulder and a test proving my gun doesn't match either one of them. We heard Collin's pull a wild bluff that failed, and I'm certain the real bullet that killed West is still available for any investigation into her murder." He glanced towards Collins who gave an enthusiastic nod. "And as far as the clandestine operation business, that's not news. These people are spooks; that's what they do. I'll wager that operation's been ongoing long before today, and I'm sure it isn't the first and definitely won't be the last. Operations the Prime Minister doesn't know about, hasn't known about, and if I'm any judge of how a politician's mind works, doesn't *want* to know about. It's all about deniability."

"Why are you defending Sir Jason, Chief Inspector, have you forgotten he was going to have you charged with *murder*?"

"Water under the bridge," Harrigan replied flippantly. He took several unnecessary paces away from the others before continuing to espouse thoughtful conjecture to nobody in particular. "Then again, if Sir Jason isn't able to arrange for me to meet with the Joint Intelligence Committee some time tomorrow and fill me in on what it is they're trying to hide, things might change. Maybe I'd have to reconsider my position on what action a police commissioner should take in these circumstances." He paused just long enough for Collins to take in what he'd said before turning and staring unblinkingly at the MI6 man.

"I'll see what I can do, Chief Inspector," Collins said quietly.

"Wrong answer. You'll have to do more than that." Harrigan replied firmly.

Collins paused before forcing his response through clenched teeth. "I'll contact you tomorrow and give you the time and place."

Harrigan turned to Reece. "See? All fixed. *Now* I think it's time we got out of this place."

"Before you leave, I do have one last question," Sir Jason said quickly. "The gun, how did you do it? Switch it I mean."

"I suppose it doesn't matter now, quite simply, you were focusing on the wrong gun. The one you confiscated and fired today *is* mine. The weapon used in the carpark, wasn't.

"You're going to have to explain that," Collins said, deep furrows filling his brow.

"As it so happened, the day before the carpark incident, the firing mechanism on my weapon didn't feel quite right. I knew a bloke in the East End who knows about these kinds of things. I took it to him to see what he could do and he gave me a loan weapon while he fixed it. As it turned out, it was nothing serious, just an adjustment of some kind. That's why it didn't match. Just coincidence."

Without uttering another word, Sir Charles Reece sighed heavily, shook his head and turned towards the exit.

As they walked to the car park, Harrigan took the opportunity to make a short, cryptic telephone call to Sarah.

It wasn't until they were standing either side of the Metallic Regency Red, Jaguar Sovereign 4.0 Litre saloon that Reece spoke again. He opened the driver's side door but instead of entering the vehicle, he stood in the opened space and looked across the turret at Harrigan. "That story about having your gun repaired, was there any truth to that?" He asked.

"Not a word."

"And Collins was correct about you swapping your weapon?"

"Of course he was."

Reece was about to enter the vehicle when he suddenly bobbed his head up again. "Then why that ridiculous gun repair story?"

"Do you *really* believe I'd give that blow-hard stuffed shirt the satisfaction of knowing he was right!? And besides, he's a spook and spooks love ridiculous sounding stories, it gets them all aroused. He's probably already got his people running all over the East End looking for the gunsmith."

The two men entered the vehicle. Reece didn't attempt to start the motor, instead he lay back against the soft leather and looked at his passenger.

"I know I'm going to regret this, but when *did* you swap your weapon? You were in my line of sight the entire time."

"I swapped it this morning when I removed Sarah and my weapons from the safe before we left the hotel. I took Sarah's and gave her mine. She doesn't know by the way."

"Why did you do that? If as you claim, you didn't kill West, how'd you know Collins would come to my home and accuse you?"

"I didn't know. I had my suspicions that the midnight telephone call luring me to the Castle Tower Gardens was some sort of setup, that's why I told Sarah to stay in bed. We're dealing with some dangerous people and I didn't want her hurt. When no one showed up, it confirmed my suspicions. Obviously someone wanted to put me in the gardens just after midnight with witnesses who could testify about my movements."

"Taxi drivers outside the hotel and hotel staff?"

"Exactly. I didn't know who was behind the ruse, but I was fairly certain Collins would've hung onto the bullets I put into Errol's shoulder. Bullets, which, with a little imagination, could easily be used against me. I figured if the opportunity arose where he could use them to pull some stupid stunt like he did today, he'd jump at it. I thought it prudent to distance myself from the corresponding gun and swapped weapons on the off chance."

"And all that "*please don't let him take my gun away from me*" nonsense before we left my house was just a ruse to throw Sir Jason off the scent?"

"Yes. If I'd've handed over my gun willingly, Collins would've smelled a rat."

Reece drove the vehicle from the carpark and turned towards the Royal Garter. "Why'd you assume he'd hang onto the bullets?"

"Because he's a sneaky, lying spook. And besides, it's what I would've done."

Reece nodded. "Now *that,* I believe."

"Of course you do."

The journey to the Royal Garter hotel was taken in silence. Reece turned the vehicle into the porte-cochère and stopped the motor. "This has been a very, um, *educational* experience, Chief Inspector." He began unfastening the seat belt. "I didn't get much of an opportunity to speak with Sarah this afternoon before we left for the Yard. If you have no objection, I would like to invite myself up to your room for an hour or so and have a relaxing cup of tea before I head home."

"Er, well, Sir," Harrigan replied, "I—"

"Is there a problem?"

Harrigan paused longer than he'd wanted to, struggling to find the suitable words to change Reece's mind. After all, he thought that saying, *"This afternoon, as Boris Akmatbayev, Russian attaché and soviet mobster was about to legally leave the country, my team kidnapped him and are detaining him in my room",* probably wouldn't have been the smartest thing to say, especially after the events of the last few hours. "Is there a problem?" Harrigan repeated and paused a second time. "Let's just say I was thinking that maybe you've had enough, *education* for one day."

"Good Lord, Harrigan, what are you up to now? No! On second thoughts, forget I asked." Reece re-buckled his seat belt and started the motor.

The Concierge, dressed in tails and top hat opened the vehicle passenger door with his white gloved hand. "Good evening, Sir".

Harrigan raised his finger, gesturing he needed a few more seconds before alighting.

"One more thing, Sir, before I go. The investigation into West's murder, including the autopsy, is directly relevant to my team's investigation and should be brought under our jurisdiction. I'd appreciate it you'd see your way clear to make a phone call or two and make it happen. It'd save a lot of time."

"I'll see what I can do. Is there anything else?"

Harrigan allowed the sarcasm in Reece's question to go through to the keeper. "Well, Sir, now that you ask, there's a new Inspector at the Yard, John Russel, recently down from Poltamere in the Lower Lakes District. I'd appreciate him being seconded to UNIIA for as long as I need him."

Reece took a small notebook from his coat pocket. "Russel, from Poltamere," he said aloud as he wrote. "Does he have your contact details?"

Harrigan nodded.

He returned his notebook to his inside pocket and put the gearshift into the drive position. "Now, if there's nothing more…?" Reece's fading voice told Harrigan it was time to leave. He twisted his body and placed his left foot onto the concrete driveway.

"I'll tell Sarah you'll catch up with her later."

"Thank you, Chief Inspector."

***

Collins had telephoned Littlewood immediately Reece and Harrigan left the laboratory. He had not been surprised to learn that even though it being a Sunday, Littlewood was at his office. *"We need to talk,"* he'd told Littlewood. *"But not over the telephone. I'll be at your office in fifteen minutes."* Not wanting the personal hassle of competing with the London traffic, he'd left his vehicle at the Yard and taxied the one and a half mile journey to Horseferry Road.

Littlewood had listened attentively to his visitor's seven-minute description of the afternoon's events and then sat silently for longer than Collins appreciated.

"So, the bottom line is, you pulled a bluff play to put Harrigan in your debt, and he called you on it," he said eventually, an undeniable tone of sarcasm, even derision, filling every word.

"Well, it's not as simple as that," a clearly offended Collins snapped.

"It's not? Really? Then maybe I've missed something. I'll recap what you've just told me and you can explain where I've gone wrong." He paused for several seconds as he aligned his thoughts. "As I understand it, after the body of Connie West, with a single gunshot to the head, had been discovered in the Tudor Palace Gardens near Harrigan's hotel, you hatched a plan to fit Harrigan up for the murder. You would offer Harrigan a deal to drop the charges in return for Harrigan closing his investigation into the Brewer Lane shootings naming Akmatbayev responsible. So, having witnesses who could put Harrigan in the park, and after substituting the bullet that killed West with a bullet you *knew* had previously been fired by Harrigan's weapon, you fronted him at Police Commissioner Reece's private residence, immediately confiscated his weapon, and the three of you went to your forensic laboratory for a comparison test. But the bullet fired from the confiscated gun, fired with Reece as a witness no less, didn't match. Proving Harrigan wasn't the killer. Have I got it right?"

"Yes, but I told you, Harrigan explained that. He was using a loan gun from—"

"And you believed that cock and bull story!?"

"It could be the truth. Right at this moment, I have two agents attempting to verify his story."

Littlewood smiled, shook his head and leaned into his soft leather chair. "And as if all that wasn't bad enough, you were forced to admit trying to frame Harrigan in order to shut down his investigation. And then, to top it all off, you agreed for Harrigan to meet with the entire Joint Intelligence Committee tomorrow where he'll be given details of your deal to supply weapons to the Kajmanistan insurgent Islamist rebels. In other words, the enemy."

Collins decided silence was his best response.

"Well!?" Littlewood demanded with raised voice, attempting to pressure Collins for a reply.

Collins gave a slight, silent, shrug of indifference.

"What a cock up. Maybe Harrigan should be in charge of MI6." Littlewood made no attempt to hide his disgust.

"You're overreacting, David." Collins said, taking advantage of the change of direction. "Harrigan isn't interested in you or your containers of assault rifles; he just wants to identify the person or persons behind the Brewer Lane shootings. That's all. Once he's done that, he'll be gone. So relax, I'm the only person who knows, that you know where the guns are going and *I'm* not about to tell anyone."

Littlewood struggled to keep his tone civil. "Harrigan has already interviewed me, and he not only suspects my involvement in some form of illegal movement of the assault rifles, but also Yoon's drugs hidden in the containers. He's also aware that Connie worked for me in the office and was feeding me information about Yoon and Al-Yousaf, so it's much too late to tell me to relax."

"Are you telling me West was at the *Sister's Basement* on *your* orders!?" Collins asked, feigning surprise.

"Of course, I needed to know what those two were up to."

Taking advantage of Littlewood's slightly more conciliarity tone, Collins decided it was time to throw a little sugar. "You always have been one step ahead, David." He paused, waiting for the compliment to take its full effect. "Anyway, none of that matters anymore," he added quietly. "Tomorrow, once Harrigan understands the concerns of the committee, he'll move on. And to be sure he does, we'll make certain there'll be enough evidence the shootings were solely about Akmatbayev protecting his North London territory for him and his team to uncover, and that will be that. We can throw in the West murder as well if needs be. Two birds as they say."

"Any idea who *did* murder Connie?" Littlewood asked. "Was it one of your lot?"

"I told you, it was Akmatbayev, and that's all I'll say about it."

"Hmmm," Littlewood pondered aloud. "And what makes you so sure Akmatbayev will sit back and let you set him up? I've never found altruism to be a quality possessed by Russian crime bosses, quite the opposite in fact. What's in it for him?"

"Quite simply, he has far more important things on his mind at the moment, cementing his political and economic power before the eventual collapse of the Soviet Union. And if analysts are correct, Russian organised crime bosses will be the main beneficiaries of the Soviet breakup, and he needs to be there. No honour among thieves and all that. And in an almost bizarre twist of fate, being held responsible for the Brewer Lane shootings, an undeniable demonstration of strength on foreign soil, could even bolster his bargaining position."

Littlewood stood from his desk, walked to the window and stared down at the Horseferry Road traffic. "And you're certain you can steer Harrigan towards Akmatbayev?"

"Without a doubt."

"I wish I shared your confidence. Harrigan's outsmarted you once already, and I don't think he'd have much trouble doing it again." He turned away from the window and rested his larger than was healthy backside against the window sill. "What if Harrigan gets to Akmatbayev first and Akmatbayev convinces him he had nothing to do with the shootings? If Harrigan decides Akmatbayev is in the clear, I question your ability to convince him otherwise."

"All hypothetical and totally irrelevant. The fact of the matter is, Harrigan won't, can't, get the opportunity to talk to Akmatbayev."

"*Won't? Can't?* That's sounding far too over-confident for my liking, Jason." Littlewood moved back to his leather chair. "Just how can you possibly know that?"

"Because, right at this very moment, Akmatbayev is in his private jet, sucking on a bottle of vodka on his way to Moscow and beyond Harrigan's reach. As I said earlier, Akmatbayev won't be returning to the UK any time soon. And if at some later date he does wish to visit the UK, he will be a powerful figure in world political circles and completely untouchable by local authorities. Trust me, David, I know what I'm doing; Harrigan has no trump cards left."

Chapter Twelve

Harrigan gave a silent nod of acknowledgement towards his colleagues as he entered his apartment and walked directly towards the bar area. He glanced briefly at the half empty vodka bottle on the dining table before taking several ice cubes from the accompanying ice bucket. He poured his beloved Ballantine's slowly over the ice cubes now resting at the bottom of a large tumbler and filled it almost to the top. He took a long draught and refilled the tumbler. He returned the bottle to the bar top, crossed the room, and stood for several seconds staring down at the bruises on Benecke's neck and her swollen and obviously painful jaw.

"What happened to you?"

"I walked into a door."

He nodded, turned, walked to the dining table and sat down opposite Akmatbayev.

"You are crazy man, Chief Inspector," Akmatbayev said in a sinister, and a much heavier Russian accented tone than when they had last spoken. If it was meant to intimidate, he should've saved himself the trouble.

Harrigan raised his tumbler. "Cheers."

Akmatbayev was clearly unimpressed by Harrigan's flippancy. "I make one telephone call and you, and your comrades, will no longer be able to continue with your little game. I have not done this because I'm interested in vat you vant. But I varn you, don't push me too far."

"And let me warn you, Boris, apart from the fact we have your mobile telephone, UNIIA doesn't play by the same rules as other agencies. You could make all the calls you like, you'll still leave when I say you can leave and not a minute sooner."

"You not understand vat I say," Akmatbayev scoffed, "I'm not talking about the rules. I have many loyal people looking after my interests in this country. They vill take much upset when they learn of how I've been treated." He drained his vodka glass and refilled it, not bothering with ice. "And they'll be upset for very long time." His cold unblinking eyes left no doubt in anyone's mind what this Russian mobster was actually saying.

Not that it bothered Harrigan. "We'll deal with that when the time comes, but for now, I have a few questions to which I need answers. When I'm satisfied with what you tell me, you can be on your way. It's entirely in your hands." Harrigan turned to Sarah. "You have arrangements to get Mister Akmatbayev back to his 'plane when we're finished here?"

Sarah explained his pilot was waiting at a private airstrip in an unknown location and Akmatbayev's Mercedes is in the carpark downstairs.

"Is Igor with the car?" Harrigan asked.

"No," Sarah continued. "Mister Akmatbayev wasn't all that keen to come with us, at first, and Igor suffered a few injuries during the tussle—"

Benecke involuntarily touched her bruised neck. *'Tussle? Fucking tussle!?'* she thought.

"—so we loaded him into the 'plane."

"Igor is dead," Akmatbayev declared.

Harrigan looked at his team. It was Lo who replied. "I had no option but to fire at him during our, um," he looked quickly at Benecke, "tussle, but I didn't hit any vital organs; he'll survive."

Harrigan nodded and turned back to the man opposite.

"Igor is dead." Akmatbayev's reinforcement of his previous declaration, brought a frown to Harrigan's forehead. With a slight shrug and holding his arms and

312

hands outstretched from the elbow in an explanatory motion, Akmatbayev answered Harrigan's unspoken question. "Igor vas paid to protect me. He didn't protect me. The pilot knew vat had to be done."

"So Igor's now floating face down somewhere in the North Sea?"

"Maybe, maybe not, is not important." Another drink of vodka. "You said you had some questions?"

Deciding any questions about Akmatbayev's employees' pension plans would be a little too frivolous for the occasion, funny, but frivolous, Harrigan moved directly onto the business of the day. "Last time we spoke, you denied having anything to do with the Brewer Lane shootings. You did admit you were intending to eliminate Yoon and Al-Yousaf, but not yet, and then someone beat you to it. Is that still your story?"

"Of course."

"And Natalya Zhestakova?"

"I told you, I only meet her last veek at Russian language school. And like I also told you, I know nothing of Mercedes used in shootings either."

"What about the murder of Zhestakova's landlady and the large man in the heavy overcoat who passed Benecke and Lo in the hallway of the crime scene building?"

"I have no idea vat you talk."

Harrigan drained his glass and refilled it before continuing. "Okay, let's assume for a moment I believe you. If you have no connection with Brewer Lane, why is the director of MI6 and the Joint Intelligence Committee, intent on steering our investigation towards you? What is it they don't want us to uncover if we dig too deeply?"

"I don't know. They are spooky spooks. They hide many things."

"You don't know? It's hard to believe that with your contacts, you wouldn't know why someone's trying to fit you up for murder. So I'll ask you again, what is it they are hiding, and before you answer, even if I only suspect you're holding something back, you won't be going anywhere; not now, and not at any time in the near future."

"I think I have given you too much credit, Chief Inspector, you don't seem as smart as I first thought. Tell me, why vould they try and blame me for something I didn't do if I knew the secret they are trying to hide? I vould just spill beans as you English say."

"And that's exactly my problem. If, as you say, you don't know their secret, why are you not protesting to the highest authorities their efforts to blame you for the Brewer Lane murders?" It was a rhetorical question but Harrigan paused anyway. "Do you know what I think? I think you're either mixed up with whatever they're trying to hide and can't spill the beans without implicating yourself, or, maybe you're trying to hide something *else* not directly connected to their secret activity."

"Something else? Like vat?"

"Like some side deal, maybe with Admiral Collins?"

The Russian emptied the contents of the vodka bottle into his glass and stared unblinkingly into Harrigan's eyes. Very few men are able to hold Harrigan's stare; Harrigan was impressed.

"And this is why you have brought me here? To answer this question?"

"Yes. And until I'm satisfied with your answer, this is where you'll stay."

Harrigan's ultimatum gave both men pause to raise their glasses and break their locked stare without either losing face.

Akmatbayev sought solace in the clear liquid as his conflicted thoughts argued silently within him. A little voice on one side of his brain fought against giving any

314

information to this person he viewed as his enemy. The second little voice, the narcissistic, self-indulgent voice, the one which continually drove him to vomit his evil into the world, was telling him something completely different. *'Now listen, Boris,'* the second little voice said. *'Forget all that can't talk to the enemy nonsense. You know very well that right at this very moment, the top echelon of the vory v zakone—* ("thieves-in-law", organized crime leaders who emerged from prison groups in Soviet prison labor camps or gulags as they are commonly known) *—are not only preparing their plans to tighten their grip on the Russian economy after the USSR collapses, but also, infiltrate top political and economic strata. You have many enemies within the vory v zakone who would like to see your power and influence extinguished, and unless you get back to Moscow immediately, they will have their way. So, tell this Harrigan whatever you have to and get the hell out of here as quickly and quietly as possible. You can always deal with Harrigan at a later date.'*

Ever grateful for the sage advice from his second little voice, Akmatbayev addressed Harrigan. "Yes, Chief Inspector, you're right, I do know Collins and his comrades are involved in some hush-hush deal with David Littlewood and his containers of veapons. But I don't know details. Maybe something about destination of veapons I think; but I only guess."

"And what is your role in their little scheme?"

"I have no role," Akmatbayev replied.

"Then that brings me back to my first question. If you have nothing to hide, why let Collins accuse you of the Brewer lane shootings?"

Desperate to hide the truth, Akmatbayev's mind searched frantically for an answer to satisfy his vigilant and shrewdly judicious imquisitor. He raised his glass to his mouth, but before taking a sip, returned it to the tabletop, issued a loud, oh well I suppose I'll have to tell you sigh, and looked directly into Harrigan's eyes. "Very vell, Chief Inspector, I tell you. The fall of USSR and end of cold var is very close. Once this happens, nations around vorld, including UK, vill be looking to get foot in door. I intend to be in charge of doorman. When UK comes knocking, I want them in my debt. What better way to achieve this, than to accept blame for shootings I will never be held accountable for, and helping your intelligence agencies and your government keep their little secrets from their people."

"And that's it? There's nothing else?"

"Nothing else!? If what I have just told you ever gets back to my enemies in Russia, my years of planning and my life, will be over. As this is not directly involved with your Brewer Lane investigation, I expect you to keep your word and not repeat what I have just told you."

"I hate to rain on your parade, Boris, but how is this not connected with our investigation? It has everything to do with it."

"No, you not understand what I tell you. I don't care what you investigate. You blame me, you don't blame me, who cares? What is important is I agreed to allowing Collins make me scapegoat; that's what puts him and his government in my debt, and *that* is what must remain between us. If you and your team prove Collins wrong and someone else is found guilty, that's not my problem. My agreement with Collins will still stand."

"And there's nothing else? No other side deal going on that I need to know about? Something maybe involving Collins?"

"Nothing that relates to your investigation, no."

"Well, I'll take that as a yes." Harrigan turned towards his team with a tacit *anything else* question. They all shook their heads. He turned back to Akmatbayev. "Is there any way I can contact you if I have more questions?" He wasn't all that hopeful of a positive answer. He was wrong.

"Of course," Akmatbayev replied. "Agent Throgmorton, you have my pen?"

Sarah handed Akmatbayev his not unsubstantial pen taken from him in Runway Lane, and the hotel notepad from the compendium. He clicked the button on top of the pen and then twisted the body to extend the ball point. He spoke as he wrote. "If Muhammad Mahmood trusts you with his contact details, that's good enough for me." He tore the page from the pad and handed it to Harrigan. "Ask for Anna, she'll get message to me."

Harrigan looked at the note. "I'll give you my contact details. In case you think of something else."

Akmatbayev laughed. "Oh, there's no need. Do you really think I don't already have them?" He laughed again.

Harrigan smiled at Akmatbayev's blatant honesty and rose from his chair. "As your driver is probably still floating somewhere in the North Sea, I'll have Lo drive you to wherever you need to go to meet your 'plane."

"There's no need for that. My helicopter will be landing on helipad on top of this building in a few minutes. I'll take lift."

"What!?" Harrigan is rarely thrown off balance. "What do you mean, landing on top of this building? Even if you do have a helicopter standing by, no-one else knows you're here. How does your pilot know where to come?"

Akmatbayev laughed one more time, well, maybe "laughed" is an exaggeration, it was more a chuckle of superiority. "Do you really believe Americans are only ones with Global Positioning System? Soviet Union began developing GLONASS fifteen years ago; we just don't shout from rooftop." He held up his biro. "You see this pen? This sends signal to our satellites; my people have known my whereabouts the entire time. I just click this button on top of pen once, and that signal says come and get me. If I get into trouble, I click twice and my people would be here in minutes, and you would all now be dead." He stood from the chair. "I leave now. Agent Lo, you will accompany me to rooftop?" He nodded a polite goodbye to Harrigan, Sarah, and Benecke.

"What about your Mercedes? We can't just leave it in the carpark," Sarah asked hurriedly.

"My Mercedes in car park?" Akmatbayev repeated. "Don't worry about that, one of my people picked it up soon after we arrived. Come along Special Agent Lo."

While waiting for Lo's return, Sarah briefed Harrigan on the events in Runway Lane, including how Benecke had suffered her injuries. Benecke quickly dismissed Harrigan's suggestion she should seek medical attention or at least take things a little easier for the next few days.

With Lo back in the room, Harrigan briefed the team of Collins' clumsy attempt to frame him for Connie West's murder, and of his reluctant agreement for UNIIA to take over the West murder investigation. "That'll be your task first thing tomorrow, David. Commissioner Reece has arranged for the body and all other relevant evidence to be sent to UNIIA's forensic people; their details are in your leather pouch from Whitlock. Also, Collins says he was informed of West's body by an anonymous caller. I'd be very interested in learning who knew to, and how to, contact MI6 and not the local police."

Lo nodded.

"Benecke, you go with Lo, but take it easy, we need you one hundred percent fit."

The news John Russel is to be seconded to UNIIA and used as and when required, brought a probably predictable flush of disapproval from Sarah. It had been even more pronounced when Harrigan told her to contact Russel in the morning and work with him on the murders of Zhestakova and Spinks. "And," he'd added. "Find that bloody Mercedes!"

Sarah's opportunity to respond was ambushed by the ringing of Harrigan's mobile. "Harrigan."

"Mister 'arrigan, it's Billy; Billy Grey, at th' Dark Knights."

"Yes, Billy, I know who it is."

"Sorry t' bovver you, but Mister Alv'rez tol' me t' tell you t' get down 'ere real quick."

"What's the problem?" Harrigan hadn't tried to hide his lack of enthusiasm. Right at that moment, visiting the Dark Knights strip club had been the last thing on his things to do tonight list.

"It's Fan Yoon, 'e's been shot, dead. 'im an' 'is man, 'ung. Bowff of 'em, dead."

"Have you called the police?"

"No, not yet. Mister Alv'rez said t' call you first."

"Good. I want to keep the police out of this for a while. Any witnesses?"

"Only Mu'ammad Al-Yousaf. 'im an' is man. They was all 'avin' a meetin' in one of our speshal meetin' rooms, when two big fellas wearin' 'eavy overcoats and 'ats, burst in, an' b'fore we could stop'em, shot Yoon an' 'ung an' then disappeared."

"They didn't try to gun down Al-Yousaf?"

"No, Mister 'arrigan, just Yoon and 'ung."

"That's interesting."

"That's what I fought too. Whatcha want us t' do?"

"I want to keep a lid on this, Billy. Lock the door of the meeting room, and any staff member who knows about it must remain schtum! Say nothing to anybody; and don't call the police. I'll be there with Special Agent Throgmorton within half an hour."

"Right oh, Mister 'arrigan."

"And, Billy, tell Alveraz to wash off that stinking perfume before we get there, it makes me want to throw up."

"No need t', Mister 'arrigan. 'e ain't wore it since you was last 'ere. 'e's stop talkin' like a Spic, too."

Harrigan returned the telephone to his coat pocket, relayed the gist of the conversation to the others, and drained the last of his Ballantine's.

"Come along, Sarah, there's no need for the four of us to go." He turned towards Lo and Benecke. "We'll catch up at breakfast. Eight o'clock?"

They nodded.

***

Traffic was reasonably quiet, for London traffic that is, and because of Harrigan's obvious lack of enthusiasm for conversation, Sarah allowed her mind to enter the dangerous territory of lover insecurity. *Why did Bill team me up with John Russel when he knows of our previous relationship? He could easily have sent Benecke. Is he deliberately putting temptation in my way? And what about how quickly he contacted Patricia Hedrich when he learned of her husband's death?*

As if able to read her thoughts, he gently placed his hand on her thigh and gave a playful, *you're not going to get rid of me that easily*, squeeze. She smiled and pushed her insecurities to the back of her mind. Twenty five minutes later, she stopped the Escort outside the Dark Knights.

With the exception of the two dead bodies in the private meeting room at the rear of the club, it was business as usual. Four gyrating strippers wearing nothing but micro G-string thongs in which was stuffed a multitude of mostly ten pound notes, the minimum allowed, performed acrobatic maneuvers on single stage platforms positioned strategically across the room. Their sweating, near naked bodies glistened beneath blazing spotlights, their more than ample breasts showing appreciation of the beat of piped music. The full impact of the room's ultraviolet lights, somewhat minimised by the marihuana smoke haze, became more obvious around the tables situated furthest from the lighted stage areas. Treating the near naked strippers and their enthusiastic followers simply as ambience, patrons in the darkened areas openly satisfied their heroin and cocaine needs, unmindful of the couples of all sexes indulging in various stages of sexual gratification around them.

Harrigan, Sarah and Billy Grey stood near the doorway immediately inside the meeting room. There were two chairs positioned one at either end of the eight seat table. The bullet ridden body of Fan Yoon was slumped in the chair at the far end of the table. Hung, one of the bodyguards Harrigan had met at the Yoon family home, lay on the floor alongside Yoon, his eyes staring at but not seeing the nicotine stained ceiling.

Harrigan stood behind the empty chair nearest the door. "Al-Yousaf was sitting here?" He asked Billy Grey.

"That's what Al-Yousaf told me, Mister 'arrigan. I never saw nuffin' an' never 'eard nuffin'."

"Not even the gunshots?" Sarah asked.

"No, Miss, nuffin'. It were Al-Yousaf what found me and told me what 'appened. 'e said 'im and Fan was talkin' when the door sudd'nly flung open an' two men busted in. One of th' men 'eld a gun against Al-Yousaf's 'ead an' th' uvver one raced t' th' uvver end of th' table an' pumped free bullets into Yoon and free bullets into 'ung."

"Did Yoon or Hung say anything before they died?"

"I dunno. Like I told you, I weren't there."

"Where's Alvarez?" Harrigan asked. "Knowing how he loves to be involved in everything around him, I'm surprised he's not here getting under my feet."

"'e told me t' 'andle it. I don't fink 'e's forgotten what 'appened last time you was 'ere." Billy Grey said with a roguishly mischievous smile.

Harrigan briefly inspected the two bodies before picking up four shell cases lying near the dead Hung. Sarah picked up the two near the wall.

Harrigan took out his mobile telephone and dialed a number. "Hello? Jackie? It's Bill Harrigan... at UNIIA, that's right... uh huh, it certainly has been a long time... no it's not a social call. I've got a couple of bodies at the Dark Knights and I need a forensic autopsy done, are you available?... yes, we do have our own medical examiners, but I want this done on the QT... you're right, you probably don't want to know. Do you know the Dark Knights club?... good. Ask for Billy Grey, he'll take you to the bodies... what was that?... no, you're not looking for anything in particular; we know time of death, and how they died. What I do want though, are the bullets from the bodies; I need to identify the weapon used... yep, that'll be fine, I have this phone with me at all times. Thanks Jackie, I'll hear from you soon."

"Ask 'er 'ow long b'fore she gets 'ere," Billy said urgently in a reasonably loud half whisper.

"Hang on, Jackie! Billy wants to know...you heard?... half an hour? thanks, I'll tell him. And we must catch up for lunch, on me... of course I'll bring Sarah, but tell me, how'd you know Sarah and I were together?... I might have guessed, you're not the first person to tell me that." He rang off.

As he returned his mobile to his pocket, Sarah heard him mumble something about "I'll bloody give her the dogs were barking it."

***

It was ten minutes after eight the next morning when the UNIIA team finally settled around a window table in the breakfast lounge. Due to the unseasonal warm and dry weather being experienced in London, the heat from the sun streaming through the window threw some doubt over the wisdom of selecting that particular table.

In between mouthfuls of tomato sauced little sausages, fried eggs and crispy bacon, Harrigan, with more than a little help from Sarah, updated Benecke and Lo of the events at the Dark Knights.

Once fully updated, Benecke pushed aside her almost empty bowl of muesli and replaced it with a side plate of various raw fruit pieces, and, leaving Harrigan to enjoy what was left of his breakfast, turned to Sarah. "The cartridge shells were identified as SP-4's?"

Sarah nodded.

"That explains why no-one heard the shots. The SP-4 cartridge is used in the Soviet PPS hand gun and has a piston fitted between the powder charge and the bullet, almost eliminating the noise. The PPS is a very efficient, compact weapon that doesn't need a silencer and favoured by many assassins."

Harrigan remained silent, choosing this time to simply nod with a look of encouragement for Benecke to expand on her comment.

"I'm a little surprised the shooters didn't pick up shells that could be so easily identified. It's not that they didn't have time. It's almost like they wanted us to find them."

"So we would identify the weapons used as being Russian, again pointing us towards Akmatbayev?" Lo suggested, joining the conversation.

Benecke nodded. "And who's been most responsible for doing that?" She asked as if playing the straight man in a comedy duo.

"Collins," Sarah completed. The only thing missing was the "boom boom".

Silence fell over the table as three pairs of eyes were mesmerized by Benecke's long, black, well-manicured, dark suede lacquered finger-nailed forefinger and thumb, purposefully selecting one mandarin segment from the plate in front of her. "Yes, Collins," Benecke replied before allowing herself some quiet time to enjoy the sweet, plentiful juice of the mandarin.

"But would Collins really go as far as murder just to steer us towards Akmatbayev?" Lo asked. "It sounds like a bit of an over kill to me, if you pardon the pun."

"He is playing for high stakes," Sarah replied.

The clattering of discarded utensils on Harrigan's empty plate brought the meandering, even rambling speculation to a halt. After laying his serviette on the unemployed cutlery he leaned back from the table. "Need I remind you all that we're still not certain who the original target was in the Sister's shooting." He took a sip of his long black coffee. "I have a meeting with the Joint Intelligence Committee later this morning and I'm pretty sure they'll confirm the only reason for their interference is to prevent us uncovering some highly confidential cloak and dagger operation they're desperate to ensure remains a secret. Whether that means they're prepared to commit murder on home soil or not is another question."

"If you're right, wouldn't that eliminate Collins as a suspect in the Brewer Lane killings?" Sarah asked.

"Maybe, but he's certainly up to something. What that is I don't yet know, but I bet my family jewels, Akmatbayev will be involved somewhere along the line."

"I prefer you didn't," Sarah interrupted quickly.

"Didn't what?" It took three seconds for his frown of wondering to quickly change to a light bulb moment. "Oh, yes, sorry. I bet a thousand quid; that better?"

"Much."

"Before the J.I.C. meeting, I'll be meeting with Eian Jones and find out how it was possible Connie West could escape so easily." He drained his coffee and pushed his chair a little way from the table. "Okay, to recap what we agreed last night. Sarah, you'll be with John Russel investigating the deaths of Navratilova and Spinks and chasing up the missing Mercedes. And see what you can dig up on the couple in the unit block who claimed to be freelance journalists and who saw everything. If they were journalists then I'm the Mother Superior. Lo, Benecke, you're on the West case. Wilkinson has agreed to bring Al-Yousaf down from Birmingham so I can question him at Stonegate about the murder of Fan Yoon, after which, I'll have a word with the Yoon family. Any questions? Good," he continued, not leaving any time for them to respond. "Time to get our skates on."

Chapter Thirteen

A little over thirty minutes after Harrigan had left their room, Sarah jumped a little nervously at the jangling of the telephone.

"Special Agent Throgmorton."

"Sarah, John Russel, I'm downstairs. I have the Zhestakova and Spinks files as you asked."

"I'll be right down. I'll meet you in the Seamed Stocking Bar."

"The Seamed Stocking bar? I'm not sure it's a good idea to be discussing highly confidential files in such a public area. Maybe it'd be better for me to come up to your apartment?" Sarah was certain she'd heard a hint of optimism in his voice.

"I'll see you in the Seamed Stocking bar, John. I'll have a skinny latte."

Acknowledging the all too familiar sound of a slamming door in the face, Russel ended the call and sought out a table beneath one of the few reasonably bright lights.

When Harrigan had first told her of her pairing with John Russel, she'd decided to make it very clear to Russel that no matter what he might, no, *would* try to do to get her back into his life, there was no prospect of anything developing between them. So it was somewhat ironic, or maybe better still, contradictory, when she hurriedly decided to change into something a little more, for the sake of modesty let's say, *presentable*.

"Wow, you look stunning," the standing John Russel said. "That is, if I'm allowed to say that without being charged with sexual harassment." He stood behind the empty chair opposite his and removed it from under the table.

"Thank you, John, and yes, you're allowed." Once seated, she quickly took hold of the chair seat with each hand and maneuvered it into place without Russel's assistance.

He'd taken two steps towards his own chair, before stopping and turning back towards her. "It might be a little ungentlemanly to ask, but isn't that Ralph Lauren's Safari perfume you're wearing?"

"Er, um, yes," Sarah replied, the inadequacy of her reply reflecting her surprise at his keen observance. "I'm impressed."

"No need to be," he said retaking his seat. "It's my favourite, and to be honest, the only one I know. But it certainly suits you."

She nodded a polite acceptance of the compliment.

They sat silently while their coffees were served, after which, in an attempt to interrupt the flow of John's flattering, if not even a little nauseatingly transparent comments, Sarah was first to speak. "You said you had the files?"

They read each file in turn, and except for the *"You finished?" "Yes". "Then we'll swap"*, conversation, nothing else passed between them until both files had been read.

Sarah closed the Spinks file. "Almost identical. The victims lived in the same apartment block, they slipped in the bath and despite the difference in their height both suffered identical head injuries, and neither had fastened the security door chain and in Spinks' case her extra security bolts. Their rooms each held a distinct smell of foreign cigarettes, the same smell of the man looking suspiciously like a Russian stereotype who passed Lo and me in the hallway, and there's no trace of usable forensic at either crime scene. Too identical for it be coincidence or anything other than murder, and too identical for it to be committed by anyone other than a professional."

"Agree, agree, and agree," Russell said.

They spent the next ten minutes discussing the feasibility of the Mercedes used in the shootings being registered in Zhestakova's name and address without her knowledge, and Spinks' involvement in withholding mail for cash.

Russel argued the theory was too far-fetched explaining it would've been easier to just register the vehicle in a false name and address. "If the perpetrator or perpetrators had the resources to manufacture the elaborate Zhestakova Spinks plan you're suggesting," he reasoned. "They wouldn't've had any trouble arranging false documentation." To further re-enforce his doubts, he'd gone on to point out there'd been no suspicious mail or amounts of cash found in Spinks' apartment, and the Yard's investigative team had found no evidence of a bank account in her name.

Sarah countered with the fact that because of the high probability of any mail being *returned to sender,* any false name and address had to be an actual postal address, and as such, would create a paper trail back to the perpetrator. And as far as the lack of evidence in Spinks' apartment, whoever killed her could easily've searched her apartment and removed any cash or other evidence. Removing all evidence and killing the only two witnesses was by far the safest option to eliminate any risk of detection. And considering whoever's behind the killings had no problem having seven people murdered at the Sisters, two more deaths would seem almost insignificant. "I hate to admit it, John," she concluded. "But unless we can find the missing Mercedes and hopefully some forensic, whoever was behind these two killings might remain a mystery forever."

"I circulated the Merc's details the morning after the Brewer Lane shootings, but so far, there's been nothing,"

John replied. "And if your Zhestakova Spinks theory *is* correct, I doubt whoever's behind all this is about to leave the vehicle where we can find it. Still, hopefully we'll get lucky." The ringing of his mobile severed any further conversation.

"Russel…you've found it!? where?…Kilmarnoch? that's in Scotland!…no, don't touch it. Just secure the vehicle, we'll send our own forensic team. And hold the breakers yard's owner and employees for questioning… I don't know. By the time we get a flight to Glasgow and then drive to Kilmarnoch, maybe, four to five hours?… yes, around four o'clock. I'll have a UNIIA agent with me… UNIIA. U.N.I.I.A.!…you haven't? I'll explain when we get there. Thanks, see you soon."

"Don't tell me…" Sarah said, her voice trailing away.

"Yep. A couple of police constables visiting a Kilmarnoch Breakers and Crushers Yard on a routine check for stolen vehicles, noticed a late model Mercedes that hadn't even been stripped parked near the crusher. They smelled a rat, and although the registration plates had already been removed, they used the V.I.N. to identify it."

"Well, you did say we might get lucky." Immediately realizing the unintentional double entendré in her 'getting lucky' statement, she continued more urgently than she'd wanted. "It'll probably be an overnight trip, so why don't you go to Kilmarnoch on your own, and I'll stay and follow up the Zhestakova Spinks angle. There's really no need for both of us to go."

"It's a UNIIA case, Sarah, so you need to be there. And besides, the DCI told us we must not separate. Let's get our overnight bags and be on our way."

"Okay, but John, I hope I don't need to remind you not to get any ideas about you and me—"

"Do you really think I'd do anything to put your boss off side?"

"That didn't really answer the question", she thought to herself, followed immediately by a twinge of guilt for not pursuing the matter.

***

At exactly ten forty-five, Harrigan and Eian Jones took their seats in Briefing Room C at the Cabinet Office Building in Whitehall. Introductions were completed, together with a none too subtle *"woman scorned but I'd still like a naked romp with you"* welcome from Dame Joan Hamilton-Westbrook. It would be true to say that Eian Jones' presence was more reluctantly tolerated than welcomed.

As Chairman, Sir John Fitzwilliam began by reminding Harrigan of his responsibilities under the Official Secrets Act. With a tone of abject disapproval at having to share the forthcoming information, he detailed their arrangement with the Kajmanistan Islamist rebels currently supporting Middle Eastern states in the increasing conflict with the West. The guaranteed unimpeded movement of the containers was also included. Notwithstanding Fitzwilliam's repeated defence of the operation on grounds of National Security, guaranteeing Britain's access to oil irrespective of which Middle East state wins the conflict, he conceded many in Britain would not view the operation in the same favourable manner as the committee. Hence the need for absolute secrecy and the reason they didn't want Harrigan digging too deeply into the Brewer Lane deaths. Especially the death of the arms dealer, Al-Yousaf.

"Where are these containers delivered?" Harrigan asked.

Fitzwilliam stiffened. "I fail to see how that information has any relevance to the Brewer Lane investigation, and I'd prefer that detail remain confidential."

"I'll decide what is and what isn't relevant, Sir John." There was no hint of compromise in Harrigan's tone. "And besides, now I know about the containers, how long do you think it would take my team to find out where they are being sent?" He prepared to push back his chair. "But, if you don't want to share that information, I'll take my leave and all bets are off."

"Urbadistan!" The urgency in Fitzwilliam's reply echoed throughout the room. "The containers are sent to Urbadistan."

"Never heard of it," Harrigan replied, settling back at the table.

"Urbadistan is a moderate, or small "i" Islamic State on the Caspian Sea bordering Kajmanistan, Uzbekastan and Russia. It has no allegiance or political ties to any other country, and no oil or manufacturing wealth. With the exception of military movements, the economy relies solely on selling access to its strategic location to whoever needs it. A neutral staging area if you like."

"I'm surprised I haven't heard of it. I would've thought a country like that would draw a lot of media interest."

"It does. But it's also a great source of information, and even the media realise that to publicise such a valuable information asset would work against them, not to mention the pressure applied by their respective governments." Fitzwilliam paused to give Harrigan the opportunity to respond, but no response was forthcoming. Fitzwilliam continued, making clear that no one outside that room knew of the operation, including Littlewood and Al-Yousaf. As far as they were concerned, the arms were being delivered in accordance with UN embargo agreements.

Harrigan didn't miss Collins' most probably sub-conscious, slight, shuffling movement in his chair.

"It takes an enormous amount of time and effort to set up such a deep cover operation," Fitzwilliam concluded.

"And the murder of Muktar Al-Yousaf means we now need to ensure his brother, who is not the most stable person to deal with, continues with deliveries to our Urbadistan distributor with the least amount of disruption."

"When you say no-one outside this room knows about your arrangements with the rebels, does that include Number Ten?"

"*Especially*, Number Ten."

Harrigan looked at Jones, a hint of doubt in Jones' innocence in all this playing in the background. Jones shrugged. "Hey, it's no use looking at me like that, Bill, I might be a committee member and I had my suspicions, but this is all news to me too."

"We thought it best Eian was not involved," Fitzwilliam explained. "We were reasonably certain he wouldn't agree."

"You can say that again," Jones exploded. "My God, supplying weapons to allies of the enemy! What the hell are you thinking!?"

"It's for the greater good," Sir Lindsay Springburn replied, his tone quiet and unemotional.

"For the greater good? what sort of fuc—"

Feeling Harrigan's steadying hand on his arm, Jones cut himself short.

"Leave this to me, Eian, remember what the doctor told you, I don't want you blowing your foo foo valve."

Jones sighed heavily and leaned away from the table.

"So, you're saying the sole reason you want UNIIA off the case, is to avoid us stumbling across your extremely dubious national security operation and letting the cat out of the bag?"

The committee members glanced quickly at each other before nodding enthusiastically.

Harrigan folded his arms and looked directly into the eyes of each committee member in turn, pausing a little longer when he came to Dame Joan Hamilton-Westbrook.

Despite her determination to despise him for rejecting her advances, she was unable to halt the surge of erotic excitement running uncontrollably through her body.

"Okay," he said eventually. "I have no interest whatsoever in your spooky spook—"

"Spooky spook? That's an Akmatbayev expression!" Collins thought, a slight hint of panic fleeting briefly, ever so briefly, across his eyes. But not briefly enough to avoid Harrigan's watchful eye or his satisfaction of Collins taking his carefully considered bait.

"— activities, and if your operation has no bearing on our investigation, it will go no further." He stood from the table. "Thank you, Gentlemen, Ladies, and if there's nothing else I'll take no more of your time." He paused long enough for any response. The room remained silent.

Jason Collins excused himself and escorted Harrigan to the door. "No hard feelings?"

"We're both big boys, and if we're going to hold grudges, we're in the wrong job." Harrigan sighed. "Okay then, it's time to pay another visit to Fan Yoon." He hesitated for several seconds, watching Collins closely for any reactions that suggested he already knew of Fan's death. There were none. "So, unless we uncover some deep, dark, secret relating to the dispersal of the weapons you haven't shared, you won't hear from me again." He took two steps towards the exit, stopped, and spoke to the empty space before him. "There isn't some other deep, dark, hidden secret I should know about, is there, Admiral?"

"No!" He called almost too quickly towards the back of Harrigan's head. "Not that I know of anyway," he added, just a little too late.

Harrigan remained stationary, his head tilted forward slightly as if in deep thought. "Hmm, okay, if you say so." He continued towards the door. "G'day, Sir," he called.

A pale faced thoughtful Admiral Sir Jason Collins slowly returned to the unusually subdued gathering seated around the meeting room table.

***

Harrigan sat in the Red Lion staring blankly into his pint of Bass. Apart from two black suited expressionless gorillas he didn't recognise filling much of the front verandah, there had been no other sign of life at the Yoon stronghold. No BMW's in the driveway, no lights on inside, no small Chinese lady in her pale blue dress. In response to his questioning of the biggest primate, the only reply he received, irrespective of the question, was *"All Gone"*.

His interrogation of Muhammad Al-Yousaf at Stonegate Police Station had been equally unproductive, but to be fair, at least Al-Yousaf's answers related to the questions asked.

"No, I didn't have him killed."

"No, I don't know who shot him."

"No, I don't know why he was murdered."

"No, I don't know why they left me alive."

"No, he didn't put drugs in the containers."

"No, we were friends, not business partners."

… and so it continued until sometime around three p.m.

Al-Yousaf had left for Birmingham immediately; Harrigan spent fifteen minutes, maybe twenty, with Wilkinson talking both on a personal level and generalities of the case. He'd thanked his old boss for his assistance and left the office ignoring Wilkinson's, *"You're sorely missed around here, Bill, any chance you're ready to return to where you belong?"* question.

Needing some quality thinking time, he'd then driven to his Finchenham home, parked his car immediately outside his front door, and walked to the Red Lion.

He swirled the brown liquid despondently. While pleased with the outcome of the Whitehall meeting, his subsequent lack of achievement was disappointing at best. And his earlier discussion with Jones hadn't achieved much, either. Jones' people had seen Connie West more as a person in protective custody than house arrest, and when she'd told the two agents the events of the last few days had left her exhausted and in desperate need of sleep, it didn't raise any alarm. There was no second door in the bedroom, and after ensuring the windows and window grills were securely fastened, and after assuring her there'd always be at least one of them outside in the living room, closed the door and didn't disturb her. They'd heard no noise from the room during the entire night and had assumed she'd slept right through. Considering the danger she'd been in, the possibility of her running away hadn't entered their heads.

He drained the last of his second pint and prepared to raise himself from the soft red chair in front of the empty fireplace.

"There's no need to get up, Sir, this one's on me."

He turned hurriedly towards the soft, smiling female voice, and instinctively reached for the pint of Bass being held in front of him. "Patricia! Patricia," he repeated. "What are *you* doing here?" It was more a demand than a question.

"Well," she replied with feigned indignation. "I've had more friendly welcomes."

He stood quickly and pulled the second red chair closer to his. "No, no, I'm sorry. I was surprised to see you, that's all. Please, sit down." Seeing the Gin and Tonic in her left hand, he raised his pint. "I'll get the next one." They smiled. "How'd you know I'd be here?"

"I start back at Stonegate next Monday, and popped into the station to arrange a couple of things and the Super

335

told me." She paused. "You didn't mind me coming, did you? Don't forget you still owe me a lunch."

"No, not at all, but I'm afraid it's much too late for lunch."

"The Super also said you will be spending the night at your home, so I thought maybe you could buy me dinner instead."

"Er, yes, that would be, er, that'll be fine."

"Great, will you be bringing Sarah?"

"Sarah? Oh, well, um, Sarah's in Scotland at the moment chasing up a lead, so I'm on my own. Maybe we should take a raincheck until Sarah's back?"

"I'm not into rainchecks, Sir, never have been."

Harrigan had no evidence to back his thoughts, but his gut told him the news Sarah was away hadn't been news to her at all; probably Wilkinson again. "As it seems you will be joining me for dinner, maybe you should drop the *Sir.*"

She stood slowly, the movement of her full red lips more of an accompaniment to her inviting, knowing look than a smile. "See you here around five? We'll have a few drinks first?" She placed her hand on his shoulder preventing him from standing. "No, don't get up, Bill. Five?"

"Five."

Unaware of Sarah Knight's eyes burning a hole in the back of his head, he unsuccessfully attempted to take his eyes off the slightly exaggerated purposeful sway of her hips as she walked towards the door.

The vibration of his mobile in his pocket broke the spell.

"Sir, Benecke. There's been some sort of mix-up with West's body, but we're assured it will be delivered later tonight. Our doctor will do the autopsy first thing tomorrow."

"Thanks, Angelina, keep onto it. I won't be back tonight, we'll catch up tomorrow."

"Very good, Sir."

The line went dead.

***

The approved UNIIA forensic team, stationed in Edinburgh, had completed their initial on site investigation of the Mercedes by the time Sarah and Russel had arrived. Despite their optimism, no relevant forensic had been found and the only fingerprints belonged to Douglas Morgan, the Breaker's yard owner and Jimmy Duff, his only employee.

"I'd like to get the vehicle to our Edinburgh facility as soon as possible, so if you have no objection?" Forensic team leader Alison Wilson, saw no need to complete the question.

Sarah nodded. "How long before we get the result?"

"Five days, maybe seven."

"*Five* days!? Alison, we need those results urgently!"

"Maybe seven," she replied mechanically, took her mobile telephone from her bag, nodded to Sarah and Russel and hurried away.

"Five fucking days! Bill's not going to be happy." Sarah's extremely limited use of the *"F"* word seemed to give it much more authority. John Russel, quite wisely, thought it better not to remind her it could be *seven* days, and resisted the immediate temptation to offer an, *"I love it when you talk dirty"* comment.

"We'll interview Morgan at the Kilmarnoch police station, I have no doubt the local boys will want to talk to him after we've finished," Sarah continued.

"And Jimmy Duff?"

"Yes, him too."

***

The evening at the Red Lion had been more enjoyable than Harrigan had anticipated. Patricia Hedrich had been the perfect companion, showing unbridled interest in Harrigan's recent adventures at UNIIA. And later, with the exception of her and her late husband's relationship, had given scant details of her own personal life. For the first ten or so years, the marriage had been one of excitement and fulfilment, but, like most marriages she'd surmised, it had gradually sunk into one of companionship rather than one of love and physical closeness. Over time, she'd come to realise she was too young to be content with simple companionship.

It would've come as no surprise to all who knew him, due to his undisputable lack of ability to understand the wiles and inner workings in the minds of the fairer sex, although enjoying the obvious flirtatious nature of the evening, he failed to pick up on the more subtle meaning behind Patricia's words.

But to be fair, the reality of the situation hadn't *fully* by-passed him. With the meal finished and a more than was advisable quantity of G and T's and pints of Bass devoured, Patricia's announcement she was unable to drive home and suggested they go home to his place for a coffee caused suspicious arousal.

And in the interest of putting all the cards on the table, after he'd put the key in the lock and stood aside from the opened door, as she brushed closely passed him, it wasn't only his suspicions that had become aroused.

***

It became apparent after just a few minutes questioning, that Jimmy Duff was a general hand who lived by a code of seeing nothing, hearing nothing, and as he said more than once, "Douglas pays mah wages 'n' ah do whatever he tells me."

With a local police sergeant in the interview room and his licence to continue trading on the line, while trying to appear cooperative with the visitors' investigation, Douglas Morgan was reluctant to give the local police any more ammunition than was necessary. It was agreed before the interview, Sarah would be the only one to ask the questions.

"Do you seriously expect us to believe, a strange man drove a near new Mercedes with UK registration into your yard, didn't give you his name, gave you one thousand pounds in cash to crush it, no questions asked?"

"Aye."

"Is that the way you usually do business?"

"Na. But times are tough 'n' when someone wants tae give me a thousand poonds tae crush his motor, well..."

"It could've been stolen."

"Aye, 'n' it could've bin his, tae."

"Aren't you required to record all transactions and check the bona fide's of the person bringing in the vehicle?"

He glanced quickly at the police officer. "Like ah said, times are tough."

"Can you describe this man?"

"Ah ne'er took much notice. Likely aroond six foot, well dressed in suit 'n' tie, a full heid o' locks, 'n' posh. The kind o' gent you'd expect tae have a motor like this."

"He didn't ask to watch the vehicle go into the crusher?"

"Nae. 'e was in a right hurry."

"Would you recognise him if you saw him again?"

"Aye, ah think sae."

Sarah looked at Russel. "Anything you want to ask, John?"

Russel shook his head, and then changed his mind. "Yes, there is just one thing. Tell me Douglas, it was obvious the customer wanted the car crushed immediately, what took you so long?"

"Well, sir, 'twas a braw motor, 'n' ah was considering whether ah could, ye know, maybe make a few extra shillings by taking aff some o' the more saleable bits 'n' pieces, if ye git mah meaning."

"Greed, Mister Morgan," John Russel replied. "A basic human flaw. If you'd dispensed with the vehicle immediately, like the gentleman wanted, we wouldn't be sitting here now." He turned to Sarah and offered an *"I've nothing more"* nod.

"Very well, Sir, thank you for your cooperation. We'll arrange for you to sit with a sketch artist."

"Does that mean ah kin go now?"

Detective Sergeant Sandy MacLeish rose to his feet and answered the question. "I'm feart nae, Mister Morgan. 'tis oor turn now."

"Thank you, Sergeant, we'll leave Douglas in your capable hands?" Sarah said. It was a half statement, half request. "We'll arrange for our sketch artist to come up from Edinburgh tomorrow. I'll be returning to London in the morning; Inspector Russel will stay here a while longer." Her raised eyebrows as she turned towards Russel clearly asked, *is that okay with you?* in such a manner there could be only one response. He nodded.

"Na need tae worry aboot Douglas, we have plenty o' questions for him. What aboot Duff?"

"I can't see him being further use to us. Just make sure he stays available." Again she glanced at Russel. Again he nodded.

"Thank you again, Sergeant, it's been a long day."

"I'll have one o' th' constables drive ye tae yer hotel."

It was a ten minute drive to The Highland Park hotel, and once booked in and leaving the porters to take their overnight bags to their rooms, Sarah and Russel went to the bar. The gold lettering on the glass doors said "Lounge", but with its faux leather chairs, cheaper end of the market circular wooden tables, two tone fawn and brown painted walls, and soft, low hanging yet soulless lighting, intimacy wasn't the first word that sprang to mind. It was a bar.

Sarah placed her bag on the table furthest from the door, and looked at her watch. "It's quarter to nine, did you notice what time the restaurant closed?"

"No, but probably nine thirty, we'll have one drink and then go and eat?"

"I'll just have a tonic water, I'm not in the drinking mood."

"You sure?" Russel pushed. "I'm having one."

"Yes, I'm sure." She took her mobile from her bag. "I'd better update Bill."

She dialled the number and watched him as he walked towards the bar. It took longer than usual for the mobile to be answered. "Oh, I seem to have dialled the wrong number, I'm sorry to… what was that?… yes, this is Sarah Throgmorton; who are you?… Patricia Hedrich? what? w… why are you answering Bill's mobile?… what do you mean, he's in the shower!? where are you?… at his house!?… you had dinner at the Red Lion, you're now both at his house and he suggested you should stay the night!?… of course I sound upset!… you'll tell him I called?… thanks for nothing!"

She sat motionless, her knuckles turning white from the grip of her now silent mobile, her shattered heart falling into the depths of despair.

"Sarah? Sarah, talk to me; what's happened?" Russel placed the tonic water in front of her and rested his hand on hers. He reached for the mobile. "Here, let me take that. Sarah, what is it? Talk to me!"

A breaking heart makes no sound, choosing instead to manifest itself in the eyes and face of the forsaken lover as the knot in the stomach tightens, and the feeling of loss, confusion and helplessness blend themselves into the emotional cocktail so familiar to all those who have loved.

"What? Oh, sorry John, it's nothing. It's nothing, really." She sat silently, her heart racing, forcing a flood of blood around her body causing a painful pounding in her ears. "Damn him!" She said angrily, "Damn him to hell!" Her anger pushed aside all other emotions as it grew rapidly, and was inevitably, as in a woman scorned, soon replaced by savage revenge.

She grabbed the tonic water violently. "Here take this back and get me a double G and T."

"A, a double? I thought you were anxious to go to the restaurant?"

"I said a double!" A blaze of fiery determination filled both her eyes and tone in absolute harmony. "The night is young, John. The bar stays open until midnight and later, if we get hungry, the hotel has twenty four hour room service. We can have something sent up to our room when we're ready to eat."

Chapter Fourteen

It was much later than Harrigan had wanted when he left the café in Finchenham High Street the following morning and drove towards the Royal Garter. There being no food in the house, he and Patricia had gone out for breakfast. It had been a pleasant and satisfying breakfast, rounding off the events of the previous sixteen hours which, like the breakfast, could also only be described as pleasant and satisfying. They'd said their goodbyes, Patricia gave him a quick kiss on the cheek and with a mischievous, *"'til the next time,"* they parted ways. It was ten minutes to ten.

A few minutes from Thistle Lane his mobile rang. It was Benecke.

"Sir, you need to come to the mortuary immediately."

"Can it wait a few minutes? I'm almost at the hotel, I need to drop off a couple of things."

"No, Sir, it can't."

"Really? What's the great urgency?"

"We've just seen the girl on the slab, it's not West."

"It's not West!?"

"No Sir. The only thing Connie West and this young lady have in common is they're both dead."

"Give me twenty minutes." He threw his phone on the passenger's seat and gunned the motor.

***

As Harrigan sped away towards the mortuary, Sarah entered their room at the Royal Garter, poured herself a large Chardonnay and went to the bedroom. She threw her overnight bag onto the floor near the front door. She wasn't there to unpack; quite the opposite.

***

"You're right," Harrigan said as he looked down at the body, "That's not Connie West." He turned around angrily and had there been an empty tin lying innocently by he would've kicked it into the next dimension. "I'm so fed up with this bloody case! Nothing makes sense! If the person behind this is deliberately trying to send me around the twist, they've almost succeeded. Surely, nothing else can go wrong."

Benecke spoke quietly. "We managed to eventually get hold of Jason Collins. He was as surprised as we were. Well, he sounded surprised; whether he was or not is another matter."

"And what did he have to say for himself?"

"There'd been some problem with the usual mortuary vehicle service so arrangements were made with the people at Bierman's Family Funeral Services who were picking up a second body, to pick up West as well and deliver it here early today. Bierman's are currently trying to get to the bottom of the mix up."

"Mix up my arse! This has Collins written all over it." He paused for several moments. "Okay. You and Lo get the name of that company and see what you can find out. My tip? The other body has already been picked up from the funeral home by the family for cremation elsewhere, and the paperwork and all identification is bullshit. Want to have twenty pounds on it?"

"No thank you, Sir," Benecke replied quickly. "But if you do find someone to take you up on the bet, put twenty on it for me too, will you?"

Harrigan smiled. "I'm going back to the hotel to freshen up and hopefully Sarah will be back. If she is, we'll visit Collins and this time, I'll get the whole flaming truth out of him."

"You haven't heard from Sarah yet?" Benecke asked.

"No. I've tried to ring her but she's not answering. I did manage to contact Russel. He's waiting for a police sketch artist to arrive from Edinburgh. Sarah left on the first flight this morning. That's probably why she's having trouble getting a signal."

***

"Hello?" Sarah said into her mobile telephone as she laid the biro on the half written letter. "…No, I have no regrets about accepting your offer… no, I haven't told him yet. I'm writing him a letter now… in an hour and a half? Can we make it two hours?… Thank you, Uncle, see you then. 'bye."

She stiffened at the sound of the apartment lock clicking open.

"Sarah, you're back," Harrigan said with relief. "I was getting worried. I've been trying to reach you." He picked up the two packed bags waiting near the door. "I'll take these inside for you, then we can have—"

"Leave the bags there, Bill, we need to talk."

He returned the bags to the floor and walked towards her. "We do? That sounds ominous."

She gave a loud, albeit slightly hesitant sigh. "I telephoned you last night; Patricia Hedrich answered, said you were both at your home and you were in the shower." She stood and walked to the balcony doors and swung around sharply. "How could you, Bill!"

"Hang on, let me explain—"

"Explain!? There's nothing to explain. Jesus, Bill, it didn't take you long to jump into her pants at the first bloody opportunity."

"Sarah! Will you stop talking and listen for a minute!" He moved urgently towards her, but she was not having

345

anything to do with it. She stepped to the side and walked towards the bar. "As soon as we learned of the death of her husband, I feared something like this would happen. Everyone knew how you both felt about each other but I thought—"

"For God's sake, Sarah, let me speak!"

But her mind was closed. "I blame myself, really," she continued, ignoring his request. "I should've waited longer after Margaret's death, but I just loved you so much and wanted to be with you so badly. I should've been more patient; given you more time to grieve, but I didn't." She poured herself a large Chardonnay and continued talking to the wall behind the bar. "You never *really* loved me, not the way I loved you. To you, it was more like friends with benefits than a true love affair." She turned and looked directly into his eyes. "And if you're honest with yourself, you know I'm right."

Unnerved by the hurt in her eyes, he tried once more, this time his tone soft; caring. "Sarah, listen, please, give me a chance to—"

But she wasn't in the listening mood and interrupted him one more time. "There's no easy way to say this, so I'll just say it." She drained her glass. "It's over, Bill. We're over." She paused briefly. "I'm leaving."

Harrigan stood silently, his head bowed, staring at the floor.

"But you don't have to feel guilty." The sudden change in her attitude from broken hearted lover to that of defiant avenger shook him. "After last night's call I was shattered, heartbroken. But my sorrow was soon overtaken by anger, maybe even hatred, and finally to the realization that two can play at that game, a *what's good for the goose* sense of freedom. I didn't go to the restaurant as I'd planned, I returned to John in the bar instead. We stayed until almost closing time, and then sometime later, much later as a matter of fact, we telephoned the twenty four hour room service." She walked away from the bar, and purposefully gave him a wide berth on her way to her suitcases.

Harrigan poured a tumbler of Ballantine's, but left it on the bar top.

"And before I leave, there's one last thing I need to tell you. Uncle Charles rang me last night while John and I were in the bar. A new deputy assistant police commissioner position has arisen at the Met and the hierarchy want it filled post haste. There'll need to be a display of normal process, but the job was mine if I wanted it. He needed an immediate answer. I said yes. I'm finalizing the paperwork later today."

"So that's it? You're just going to walk out? Can't we even talk about this?"

"There's nothing to talk about. Even before last night, I'd begun to doubt the long term future of our relationship. But putting all that aside, the clock is ticking, Bill, and if I am ever to have a family, I need to start now. It's time I returned my life to some semblance of normality. Regular hours and one address, something I'll never have following you around the world living out of a suitcase. The job offer from Uncle Charles is too good an opportunity to refuse." She continued talking over her shoulder as she walked towards the two suitcases. "My UNIIA badge, Glock and letter of resignation are in the safe. I'll leave you to talk to Whitlock."

He moved quickly towards her. "We agreed at the start that if UNIIA is disbanded after the trial period, we'd go back to the Met! You've changed your mind on that too? For God's sake, Sarah, we're both adults. We can get past whatever happened last night; we can work through this."

She gave a slight smile. "And how long do you think our marriage would last with you being a chief inspector and me a deputy assistant commissioner?"

"It wouldn't bother me."

"Well, it would bother *me*." She placed her hands softly against his cheeks and gave him a short, soft kiss. "I love you, Bill, more than you'll ever know, and I'm sorry; but this is the way it has to be."

He opened his mouth to speak but no words appeared. He could do nothing but watch silently as, after picking up her bags, she turned and walked away.

As the apartment door yielded to the force of the automatic door closing device, the echoing sound of the loud click of the door lock took sinister pleasure in underlining the finality of Sarah's parting words.

He stood motionless for several moments, staring at the emergency exit diagram on the back of the door. He turned slowly, returned to the bar, and emptied the contents of the tumbler in one long draught. After reaching across the bar to gather the half empty Ballantine's bottle, he walked towards the balcony.

***

The slightly built middle aged man in the black suit, tie and white shirt, glowered over the rimless glasses balanced on his long, slightly hooked nose. "And I'm telling you once again, Special Agent Benecke, accusing Bierman's Family Funeral Services, a fourth generation family business, of delivering the incorrect body to your pathologist, is absurd! Even offensive!"

Benecke turned to Lo. "Tell me, Special Agent Lo, do you think I was being offensive?"

Lo pursed his lips and slowly shook his head.

Benecke returned her gaze towards the desk, placed her knuckled fists on the desk top and leaned forward. "You see that, Mister Bierman? My partner didn't think I was being offensive." She leaned forward a little further. "But believe me, I *can* be." With the speed and stealth of a shining black panther claiming its prey, she reached across the desk, lifted him from his chair by the coat lapels and pulled him towards her. He groaned as his groin area slammed into the edge of the desk. His glasses clattered as they fell to the hard wooden surface. "I don't give a Goddamn whose fault it is, all I know is the body delivered is not that of Connie West, and unless you take us to the correct body immediately, the one you *should've* delivered in the first place, you'll soon discover just how offensive I can be!" She threw him violently back into the unsuspecting chair, which, caught off guard, almost toppled over. Almost.

Bierman waved his shaking hands over the desktop, searching for his spectacles. "I would if, if that were, er ... possible, but I can't." He swallowed nervously. "It's not here. The family's funeral home picked it up early this morning." He replaced his recovered glasses. "Very early in fact, I had to come in especially to give them access."

"And you didn't check the body before you released it?" Benecke asked.

"Why would I? I was just transporting the bodies."

"Do you have a contact number?"

He reached down quickly to his left, opened the bottom drawer and retrieved a brown manila folder. He handed it to Benecke. "Everything's in there. The letter of authorization from the family and the signed pick-up documentation. It's all in order."

She opened the file, speaking as she scanned its contents. "Tell me, Bierman, how did you become involved in this mess in the first place. Why didn't the…" she paused and glanced at the letter of authorization. "…West Country Funeral Home go directly to the Central London Morgue?"

"I don't know. That would've been the normal practice, but when I receive a telephone call from MI6, I'm not about to start asking questions."

"MI6?"

"MI6."

Benecke gave the paperwork to Lo. "We need to get that body back."

Lo nodded knowingly and left the office.

Benecke stared down menacingly at the apprehensive little man. "We're investigating multiple murders, Mister Bierman, and if we find any evidence that makes us even doubt you haven't been completely truthful with us, we'll be back. And if we do have to come back, I assure you, you're not going to like it; not even a little bit. So, one last time, is there anything else I should know?"

His hesitation was brief, but it was definitely there. "N… no, Special Agent, there's nothing else."

Bierman waited until his visitors had turned into the high street before picking up the telephone handset. The private number answered after two rings. "Sir, it's Maurice Bierman. I've just had a visit from two UNIIA agents… no, Sir, I told them exactly what you told me to say; nothing more, nothing less… I'm not sure if she believed me or not. The big black woman did all the talking and she's hard to read… I'm not sure, all she said was if she found out I'd been lying they'd be back… yes, Sir, let's hope so… of course. I'll tell them exactly what I said before."

He returned the handset to its cradle. This wasn't a world of courteous goodbyes.

***

Harrigan sat on the balcony, looking across the London landscape. Looking, but not really seeing. He refilled the tumbler and once again, maybe a little unsteadily, raised it to his lips. The exceptionally warm dry weather made sitting on his apartment balcony less pleasant than would normally be expected. Not that he noticed, his mind was elsewhere. He'd learned over his years in law enforcement, that every case throws up adversities; nothing goes right all the time, a lot like life, really. But *this* case? This case was *all* bloody adversity; proving the old saying, *when one door closes another one slams in your face.* And now this Sarah thing? For the first time in his life he just wanted to give up and move on. Maybe it had been the heat or even the whisky that had allowed his mind to wander into the unfamiliar territory of self-pity; not that it mattered, he didn't stay there long.

"Fuck it," he said loudly, much to the disapproval of the elderly couple drinking tea on the balcony of the next door apartment. They both glared disapprovingly at the near empty bottle of Ballantine's. On second thoughts, it had been the wife who'd glared at the bottle with disapproval; the husband's stare was more one of jealousy.

"One final throw of the dice and that'll be it!" He announced.

He telephoned Eian Jones and asked for two favours. He needed tickets on the next flight to Urbadistan for Lo and Benecke, and after telling him about Sarah, said he needed Godfrey Windsor on call to replace Sarah as required. Jones had no problem with the Windsor secondment. The flight tickets were a different matter. But accepting the futility of questioning Harrigan's motives and ignoring the now almost familiar gut wrenching feeling in his stomach, said he'd get back with the flight details.

Harrigan refilled the empty tumbler.

He'd not had time to take even a sip, before the ring tone of his mobile lying on the table shattered the moment. His angry stare was water off a duck's back to the defiant instrument, it'd become immune to angry stares. Fighting all natural instincts, he ignored the incessant ringing, a smile of pride and achievement crossing his lips as the telephone fell silent.

But the smile was fleeting at best, mobile telephones don't give up that easily. He snatched it up from the table top, almost dropping it in the process.

"Harrigan!"

"Sir. Benecke."

He listened silently while she recounted the events at Bierman's Funerals. "We've not been able to contact the West Country Funeral Service and to be honest, we doubt it even exists," she concluded.

"S'okay, forget about it f'now, I'll chase it up later. Get back to the hotel, we need t'talk."

"Are you alright, Sir? You sound a little, er, different than usual."

"I'm fine, jus' a bit tired.

Concerned Harrigan's slightly slurred and somewhat stilted speech could be a health warning, she asked to speak to Sarah.

"Sharah's not here. She's left."

He pressed the little red button and threw the mobile onto the table. It slid off the far side and clattered onto the tiled floor.

***

"My God, Collins, you did what!? Have you completely lost your senses?"

Collins glared at his visitor across the desk in his London apartment's private study. "I give you substantial rein," Collins replied quietly. "But don't forget who you are talking to; at least show some semblance of respect."

"Yes, of course, I apologise. I just find it incredulous you think Harrigan believed your ridiculous lost body story. My God, Admiral, it's sheer idiocy."

"He doesn't have to believe it. The incident is fully documented, and if he wants to dispute it, let him try. He won't get anywhere."

"I hope you're right."

"Oh, I'm right. And I agree, it was a little far fetched, but after Harrigan called my bluff on the Connie West murder story—"

"Another one of your fuck ups."

"Yes, but had it worked, Harrigan would now be well and truely out of our hair. It was worth the risk."

"That's debatable."

Collins gestured dismissivelly. "Water under the bridge. Believe me, my friend, Harrigan is almost at the end of his tether, and now Sarah Throgmorton has walked out on him, it won't be long before we get the result we want and he'll be on his way."

"Maybe. I must say the timing of that Deputy Assistant Police Commissioner position coming up at the Met was a stroke of good fortune. An offer she couldn't refuse."

"A stroke of good fortune? Hmm, yes, I suppose you could say that." The smugness of his tone should've caused Collins' visitor to smile. It didn't. Collins continued. "But you didn't come here to discuss that. What is it you need to tell me?"

"Harrigan is sending Lo and Benecke to Urbanistan, presumably to follow the weapons trail."

The colour drained from Collins' face. "What!? Are you certain?"

"Absolutely."

Collins stood and walked slowly around the room before returning to his chair. "That can't be allowed to happen."

"There's no need to concern yourself, it's been taken care of."

"Taken care of? What does that mean exactly?"

"Let's just say, measures have been put in place."

Collins shook his head violently. "I don't want to know."

"No, you don't."

Without another word, the visitor left the room, gave a polite nod of farewell to the smiling Lady Annabelle, and left the apartment.

Chapter Fifteen

It was five minutes to six, Wednesday morning Urbadistan time, when Benecke and Lo landed at Al Fadmur airport. Lo had taken full advantage of the spacious reclining business class seats and slept most of the journey. Benecke had attempted to do the same, but the feeling of uneasiness she'd tried unsuccessfully to throw off had kept her awake. It had been abundantly clear when they'd arrived back at Harrigan's apartment mid-afternoon yesterday, their boss had given his favourite Ballantine's a decent workout. Unbeknown to Benecke, after seeing the two empty bottles lying abandoned on the balcony table, Lo had felt a surge of admiration towards Harrigan's ability to continue functioning. But functioning he was. He'd explained Sarah had been offered a *too good to refuse* position at the London Met and had left the team. Despite Benecke instinctively knowing there was much more to it than that, she'd said nothing. He'd explained about the trip to Urbadistan, their Khususia Air airline tickets were waiting at Heathrow Terminal 4, and accommodation had been booked at the Medwin Sumunhur Hotel. He'd also handed Benecke a note with the name and ETA of the next arms-carrying vessel to arrive at the Port of Sumunhur, complete with the container number.

The quizzical expression on Benecke's face while reading the information had led Harrigan to continue. "Information gathered by Eian Jones from a confidential contact."

She'd nodded understandingly. "The ship is due in four days give or take. Tell me again, Sir, what is it we're looking for exactly?"

"Anything that verifies Collins' Kajmanistan Rebels story."

"You doubt his telling the truth?"

"I doubt everything that comes out of the man's mouth."

"Why would he lie about a thing like that? If he was going to make up a story, surely he'd think of something better than to confess to a highly questionable action that could blow up in his face and damage the UK USA relationship if it ever got out. It doesn't make sense."

"It does if he's hiding something of greater importance. Just sniff about and see what you come up with. And for God's sake you pair, be careful. Don't take any unnecessary risks and if you suspect you're in danger, hightail it out of there. Urbadistan might be neutral territory, but it *is* the Middle East. Okay, your flight leaves at six fifteen, so you'd better get moving."

The Al Fadmur terminal building was of a standard a seasoned traveller would expect from an international airport. Retail outlets inside the terminal however, was where any similarity ended. Urbadistan, by design, is not a tourist destination. El Basna, the capital city, is situated some ten miles north west from the major airport and twenty three miles north of Sumunhur. The city has all the appropriate facilities for the needs of the, in global terms, relatively small permanent resident population.

Sumunhur itself, is an area of approximately twenty five square miles, and with the exception of general maintenance facilities and one fuel station, is covered mostly by large, enclosed, and heavily guarded storage facilities. Each facility included basic employee living quarters which partly explained the lack of pedestrian foot traffic. The top end luxury Medwin Sumunhur Hotel caters exclusively for local and visiting businesspeople and their guests. All accommodation contains a medium size sound proofed meeting room, complete with electronic device detectors. Beyond the meeting room, the entire apartment is also covered with electronic device detectors and a telephone scrambling device which can be activated for a not unsubstantial fee.

There are three transportation routes for the dispersal of landed goods. Two well maintained road arteries, the Caspian Sea, and a large cargo airport.

"I hope they have a taxi service here," Lo said as they walked towards the baggage carousel.

Benecke didn't answer; her attention was elsewhere. Considering the low key nature of their visit, she was more than a little troubled at the sight of a man holding a large hand printed sign which read BENEKE AND LO. He wore the traditional Arabic dress code of long white Thawb, neatly trimmed thick black beard, topped off with a white keffiyeth and rope head-covering. She immediately decided the missing 'C' in her name could quite possibly prove to be the least of their problems.

Lo followed her gaze. "Well, so much for our visit being kept under wraps; seems we've been outed already," he said.

"Looks like it," she replied.

With the Al-Fadmur Airport baggage handlers being obviously more efficient than the local sign writers, their wait at the carousel was short lived. Twelve minutes later, with luggage in tow, they approached the man with the sign.

"You waiting for us?" Benecke half asked, half stated. There was a slight hint of accusation in there somewhere as well.

"You Benecke and Lo?" He responded. The complicated subtleties cleverly woven into Benecke's tone had been completely lost.

Lo jumped in quickly. "We weren't expecting anyone to meet us." He was happy to let Benecke lead but was always ready to play his role of the steady hand on the rudder at the first sign of her hackles rising. "We were wondering who sent you to meet us?"

"It's a complimentary service from the Medwin. I am Rasul. Follow me." Without offering to assist with their bags, he turned swiftly and marched towards the exit.

"Not the friendliest or most polite limousine driver I've ever encountered," she whispered to Lo.

"It's the Middle East and you're a woman. Don't worry about it," Lo replied somewhat offhandedly.

"You're such a fucking wimp sometimes!"

Lo never ceased to be amazed at how much anger Benecke could fit into a whisper. "You're so sexy when you're angry."

It took just a few moments for the glower to leave her face. She smiled and gave a half laugh.

They were good for each other. Each fulfilling the other's needs.

***

The smell of freshly brewed coffee brought Harrigan, albeit with some level of difficulty, into Wednesday morning. He turned slowly and looked at the clock; five thirty-seven. He rolled back and closed his eyes.

"Freshly brewed coffee?" With his mind very much under the spell of yesterday's Ballantine's, it was several seconds before the relevance of the question registered. His eyelids sprung open.

"Sarah?" He called as he swung his legs over the side of the bed and sat upright much quicker than he should have. Without waiting for the dizziness to subside, he grabbed the white hotel bathrobe, and not bothering to use the loops, tied the thick white woolly belt quickly around his waist. He hurried somewhat unsteadily into the main living area.

"No, Chief Inspector, It's not Sarah. Sorry to disappoint." The soft, disarming huskiness in her voice, while well-rehearsed and well-delivered, was totally wasted on Harrigan.

She stood at the counter in the kitchen area, her back to him. Her short, black, pixie bob cut hairstyle complimented the black tailored business suit. Black patent strappy stiletto heeled shoes below the cuff-less ends of each trouser leg, gave absolute authority to her air of tempting sexuality. She turned slowly. The white collared shirt and black Bolo tie completed the ensemble. She walked towards him, offering him a mug of hot black coffee in her outstretched hand.

He took the mug.

"Deirdre Wright." Her introduction was brief. Her voice soft, well educated, and holding a subtle hint of invitation.

"I guess all the 'meeting Miss Right' jokes have been done?"

"To death."

They moved to the small dining table. She sat across from him.

"How's the coffee?"

"I'm sure it'll be fine."

His short, somewhat abrupt reply left no doubt he had no intention of leading the conversation. She accepted the challenge. "I'm surprised you haven't asked who I am or what I'm doing here."

"No need. You're a spook."

"Oh? And how exactly did you come to that conclusion?"

"You entered my apartment without waking me, so you must have had a way to bypass the electronic lock; not easy to do. You knew this was my apartment, how I take my coffee and who Sarah is. You only made coffee for you and me, so you also knew she wasn't here. You wander about the apartment like you own the place. I could go on." He raised the coffee mug to his lips. "I don't know *why* you're here, but it's bound to be some sort of Intelligence Agency bureaucratic bull shit."

"Maybe. Then again, my motive for being here might be more," she paused, "sinister?"

"It could be. But if it is, it's not your *prime* motive. If it had been, you'd've done your damnedest while I was asleep, not make bloody coffee. And while we're in our show and tell moment, your partner might as well show himself. Where is he, in the second bedroom?"

"Partner?" She repeated innocently.

"Yes, partner."

"And what makes you think I have a partner?"

"Spooks are like Nuns, they always go 'round in pairs. So are you going to tell him to come out, or do I have to go in and drag him out myself." His patience had almost run its course.

"It's alright, Gavin," she called loudly. "Come and get yourself a cup of coffee!"

"I'm curious," Harrigan said. "Why the hell was he hiding?"

"You have quite a fierce reputation. I wasn't sure how you'd re-act and I wanted something up my sleeve."

At the sound of the opening second bedroom door, Harrigan spun around sharply and closely followed the movement of the behemoth in the dark tan suit lumbering across the apartment. Considering his size, his expressionless battle-scarred face and empty staring eyes, there was no doubt what Gavin brought to the table in this beauty and the beast partnership. Harrigan turned back to the table.

"Okay, you ready to tell me why you're here?"

"We need to discuss your investigation into the Brewer Lane shootings."

"There's nothing to discuss. UNIIA has total jurisdiction over its cases."

"Not when there's a question of National Security you don't."

"We have ongoing dialogue with the Joint Intelligence Committee. They're aware of what we're doing."

She didn't answer immediately, choosing to wait for Gavin to place his coffee mug on the table and stand beside and slightly behind Harrigan's left shoulder. "Have you informed the J.I.C. you've sent two of your team to Urbadistan?"

Harrigan tensed. Lo and Benecke's trip wasn't a secret, but it had certainly been kept under wraps. Only those who needed to know, knew, and she wasn't one of them. "D'you know what, Ms Wright, before we go any further, I think it's time you told me who you work for. Secret Service? Special Ops? MI6?"

She gave a short derisive laugh. "No, nothing like that. Nothing so cliché. We're the last line of defense. Our orders come from the very top. There is no paper trail; no telephone records to trace; no records of any description. We don't exist. Once advised of our tasks, we carry them out using any means we deem necessary to get the job done." She glanced up deliberately towards the stony faced Gavin before returning her gaze to Harrigan. Her eyes now icy black, their intensity accentuated by the pale, slightly Goth-like white makeup, black eyeliner, and dark red almost black lipstick. "Whatever it takes to get the job done," she repeated. His eyes were drawn towards the thick black mascara on her eyelashes as she blinked slowly; purposely. "*Whatever* it takes."

He felt the weight of the monster standing beside him increase as it leaned into him.

"So, what task brings you to me?" He tried to sound as relaxed as possible. He thought he did it pretty well.

"We've come to ask you to withdraw your team immediately."

"And if I choose not to?"

"Well, when I said *ask*, I was being polite."

In negotiations such as this, he'd learned over time that timing is paramount. He remained silent, looking down thoughtfully. At just the right moment he looked up slowly. "I had a heavy day yesterday—"

"Yes, we saw the empty bottles on the balcony table." Her interruption had a definite casualness about it. He admired her professionalism. This was just a job to her. There was nothing personal.

"It might be last night's whisky, or maybe I didn't have anything to eat, I don't know, but I'm starved. I need to make a couple of pieces of toast." He attempted to push his chair back. Gavin placed his hand on the back of the chair. It wouldn't move. "Oh come on! It's two pieces of fucking toast for Christ's sake. You wouldn't want me to die hungry would you? Think of it as a last meal request if it helps."

Deidre Wright appreciated his ability to inject nonchalance, even flippancy into the situation.

She held his stare longer than most before looking up at her partner and tilting her head sharply to her right. Gavin released the chair immediately, pulled out his own chair and began to sit, bending over as he did so.

"Thank you," Harrigan said as he prepared to rise.

There are times in life when things happen so quickly, it's all over before you realise it. Harrigan flicked the thick, white, woolly belt of his robe across the back of Gavin's neck, grabbed both ends, and pulled the belt towards the floor with all the strength he could muster. Captured by the belt, Gavin's head crashed into the table top. Grabbing a full handful of hair, Harrigan jerked the head up savagely and smashed it down again. Two, Three, Four times more. With scalding hot coffee and blood from protruding china pieces from the smashed coffee cup flowing down his face the carnage continued until consciousness eluded him. Finally, after lifting the defenseless body away from the table, Harrigan reached across the huge chest and grabbed the 9mm Browning from its shoulder holster before crashing the bloodied, broken face into the tabletop one last time. Pointing the weapon steadily towards the surprisingly calm Deirdre Wright, he shoved the limp body sideward. It fell noisily to the floor.

She drained the last of her coffee and slowly returned the cup to its saucer. "Come now, Chief Inspector, was all that *really* necessary?" She was calm, unmoved, her lack of concern for her partner obvious.

Harrigan gestured with the Browning for her to stand. She obeyed. He stood behind her and ran his hands over her back, and up and down both the outside and inside of her legs. He reached around her and felt her frontal areas; *all* her frontal areas. Satisfied she was carrying no weapons on her person, he stepped aside and gestured again with the Browning. She sat. He removed her black leather shoulder bag from the back of her chair and returned to his seat. After laying the browning on the table he emptied the contents of the bag. Finding nothing of consequence, he bundled everything back into the bag and slid it across the table. "Was it necessary?" He eventually repeated her earlier question. "A beautiful and obviously intelligent woman, accompanied by her not so smart gorilla, break into my apartment while I sleep. I awake to the smell of freshly brewed coffee being prepared by a woman I have never seen before. She beckons her gorilla to come out of hiding and tells me I am to withdraw my team from the field immediately or suffer the consequences. What was I supposed to do? Sit here waiting to discover what form those consequences would take? Sorry, I don't do things that way. I prefer the 'act first, apologise later' approach. So *yes*, Ms Wright, to answer your question, it *was* necessary." He pushed the untouched and now tepid mug of coffee further to his right. "You didn't believe I would actually drink that, did you?"

She gave a, *'it was worth a shot'* shrug. "So what now?" She asked. There was no emotion. It was strictly business. A matter of fact question.

He glanced briefly down towards Gavin before picking up his mobile telephone lying on the table. He assumed he must've picked it up from the tiled floor of the balcony and put it there before going to bed last night. He didn't remember. "I'll call an ambulance for your partner, and while we're waiting, we can talk."

He made the call and put the 'phone into the pocket of the white gown. "They'll be here in around twenty minutes."

"Why don't you put some other clothes on?" She asked. "In case you're not aware, that white woolly gown doesn't do anything for your tough guy image. If you want the truth, it looks damned ridiculous." She moved her gaze slowly down the opened robe, stopping as it focused on the area of manly private bits. "I'm glad you don't sleep naked." She paused briefly allowing her gaze to intensify. "On second thoughts, maybe I'm not." Her tone was personable; friendly even. She stood from the table. "I'll make the coffee." She strode towards the kitchen area. "Proper coffee this time, I promise," she called over her shoulder.

Harrigan smiled, it was as if she was an old, intimate friend come to visit.

He felt a twinge of sympathy for the bloody, broken, shattered body of her partner. As far as she was concerned, it was as if it didn't even exist.

He left the bedroom door open, listening for any sound not consistent with the making of coffee. Not that he was expecting any further trouble for now. Not with the paramedics on the way.

With Deidre's earlier, *"We don't exist"* comment constantly front of mind, he hadn't been able to shake the possibility she could be one of Eian Jones' Unit 29 operatives. If she was, did that mean Jones was behind this? After all, he was one of the few people who knew Benecke and Lo were in Urbadistan, and he'd clearly doubted the wisdom of sending them there.

"Well, there's only one way to find out." He pulled on his trousers. "You live in London?" He called through the open door as casually as possible.

"Yes!" Her voice echoed back through the apartment. "Why do you ask?"

"Just wondering! I rented a unit in London a couple of months ago, and it was the best accommodation I'd found for a long time. I wrote the unit number down so I could ask for it if the need ever arose again." To heighten any suspense filled anticipation she might be experiencing, he allowed several silent moments to pass before continuing. "29! Unit 29!"

The sound of clattering coffee cups stuttered briefly. Very briefly; but stutter it did. He returned to the apartment living area. "Coffee ready?" The innocence in his tone didn't fool her for a moment.

She gestured with the coffee cups and glanced towards the London skyline. "Outside?"

"After you."

The rain falling was blessed relief from the above average London temperatures. Luckily, after moving the table and chairs closer to the apartment wall, they were able to stay dry. She sipped her coffee slowly before returning her cup to its saucer. "You are a truly amazing man, Chief Inspector. You know things. Things you shouldn't."

Her response was the closest she could come to affirming her Unit 29 status.

"So we're on the same side?" He pushed.

"I don't have sides. I just follow orders."

"Orders from whom?"

"I have no idea. Tasks are simply relayed to me by a voice on the telephone. A non-traceable telephone. The original orders could be issued by Mickey Mouse for all I know."

"And you just obey the orders? No questions asked?"

"No questions asked."

"No matter what you're told to do?"

"No matter what."

"And you're happy with that arrangement?"

"You show me someone who's happy in their job, and I'll show you a liar. We all do what we have to do."

A knocking at the door brought a halt to any further conversation.

Twenty minutes later he held the apartment door open as the paramedics wheeled the still motionless Gavin into the hallway and towards the goods only lift. Deidre pushed a small handwritten note into his hand as she brought up the rear. "If you're still alive when all this is over, call me."

He shoved the note into his trouser pocket. The heavy duty automatic door closer denied him the satisfaction of slamming the door, doing nothing for his mood. He hurried across the room to the land line telephone.

It took almost ten minutes for the concierge to connect his call.

"Hello? Medwin Sumunhur Hotel?... Chief Inspector Harrigan in London. I need to speak with one of your guests... Benecke or Lo..." It seemed like hours before the receptionist returned to the telephone. "...the booking was cancelled!!?? When?... I see. Who cancelled it?... the Serious National Crime and Intelligence Agency? Do you have a name?...pity. So you wouldn't know where they are now?... no, of course. Thank you."

He dialled again. *'Come on, answer the bloody thing!'* "Eian? Bill. What the hell's going on? I tried to contact Benecke and their booking was cancelled... about two hours before their flight landed... by your bloody office!... I didn't say you did, but someone there did and... okay, an hour." At least the telephone had the courage to accept Harrigan's temper filled slam.

With ablutions completed, his Glock in the shoulder holster and freshly brewed coffee in hand, his journey to the balcony was interrupted by a loud knock on the door. He put the coffee on the coffee table.

He didn't recognise the man on the other side of the door's peephole. He stood to one side. "Who is it?"

"Ricardo Gianni."

"That supposed to mean something?"

There was a short silence. "Look through da hole."

Harrigan pulled the Glock from the shoulder holster and opened the door ajar as quickly as he could. The man stood motionless, staring at the barrel of the weapon aimed at his forehead. CIA badge held high.

"What da fuck!" The words spewed out of his mouth of their own volition. But that was okay. It was what had to be said.

Harrigan lowered the Glock and opened the door wide. "Come in." He regathered his coffee. "If you want coffee, I'm fresh out of good deeds so you'll have to make it yourself." He nodded towards the kitchen area. "The stuff's over there."

Several minutes later, Ricardo Gianni, *"I dropped 'the third' when I joined the Agency"*, with coffee in hand, joined Harrigan on the balcony.

At Harrigan's invitation, Gianni had been more than willing to detail who he was, and the background as to why he was there.

He'd been with the CIA for over fourteen years and a Field Agent for the last nine. He came to the London office eight months ago.

He knew that despite the Brewer Lane murders seeming to be a local matter, UNIIA had been called in to investigate. He knew about the arms going to the Kajmanistan Rebels and the Yoon drugs in the shipments. He knew Littlewood supplied the arms to Al Yousaf and they were shipped to Urbadistan. The USA was not best pleased with the arrangement, but it was only assault rifles, and although the Kajmanistan Rebels supported the non-American aligned states, they were not major players in the Middle Eastern conflicts. It might even play to USA's future advantage if one of their allies had an in with the opposition. Despite using all available resources of the CIA, he'd been unable to trace the identity of Al-Yousaf's customer. This had led the CIA, not surprisingly, to suspect someone in the UK Government most probably had a hand in it somewhere. How far up the chain of command it went they had no way of knowing, but considering the growing unrest developing in the Middle East and the vital allied relationship between their two countries, no further investigation had been undertaken.

"And besides," he concluded. "Reports from people on the ground indicate only a token number of weapons are being supplied. A handful, more or less; here and there. A hornet's nest not worth stirring. Not officially, anyway."

"A *handful*?" Harrigan asked.

"That's our information."

"Hmph. That's interesting." He raised the coffee mug to his lips but didn't drink. He stood suddenly, went inside and tossed the mug into the sink. The black liquid spilled up the sides of the sink and over the draining board. He grabbed the Ballantine's and two tumblers.

"Scotch?" He asked.

"I'd prefer Bourbon."

Harrigan filled both glasses and placed one in front of his visitor. "You'll have Scotch." He took a long draught and stared at the tumbler as he placed it on the table. He continued without looking up. "How do you know all this stuff? Yoon, Al-Yousaf, Littlewood, Urbadistan and all the other." He twisted the tumbler several times before raising his head slowly. "That was supposed to be highly confidential information known only to a select few."

"We're the CIA."

"Don't give me that crap. Tell me how you know or I'll toss you over that fucking balcony rail."

Gianni recognised the hollowness of the threat, but he also knew Harrigan was a person not to be pushed too far. "I had a mole in the operation."

"A mole?"

"Yes."

Harrigan sat silently, then smiled and shook his head. "Don't tell me. Connie West. Right?"

"Right."

"And it was your lot that helped her get away from Jones' people?"

"Right again."

"And she's alive and well?"

"Alive, safe, and being well looked after."

"She's a bit young to be an agent, so she's what, an independent informant?"

"Close enough. I also know about that ridiculous business when Jason Collins threatened to charge you with her murder unless you closed the Brewer Lane case."

"And if he had charged me, you wouldn't have lifted a finger to help?"

"You're playing with the big boys now, Chief Inspector."

Harrigan emptied his glass. "As interesting as all that is, you still haven't explained why you're here."

"It's quite simple really; I was curious why you sent your two colleagues to Urbadistan."

Harrigan frowned, his expression asking the tacit question, *"How did you find out about that?"*

Gianni's response came by way of an equally tacit, *"I told you; we're the CIA"* shrug.

"If this is, as you put it, *a hornet's nest not worth stirring,* why were you curious?"

"I couldn't find any logical reason for anyone to set up such an operation for just a handful of assault rifles. When I learned of the Urbadistan visit, I figured you must be wondering the same thing. I thought I'd ask."

"Collins' desperation to have me wind up the investigation has bothered me from the start. I have my suspicions, but nothing I can prove. I sent Benecke and Lo to try and find an answer. A last resort."

"Have they found anything yet?"

Harrigan took his tumbler to the balcony rail and stood in the drizzling rain. With his back to Gianni, he spoke to the grey, miserable, London landscape. "I don't know. They've disappeared." He drank from his tumbler and turned. Leaning against the railing, he told the man from the CIA about the hotel booking cancellation. "I have no contacts in Urbadistan, and to be honest, probably for the first time in my life, I'm at a loss what to do next."

There was sadness in Harrigan's tone Gianni hadn't expected. A sadness foreign to his reputation. He took his mobile telephone from his inside pocket and stood from the table. "I might be able to help. Come out of the rain. No promises, but I'll make a couple of calls."

"You have people in Urbadistan?" Harrigan asked with fierce, enthusiastic optimism.

Gianni turned his head slowly towards Harrigan. He wasn't given the opportunity to speak.

"I know. I know. You're the CIA. Sorry I asked."

***

Rasul's continued less than professional behaviour had done nothing to ease Benecke's doubts as to his Bona Fide's. Seeing the fuel station coming up on the left, she asked Rasul to stop there, she needed to purchase a couple of things.

Rasual didn't agree or disagree to her request. "You'll be able to buy everything you need at the Hotel. We're almost there."

She stifled her proposed angry response at the sight of the fourteen storey hotel coming into distant view to the right. She allowed her anger and fears to subside and relaxed into the leather upholstery. But relief was to be short lived. Two minutes later, the stretched limousine sped past a road clearly sign posted as the hotel turn off. She quickly crossed the passenger area and kneeling on the opposite seat, spoke to the driver through the open dividing screen.

"Wasn't that the turn off!?" She demanded.

"There's a dedicated limousine facility at the rear of the hotel," he replied calmly. "Just a few more minutes."

He turned at the next street on the right. The road was much narrower than the one they'd just left. There were no pedestrian pathways, and all roadside buildings or human activity on either side had disappeared. The wide open space of the private and cargo airport soon became visible to the left.

Despite keeping sharp lookout for a rear service vehicle or limousine roadway leading to the hotel, Lo could see none. The sense of guilt for taking Benecke's fears so lightly, propelled him towards the dividing screen. "Hey, Rasul! What's going on?" He reached through the opened screen and grabbed at Rasul's shoulder. "Turn around immediately and take us—"

Rasul pushed the accelerator to the floor throwing Lo backwards. He grabbed the bottom edge of the partition opening to prevent himself falling to the floor.

Rasul calmly reached for a black button on the dash. With the sound of the rear cabin's door locks snapping into position ringing in his ears, Lo felt the thick glass partition begin to rise. He tried desperately to hold it down. But it was too powerful. He was left with no option but to release his grip before his fingers were trapped at the top. With no weapons, no telephones and no passers-by outside whose attention they might've been able to attract through the tinted windows, he returned to his seat and looked at Benecke. "Well, it looks like we've found what we were looking for," he said.

Busily scanning the passing terrain, seeking out any abnormality that might be useful in the future, Benecke allowed Lo's statement of the obvious to pass her by without comment .

Chapter Sixteen

Harrigan pushed the doorbell button of Jason Collins' penthouse apartment more violently than was necessary. Not surprising, considering the day's events. Ricardo Gianni had promised to contact him as soon as he'd learned something from Urbadistan. They'd swapped telephone numbers before the CIA man left his apartment. Swapped is probably not quite accurate. Gianni already had Harrigan's number; it was that CIA thing again. Although grateful for Gianni's offer of assistance, he couldn't just sit around and wait. He'd contacted Jason Collins' office and agreed it would be best if they met at Collins' apartment. *"Walls have ears, Chief Inspector. Shall we say two this afternoon?"*

Eian Jones had also telephoned and assured Harrigan no one from his agency had cancelled the Medwin Hotel booking and offered further assistance. *"No, there's nothing else at the moment thanks, Eian, just keep Windsor checking Collins' finances."* Truth be known, Harrigan *could've* used Jones' contacts, but despite best efforts, he couldn't shake his suspicions about Jones being somehow involved in the Deidre Wright visit. He and Jones might've had a close working relationship; maybe even a friendship; but he was also a spook. Harrigan had learned over the years, you trust the word of a spook at your own peril.

He was about to leave his apartment when an unexpected call from Inspector John Russel regarding forensics on the Mercedes found in Scotland capped it all off. The report from forensics was disappointing. Nothing of any significance had been found. It had always been a long shot. Any thought Russel might have had about delivering his overly rehearsed speech about his and Sarah's dalliance in the Highland Park hotel was brutally cut short by the sound of the sudden loud *click* in his telephone. He looked briefly at the silent handpiece, allowing a twisted smirk to linger on his lips before replacing it in its cradle. He'd enjoyed the chase. It had been a long, hard journey; Sarah had been difficult prey. But it was now time to seek out another piece of forbidden fruit ripe for the picking. Of course, with his wife, a lieutenant in the British Army Intelligence Corps returning home next week from her two-year posting in the Gulf, it will be more difficult. He looked forward to the challenge.

The sound of the security chain being unfastened forced Harrigan to take an involuntary step back.

Lady Annabelle's captivating smile had an air of genuine sincerity one does not expect from the upper classes. "Welcome, Chief Inspector. The Admiral said you'd be here around two." She glanced at her watch. "And punctual as well. I like that." The perfectly timed, deliberate pause that followed, emphasized the true meaning behind her next statement. "Jason is running a little late."

Harrigan guessed Lady Annabelle to be in her late forties, but with people of means it's often difficult to tell. Especially when they wear casual chic blue jeans, a white loose-fitting V necked sheer sleeved blouse, heeled strapped shoes, perfectly applied makeup and just the right amount of tan.

She opened the door wider and gestured for him to enter. "Please, go through to the terrace."

The traditional conversation about the view and the weather passed between them while Harrigan poured their coffees from the tall, elegant coffee pot. Despite the drizzling rain, the covered terrace and radiant electric heater gave the area a satisfactory level of warm comfort.

"My husband mentioned you and your partner have recently separated. I'm sorry to hear that."

Harrigan sipped his coffee and gave a slight nod of appreciation of her concern.

"But don't worry, we all find the right one," she continued. And again, after a calculated pause added. "Eventually."

Harrigan wanted to frown; but didn't. He'd already noticed she'd referred to Jason Collins as *The Admiral*, *Jason* and now *husband*. He'd not put much stock in it at the time. But the *Eventually?* The sound of a key being fitted to the front door lock disrupted his thoughts relating to the standing of their marriage.

"Here he is now." She placed her hands on the tabletop and sat straight backed. Acknowledging the clear message, he rose quickly, stood behind her chair, removing it as she stood. She nodded gracefully and walked into the apartment.

"The Chief Inspector is already here!" He heard her call.

"Bring him to my office." It was more an order than a request.

There being no dedicated visitor's chair, Collins waved off handedly towards the smallish but exceptionally comfortable soft leather lounge chair on the far left several meters from the rosewood desk. Collins lowered himself slowly into the high backed leather chair on the other side of the desk, laid his arms along the highly polished wooden arms, and stared blankly at Harrigan. He'd tried for that look of superiority so popular with high ranking officials. It didn't work.

"Very well, Chief Inspector, what's all this about?"

Harrigan positioned the small leather armchair close to the desk and directly opposite Collins. It was slightly lower than Collins' chair which gave the other man the dominant position. In an effort to counter this disadvantage, Harrigan sat as 'tall' as he could, crossed his right leg over his left, and placed his hands on his thighs. "Tell me everything you know about the cancellation of the hotel booking for my people in Urbadistan, *and*, of their current whereabouts."

Collins pulled his head straight back, and even with a furrowed brow, still managed to open his eyes wider. "Good heavens, man! What in the blue blazes are you talking about!? Are you saying your people have disappeared?"

Harrigan closed his eyes slowly and clenched his teeth twice, causing his jaw bones to pulsate. Several silent moments passed before Collins was forced by Harrigan's dispassionate unblinking stare to move nervously in his chair. His voice was calm, soft, not a whisper but definitely below normal volume, and complimented by an unmistakable Arctic chill.

"Collins, I've had a most trying day and have neither the time nor patience to listen to your lies. Now, I'm going to ask again, more simply this time, and if I'm not happy with your answers, I promise, you will have a worse day than *I've* had."

"That sounds like a threat, Chief Inspector."

"Of course it sounds like a threat!" Harrigan was somewhat put out Collins questioned it might've been otherwise. He took a few deep breaths. "Okay, let's try again. You knew Benecke and Low had travelled to Urbadistan. Correct?

"Correct."

"You knew they were staying at the Medwin Hotel. Correct?"

"Correct?"

"Did you know their booking had been cancelled?"

"Not until they failed to arrive as expected. We assumed there'd been a change in plans."

"And you have no idea of Lo and Benecke's current location?"

"None whatsoever."

"And how did you come by your information?"

"We're MI6. It's our job."

Harrigan smiled. "You know, you sound just like Ricardo Gianni, the CIA man who visited my apartment this morning."

Harrigan's timely mention of the CIA had the desired effect. Collins' sham air of unconcern deserted him immediately. "The CIA!? You have involved the CIA!? My Lord, do you know what you've done?"

"*I* didn't involve them. *He* knocked on *my* door."

"And you let him in." It was a statement, not a question.

Harrigan shrugged and answered anyway. "Why wouldn't I?"

Collins shook his head and lowered his voice. "Do you realise the magnitude of the damage this could do to the US UK relationship if they get wind of our arms deal with the Kajmanistan rebels?"

"They already know. Well, most of it, anyway."

"You *told* them!?"

"I didn't have to; they've known for quite some time."

Harrigan recounted almost verbatim, Gianni's earlier summary of the CIA's knowledge of the operation.

"So they only *suspect* the UK Government might be involved?" There was clear optimism in Collins' voice.

"That's what he said."

"And he has no idea of *my* involvement?"

"Not yet." Harrigan had no difficulty infusing a tone of threat into his two-word answer.

"Not yet? What do you mean, *not yet*?"

"It means that unless you can explain to me why only a handful of rifles are going to the Kajmanistan rebels, and who you're sending the bulk of the weapons to, your involvement in all this will be tomorrow's headline news."

An unemotional poker face is one of the most valuable weapons in the intelligence community's arsenal. Collins had it down pat. Except that is, for the ever so slight pause before answering. Harrigan let it go for now. "What a preposterous accusation! Who in the devil told you that poppycock? Gianni?"

"Who else? The CIA have people on the ground in Urbadistan. Like the MI6 apparently. I must admit, I'm a little surprised your people haven't reported it."

"They haven't reported it because there's nothing to report. I have direct contact with Khalid Ibn Qasim, leader of the Kajmanistan rebels. I assure you his people receive *all* the weapons. I'm sorry, Chief Inspector, you've been misled."

"As I understand it, for the reason of deniability for other members of the Joint Intelligence Committee, you're the only person who has contact with this Qasim character?"

"The only one."

"And I assume your contact is by telephone or other "at arm's length" means?"

"Not by telephone, too easily intercepted. But yes, other means."

"How do you know you're actually conversing with Qasim?"

"We have passwords, codes, specific phrases."

Harrigan's silent thoughts were interrupted by the sound of the closing front door. His questioning frown called for an answer.

Collins glanced at his watch. "That'll be Annabelle off to her aerobics class at the Cornelia Refugium."

"I might as well be off too," Harrigan said beginning to rise. "It seems I have a lot more digging around to do." But then, purposefully, he appeared to change his mind and settled back into the soft leather. "Before I leave, let me remind you my brief is the Brewer Lane shootings. Nothing more; nothing less. I have no interest in your assault rifles, who gets them and who doesn't, or who's on top and who's paying."

"Yes I know. That's what you told the J.I.C."

"What you don't know, is, despite our best efforts, we've been unable to gather sufficient evidence against any of the three logical suspects. The Yoons, the Al-Yousafs, or Boris Akmatbayev."

"Get to the point, Harrigan."

"The point is, sending Lo and Benecke to Urbadistan was a last desperate throw of the dice. If they'd come back empty handed, which was quite likely, and nothing else had come to light in the meantime, that would've been it. My report would've named the three suspects, explain the lack of evidence and our investigation would've been closed. The case would remain open but I suggest it would soon find itself languishing at the bottom of the cold case files, never again to see the light of day. "

"And you're telling me this because…?" He allowed his voice to fade away.

"Because I strongly believe Benecke and Lo's disappearance is no accident and their safety is in danger. But, if they are returned unharmed, the closure of our investigation could quite possibly still be the outcome."

"Am I to take it from that you think I had something to do with their disappearance?"

"You can take from it whatever you like." He rose once again. "But be warned, don't take too long."

"Meaning?"

"Meaning until my team has been returned, unharmed, I am about to dig much further into your little operation and if you've lied to me, whatever I find out will be exposed for all to see."

"You seem to be forgetting you're bound by the Official Secrets Act."

Harrigan stood, and with fists closed, leaned all his weight onto the desk. With a touch of Déjà vu, Harrigan's dispassionate, unblinking stare and calm, soft voice, re-introduced the Arctic chill into Collins' total being. "Be warned, Collins, the safety of my team ranks much higher than any Official Secrets Act." Harrigan leaned slightly further forward. "*Much* higher." He allowed time for his intimidation to take full affect, turned away from the desk and strode towards the door.

"Wait!"

He stopped at the sound of Collins' voice but didn't turn.

"Wait," Collins repeated quietly. "Please—" With Harrigan still facing the door, his gesture towards the small leather chair still waiting patiently on the opposite side of the desk was somewhat meaningless "—come back."

As Harrigan returned to his seat, Collins removed a bottle of Aberlour Highland single malt whisky and two tumblers. "Sorry, no Ballantine's."

Harrigan offered a *beggars can't be choosers* shrug.

He half-filled each tumbler, pushed one across the table to Harrigan and returned the bottle to the bottom drawer. There was no ice. There had been no salute before each took a large sip and returned their tumblers to the desk. Collins breathed a heavy sigh of resignation.

"I don't particularly like you, Chief Inspector, although you probably already knew that. You're too brash; you lack respect; you use the laws of the land as guidelines to be obeyed only when it suits—"

'When are you going to get to the bad bits?' Harrigan kept his thoughts to himself.

"—but I believe you are honest, well, *basically* honest anyway, and what I'm about to tell you must not leave this room." He paused, allowing time for Harrigan to comment. He didn't. Collins continued. "Your CIA man was correct. We send only a small amount of weapons to the Rebels, as a cover. The majority are earmarked for Akmatbayev." Once again, Harrigan ignored the opportunity to speak. This revelation was more a verification of his own suspicions than news.

Collins took another sip of the single malt. "It's common knowledge Russian organised crime bosses wield the real power in the USSR. Power held and enforced by fear and intimidation. With the fall of the Berlin Wall and other indications of a softening of the iron curtain, the collapse of the Soviet Union seems inevitable. Crime bosses have no intention of letting such an event weaken their power and are strategically positioning themselves for when the time comes. As I'm sure you are aware, Boris Akmatbayev is not only one of the most powerful crime bosses he also has very strong political contacts. If he is to maintain control of his domain, both in Russia and what are currently satellite states, he needs increased man power and weaponary. For his plans to succeed, it's essential his Russian underworld competition remain unaware of his build up of weaponary. Hence, he purchases them from us. He has the manpower, and very shortly, thanks to me, ample weaponary."

"And in return?"

"Continued access to oil and gas. In round figures, we import fifty percent of our oil and gas from Russia. With the trouble in the middle east, and the North Sea Piper Alpha oil rig disaster eighteen months ago, we must do whatever it takes to guarantee supply."

"Two bob each way."

Collins frowned. "Two bob each way?"

"You assist the Kajmadistan rebels in case things go wrong in the middle east, and the possible powerbrokers behind the new Soviet bloc if the USSR collapses."

"A little crude, if you pardon the pun, but yes, more or less."

"You wouldn't do this on your own. Who else in the Government know about the Russian connection."

"Two other persons, but I won't give you names. Suffice to say they are both at the top of the tree."

"Number Ten?" Harrigan pushed.

"I've said enough. Except, there is nothing in writing, nothing to link anyone else to any discussions we've had, and if it all goes wrong, *I'll* be the one for the high jump." He drained his tumbler. "So maybe now, Chief Inspector, you understand why I have been so eager for you to close the Brewer Lane case. Whileever you and your team continue sniffing around the arms shipments, talking to Akmatbayev, Littlewood, and my colleagues on the Joint Intelligence Committee, there is a danger you'll stumble on something that could blow everything wide open."

Harrigan stared thoughtfully at the ceiling before looking back at Collins. "So, all Littlewood and Al-Yousaf knew was the weapons were for a customer with delivery address in Urbadistan?" He was more thinking aloud than asking a question but Collins answered anyway.

"Yes."

"And your J.I.C. colleagues believe all weapons are going to the Kajmadistan rebels?"

"As far as I'm aware, yes."

"But it's possible one of them could know more?"

"Anything's possible. But to be honest, I doubt any of them would *want* to know more."

"And the murders of Natalya Zhestakova and Hazel Spinks, the second Yoon brother, the Mercedes registration, and the two people on surveillence opposite the Sister's, none of your doing?"

"None of my doing."

"One last thing. Who do *you* think was behind the Brewer Lane shootings?"

"Akmatbayev." His answer was definite and immediate. "He didn't appreciate the Yoons trying to muscle in on his European territory. He shot the others at the table to muddy the waters. When the second Yoon brother was killed and Al-Yousaf left alive, it only served to cement my view."

Harrigan nodded slightly, swallowed the last of his Aberlour and stood from the desk.

Collins also stood. "I'll contact my people in Urbadistan, and see what they can discover about Benecke and Lo's whereabouts."

"I suggest you try harder than that."

Collins had almost closed the front door when Harrigan turned. "Oh, I meant to tell you. Connie West, your informant in the Al-Yousaf, Yoon group. She also works for the C.I.A. They have her hidden away safely. I don't know where." He turned towards the lift. "I thought you'd like to know."

Collins returned to his desk, poured a full measure of Aberlour, and rang a programmed number on his mobile. "We need to talk... now!... Because I've just had a visit from Harrigan and he knows about the Russian connection… no, he doesn't know of our arrangement, but he has a way of digging out the truth… no! I'll come to your apartment. I'll see you in an hour." He returned his mobile to his coat pocket, downed the contents of the tumbler in one swallow and hurried out the room.

The small leather armchair waited patiently to be returned to its rightful place.

***

"Good afternoon, the Cornelia Refugium, Wilhelmina speaking. How may I help you?… Chief Inspector Harrigan? Yes, Sir, I remember you… an aerobics class? No, not today… Lady Annabelle? No, she's not. In fact, we haven't seen her for several months… I'm positive." Wilhelmina paused briefly. "Dame Joan is here, I'm certain she would like to see you. Should I put you through? … Another time? I'll tell her you rang. 'Bye Inspector."

***

The Black cab pulled into the curb outside the white trimmed four storey greyish brown brick apartment block at number fifteen, MidPuckle Road, Camden. Lady Annabelle paid the driver, and not bothering to wait for any change, left a handsome tip and hurried towards the front entrance. It was exactly two minutes and twenty-three seconds from the time she pressed the buzzer on the security panel beside the front door until she entered apartment four.

"Annabelle, what are you doing here?" A slight hint of annoyance took the edge off his attempted show of concern.

"It's that damn Harrigan! He's with Jason! He's going to discover that you and I are—"

"Annabelle, relax. Jason has already telephoned me. Harrigan knows about Akmatbayev and the weapons. Nothing else."

"What about our relationship. And the *money*?"

"I told you, all he knows is about the weapons going to Akmatbayev; that's all! Nothing more!" His tone did nothing to ease the look of panic in her eyes. He continued more calmly, desperately trying to put her at ease. "Trust me, you have no cause to worry. Where the weapons are going has nothing to do with the Brewer Lane shooting, and that's all Harrigan cares about." He glanced at his watch. "I don't mean to rush you, but I'm expecting someone here shortly. So, if there isn't anything else?" It was more a suggestion she leave, than a genuine question.

"I don't think I can carry on like this any longer. I'm tired of all the secrecy; the hiding away. And now with this Harrigan person lurking around every corner, I—." She cut herself short, went swiftly to him and cradled his hand in hers. She pressed it hard against her breasts. "It's time to tell Jason about our affair, of our love for each other; of our plans to begin new lives together. Just you and me. Please, Darling, tell me you agree."

Godfrey Windsor released his hand and took a pace backwards. "No, Annabelle. Not *our* plans; *your* plans," he corrected. "*Your* plans." There was a coldness in his voice.

Ignoring the tightening knot in her stomach, the increasing pounding in her ears and denying the true meaning behind his words, she spoke quickly, a quiver in her rambling voice. "No. No. No, not *my* plans, *our* plans! You told me you loved me. You told me I was the most desirable woman you had ever been with. You said your life would be meaningless if I wasn't part of it."

"People say many things in the heat of the moment. And yes, maybe I did say I enjoy you being in my life—"

"In your *bed* more likely!"

"—but really, did you honestly believe our relationship would be more than it was?" He glanced once more at his Rolex.

An outward display of emotion is simply not done in the best of British circles. It is stoicism, stiff upper lip, lay back and think of England. Dignity at all times. She stood defiantly in the centre of the room, head held high, a statue of virtue. "So now you have bedded me as often as you've desired and my usefulness as a spy against my husband has come to an end, you have no further use for me and wish to discard me like you would a soiled cloth?"

"I didn't say that. But—"

"Well, unfortunately for you, I'll not give you that satisfaction." She paused dramatically, turned proudly, and with a deliberate but discreet further tilt of her head spoke with the bravado of the victor. "Good-bye, Godfrey."

The drama of her exit was somewhat diminished by the sudden knock on the door. Almost without pause, while not actually *flinging* the door open, she did manage a fling that was proper and in keeping with her status.

At the unexpected sight of his wife in the doorway, Jason Collins' footing became a little unsteady. Shock does that sometimes. They stood facing each other. Annabelle was the first to speak.

Her words were spoken slowly, each delivered independently of the next. "Get out of my way."

Once again, Collins' legs moved of their own volition and took two steps to the left.

Godfrey Windsor came to the door, seemingly unaffected by the drama of the situation. "Jason. You're early. Come in."

Collins glanced briefly at Windsor, and then back to his disappearing wife, her stiletto heels echoing on the tiled stairway.

Windsor was well into his apartment before speaking. "I didn't hear the street door buzzer." It was a sort of throw-away line that while delivered casually, demanded an answer be offered.

"A resident was going out so I didn't bother."

"Pity." Windsor stood beside the small but well stocked bar. "Sherry?" He poured himself a full measure of Fino Sherry.

"What was Annabelle doing here?" Collins demanded as he approached.

"She was concerned about you. She said Harrigan had come to your apartment and his visit seemed to disturb you more than it ought. As I recall, *unnerved* was the actual word she used. Because your reaction was so out of character, she became extremely worried and knowing of my connection with Eian Jones, contacted me. I thought it best we spoke face to face. I told her Harrigan has an unnerving way about him, that there was nothing to worry about. She was about to leave when you knocked on the door." As Collins had not indicated one way or the other about the sherry, Windsor recorked the bottle, placed it on the bar and walked to the soft leather armchair in the sitting room area.

Collins remained silent as he moved to the bar. He read the label on the sherry bottle, removed the cork and spoke as he poured; his voice calm; his words measured. "Annabelle has never given a tinker's cuss about my feelings. Not even *before* we were married. So, would you like to try again or just admit you and Annabelle are having an affair?"

"A gentleman doesn't kiss and tell, Jason. Maybe you should ask Annabelle."

Collins took that as a *yes*. "How long has this been going on?"

"Really old man, you should be discussing this with your wife. And besides, considering your dalliances with professional ladies and your non too subtle trysts with Joan Hamilton at the Cornelia, you are in no position to be judging the sexual activities of anyone, especially Annabelle."

Collins sipped the sherry. His arrangements with professional ladies had never really been hidden; an open secret if you like. Windsor's knowledge of his meetings with Joan Hamilton-Westbrook was more worrying, but a matter for another time. Sexual activity in his marriage had always been more of a duty than pleasure; for both he and Annabelle. And truth be told, the fact Annabelle was in an affair didn't affect him one way or the other. Maybe even excited him a little. *"But Godfrey Windsor! Why that cad? He was more a toy boy than a serious lover! There was no shortage of younger, more beautiful women of his own age who'd enjoy his company. So why Annabelle?"* The questions raced through his brain. Over and over. He emptied his sherry glass in one swallow and raised the bottle a second time. He'd almost removed the cork when, without warning, he froze. His mind whirred as he stood motionless. The seconds ticked by. A dense cloud of silence filled the room. And then, as quickly as it had begun, the silence was shattered. He slammed the bottle heavily onto the bar top. The sound of the slight stem of the sherry glass breaking as it tumbled onto its side contrasted sharply with the fury of the moment.

"My God, Windsor! You've been using Annabelle to spy on me. That's it, isn't it? That's how you learned of the weapons going to Akmatbayev and not the Kajmanistan rebels."

Windsor's smile filled with a cruel smugness. If cruelty can have a smugness that is. "Do you *really* think I was after her body?" And as an afterthought. "As well kept as it is."

"And the blackmail? Akmatbayev and me forced to pay for your silence with each delivery or the UK's alliance with the USA will be destroyed and our international reputation damaged for all time. She in on that too?"

"Not directly, no." Windsor rose slowly and stood several feet away from Collins. He was younger, taller, and confidently threatening. "You came here to talk about Harrigan's visit to your home. If that's what you still want, then I suggest you start talking. If not, it's time for you to leave. It's your call."

He was right of course. The current matters of argument between them could wait, getting rid of Harrigan must take priority. Collins' years of civil service and diplomatic training allowed him to easily regain his composure. He walked to the living area and stood facing a simply framed confused painting of bold colours, movement, and individuality created in the Jackson Pollock style. He'd always considered Pollock paintings to be more that of a painter's drop sheet than actual art. He was a 19th century Marine Art man himself. He spoke to the drop sheet. "Harrigan's people have gone missing in Urbadistan. He won't sign off the Brewer Lane case until their safe return." He turned towards Windsor and recounted his earlier conversation with Harrigan. "I have offered to have my people on the ground try and locate them."

"And the C.I.A. are sniffing around?"

"That's what he said. I don't think they know anything of importance just yet, but it does place an urgency on finding Benecke and Lo and returning them unharmed. If they are still alive of course."

"Don't concern yourself about that; they're still alive."

"Really? And tell me, just how do you know…?" There was no need to complete the question. "*You! You* took them!?"

"I can't take all the credit." Windsor picked up both the stem and bowl of the broken sherry glass and carefully placed them in the waste basket. "Akmatbayev played his role." His calmness only added to Collins' anger. With unnecessary ferocity, his visitor strode across the apartment, grabbed the closest tumbler from behind the bar, snatched up the bottle of Chatelle Napoleon and carelessly splashed more than was decent into the undeserving whisky glass. Windsor took the opportunity to twist the knife. "I rarely agree with much of your idiocy, but you're right in one thing; Harrigan has to be stopped. But after your somewhat puerile attempts, to firstly seduce him using Joan Westbrook, and then accusing him of a non-existent murder, Boris and I decided to take the adult route. Take something, or in this case, someone, he cares for and hold them for ransom. And by what you've just told me, it seems we were right." The pause, taken as Collins was mid-draught denying him the opportunity to respond, was timed to perfection. Windsor continued. "So, all you have to do now is contact Harrigan, tell him your people have located Benecke and Lo, they are in good health, for now, and will be released immediately after he signs off the Brewer Lane case. Job done."

"And if he doesn't agree? If he wants them released before he signs off?"

"Then one of them will be killed. Probably Lo. Benecke means more to Harrigan than Lo and is a more valuable final bargaining chip."

The unexpected, somewhat sociopathic iciness in Windsor's tone stunned Collins into momentary silence. "Where are they?" He demanded forcefully, attempting to cover his lapse of composure.

Windsor took the almost empty glass from Collins' hand. "You don't need to know where." He began to turn away. "Time for you to go. Let me know what Harrigan says."

Collins grabbed back the glass. "When you first threatened to blackmail Akmatbayev and me, he wanted to kill you. I talked him out of it. I persuaded him that as we didn't know your source of information, and it was almost certain you had an accomplice, killing you wouldn't've solved the problem." He drained the glass. "I was wrong."

Like his wife before him, Collins chose to use the stairs. He selected a stored number in his mobile telephone. Yes, he had to contact Harrigan, but first, there was someone much more important he must speak with.

**

"You are indeed a man of surprises, Chief Inspector. A known member of the most exclusive private dining and meeting places in London. Probably Europe." Lady Annabelle luxuriated in the soft semi aniline dark green leather armchair, admiring the view of the Thames. She might very well reside within the top order of the pampered and privileged aristocracy, but until today, had been denied the most sought after experience of society's elite. Unfortunately, her breeding didn't allow her to question Harrigan's obvious high status in Ali's.

Harrigan nodded graciously and sipped his Ballantine's. "You said on the telephone you had information in which I'd be very interested." Nodding graciously is one thing; beating around the bush was another. He had no time, or, if truth be told, inclination for polite niceties.

"Straight to the point. I like that." The impatient reprimand in Harrigan's eyes was unmistakable. "Of course, I'm sorry." She finished her Gin and Tonic. The silent hand of Rashid, their personal waiter for the evening, replaced her empty glass with a chilled Gin and Tonic with lime wedge.

He listened closely as she spoke willingly, albeit with a touch of embarrassment at the more personal aspects of her relationship with Windsor. They had met a little over two years ago at some charity fund raising evening. He'd been one of her husband's invited guests and innocently seated beside her at the table of eight. His invitation to dance seemed casual, even dutiful at the time, but it was now clear she'd been targeted. Their affair began almost immediately, and it wasn't long before their pillow talk included snippets of information relating to the Joint Intelligence Committee and MI6 she'd casually overheard from her husband. Nothing of great import. As their relationship grew, her information seeking became more serious. Of more consequence. Her desire for a permanent relationship with him grew also, but he'd always used the difference in their wealth as an excuse. He didn't intend to be a kept man. When she'd told him about the arms being supplied to Akmatbayev, he'd said that was his opportunity to build his finances and the blackmail had begun. Believing this opened the door to their future together, she was only too willing to spy on her husband, even to the degree of having an electronic listening device fitted into his home office.

In answer to Harrigan's question, she didn't know how much he'd been paid, but did say when Eian Jones moved to UNIIA, he'd become bolder and had increased his price considerably.

Harrigan had already learned of the arms going to Akmatbayev, but the information about the blackmail and Windsor's increased demands during Jones' absence was extremely valuable; extremely valuable indeed.

He looked at his watch. "It's a little after seven thirty, time for dinner. Would you care to join me?"

She gave that handsome laugh so common with ladies of high society. "You ask if I would care to take an evening meal at *Ali's?* I've been led to believe you were much smarter than that Chief Inspector." She laughed again. A full, genuine laugh that lit up her eyes. He wondered how long it'd been since she'd done that.

Chapter Seventeen

Two 'home baked' English Muffins at the Alfresco Royal coffee shop in the King's Cavalry Gardens on the Victorian Embankment isn't much of a breakfast, but Harrigan wasn't all that hungry; he'd get something more substantial later. The thundery showers persisting from yesterday's welcomed rain, had meant Harrigan had forgone the alfresco part of the morning and chosen a table beside a window over-looking the gardens. He absently pressed his thumb on several of the crumbs on the white china plate before pushing it aside. He licked his thumb clean and glanced at his watch. Nine forty-five, Eian Jones would be there at ten.

It had been a little before eleven the previous evening when Lady Annabelle had said goodnight and exited the taxi outside the Cornelia Refugium. *"I've arranged two nights accommodation at the Cornelia,"* she'd explained. *"It'll do Jason good to stew for a day or two. In fact, now he's aware of my activities with Godfrey, it will enable us to have a two-sided open marriage. And before you ask, Chief Inspector, yes, we will stay together. We married because his family had the titles, and my family the wealth. It has worked well over the years, and I see no reason for it to change."*

During the taxi trip to his hotel, he couldn't help being surprised that the thought of being punished for her involvement in blackmail, maybe even worse, hadn't crossed her mind. Then, he'd supposed, why would it? Her privileged life had placed her above all that crime and punishment stuff of the common folk.

Eian Jones' voice broke into his reverie. "Sorry I'm late, Bill, I don't walk as quickly as I used to."

"I'll let it go this time, Eian," Harrigan smiled.

Being a regular at the Alfresco, there was no need for Jones to call the waitress. He placed his order and a third cup of long black coffee for Harrigan. "Any news of Benecke and Lo yet?"

Harrigan shook his head. He needed to satisfy himself Jones was still one of the good guys before letting the Collins' *sign off the Brewer Lane case and get your people back safely* cat out of the bag. He proceeded cautiously. "Prior to taking up the Brewer Lane case, you explained UNIIA had been brought in to investigate because you suspected your colleagues on the J.I.C. were up to some jiggery pokery they didn't want you to know about."

"Yes, and you proved me right. Sending weapons to the Kajmanistan rebels is something to which I, as a member of the J.I.C., would never have agreed."

They sat back silently as their order was delivered.

Jones continued speaking while placing one cube of sugar into his white decaf. "And for the record, if the reason you asked me to meet you here was because you suspect me of having something to do with Benecke and Lo's disappearance, you've not only wasted your time, but mine as well."

Harrigan had forgotten how easily they could read each other's minds.

"I must admit that as it was your people who made the travel arrangements to Urbadistan, the thought had crossed my mind." Harrigan sipped his coffee before continuing. "You said before I'd proved you right about your colleagues on the J.I.C. being up to no good. You were half right."

"Only half?""

"It's true weapons are going to the rebels, but just a handful here and there. The majority are being delivered to Akmatbayev in preparation for the aftermath of the fall of the USSR."

Being the ultimate professional, Jones displayed no emotional reaction to the news. He sat silently tearing a generous piece from his croissant.

With the exception of the Godfrey Windsor blackmail and any mention of Annabelle, Harrigan relayed to Jones all relevant details relating to the Brewer Lane investigation and the undercover arms deal. "As far as I'm concerned," Harrigan concluded. "What you do with the arms deal information is entirely up to you. My task remains the Brewer Lane shooting; nothing more; nothing less. But whatever you decide, you can't say you got the information from me. Under the Official Secrets Act I probably shouldn't have said anything, but fuck it, I thought you should know."

Jones had mostly listened in silence, interrupting once about halfway through with a *"Christ, what a mess"*, spoken through a heavy sigh.

"Don't worry, your secret's safe with me." Jones ordered two more coffees.

Harrigan moved the conversation onto a more pressing matter. "You asked me earlier if I had any news about Benecke and Lo. I shook my head."

Jones acknowledged the statement.

"I lied." He outlined the Jason Collins' ultimatum.

"So," Jones summarized. "Benecke and Lo are being held somewhere, you don't know where, by a person or persons unknown, and will only be released if you close down your investigation into the Brewer lane shootings."

"Yes. And he wants an answer within forty eight hours. Well, closer to thirty hours now."

"Does that mean Collins is holding them?"

"I don't think so. It sounded more like Collins was passing on instructions."

Jones sat thoughtfully before responding. "The taking of two UN agents is serious business, so the stakes must be high. Because Collins is involved somewhere along the line, it would be reasonable to assume it is connected to the arms going to Akmatbayev. If your assumption Collins is following orders, they can only be coming from the two unnamed persons in the UK government, or Akmatbayev. Take your pick."

"There is one other person." Harrigan said quietly.

Once again, Jones leaned back as their coffees were placed on the table, his frown asking the obvious question.

Harrigan pushed the coffee to one side and leaned on the table. "Godfrey Windsor."

Eian Jones is a hard man to shock. It's even harder to draw him away from his poker face. But an involuntary nervous laugh will give you away every time. "Godfrey? You're kidding, right?" Harrigan sat stony faced. "C'mon, Bill. For fuck's sake; tell me you're not serious!"

"I wish I could old friend. When Godfrey learned of the actual destination of the weapons, he—"

"How'd he come by *that* information?" Jones interrupted.

"That's not important."

"Okay then, how did *you* come by the information about Godfrey?"

"That's not important either." Harrigan pulled his coffee back in front of him. "As I was saying, realizing Akmatbayev's plans would be thwarted if the political powers or his gangster mates learned of his growing armory, and the ruination of Collins' and the UK's reputation if the press ever got wind of it," he paused momentarily. "Um, how shall I put this? I'll just say I guess the temptation was too great for him to let pass."

"He was *blackmailing* them!?"

"I'm afraid so. And as far as I know he still is."

"When did it start?"

"I know it was when he was your 2ic before you were seconded for the UNIIA trial. Other than that, I couldn't say." Harrigan sipped his coffee. "One other thing that might be of interest, when you went to UNIIA and he moved up, he increased his price."

With eyes closing, Jones' head tipped downward. Harrigan hadn't noticed before, but he thought his friend's skin had an unnatural greyish tinge about it. He wondered if his recovery from major brain surgery to remove the tumor was going as well as he makes out. Still, it'd be pointless asking him.

Jones raised his head slowly. "So, what're your plans now?"

"As far as Windsor, I have no plans; he's your department, nothing to do with me. The only thing I ask is that you take no action until I have Benecke and Lo back."

Jones nodded agreement.

"As far as Benecke and Lo, I plan to do whatever it takes. If I must sign off on the Brewer Lane case, so be it. But I'll give it another twenty four hours, hopefully Gianni's men on the ground over there will come up with something."

***

Benecke and Lo sat side by side on the basic double bed in a small underground room best described as a cross between a London bedsit and jail cell. An electric light bulb, embarrassed by its nudity and which Lo had guessed was probably 40W, dangled in the centre of the room from a twisted electric cord. There was no natural light. A shower, wash basin and Islamic toilet were also provided, notwithstanding the absence of any privacy provisions.

A wooden table, two wooden chairs, microwave and small freezer filled with frozen meals completed the list of personal comfort items. There was no cutlery. One metal cup hung over the wash basin.

The heavy metal door had no door handle on the inside and the peephole was for use by those in the corridor to see in.

Assuming the room would be bugged with a listening device, they sat silently, each committing to memory every detail of the trip from the airport.

After the locking devices in the limousine had been activated, it had been another four, maybe five kilometres before Rasual turned into the entrance of a well-fortified industrial storage complex backing onto the airport. Not that its fortification was out of place, all such complexes in Sumunhur were well fortified. Being situated on the edge of the Sumunhur area, the closest neighbouring unit was over two kilometres away. The limousine stopped immediately in front of the heavy metal gate. Unbeknown to Benecke and Lo, reverse spikes in the driveway activated automatically, blocking any retreat. Two guards in grey uniforms, Benecke guessed to be of Russian appearance, remained seated in the guard house to their left. The guards and Rasual nodded to each other as the sliding gate moved reasonably quickly to the right. It was quite apparent Rasual and his vehicle were well known here.

They drove along the concrete driveway and onto a large pavement area, also concrete, in front of a huge storage shed displaying the sign, U73

Lo estimated the rectangular building covered an area of at least 5 football fields; Benecke said 6. Lo knew better than to argue.

Having driven through the vehicular entrance in the centre of the building, their vehicle stopped in a large central vacant area most probably used primarily for loading and unloading shipping containers.

To their left were hundreds, no, probably thousands of unmarked wooden crates, stacked five rows high in an interlocked formation. Lo guessed each contained five or six assault rifles and accessories. To Lo's amazement, Benecke agreed. Two long workbenches stood in front of the crate stacks, behind which stood two men in Arab dress. With a limited few seconds glance before a guard cradling a Russian AS Val silenced assault rifle opened a back door, it appeared the two workers were testing each rifle, ensuring they were in perfect working order. Lo and Benecke learned later these men were residents from El Basna, and as such, were probably also involved in smuggling out the Yoon family drug shipments.

After retrieving their luggage from the boot of the limousine and it being inspected by one of the guards, with bags in hand, Lo and Benecke were marched towards the far right corner of the building. Hidden by a small mechanical workshop and an array of trucks, trailers, passenger vehicles, forklifts of varying sizes and an assortment of smaller implements and work tools, it wasn't until they had almost reached the end of the building before a flight of steep concrete steps leading downwards came into view.

At the bottom of the steps, to the right, a poorly lit underground corridor ran across the building. There were four numbered doors. One and three on the left; two and four on the right. The corridor came to an abrupt end at an unnumbered fifth door. Unlike the others, it was fitted with a substantial combination security lock and a peephole looking in.

Lo and Benecke spent the next few hours looking for any listening devices and attempting to develop a plan of escape. They found no listening device and the best escape plan they could come up with was to sit and wait and play it by ear.

There being no TV, radio or reading material, and having accepted a ke sera sera philosophy, they laid on the bed for another hour. It was Benecke who broke the silence.

"You know, Lo, there is *one* thing we could do."

"Oh?" His one word reply actually asking, *"and what would that be?"*

She rolled towards him, stared directly into his eyes and slightly, ever so slightly, raised her eye brows.

"Oh?" He repeated. A one and a half second moment of awkward silence crawled by until brought forth by a moment of awakening, a slow drawn out, "Oh" of understanding filled the void.

And why not? The UNIIA work environment presented little opportunity to meet others. Everyone has needs, and their 'friends with benefits' arrangement had served them well for several months now. Besides, who knew what the future had in store for them. Or indeed, if they had a future.

By agreement, Lo showered first, using toiletries and a towel from his luggage.

With his second brain now well in charge, a shudder of excitement surged through him as Benecke's still wet, naked body pushed hard against his.

***

To say Harrigan was disappointed with the most likely outcome of this investigation would be an understatement. It would be the first unsolved case of his career. In fact, disappointed isn't quite right; *pissed off* is much closer to the truth.

Eian Jones had left the Alfresco Royal some ten minutes earlier, leaving Harrigan at somewhat at a loss with nothing to do but wait to hear from Gianni. Waiting had never been one of his stronger suits. So, he did what any man of action would do in his place. He walked to the Strand and hailed a cab.

"Ali's please driver. The one in Abbey Towers, Millbank Road."

With two Ballantine's under his belt, and midday approaching, Harrigan opened the menu. He hadn't decided between the garlic butter baked salmon or the Filet Mignon when his mobile telephone vibrated in his pocket.

"Harrigan... Gianni? ... You have? ... Can you rescue them?... No, of course, not on the telephone... I'm at Ali's... no, the one in Abbey Towers, Millbank Road... yes, I'm a known customer... it's a long story... okay, just call me when you're in the lobby. You want me to order you something for lunch?... Baked salmon or steak?... Okay."

The white coated Mahindra, placed the third Ballantine's on the clear glass coaster.

"Are you ready to order, Chief Inspector?"

"Yes, thanks, Mahindra. I'll have the Garlic butter baked salmon and Filet Mignon, medium. I'm waiting for a guest, so, make it for about an hour?"

"Of course, Chief Inspector."

He raised his glass. "This one I'm going to enjoy."

***

With The usual commentary of adulation for Ali's, the questioning of how Harrigan became the number one known customer, and recognition of Harrigan's many unique attributes completed, Ricardo Gianni came to the point of his visit. Harrigan listened intently to Gianni's account of Benecke and Lo's movements in Urbadistan, disposing of the hyperbole and mentally recording only the basics. Gianni's people at the airport had seen Benecke and Lo enter Rasul's Limousine; after leaving the airport they turned onto the El Basna highway and towards the hotel; their man at the fuel stop saw the limousine drive by and it didn't arrive at El Basna. The only turnoff between the fuel station and El Basna leads to the rear of the airport and Unit 73. Rasul's limousine is known to visit that unit regularly. "We're reasonably confident your team is being held there," he concluded.

"Who owns the unit?" Harrigan asked, probably a little too eagerly.

"We don't know. As you would imagine, Sumunhur storage facility ownership is a well-guarded secret. But we do know containers from the Al-Yousaf organisation are delivered there, so it's a safe bet it's a distribution centre for the assault rifles."

"I have to say, you seem remarkably relaxed about all this."

Gianni sipped his bourbon on ice. "We all use Urbadistan for our own dirty little secrets. My country, your country, east and west, everyone. Of course, we go through the motions, pretending to spy and acting aghast behind closed doors. It's all part of the game. It's how the system works."

Harrigan shook his head, gave a slight *'hmmph'* and drained his glass. "So, what's the plan? How do we get Benecke and Lo back?"

"Before we get to that, we need to talk about what it is you're not telling me."

Their conversation was interrupted while Mahindra renewed their drinks. It was agreed lunch would be served in ten minutes.

Under normal circumstances, Harrigan's response to Gianni would've been along the lines of *'Something I'm not telling you? I'm not sure what you mean.'* Of course, Gianni would've known it was bullshit, and the meaningless word games would've begun, and in the end achieve nothing. This was no time for those particular games. And besides, he needed the C.I.A. man and whether it was because of his New York or Italian accent or maybe a little of both, he rather liked him; for a spy that is. But on the other hand, he couldn't tell him the UK government was supplying weapons to a Russian mobster for future favours. Even Harrigan drew the line at treason.

Gianni sat back silently, watching the activity on the Thames and sipping his bourbon. He understood Harrigan's dilemma; he'd been there himself. There are things you can say and things you can't. He had no doubt Harrigan would figure it out.

Harrigan held his glass in both hands and stared into it as if searching for an answer. "I understand why you'd think I might not have been totally honest with you, but there's little more I could add to what I've already said. But now that you ask…" He removed his left hand from the glass, swivelled his Ballantine's slightly and took a large sip. "Tell me, that Unit 73, I assume it's a large building?"

"Very."

"And if rifles *were* being held back from the shipments, it'd be an ideal place to store them?"

"I would say so."

"So how about this. Suppose, and this is just a theory, suppose the Kajmanistan Rebels are using a sufficient amount of weapons so as not to raise any suspicions by the UK Government, and are actually storing weapons for a third party to assist the Arab nations if things don't go their way in the growing conflict with your lot and your allies."

"Third party?" Gianni could see where this was going and was willing to play along. "Do you have any such third party in mind?"

"Not off hand." He stared thoughtfully at the ceiling, eventually returning his gaze towards Gianni. He gave a slight shrug of his shoulders. "Russia, maybe?"

"Why would the USSR want UK weapons? They have plenty of their own."

"I didn't say the USSR. The USSR is about to collapse and it's really no secret the Russian mobsters have no intention of lessening their grip over the economies of Russia or the current satellite states. To achieve this, enforcement will undoubtably be a major component and that will take weapons. But there's no way creating a stockpile of *Russian* made weapons could be kept a secret. They couldn't risk showing their hand."

"Hmmm, interesting." Gianni took a sip of bourbon and returned it to the table. "We know your government is supplying weapons to the Kajmanistan Rebels to ensure oil supply from the middle east. But what *you're* suggesting, is the Rebels, unbeknown to the UK suppliers, could be using most of those weapons to shore up support from whomever will control the economy of a new free market Russia and post-Communist states?"

"Why not? And what better place to store them than Urbadistan?" Not for one moment, did Harrigan believe Gianni had been fooled or even doubted he'd just taken the actual situation, and basically swapped around the roles of the UK Government and the Rebels. He'd been around long enough to recognize purposeful misdirection when it was offered. But as it solved any potential relationship problems between their governments, Harrigan had no doubt Gianni would go along with it.

And once again, he was right.

You cunning bastard. Gianni kept his thoughts to himself.

Any further discussion was put on hold while Mahindra and two other white coated attendants served their meals.

Aware of Harrigan's dislike for what he'd often described as, *"that sissy Bon Appetite thing"*, Mahindra bowed slightly and left as quietly as he'd arrived.

With neither men proponents of small talk, their meal was taken in silence.

Gianni carefully placed his cutlery together on the empty plate and was the first to speak. "That was the best Filet Mignon I've ever had," he announced.

Harrigan had always found a comment on the quality of the meal when dining in a place of Ali's reputation to be annoyingly superfluous. The only thing worse was the inevitable follow up question about the other person's meal. Gianni didn't disappoint.

"How was the salmon?"

"You haven't answered my question yet," Harrigan said, ignoring the salmon question. He drained his coffee and rose from the private dining table.

"About a plan to rescue Benecke and Lo?"

"That's the one."

They relaxed once again in the green leather armchairs. Gianni picked up the replenished bourbon tumbler waiting patiently on the side table.

"Go on then," Harrigan urged.

It was Gianni's turn to swivel the liquid and stare into his glass. "I have a plan. Well, the bones of one anyway." He raised the glass to his mouth, stopped, and returned the bourbon to the table. "Urbadistan being Urbadistan, we're not able to mount a showy frontal attack, going in with guns blazing, it requires something much more devious."

"I have no problems with devious."

"Good. And if my plan works, you, me and our governments will be able to put this whole thing behind us."

"Just to make it clear, Gianni, I don't give a monkey's fuck about your government, the UK government, any bloody body's government. All I want is Benecke and Lo's safe return so I can wrap up the Brewer Lane case and get the hell out of here."

"Yeah, I know. But I think you might enjoy this. Grab your Ballantine's, sit back, and I'll explain."

***

The private meeting room at King Charles St, Whitehall, Westminster, was as grandiose as one would expect it to be for a senior office holder of the UK Government. The mahogany furniture created by master craftsmen and high backed green leather chairs, all of unnecessary dimensions, stood with an air of undeniable arrogance. The heavy maroon drapes and hand carved picture frames with gold leaf trim surrounding portraits of dignitaries of yesteryear mocked the sweat of the everyday man and woman. Admiral Sir Jason Collins sat across from a granite faced, perfectly groomed man of advancing years.

"My God, Collins, you were given one simple task. Weapons for oil. And what was the only condition? Secrecy! No-one was to know. Especially our American allies. And what have you delivered? You've not only allowed those meddlesome U.N.I.I.A. people to get involved, you also have the C.I.A. sniffing around!"

"Supplying thousands of assault rifles to a Russian mobster under the table is no simple task, Sir Reginald. And to be fair, until Harrigan was given the Brewer Lane investigation we had it all in hand."

"Do you realise how pathetic that sounds? One man! Your excuse is one man is smarter than the whole of MI6?

"No ordinary man. He doesn't play by the rules. He—"

"Doesn't play by the rules!? Good Lord man, you're head of MI6, and you're telling me you don't know how to defeat a man who doesn't play by the rules!?" He paused, his pacemaker appreciative of the rest. Several moments later he continued, the calmness in his voice more threatening than his previous tone. "You have forty eight hours. If you haven't resolved this situation successfully by then, I'll have no option but to go to number 10. The PM will have to be informed."

Collins opened his mouth to object but was denied the opportunity.

"Forty eight hours. Good-bye, Admiral."

Jason Collins had difficulty holding his head high as he walked along King Charles Street towards the Triple Arch Bridge. Being a high ranking naval officer and a Knight of the Realm, he didn't take kindly to being spoken to in such a disrespectful manner. But the PM giveth position, and the PM taketh away. Unfortunately, accepting being treated as an underling by the PM's senior representative is all part of the giveth and taketh process. But even more galling is the telephone call he must now make.

"Chief Inspector Harrigan?... something's come up and we need to talk, urgently... no of course, you're correct; *I* need to talk... the Seamed Stocking bar in your hotel? Yes. that'd be fine. Shall we say two thirty?... *tomorrow!?* I said, I need to talk with you, *urgently*!... Well maybe you should care. Need I remind you if you don't sign off on the Brewer Lane case by tomorrow, one of your people will die... you'll call me tomorrow!?... hello?... hello!?"

***

Four hours after Gianni and Harrigan's luncheon meeting at Ali's, Boris Akmatbayev entered the top floor suite of Moscow's Intourist Hotel to attend a hastily gathered summit meeting of the six top leaders of the notorious 'vory v zakone'.

"Okay. Vat's so important we need urgent meeting?" Akmatbayev took up position at the end of the medium sized rectangular table, completing the sextet.

"Thank you for coming, Boris." There was no hint of welcome in the voice of seventy eight year old Aleksandr Mogilevich, recognised as the top mobster in all the USSR. A godfather like figure some would say. Grossly obese, often described as 'a giant of a man', he sat at the other end of the table facing Akmatbayev. His face was heavily tanned. The naturally down turned ends of his lips, coupled with thick black eyebrows covering eyes as cold as his own soul, struck fear into the hearts of all who knew him. There were a few exceptions, of course, and Boris Akmatbayev was one such exception.

"So, what's so important?" Akmatbayev repeated the question.

"For many months, we have been planning the distribution of territories after Soviet dissolution. We all thought, apart from some tidying up around edges, we were all agreed. Yes?"

Akmatbayev nodded.

"Unfortunately, it has been brought to our attention, one of us is planning to take over much more territory than was agreed."

Fearing the worst, Akmatbayev took his large biro from his inside pocket and pressed the top button twice. He must now play for time until his team arrived. "That's interesting, but it doesn't answer the question of why I was summoned so urgently. If what you say is true, why not just deal with the guilty person?" There was increased intensity in his actions as he pressed the button a second time.

"It gladdens my heart to know you see it that way." Mogilevich produced a PSS pistol from beneath the table and aimed it at Akmatbayev's heart.

"Wait! Aleksandr, I can explain!"

Mogilevich spoke through a humourless smile. "Do you really think we didn't know about your sneaky pen? Your people won't be coming, they have been—" he paused, "decommissioned."

The colour drained from Akmatbayev's face. As he looked into the soulless eyes, for the first time in his life he felt the fear he'd always considered to be the province of others. It was also the last time in his life he would feel anything. His bloodied body went limp as five bullets tore into his heart.

Mogilevich pocketed the pistol and telephoned his clean up team waiting in the apartment below.

He then dialled a second number. "Hello? Is done. Your people vill be released tomorrow." He didn't wait for a reply.

In absolute silence, the five men slowly raised their substantial bodies from the table and left the hotel.

***

Lo swung his legs over the edge of the bed, picked up his underpants from the floor and slid them on. He retrieved his watch from the wooden table in the centre of the room. Eleven o'clock; Urbadistan time. Rising an hour before midday was a new experience for them both. But, with literally nothing else to do, together with a few hours of more than strenuous activities during the night, probably offered sufficient justification.

"What time would that be in London?" Lo asked.

"Not sure. Somewhere around six a.m.?"

When isolated from the rest of the world, topics of meaningful conversation become very thin, very fast.

And let's face it, being underground, they couldn't even talk about the weather. The elephant in the room topics, why they were kidnapped, who was behind it and prospects for their future had been thrashed to death yesterday. It would've been easy to continue that conversation this morning, but it had done nothing to boost morale, and they'd individually decided it best be left alone. Secretly however, the feeling of powerlessness, even impotence to effect a change in their situation was both emotionally and mentally crippling.

Benecke decided to take a shower. Lo sat at the wooden table, nursing a metal mug of water.

If only they had known what the next few hours would bring.

Chapter Eighteen

As Rasual's limousine turned into the driveway, the two gate guards at Unit 73 looked at the clock on the wall. 11.30 a.m. They turned to each and frowned; they hadn't been expecting him.

Rasul played his role of innocence well after bringing his limousine to a stop mere inches from the heavy steel security gate. Being an unscheduled visit, one of the guards left the guard house and walked towards the driver's door on the left of the vehicle. They say familiarity breeds contempt and the Russian AS Val silent assault rifle slung carelessly over the guard's shoulder seemed to prove that point. So much so, as he leaned in to speak to Rasul, he failed to notice the right side rear door open and the sudden appearance of a grey uniformed man. Not until it was too late that is.

"Don't make sudden moves." The man looking over his own AS Val pointing at the guard's head and speaking in fluent Russian, was deterrent enough for the guard not to tempt fate. He stood frozen; both hands remaining on the turret. "Now, tell your partner in guardhouse not to do anything foolish; put his hands on head and stand slowly. If there is *hint* he is not comply with request, my comrade in rear of vehicle will blow hole in him size of Siberia. And that will happen just seconds before *your* brains are cast to wind."

At the sound of the guard's raised voice, his partner looked up from the desk and instinctively reached for his weapon. But the fear and desperation in the words of warning allowed common sense to prevail. His hands went to his head and he rose slowly.

With hands still raised, the guard at the vehicle marched at gun point into the guardhouse. The eyes of the grey uniformed man in the rear of the vehicle aiming at the guardhouse, followed their progress through the small building's large window, his excited trigger finger waiting impatiently for the call to action. Rasul sat motionless with his hands on the steering wheel. The mostly unblinking stare of the vehicle's third occupant holding his assault rifle aimed at Rasul's back through the cabin partition, remained fixed on Rasul. It would be fair to say it was more this man's rifle than Rasul's thespian prowess that contributed to his stella performance. Both guards, now with hands on heads, were marched to the far end of the building. Once standing hard against and facing the wall, the As Val kicked twice and both men fell to the floor. The man from the vehicle then took his position at the security desk. He closed the naked model magazine, moved it to one side and pressed a large red button. The gates began to open.

As he'd done the previous day, Rasul drove along the concrete driveway and stopped the vehicle in the centre of the building. He felt a slight rock as the man in the rear alighted and appeared at the driver's window.

"Give keys."

Rasul obeyed quickly.

"You wait. You move, I shoot." He turned from the window and walked to the two local men working at the benches on the left.

"You go home now. No come back. Job over. Your money in bank."

The two local men ceased what they were doing, bowed slightly and hurried to the private vehicle parked at the far end of the building. They'd lived in Urbadistan their entire lives and had worked for many owners of units in Sumunhur over the years. Unit owners were reluctant to employ outside labour but these two men were in demand. They had a code. Work hard; see nothing; hear nothing; say nothing. It should come as no surprise they were known around the area simply as, *'The Monkeys'*.

With the barrel end nudging him in the back, Rasul led the way down the concrete stairs. They stopped at door Number 1.

"You knock."

Rasul knocked.

The door was opened by a none too steady, unshaven man, dressed only in a singlet and trunk style underpants.

"Rasul? Vat you vant?"

Not the most memorable last words, but last words all the same. The As Val coughed and 'singlet man' fell to the floor. His roommate, sitting at the table, stood quickly. That was unfortunate in two ways. Firstly, he should've been on duty on the main floor, but months of boredom had led to his breaks becoming longer and longer and finally, well, he just should not have been there. And the second unfortunate thing? A standing target is easier to hit than one crouched over a table.

The grey uniformed man looked at Rasul. "You close door."

After dragging the first body further inside the room, Rasul pulled the door closed.

With the exception there being only one person per room, the killing process was repeated at doors 2, and 3. The sound of the opening door number 4 behind him, followed by a slightly slurred but still clearly Russian demand didn't surprise the man with the weapon.

"What's fucking noise out here?" A man holding a half full vodka glass stepped into the corridor. It'll never be known whether or not he'd realised the answer to his question before the three bullets, perfectly grouped, struck his chest. Rasul struggled with the dead weight as he moved the body from the corridor to the room. Exhausted, he dropped his burden just far enough into the room to allow the closure of the door. He took several breaths before standing slowly and preparing to leave. Sad to say, Rasul didn't get a chance to say any last words; memorable or not. The As Val coughed one more time. The man shouldered his weapon, closed the door behind him, and turned to face the door with no number. He reached for the electronic lock keypad.

Lo and Benecke had heard noises in the corridor, but having no means of seeking out the truth and being near midday they assumed it was a staff change of shift. Benecke did say the coughing noise sounded more like a silenced rifle than someone needing a cough drop. Lo shrugged off the comment and went to the sink to refill the metal cup. To describe their mood as relaxed wouldn't be quite correct. Sure, there was an air of relaxation about it, but it was more patient resignation to their situation than anything else. But whatever it was, it all changed when they heard the beeping from the keypad. As professional as they were, the sound was so unexpected, it took a few seconds for them to react. Not that they could do much. They had no weapons and were not close enough to mount a challenge to whoever was opening the door. Benecke stood from the table and Lo threw the cup into the sink, actions that were so lame, they swore it was a secret they'd take to the grave. Which, for all they knew could be any minute now.

The door swung open, revealing a large, grey uniformed man standing astride in the doorway nursing an evil looking AS Val rifle. Much to the captives' relief, the barrel was pointing to the ground.

"Get your things. You go now."

Questions including, *'who are you?'*, *'why are we here?'* and *'why were we kidnapped?'*, each one as desperate as the others to be asked, sprang into their minds. But Benecke and Lo were having none of it. It took them less than sixty seconds to sweep their few personal belongings back into their cases and close the zips.

The man stood to one side and gestured with his weapon for them to enter the corridor. As grateful as they were to be leaving, neither could dismiss the thought that maybe they were about to be shot in the back as escapees. But at the last minute, the man turned and led the way.

Once near Rasul's limousine, the man handed the car keys to Lo. "You take car. Drive to back of service station on highway near end of road. You vill be driven to airport from there." He stood back from the vehicle.

They threw their bags into the rear passenger cabin. Benecke took the keys from Lo and opened the driver's door. She turned to the man. "What about the guards on the front gate?"

He ignored the question. "You go now. Hurry, or might miss plane."

The vehicle lurched forward, sped away, and, much to Benecke's relief, through the opened security gates. They turned towards the El Basna Highway.

Given the events of the last forty eight hours, it would be reasonable to assume the conversation in the car would be fast, furious and mostly both talking over each other. But whether it was the sheer relief of escape or fearful apprehension of what might lay ahead, probably a little of each, not one word passed between them. It wasn't until Benecke stopped the limousine behind the service station was the silence broken.

"So, what happens now?" Lo asked, immediately realizing the ridiculousness of the question.

"How the hell would I know!" Benecke snapped. Sure, it was a stupid question, but Lo was somewhat taken aback by the viciousness in her voice. And apparently, he wasn't the only one. There was a slight delay before she quickly turned her head towards him and mouthed a silent, "*sorry*".

His soft smile and slow affectionate blink told her everything was okay.

A black Chevrolet Suburban turned the corner at the end of the service station and stopped behind them. A tall, well-built black bearded male walked towards them. He wore a western style black suit, white shirt, black tie and traditional Arabian Kaffiyeh headdress.

Benecke and Lo were already standing outside their vehicle when he reached them. The tone of urgency failed to diminish the richness of his deep, educated voice. "Bring your bags and I'll fill you in on the way to the airport."

Benecke soon came to the conclusion that his idea of *'fill you in'* greatly varied from hers. He introduced himself as Idris. Once at the airport, he would take them through the V.I.P. entrance used only for persons of importance wishing to remain anonymous. Of course, he'd added, this anonymity comes at a hefty price. After turning onto the El Basra highway, he wasted no time in establishing their relationship. He didn't know, and didn't want to know, who they were, who they worked for or why they were visiting Urbadistan. Once inside the airport grounds, he will take them to a waiting chartered plane. And that was the total of the 'filling in' process. No surname; no mention of who he worked for; who owned or who chartered the plane, or, which, in the scheme of things was probably of most interest to them, the flight destination.

This information was received once seated in the Beechworth 1900. The tube-like design of the aircraft had the feeling of being inside a giant cigar tube. The two rows of single seats, one either side of the aisle, did nothing to ease the claustrophobic atmosphere. Although being the only passengers on the nineteen seat aircraft, they were shown to their seats in row five.

Seyyal, the flight attendant, continued the anonymity theme throughout the entire journey giving basic details only. All she knew of their travel arrangements was this flight will terminate in the Iranian city of Tabriz in approximately three hours. She handed each a sealed envelope, in which were details of the rest of their journey and all necessary documentation. The envelopes were not to be opened until they had left this aircraft. After serving them coffee and sandwiches, she returned to the left side front seat.

Benecke and Lo gave each other an almost comical *'so far so good'* shrug.

Lo looked at his watch and calculated a rough estimate of London time. 11 a.m.

***

Harrigan sat at his balcony table at the Medwin's Royal Garter International hotel, nursing the mug of stronger than usual coffee. He looked at his watch. Ten forty-five; perilously close to the midday deadline to tell Collins if or not he would sign off the Brewer Lane case. It wasn't in his nature to give into blackmailers, but there was no way he was going to put the lives of his team at risk. In the event Gianni's plan didn't come off, he'd spent the morning preparing a draft of his report. He sipped the coffee and allowed his mind to drift back to yesterday's luncheon at Ali's.

After listening to Gianni's, outrageous, but brilliant rescue plan, Harrigan had intended to return to his hotel room and wait for Gianni to contact him and report, one way or the other. The basis of the plan was simple. Because of Akmatbayev's paranoid secrecy regarding his stockpiling of weapons, Gianni was convinced it wasn't only the Kremlin he was trying to fool; his main target was his Russian mafia colleagues. "He sees the dissolution as his opportunity to oust Mogilevich and move into the top job."

Harrigan had agreed.

Gianni then laid out his plan. "We do a deal with Mogilevich. In exchange for his people rescuing Benecke and Lo, we will supply him the identity of who is planning to overthrow him. A person who is currently building a large arsenal of weapons. Once the rescue has been successfully completed, our people will move in, clean up whatever mess is left behind and remove and destroy the weapons. Mogilevich keeps his position, we disappear the weapons, and you conclude Akmatbayev was responsible for the Brewer Lane killings; I doubt he'll still be around to disagree. And maybe most important of all, diplomatic ties between our governments remain intact."

The two men had shaken hands and Gianni left to set the wheels in motion. About to join Gianni in the lift, Harrigan, with little else to do but wait for a progress report, changed his mind and stayed for another liquid refreshment.

At eleven fifteen that evening, Ali had arranged for Harrigan to get back safely to his hotel.

With perfect timing, the sound of his mobile telephone broke into his thoughts. He grabbed at the 'phone, almost dropping it in haste. "Gianni?...they have?... they are?...thank the good bloody Lord for that. What time will they get to Heathrow?...they're on their way to Tabriz, overnight, and arrive on Turkish Airlines at one tomorrow?...I owe you one. I'll call Collins and arrange to meet…you would? I don't see why not. Downstairs in the Seamed Stocking bar at midday suit you?…good, see you then. And, Gianni, thanks again."

Admiral Sir Jason Collins arrived at the Seamed Stocking Bar at exactly twelve noon. He hadn't had the best of mornings. He'd had little sleep, the wasted hours going by before Sir Reginald goes to the PM weighing heavily on his mind. And his wife was still staying at the Cornelia Refugium, refusing to take his calls. He'd been sitting quietly, not wallowing in self-pity but certainly mulling over the disintegration of his life when Godfrey Windsor had rung seeking Harrigan's answer. After learning Harrigan had not yet contacted Collins, Windsor assured him that even though he'd been unable to contact Akmatbayev, nothing had changed. Harrigan signs off on the Brewer Lane case or one of the hostages dies. *"And you'd better remind him, time is running out."* And then, to top it all off, David Littlewood had called, most displeased at the cancellation of all future weapons orders and demanding he purchase those already manufactured. He stood silhouetted in the doorway of the Seamed Stocking for a full fifteen seconds before his eyes adjusted to the darkened room and he was able to see Harrigan in the far corner.

"Admiral, thank you for coming. This is—"

"Ricardo Gianni, the C.I.A. man." Collins finished Harrigan's sentence; he didn't acknowledge Gianni. "What's he doing here? Our business is private."

"Why don't you sit down and I'll order a round of drinks." Harrigan was being as polite as he knew how.

"I didn't come here to socialize, Chief Inspector. Give me your yes or no answer and I'll be leaving." Not knowing what Harrigan might've already told Gianni about the kidnapping ultimatum, he wasn't about to offer any information he didn't have to. He leaned towards Harrigan, his voice almost inaudible. "I should tell you, I received a telephone call from the kidnapper this morning and was told to strongly impress upon you there's little time left."

"Sit down, Admiral, we have all the time in the world. Believe me, there are a few things you need to hear."

Collins remained standing.

"Suit yourself," Harrigan continued. "Maybe it *would* be better to wait until Benecke and Lo get back tomorrow and we can talk then." He signalled the waiter. "Thanks for coming, Admiral, I'll let you know what time tomorrow we'll—" There was no need to finish his statement; Collins pulled out the heavy padded chair and sat at the table.

"I'll have a Gin and Tonic".

After ordering doubles all 'round, Harrigan proceeded to detail everything he'd told Gianni. Once completed, he handed the floor over to Gianni who explained the escape plan and the current situation. Collins had shown no emotion as he listened, except for a quick glance at Harrigan during the Kajmanistan Rebels betraying the UK Government explanation. And try as he might, he couldn't stop just a smidgen of admiration sneaking through.

He didn't respond immediately, taking time to digest the new information. Harrigan on the other hand, wasn't about to give him any opportunity to come up with any bureaucratic bullshit and complicate matters.

"What that all boils down to, is Benecke and Lo are on their way home, and any potential threat to the UK USA relationship has been averted. Akmatbayev is no longer with us, all weapons destined to assist his cause will be destroyed, and as the company you created to order the weapons doesn't exist, there is no verifiable paper trail. Al Yousaf only knew the delivery destination as did Littlewood." Harrigan paused purposively. "Littlewood *didn't* know any more than that, did he, Admiral?"

"No," Collins lied.

"Good. The oil supply deal you had with Akmatbayev is, to coin a phrase, now obviously dead and buried. It'll be up to you to square it up with your fellow members on the Joint Intelligence Committee."

"And the Brewer Lane investigation?" Collins asked, trying to sound as disinterested as was possible.

"As the Yoon family was attempting to gain a drugs foothold in Akmatbayev's territory, and with the evidence uncovered during the investigation, there will be little difficulty in establishing Akmatbayev as the guilty party."

Collins drained the last of his Gin and Tonic. "Thank you, Chief Inspector, Agent Gianni." He rose from his chair.

"There is still one loose end," Harrigan said.

"Oh?" Collins frowned.

"Godfrey Windsor. He knew about the Russian connection."

There was a smugness in Collins' reply. "Like members of the Joint Intelligence Committee, he's bound by the Official Secrets Act. And besides, he can't say anything without implicating himself. I don't think he's a problem." He gave a slight but meaningful nod of farewell and turned away from the table.

Gianni drank the last of his bourbon and pushed his chair from the table. "I'd best be leaving as well."

"Back to the office?" It was a throw away question.

"Actually, I'm off to Urbadistan. I'm certain there'll be more to the Unit 73 clean up than meets the eye. And then there's the disposal of the weapons."

"Do you know there's another shipment arriving in the next couple of days?"

"Yeah. It's on my list."

"Thanks again for your assistance."

"All part of the job. With the growing turmoil in the middle east, and the almost certain dissolution of the USSR, the maintenance of a good relationship between our two Governments is vital. So, if there's nothing else…?

"There is one thing. I'd like to have a few minutes with Connie West if that's possible."

"That'll be up to her. I'll contact her and give her your number."

Harrigan stood and the two men shook hands. Both had firm grips; but neither tried to dominate. It was a mark of the respect they held for each other.

Chapter Nineteen

Monday 14th May, two days after Benecke and Lo had returned to London. Aware of Harrigan's nigh on paranoia of electronic listening devices, they were a little surprised to learn the final debriefing meeting was to be held at Eian Jones' office at Parliament Street, Whitehall.

There were five people at the six person, round, highly polished wooden table in the meeting room section of Jones' oversized office. Themselves, Jones and Harrigan and Jones' 2ic and Deputy Chief the Serious National Crime and Intelligence Agency, Godfrey Windsor.

The absence of the usual coffee pot and paraphernalia or even water jug and glasses on the centre of the table, added to the solemn, and more than tense atmosphere.

Jones closed Harrigan's final report on the Brewer Lane investigation.

"You look disappointed," Harrigan said.

"Disappointed? No, I wouldn't say disappointed, I gave you the case because I thought the other members of the J.I.C. could be involved in some operation they knew I wouldn't approve of and were keeping me out of the loop. You proved me right."

"Then what's the problem? You're clearly troubled about something."

Jones answered the question with one of his own. "I understand why you reached the conclusion you have, in your position, I probably would've done the same thing. But, off the record, do you *really* believe Akmatbayev was behind the killings?"

Harrigan sat silently. With all eyes staring at him, waiting, he sighed with indecision.

"Those bastards killed two of my people, Bill." There was genuine pain in Jones' voice.

Harrigan no longer needed time to consider his options; the decision had just been made for him. "We know he became involved during my investigation when the supply of weapons was threatened, but Brewer Lane? No. He had nothing to do with it."

"You seem very certain, Chief Inspector." There was a definite touch of allegation in Godfrey Windsor's comment.

"I am."

Jones picked up the report file and stared at the cover. "That's not what it says in here."

"Reports can say anything, and my report says everything it's supposed to. The Yoon family was making inroads into Akmatbayev's European drug territory. His target at Brewer Lane was Jimmy Qiang Yoon; the others, including Muktar Al-Yousaf, were just to muddy the waters. This is supported by the Dark Knights club killing of the second Yoon brother, Fan, several days later, while sparing Muhammad Abdul-Halim Al-Yousaf who was in the same room. It solved the drug problem while protecting the weapons supply. A man now dead planned the whole thing, so it's case closed and details of the weapons for oil operation never sees the light of day. Job done."

"So, you write a report substantiating the case against Akmatbayev even though you don't think he was responsible?"

"Correct."

"Why don't you think he did it?" Windsor challenged.

"To begin with, it doesn't make sense. If Akmatbayev had wanted to get rid of the Yoon threat, he'd've just have them killed. And if he had, most people would know or at least suspect it was him. Why would he go to all the trouble of setting up a chain of evidence just to prove it? The eye-witnesses in the unit opposite the Sister's Basement planted to point us to the Mercedes; the Mercedes in the name of a worker in the Russian language college which eventually cost two innocent women their lives; the Russian shell casings left at the crime scenes; the mysterious stranger at Friedenberg House smelling strongly of Russian cigarettes. I could go on. It wouldn't happen. And besides, he told me he didn't do it. I believed him. He did say he had planned on killing them, but needed more time to sus out the entire operation."

Harrigan waited for Jones' *"so who do you think was responsible?"* question. It didn't come. He just sat there, silent. A glassy stare in his eyes.

"Eian, you okay?" Harrigan asked.

"What? Oh, sorry, my mind was elsewhere. You carry on, I'm listening."

"I said at the beginning, if we are to solve this, we needed to establish the actual target. Up until yesterday, we hadn't done that."

"What happened yesterday?" Benecke asked.

"I'm coming to that. There were six people at the Sister's table. Connie West. She was playing several ends against the middle; a dangerous game. But the only person with a real motive to want her dead was Littlewood. If she decided to reveal the sexual deviance when she was young he would be ruined. Even imprisoned. But the gunmen paid her little attention when she fell to the floor, so it wasn't her. Sophie was gathering information for Akmatbayev, but she had only just joined the group, so it's highly unlikely it was her. Muhammad Al Yousaf had motive to kill his brother, but these killings were well planned and, to my mind, overly elaborate. I don't think Muhammad would've gone to all that trouble and besides, he didn't have access to all the right circles needed to set it up. There's no doubt Fan Yoon hated his brother, Jimmy, for being promoted over him, and is violent enough to do it. But like Al Yousaf, it's too elaborate and he lacked the contacts. And of course, a short time later he was also shot."

"Which brings us back to Akmatbayev and the Yoon family." Godfrey Windsor pushed his chair back roughly and gave a sigh of exasperation.

"Or Collins," Lo added.

Harrigan nodded. "Ah, yes; Collins. He might've preferred it if the Yoons were out of the way, but mastermind the shootings just to get rid of them? No, his focus has always been about keeping a low profile. He only raised his head *after* the shooting when we were given the case so we wouldn't stumble on to his guns deal with Akmatbayev. The last thing he wanted was a mass killing that endangered the secrecy of his operation."

"You do realise you have just proved it *had* to be Akmatbayev?" Godfrey Windsor asked the question in everyone's minds.

"I think *proved* is a bit of a leap, but yes, I had enough circumstantial evidence to blame a dead Russian gangster and to everyone's relief, write the report and close the case." He waved towards his report lying on the table in front of Jones. "Which I did."

"So, it's case closed?" Windsor asked.

"That's for your boss to decide. He called us in to solve the case and I've given a report which, all things considered, satisfies the brief."

All eyes turned to Jones.

He picked up the brown manilla folder and threw it quite forcibly towards Harrigan. As it flew through the air, the cover opened, scattering the loose pages over the tabletop. "The whole purpose of UNIIA was to create a fiercely independent agency unable to be swayed by political interference. That report destroys everything UNIIA stands for. You asked if I was disappointed. Yes, Chief Inspector, I am disappointed. Disappointed you thought I wanted such a load of politically correct bullshit. Now, do you know who was behind the Brewer Lane massacre or not?"

Harrigan nodded.

"Can you prove it?"

"It's mostly circumstantial, but yes, I have enough."

"Then for Christ's sake, who is it?"

"Yes, Chief Inspector, who?" Windsor repeated Jones' question.

Harrigan's dispassionate stare remained fixed on Windsor. "You."

There were mixed reactions around the table. Surprise from Benecke and Lo, and a steady, *I hope you can back that up* eye shift to Windsor and back to Harrigan from Eian Jones. Windsor's reaction was exactly what Harrigan had expected; no reaction at all.

Following a pause befitting the situation, Harrigan continued. "I first put you in the frame after learning you were blackmailing Collins and Akmatbayev."

That got a reaction. "Annabelle?"

Harrigan nodded. "Yes, a woman scorned, but that couldn't be the motive, like Collins, keeping a low profile only helped your cause. So I pushed you to the back of my mind. Until yesterday. I spoke to Connie West. She didn't tell me anything we didn't already know, but then she said something I'd heard before, and that got me thinking."

He waited for someone to ask what it was she said. No one spoke. He carried on. "She talked about suspicions she'd had about the two confidantes of Al Yousaf. She had no particular reason to doubt they were anything but who they said they were. It was more how easily they were able to fix things, solve any problems that arose, especially with government. She'd even wondered if they might be undercover government people or maybe working for someone with a lot of pull where it matters. She had told Muktar Al Yousaf her thoughts, but he'd just waved them away as female hysteria. Sometime later, I sat on my apartment balcony, thinking of what she'd told me and it was then I remembered Akmatbayev had made a similar, but much more positive comment. He said they were definitely moles and probably from one of the English spooky spook agencies. I remember your agency was mentioned, Eian."

"Yes, I remember that. I was there," Benecke added. "In the back of his limousine." She chose this moment to begin gathering and sorting the scattered papers.

"All very interesting, Chief Inspector, but what has any of this got to do with me?" Windsor appeared composed and even a little disinterested.

"Godfrey, before you carry on and make a complete fool of yourself, there're a few things I should explain. I know the two people in question were Unit 29 agents. I know their role, given to them by Eian, was to infiltrate the Al-Yousaf Yoon group and report back. I know that when Eian was seconded to the UN to help establish and run the UNIIA trial, you were put into the role of Acting Chief of the Serious National Crime and Intelligence Agency. It follows therefore, that any reports from the two agents were sent directly to you."

"I received no reports. Search all my records; search wherever you damn well want. You'll find nothing."

"I have no doubt any reports you received have long been destroyed. But what you did with any reports you received is irrelevant."

Windsor frowned.

"Before Eian left for the UN, the agents were instructed to keep copies of all relevant documents in a secure offsite location. Remember, they were put there because Eian suspected the J.I.C. was up to some kind of skulduggery. It was a safeguard in case something was uncovered while he was away that might prove harmful to the J.I.C., or even the government and the originals destroyed. He had no idea it was going to be you who destroyed them of course."

It was the first time Harrigan saw a crack run down Windsor's granite like expression. Just as well really, there were no copies; it was a lie. And, as the saying goes, one lie leads to another. "And once we retrieve those copies, I have no doubt they will indicate the agents suspected something untoward was happening."

Windsor looked quickly at all those around the table as he began speaking. "If we assume for a moment these reports did exist, and I'm not saying they did, a report stating they suspected something untoward was happening is hardly a motive for someone to kill them. Especially me. If the Russian connection was uncovered, it would've been Jason Collins for the high jump, not me. And I doubt Akmatbayev would've survived once his buddies discovered what he was up to. You're fishing Chief Inspector. You have nothing." He went to rise but the ever alert Lo was quickly behind him, his hands on his shoulders, forcing him back into the chair. Lo remained standing.

"I have the blackmail," Harrigan said softly.

"Do you? What, based on the words of and adulterous wife and her *'dealing with the rebels and the Russians'* husband? Good luck with that."

"And the kidnapping of Benecke and Lo, demanding I shut down the Brewer Lane case for their safe return."

"You're accusing me of that too!?"

"Of course. The morning after Akmatbayev was killed, Collins said the kidnapper had rung him with a message to pass on to me. So, with Collins and Akmatbayev out of the kidnapping picture, you're the only one left. You couldn't allow the agents to dig any further. If they discovered the Kajmanistan Rebels and Russian connection, it's odds on they would also uncover your blackmailing Collins and Akmatbayev. The natural progression from there would be you also knew where the weapons were going and didn't report it. Your career would be over, the coveted position of permanent chief of the agency a distant memory followed by a lengthy period of incarceration. You couldn't allow that to happen. Motive aplenty." Windsor's defiant expression clearly relayed the message he still hadn't been pushed over the edge. Harrigan could almost see the cogs turning in Windsor's brain, weighing up the chances of being found guilty and what options he had to make it all go away. Maybe one last push would do it. "The problem with such an elaborate plan, is the number of other people involved and no matter how careful you've been, someone will identify you. The two eye-witnesses posing as journalists in the unit opposite the Sister's, planted by you to lead us to the Mercedes, their fingerprints will be in the apartment. Jimmy Duff, the worker at the breaker's yard in Scotland described the man who brought the Mercedes in for crushing said he'd recognize the man again. And you certainly match his description. The setting up of the vehicle's MOT in Natalya's name, not easy and probably a favour called in? Not to mention the copies of the reports, Connie West and the vengeful and willing Annabelle's testimonies. And of course, Collins will be only too pleased to throw you under the bus, including, as I've said before, the kidnapping." He paused briefly. "Do I need to go on?"

Windsor sighed and shook his head. "No, there's no need. And you're correct, the plan was overly elaborate, but it had to be. To succeed, the identity of the *actual* target had to be kept hidden, and a suspect created to lead you to the *wrong* target." He nodded towards Harrigan's report. "And it almost worked." He took a heavy breath. "You know, Chief Inspector, you should consider joining the UK intelligence community, they could use someone of your ability." He gave a slight, unexpected smile. "It's funny in a way, that if you had been employed by UK Intelligence, you would've known, despite all your hard work, a person with knowledge capable of bringing down a government, knowledge I have, irrespective of the wrong-doing will never see the inside of a prison. All evidence will be expunged, or even better still, filed away in some dusty archive never to be seen again. All witnesses and investigators will not dare risk the harsh penalties of the Official Secrets Act. And like it or not, I will be promoted to a cushy little number in a country of my choice." He turned, looking over his shoulder. "You can return to your seat, Agent Lo, I'll be leaving now."

Eian Jones stood from the table. "Wait where you are, Agent Lo." He walked the few meters to his desk and pressed a button on his interoffice telephone instrument. "Do you have enough, Joan?" He asked.

The door leading to the outer office opened. "Plenty, thanks Eian." Director General of the National Security Intelligence Agency, Dame Joan Hamilton-Westbrook, looked over her left shoulder and spoke to the two well-groomed men behind her. "Alright, gentlemen. He's all yours."

Godfrey Windsor's reaction to being handcuffed and marched unceremoniously towards the door was more one of defiance than protest. Unfortunately, for him, his threats including *"I know where the skeletons are,"* and, *"you'll all live to regret this by the time I've finished"*, fell mostly on deaf ears.

With the door closed once again, Eian Jones was the first to speak. "You know he's right, Joan, he does know where the skeletons are, and if he gets the opportunity to speak—"

Joan's interruption came by way of a kind but superior laugh. She walked over to him and patted his cheek. "You know Eian, sometimes you say the sweetest things." She turned and began to walk towards the door. "Don't worry about Windsor, I know my job."

"What about Collins?" Harrigan more demanded than asked.

She broke her journey and stopped in front of, and much closer to him than was necessary. "Now, now, Chief Inspector, don't be greedy." She leaned a little closer and lowered her voice. "Of course, if you want to discuss the matter further, you have my number."

With the sight of the overly accentuated swing of Dame Joan's shapely rear now blocked by the closed door, Harrigan and Jones smiled at each other. Harrigan spoke first.

"Did you really have to throw the file that hard? The bloody pages went everywhere."

"It had to look authentic."

It was Lo and Benecke's turn to look at each other.

***

Two days after Windsor's arrest, Harrigan sat on his hotel balcony, staring at but not seeing, the sweeping London vista. The morning newspaper delivered to his room each morning, lay open at an article carried in every major newspaper. *"Russian mobster behind the Massacre at Brewer Lane"* the headline shouted. The article went on to explain it was the result of an illicit drug feud between the Yoon family and Russian mobster, Boris Akmatbayev, followed by a rehash of the events of the night. Rebecca Lane, the journalist responsible for the article in his paper, had attempted to intensify her article by questioning how a Russian mobster could be allowed to enter the UK in a diplomatic role. Like that was going to be allowed to go anywhere.

Although part of the ruse to trap Windsor, Jones' comment to Harrigan about the purpose of UNIIA being to investigate and report free from political pressure and irrespective of who might get hurt had hit home. Let's face it, it was really the only reason he and Jones had become involved in the first place. He picked up the paper and without reading it again, simply looked at the article for around twenty seconds before closing the paper and tossing it carelessly onto the table.

Satisfied he had not allowed the integrity of UNIIA to be compromised, he picked up his mobile telephone and dialled an international number.

Nelson Whitlock, UN Under Secretary for the Office of International Investigation and Harrigan's boss, looked at the clock beside his bed. He picked up his mobile telephone. "Hello?...Harrigan? Do you know what time it is here in New York?... of course you don't care... yes I've seen your report, but please, please, don't tell me you rang me at 5 am just to ask me that...good. But before you do tell me why you called, I'm glad you did. I was going to contact you today. There's something I need to tell you. Wait while I get out of bed." He pulled his dressing gown closed tightly as he lowered himself into the chair in his home office. "Hello? You still there?...I had a visit from a senior advisor of the Security Council yesterday. The council has received a communique from the UK Government advising they no longer support the UNIIA trial. I don't know what hornet's nest you disturbed over there, but they have decided the

UNIIA concept, while developed with all good intent, has the ability to seriously compromise National Security of a participating Nation…what does that mean? It means the continuation of the trial will be put to an emergency meeting of the council, probably in a couple of weeks, and a vote regarding its continuance will be taken…I agree, it only takes one major nation to withdraw support and the whole thing will collapse…there's very little you can do at the moment. You're all still on the payroll. The hotel and expenses are all covered so take a break and maybe consider your options for the future. Just in case…no, unfortunately I think you're right. I'll leave you to talk to Benecke and Lo?… thanks. I'll contact you when I know more. And Bill, I'm sorry…now, what did you want to say to me?… it doesn't? Okay then, I'll be in touch."

Epilogue

As predicted, the UNIIA trial was cancelled three weeks later. At Whitlock's insistence, as a condition of their termination and in appreciation of their service, Benecke, Lo and Harrigan were granted twelve month's salary in lieu.

Immediately after learning of the possible cancellation of the UNIIA trial, Benecke spoke to her people at the FBI. It was agreed that should the cancellation proceed, they were more than willing to take their star agent off unpaid leave and reinstate her to her previous position as Senior Special Agent. She had one condition. Lo was to come to USA with her and be recruited into the FBI. He wasn't a USA citizen and had no visas, but that wouldn't be a problem. The FBI had their ways to overcome such incidentals.

Connie West had told Harrigan she was aware just how untouchable a person of David Littlewood's standing is and has closed the book on the entire episode. It was time to start a new chapter in her life. Not being burdened with Connie West's newly found forgive and forget attitude, Harrigan visited David Littlewood. Under threat of being exposed by Harrigan, Littlewood agreed an amount of £2Million for Connie West would be forwarded to Ricardo Gianni to be passed on to Connie. Littlewood was also left in no doubt as to the consequences if he ever had, or attempted to have, contact with West again.

Eian Jones arranged a meeting with Harrigan at the Alfresco Royal coffee café. He confessed he'd lied about the success of his brain surgery, and had only returned to work to investigate his suspicions about the J.I.C. The shootings at Brewer Lane and his team being in London and available was too good an opportunity to let pass. He told Harrigan if he wanted to take over as Chief of the Serious National Crime and Intelligence Agency, he could arrange it. Harrigan thanked his friend but wasn't interested. Eian Jones passed away eight days later.

The news Harrigan might soon be available to be hired led to several offers of employment. He was still attached to the London Met, but doubted he would return there. Other offers came from MI5, MI6, Interpol, and two from Australia; one from Sydney, the other from the Australian Federal Police in Canberra. The infamous Muhammad Mahmood even caught up with him at Ali's. He declined them all. Each had told him if he changed his mind just call. But he had money in the bank, owed nothing, and had twelve months pay coming to him. He was ready for a little 'me time'.

A week after Windsor was arrested Harrigan read a small article on page five of the morning newspaper announcing Godfrey Windsor of the Serious National Crime and Intelligence Agency had taken up a position in the Foreign and Commonwealth Office, and has been given the task of establishing an embassy in the Middle East. Due to unrest in the Middle East, the exact location remains confidential at the time of reporting.

Sir Jason Collins was awarded the British Empire Medal for meritorious civil service in the Queen's Birthday 1991 Honours list.

Annabelle and Jason Collins now have an open marriage arrange with a limited number of newly found, but close friends. Their marriage is stronger than it has ever been.

John Russel's excitement in the conquering of a young constable behind his now returned wife's back was short lived. (His wife was in the army intelligence corps for

God's sake! Bloody moron.) His employment in the Police Service was terminated; divorce proceedings are ongoing; and he now works as a security guard at Sainsbury's

The identities of the shooters at the Sister's Basement was never established.

The question of Natalya Zhestakova's unidentified key remains unanswered.

Despite all good intentions, Harrigan never returned to see Bill Buckle.

***

Three months later...

News Headlines

August 6th 1990

Middle East UK Embassy destroyed during Operation Desert Storm

It has been reported by confidential sources, Ambassador Godfrey Windsor lost his life during a bombing raid early yesterday. No further details have been released.

Sarah

Nine weeks after the United Nations International Investigation Agency trial had been terminated, following the mandatory public equal opportunity and transparent recruitment process for the position of Deputy Assistant Police Commissioner had been completed, Sarah's status was upgraded from 'Acting' to 'Permanent'.

In line with a new directive issued following the release of a report from the thirty six month 'Cooperation between Ranks and Ancillaries in the UK Police Service' public inquiry, Sarah's first official duty was to visit all police stations within the Greater London area on an 'Introduction to Other Ranks Tour' (recommendation 71 (b) (viii)). Stonegate Police Station was fourth on the list.

With the exception of Superintendent Wilkinson and a couple of the old hands, the station was filled with new faces. Protocol dictated Wilkinson's office was her first port of call. After the congratulatory and courtesy exchanges had been completed, he was grateful her preference was to talk to the other ranks alone. *"It gives a more personal touch,"* she'd explained.

The old hands complied with their congratulatory obligations and continued with their work. The young faces of recruits, fresh from college, most of whom had been fast tracked, showed almost overwhelming gratitude for the opportunity to meet a member of the senior ranks up close.

The only real change since she and Harrigan were stationed there together, was with Patricia Hedrich. To ensure compliance with the recently released 'Streamlining and Efficiency Police Management Guidelines', Patricia was promoted into the newly created position Personal Assistant to Senior Ranks and given her own office. She is now fully occupied with the extra paperwork and reports required.

Sarah entered Patricia's office. She didn't knock. "Hello, Patricia." There was nothing friendly in her greeting.

"M'am." Patricia looked over the top of her computer screen. "Congratulations."

"Thank you." Sarah glanced quickly around the office.

"And to you on your new position." Sarah paused briefly. "Sorry to hear about your husband."

"Thank you. Why don't you sit down?"

"Thank you."

…and so the conversation went on; and on; and on; eventually falling into awkward silence.

"How's Bill?" Sarah asked, trying to infuse a tone of casualness. She failed miserably. Which wasn't surprising; the question was the reason she came into the office in the first place.

"Bill?"

"DCI Harrigan."

"How would I know?" Patricia said with a frown.

"Well, after that night I rang and you answered his mobile, I thought—"

"You thought *what?*"

"You'd just come back from the Red Lion where you had dinner and a few drinks, you said you would be staying the night, and he was in the shower. It was quite obvious what was going on."

Patricia pushed the keyboard to one side. "Sarah," she said, deciding this was not a "Ma'm" moment. I'll tell you what went on. Yes, we went to the Red Lion. Yes, we agreed it better I stay the night instead of cabbing it home and then back the next morning for my car. Yes, he was in the shower upstairs when you telephoned. And yes, when he came down I did my best to get his pants off. But he insisted you and he were together and would not be jumping into bed behind your back."

"Then why didn't he ring back?"

"I didn't tell him you rang. At first I thought if I was to have any chance of intimacy with him, the last thing I was going to do was to tell him you rang. But when he kept insisting I sleep in the downstairs guest room, alone, I played my woman scorned card. I don't know if you've ever played that card, but—"

She didn't finish her sentence; Sarah was already out the door.

There was no answer to Sarah's knocking at Harrigan's Finchenham home. Sarah Knight at the Red Lion told her he'd there two nights ago.

"Any idea when he'll be in next?"

"Sorry, Deary. He said he'd popped in to say goodbye and didn't know when he'd be back."

"Did he leave a forwarding address or contact number?"

"No."

She telephoned Ali's. Harrigan had been at Ali's last night. And again, he'd come to say goodbye, didn't know when he'd return, and no contact details were given. Sarah didn't know if Ali was telling the truth about the no contact details, but there was no way Ali would betray Harrigan's trust.

After several unsuccessful attempts to have immigration officials check if Harrigan had left the country, she asked her Uncle Charles if he could pull some strings. He refused.

"You're better off without him, Sarah. Trust me. And besides, as Deputy Assistant Police Commissioner, you'll socialise with a wide range of more eminently worthy suitors. People of title and wealth."

Two years later, Sir Charles Reece passed away, never understanding why Sarah had run from his office in tears.